ASSASSIN'S
ORBIT

First published 2021 by Solaris
an imprint of Rebellion Publishing Ltd,
Riverside House, Osney Mead,
Oxford, OX2 0ES, UK

www.solarisbooks.com

ISBN: 978-1-78108-915-6

A CIP catalogue record for this book is available from the
British Library.

Designed & typeset by Rebellion Publishing

Printed in Denmark

ASSASSIN'S ORBIT

JOHN APPEL

SOLARIS

For my grandmother, the late Ruth Ronald,
whose spirit lives on in the women in these pages.

And for Michelle, Alexa, and Ben, whose love
makes everything not only possible, but worthwhile.

CHAPTER ONE

Noo

Second Landing Social Club,
Ileri Station, North Ring

"This isn't a crime scene, Daniel, it's a slaughterhouse."

Forty years as a private investigator on Ileri Station hadn't prepared Noo Okereke for the carnage around her. She'd attended to killings before, if rarely, but tonight marked her first mass murder.

She was glad to see it only through virtual reality.

Her translucent telepresent figure knelt by one of the bodies: a young man she'd known for his entire life. Inside the blood-spattered room, the hovering bot serving as her proxy dropped to the level of her virtual head. She forced herself to examine the holes punched through the young man's torso—from the front, the detached investigator within her noted. His head lay facing towards her, eyes still open, face slack. Next to his right hand lay his stunner; he'd managed to draw, at least, before being cut down.

Other Constabulary bots ranged about the luxuriously appointed room, cataloging the plentiful evidence. The bots were the only things moving. The people inside—what was left of them—would never move again on their own.

Another hoverbot slid into position nearby and Detective Daniel Imoke's lean shape winked into being beside her own virtual body. "It's Saed?" he asked. For formality's sake, she guessed, and the official record; Imoke knew—had known—Saed practically since birth. Only a little less time than she had, really.

Noo gave a reluctant nod, caught herself, then vocalized for the record. "I confirm the victim's identity as Saed Tahir, employed by Shariff Security." Her business partner's grandson, and practically a brother to her own children. Her virtual form rose as she surveyed the room. Eight other bodies lay across the floor or slumped in their seats. All the victims she could see had been shot in the upper chest. Two had been shot in the head as well. *The killer was trained—wanting to be sure of their kills?*

Blood was everywhere: splattered across the top of the game table, the walls, the carpet, the bodies of the other victims. The great aching emptiness in her chest warred with the urge to vomit.

Pull it together. She took a deep breath, sent a silent prayer to the Huntress. *Guide my eyes and make swift my steps, that I may find the killers.*

Steadier now, she looked around the lounge-turned-charnel house. "He was on assignment. Bodyguard to the Minister for External Trade, Ita." She peered at each of the victims seated at the card table in turn. She knew Ita's face from the media feeds but didn't see him among the dead—no, wait. She looked more closely at one of the seated victims, spotting the New Horizon party emblem embroidered on the left breast of their yellow kaftan. She pointed. "This is Ita, I think."

Imoke's own face stayed impassive. "Unofficially, it is," he said.

Noo stood and traced the path between Saed's body and Ita's, trying to estimate where the shooter or shooters had stood. Saed's form lay squarely in the path between Ita's body and where she judged the assassin's position had been. Quick steps brought her to the spot from where death had reached out to encompass everyone within the parlor. Sure enough, Saed had managed to get between his charge and the killer.

You did your job until the very end, my boy. Cold comfort for us.

"Why can't you identify them officially? Why did you need me to come down and ID Saed in person?" she asked.

Before he could answer, the room faded around her abruptly, replaced by the dark, equipment-packed interior of one of the Constabulary's little electric vans. Noo blinked in her seat, adjusting, the transition from posh club parlor to utilitarian service vehicle catching her by surprise. A young woman in crime scene team coveralls swept the closed-network VR trodes from Noo's temples, then turned to do the same for Imoke, her twist-outs swinging as her head bobbed. "Commissioner's here, boss," the tech said, as she hurriedly stuffed the trodes into a storage cubby.

Imoke grimaced. "That was quick." He stood up slowly, head ducked to avoid cracking it on the van's roof. "They keep making these things smaller." He twisted sideways and hunched down to scoot past the bot rack. "This crate's nearly as old as you are, Sergeant," the tech quipped as she called up an augmented reality window that shimmered between herself and Noo, studied it briefly, then waved it away. The younger woman flicked her fingers, red-painted fingernails shining for a moment in the glow of the VR system lights. The rear door clicked as the lock disengaged. Imoke pushed it open, flooding the van with light, and stepped out. He turned and offered Noo his arm to steady herself as she stepped forth. Nodding her thanks, she wrapped her right hand around it as she clambered out of the van, feeling the firm, wiry muscles inside his tunic sleeve. He was still a fit man for all that he was her age, sixty-four standard, with the lean build of the football goalie he'd been in their youth. His shoulders were broad and muscular without being thick. A close-cropped fuzz of hair perhaps a quarter centimeter long—graying now—topped his long, narrow face with its slightly-crooked nose, broken decades ago.

"You've handed me a real flaming bucket of shit, Daniel," Noo said in a low voice. She glanced around, hunting for signs of the Commissioner, and released Imoke's arm. *Wouldn't want Toiwa thinking Daniel and I are banging again.* Maybe she could slip away before Commissioner Toiwa spotted her... She'd have to call Fathya, her business partner—Saed's grandmother—right away.

The van was parked crosswise in the normally pedestrian-only street outside the Second Landing Social Club, part of a row of modest five-level buildings sitting in one of the nicer neighborhoods of Ileri Station's north ring. Not that any of the neighborhoods on the station were bad, really. But the movers and players, the heads of the more successful family concerns, government officials of a certain rank, media-feed stars; they all tended to cluster in neighborhoods like this one. The district lay a scant block from Idibia Park with its lake, and water, as ever, drew humans to live near it.

The structures on either side of the club were the usual blend of offices, shops, and residences. A normally busy cafe—now cleared of patrons and most staff—sat across the street from the club. Two blocks spinward lay the nearest transit-system station. More little vans packed the vehicular alleyway behind the club; every ambulance in the north ring but one, Imoke had told her.

Noo's eyes tracked along the eternally up-sloping street, taking in the crowd of onlookers, and then up to the ring's ceiling. North ring kept daylight during third shift so the louvers covering the inner surface of the ring were open, and light reflected by the giant external mirror shone through. She spotted a cluster of people up-ring, near the Goan consulate; she zoomed on one of the augmented reality sigils hovering around the mob. *One Worlders. Idiots.*

She shook her head in disgust. "A political assassination and the first mass murder on the station in decades, and the brain-bit buttonheads are protesting the Goans? Goa's not even part of the Commonwealth. How does picketing their consulate affect the vote?"

"Seventeen years since the last mass killing," Daniel said. "And the first with a projectile weapon in twenty-eight. I had to look it up." His gaze flicked up towards the distant protest before returning to her. "Where the One Worlders are concerned, I just assume they're against all off-worlders, Commonwealth or no." He touched her arm. "I'm terribly sorry to have pulled you out here at this hour. Once I realized it was Saed, though, I thought it best to call you for the identification."

So that I can tell Fathya her grandson is dead, instead of you. She'd had her own children late, and her kids had grown up with Saed and Fari, his sister. *Shit, I have to call the kids once I tell Fathya.*

Noo took a deep breath and pushed that task off a little longer. "You were right to call," she said, looking up at his long, dark face. "Still, a bucket of flaming shit," she repeated.

Imoke turned, his attention drawn by a uniformed constable making emphatic if confusing hand gestures. "It's worse than you know," he said as he took her elbow and turned, trying to steer her towards the front of the van. She shook his hand off and stepped off to match pace with him. "Besides Ita, there's another political victim."

She ground her teeth at being herded as well as with his indirectness. *This is why we only sleep together for three months a year.* "Out with it, man," she said in a clipped tone as they rounded the corner of the van—only to run headlong into Commissioner Toiwa and her entourage.

Noo and Toiwa locked eyes as Toiwa's aide plowed into Imoke, who caught the young woman, saving her from an ignominious face-planting on the van's windshield. A uniformed constable lieutenant veered left at the last second, just missing Noo. She ignored the minions, focusing instead on the Commissioner. The stare-down between private investigator and the top police officer on the station might have continued indefinitely had Imoke, veteran witness of a previous clash between the two, not intervened.

"Commissioner, thank you for responding so quickly during third shift. I hope—" His mouth clamped shut as Toiwa's right hand snapped up, palm outward.

It might have been third shift and the middle of Toiwa's sleep period, but she was dressed as if for a meeting with the Prime Minister and the entire cabinet. Just forty-five, nearly two decades younger than Noo or Imoke, Nnenna Toiwa looked like she was about to step into a media studio, smartly turned out in a charcoal-grey jacket-and-slacks combo with a steel-gray blouse. She had sharp, imperious features, long hair relaxed and bound back, and cheekbones Noo would have killed for three decades earlier. Toiwa certainly didn't look like she'd risen from her bed about the same time Noo responded to Imoke's call. She wore low heels, in spite of which she could still look down her nose at Noo as if examining a particularly unpleasant specimen presented by an underling.

Noo's own appearance didn't normally bother her; at sixty-four her body had seen its share of living, and she'd birthed two children, leaving her roundly plump. But something about the taller, younger woman, with her gym-toned body and perfect hair, made Noo feel dumpy.

"What is M. Okereke doing at your crime scene, inside the perimeter, Detective Sergeant?" Toiwa asked, her media-feed-quality voice carrying clearly despite the background chatter, if pitched low. Her left hand gestured towards the line of uniformed constables and augmented-reality tags marking the off-limits zone. She eyed Noo from waist to head. "There's no call for a civilian to be here on the scene."

To his credit, Daniel Imoke didn't wilt in front of his boss' boss. "I asked her to confirm the identity of one of the victims," he said.

"You couldn't obtain that from the victim's djinn?" the Commissioner asked, one eyebrow arched. Noo's ears perked up; Toiwa's arrival had kept Daniel from answering when she'd asked the same thing.

Imoke shook his head. "Localized electromagnetic pulse. The attacker fried everyone's electronics, and the electronics inside the parlor," he said. Noo kept her expression still with an effort but took note. *That's just as bad as the fact they used a gun.* Using an EMP device inside a station was the mark of someone who possibly didn't care if they also fried essential systems, like fire alarms and vacuum breach sensors. *Grounders,* Noo thought, before kicking herself about making assumptions. It was true all spacers and most station-siders respected the machines that kept them all alive, but that wasn't evidence.

Only a slight widening of her eyes betrayed Toiwa's surprise at hearing this. The Commissioner turned, giving Imoke her full attention. She twisted her left hand in a circle, counterclockwise, and the air around the three of them assumed the quality of stillness that spoke of a privacy field snapping into place. "You're sure?" she asked, voice low even inside the field.

Daniel nodded. "The first medics on scene discovered the problem when they couldn't pull the victim's emergency data from their djinns. Crime-scene techs confirmed the EMP. I thought I recognized one of the victims, which is why I called M. Okereke to confirm my belief."

Toiwa turned now to Noo, her mouth still tight. "You knew the minister? Or his guests?"

Noo shook her head, snorting. "Hardly that. His bodyguard. Saed Tahir."

"Who?"

A fourth person shoved past a protesting underling and bulled her way into the privacy field. "My grandson."

Oh shit. Should have known Fathya would have her own source to tip her off.

"M. Shariff." Toiwa faltered for a second, seemingly torn between courses of response, before settling on diplomacy for now. "Assuming his identity is confirmed, my deepest condolences."

If Imoke was a goalie, Fathya Shariff was a forward, barely middling height and spare of build. Her bald brown head gleamed in the light here in the broad station corridor. Fists clenched, she ignored the Commissioner, to Toiwa's obvious displeasure, and Noo, to her temporary relief, and confronted Imoke. "Who killed my grandson, Daniel?"

Imoke spread his hands, face downcast. "We don't know yet, Fathya. But on my honor, we'll find who did this."

Toiwa stepped in between the two, pushing her subordinate against the van's front and driving Fathya Shariff back by presence alone. "I can assure you, every available resource will be devoted to this case," she told them, taking Fathya and Noo each by the elbow and drawing them with her towards the perimeter, and away from the Second Landing Social Club, scene of horrors. "Thank you, M. Okereke, for your assistance in confirming M. Tahir's identity, but your aid is no longer required." She dropped the privacy field, released their elbows, and waved Imoke forward. "The Detective Sergeant will see you off," she said, her tone brooking no dissent. "And perhaps have a word with whomever is in charge of the perimeter about what constitutes a secure crime scene."

Shariff started to protest but Noo shot her a private signal, djinn to djinn. *<Not here, not yet. We can find out more if she doesn't explicitly order us cut out.>*

Her partner and friend converted her stillborn outburst into an exasperated grunt. "Very well. I will expect a full accounting, Commissioner," she said. She glanced at Imoke. "We can see ourselves off. I'm sure the Detective Sergeant has his hands quite full managing such an exceptional crime scene."

"Thank you, I do," Imoke said, reaching forward to take both of Fathya's hands in his own. "Fathya, my deepest sorrow. Please know, and tell Fari too, that I will do everything in my power to bring Saed's killer to justice." Releasing her hands, Imoke inclined his head, then turned to take Noo's. "Thank you for coming and helping, M. Okereke," he said. The bleep of an incoming data packet via near-field channel from his djinn to hers, invisible to everyone but themselves, surprised her not at all. She murmured her thanks and they parted.

She waited until they'd passed beyond the security perimeter and were sliding through the thin crowd of bystanders before she accessed the data packet Imoke had slipped her. "Oh, fuck me, the Mother wept," she cursed beneath her breath.

Fathya Shariff had known her for forty years, but she still bristled at Noo's blasphemy, even if they professed different faiths. Noo shushed her, grabbed an elbow and sped her around the corner. Fathya glared but consented to the handling. "What's the fuss?"

"Fuss is the least of it," she snapped. "I didn't have time to really look at all the bodies. The ninth was behind the card table, all I saw was the legs."

"Who was it?" Shariff asked, frustration clear in her tone.

"The Commonwealth Consul on the station." Fathya stopped, mouth agape, as Noo went on. "This killing wasn't just political. It's an interstellar incident."

CHAPTER TWO

ILERI

"WE CALL THIS new world *Ileri,* or *Promise,* in the tongue of one of the many peoples represented here in this place of our Exile. A promise to ourselves, and to our descendants, to avoid the mistakes of the past. A promise that all here and our children to come will be seen as equal in worth. A promise to build a new home in which every person is cared for. By necessity, nearly every one of us left someone behind on Lost Earth, whether to the Unity Plague, or to the incidental horrors it spawned.

From this day forward, let us leave none behind."

— *Peter Akindele, first Prime Minister of Ileri, on the first anniversary of Settlement*

Toiwa

GOVERNMENT HOUSE, ILERI STATION, TRAILING RING

TOIWA DIDN'T THINK the governor was pissed at her, personally. But sometimes being downrange of the heads' anger was part of the job, and this was one of those times.

"How is it that a rising star of the Horizon party, which has staked its future on the referendum about joining the Commonwealth, was gunned down along with the Commonwealth Consul during an off-the-books meeting?" Governor Sahndra Ruhindi didn't shout in her own situation room. She and Toiwa stood alone by the big holoprojection of Ileri Station, looking like a child's toy atop the space elevator cable that terminated in New Abuja, the capital. Clusters of aides and staff lurked in the dimly lit corners of the room as the station's top constable briefed the top politician.

Toiwa reached into the 3D projection of station, grabbed the north ring's image, and swept her hands apart to zoom in. In seconds, a rendering of the Second Landing Club's block hung between them. She tapped it twice; an irregular splotch of red covered the building and parts of the surrounding streets. "We're still working on that, but the EMP wiped the recording devices in the club, along with all the victims' djinns. Everything in the red area, in fact. I've got officers canvasing the district and my technical teams are pulling surveillance data from outside the affected radius. I've asked both Minister Ita's office and the Commonwealth Consulate for their schedules to try and reconstruct their movements prior to the meeting, but they haven't gotten back to us yet."

"I hope you're doing something more robust than throwing beat cops at this," Ruhindi snapped. She was a sharp-featured woman, and her frown gave her face a decidedly grim cast that her robe and headscarf—couldn't quite offset. The cluster of hovering aides, hearing her tone, edged away like children trying to escape an argument between parents. "The referendum on joining the Commonwealth is just two weeks away. This assassination has to be aimed at disrupting the vote, or influencing it, and we can't let that happen."

Ah, so now it's "we". Toiwa counted backwards from five in French before responding. "My people and I understand the stakes, Governor," she said in her most placatingly calm voice. "And we can read the poll numbers. It's clear the vast majority of people want to join the Commonwealth. But there's only four of the First Fourteen worlds still independent, counting Ileri, and some people have strong feelings about staying that way."

"Hmph." Ruhindi shook her head. "Heads in the mud, thinking we can go on as we have. Things have changed since the end of the Three-Planet War. Shenzen and Goa are finally starting to bounce back twenty years after nearly kicking each other to death, and with Goa joining the Triumvirate, well." She flipped through the windows in the big projection field. "The Commonwealth shares our values. Most people understand that joining is our best path forward."

Always the politician. Ruhindi hadn't really changed in the decade since they'd met in Elleville, where Toiwa had been an up-and-coming inspector and Ruhindi the deputy mayor. "Be that as it may, Governor, we've been dealing with the ongoing conflict between Minister Miguna's One Worlders and, well, everyone else, ever since the vote was announced." Toiwa half-turned and waved at the display wall behind her, which at the moment carried feeds of two substantial protests and counter-protests, one in the station's north ring and one in the trailing ring. "To be honest, I've been expecting low-level violence to break out soon. Nothing like this, though."

"Further violence is unacceptable," Ruhindi said as she jabbed her index finger at Toiwa. "You've got to keep a lid on this, Nnenna. Aside from jeopardizing the vote, this station is our gateway to the rest of the Cluster. Disruption like that can't be tolerated. Especially not with a Commonwealth warship expected in-system any day."

And back to it being my problem. She swallowed her anger. "We're doing our best, Governor," Toiwa said aloud. "But the Constabulary was stretched thin already keeping up the public order patrols and responding to flash protests along with the scheduled ones. The resources this investigation will require are going to push things over the edge."

"Dammit, I know you're a bit short-handed since you're still cleaning out Ketti's old guard, but I didn't realize things were that tight." Ruhindi had the grace to sound a bit conciliatory; she'd been the one to ask Toiwa to come clean house after the legendarily corrupt but untouchable previous Commissioner had finally died in the saddle, so to speak. Or maybe literally, if the rumors were true. "Can you get help from down the cable?"

"We're getting some already." Toiwa called up the data from her djinn and opened a private AR window she shared with the governor. "The New Abuja homicide team is assisting Detective Imoke's investigators virtually. Likewise for the forensics teams, since none of the station team have experience with a crime of this nature." People had still been murdered during Ketti's tenure, of course, just not in large batches, and political assassinations were simply unheard of. Easier to buy people off or get them transferred planetside, or to one of the small subordinate stations elsewhere in the system. One thing she couldn't fault the Constabulary she'd inherited for was a lack of experience for crimes they'd never seen.

"I've also requested additional constables to help maintain order. The first wave is coming up on the morning shuttle, along with some specialists to assist the investigation. A larger contingent will follow via elevator tomorrow, so we'll see them in four days."

"Good." Ruhindi scanned the big display wall behind Toiwa, which had switched from video feeds of key points to some kind of data visualization. Toiwa kept her attention on the governor, who studied the data viz, nodded, and then turned back to her police chief. "You never explained how the assassins got the weapons to use. Someone's got an unauthorized fabber?"

"That seems most likely."

"Do you think the Fingers supplied them?"

Toiwa hesitated. Ileri's most prominent criminal organization was bold, aggressive, and well-entrenched on-station, but they weren't stupid. "We haven't ruled it out," she said finally. "They've got the means, and the establishment where the killing took place is one of their fronts, so that's opportunity covered. But what's their motive? The Horizon party platform and joining the Commonwealth are both positive things for them, good for their business. More support for the New Arm colonies, which expands their markets." She shook her head. "My people dropped in on them like a firehawk on a scuttlemouse. We're going through the club and all their affiliated operations like nanniescanners and I've got constables shaking down every known Fingers operative. It's hard to believe they'd expose themselves to this much attention."

"Hmm." Ruhindi nodded, drumming her fingers on the edge of the display table. "Another thing for you to chase down, then." She stilled her fingers. "I want you to tie the intelligence agencies into the investigation."

Toiwa blinked. "They don't have jurisdiction."

The governor sighed. "Nnenna, you're not naive enough to believe they aren't already digging into this. The Directorate rep hinted as much when she called me earlier, making the case that killing the Commonwealth Consul was very much part of their patch. The domestic branch will claim responsibility for Ita's killer. The military spies will natter about planetary security."

"I see," Toiwa said, her jaw clenched.

"Lighten up, Nnenna, I'm on your side," Ruhindi scolded.

Are you?

"They're going to stick their noses in, so better to fold them into the effort up front. You'll be on stronger footing to retain control." Ruhindi shrugged. "That's my advice, anyway."

She wasn't wrong, Toiwa thought. Strictly speaking,

Toiwa answered to the Constabulary High Commissioner down the cable, and not to the Governor of Ileri Station. The reality was more complicated, of course; the advice of the station's highest civilian authority carried considerable weight.

She caught the eye of her chief aide, Kala Valverdes, who lurked near the entrance with her uniformed aide, Lieutenant Marie Zheng. She shot Valverdes a brief message requesting ze ask the intel services for liaison officers. Valverdes acknowledged and popped open private AR windows even as Toiwa turned back to Ruhindi. "Thank you, that's a good point. I'll do that."

"Find them, Nnenna." Ruhindi leaned across the display table, eyes fixed on Toiwa's. "We can't let conflict between the factions break into open fighting. This must be solved quickly. The Commonwealth ship coming to observe the referendum is due any day, and that's going to further set the One Worlders off. We need this put to bed before that happens."

And do you want the real killers found, or just a plausible suspect? There was a time when Toiwa thought she'd have known Ruhindi's will, and it would have aligned with Toiwa's own. But since coming up the cable... she wasn't so sure anymore.

"Yes, ma'am," was all she said.

Ruhindi seemed to sense something was amiss, though. "Out with it, Nnenna," she said. "Something's eating you."

There was, in fact. Multiple things, but only one she felt like airing. "Fathya Shariff's grandson was among the victims," she said.

"I know."

"I'm worried she and her partner are going to make problems for the investigation. Could you persuade them to back off?"

Ruhindi laughed out loud, causing the staffers around the room to fall momentarily silent. "I haven't been here that much longer than you, Nnenna, but even I know that's a fool's errand." She shook her head. "Fathya Shariff can call in favors from just about every person of consequence on the station, and she's not without influence planetside to boot. Okereke's got her matched in the civil service and, so I hear, on the extra-legal side." She fixed Toiwa with a familiar look. "And it's her *grandson*. She and Okereke are basically family to each other. This is personal for them. You might as well ask me to stop the world from spinning."

Toiwa frowned but nodded. "True enough. Should I fold them in as well?"

Ruhindi looked thoughtful. "It couldn't hurt to read Shariff in. From what I've heard, her security firm filled the gaps where your predecessor turned a blind eye. This might be a good opportunity to build a bridge."

MEIKO

COMMONWEALTH CONSULATE, ILERI STATION, SOUTH RING

THE UNIFORMED TROOPER guarding the door from the consulate's public foyer to the semi-public office space behind waved Meiko Ogawa through after scanning her djinn. "The bot can't follow, ma'am," ze said, pointing at the autopallet bearing Meiko's scant luggage. "I can page someone to take it to your quarters if you like."

"It's no problem. I'll carry it," Meiko said, though her muscles and joints protested at the thought. The trooper seemed to pick up on her fatigue, and wordlessly scooped the small duffel up and helped Meiko shrug her thin, aching shoulders into the straps. Ze held the door open as she walked through, then firmly closed it behind her.

Sasha Kumar was waiting for her on the other side. Meiko's djinn scooped up her public profile, which gave 'Science Attaché' as her job title. That was true, though incomplete, just the same way Meiko's own public profile identified her as a planetary surveyor.

After all, they couldn't advertise that they were really spies, could they?

"You made good time," Kumar said, motioning for Meiko to follow her deeper into the block-sized Consulate complex.

"We burned at three gravities the whole way, except for five minutes at turnaround," Meiko replied. "Whatever you said to the Ileris when you asked them to give me a ride back from 351 Juliette, they certainly treated it as an urgent request."

Kumar—a short, slight woman with a mass of dark hair Meiko envied—had to slow her pace so Meiko could keep up as she wove a path from the semi-public area, where Ileri citizens sometimes came on official business, into the private, Commonwealth-citizens-only interior. "Are you all right? Do you need to rest before I brief you?" Kumar asked.

Rest sounded wonderful, but it could wait. Now was not the time to demonstrate any impairment, not with escape from exile so tantalizingly close. "I'll be fine," Meiko said. "After so long in microgravity, going to three Gs and then to standard in five hours takes a little out of you, even if you put in extra gym time." Not that she'd had much else to do in her spare time while stuck at the Ileri covert lab on asteroid 351 Juliette besides work out. But at sixty-two, Meiko knew she wouldn't be bouncing back from this the way she had even ten years earlier.

Kumar led them to a door labeled 'Secure Briefing Suite' with a full palm reader lock. A red halo lined the doorway. Kumar ushered her inside, then closed the door behind them and waved her djinn over the pickup beside the entry. The halo changed to green, indicating the auditory and EM shielding was active and the room was now secure. Meiko shrugged out of her duffel's straps and dropped the bag into a corner, then pulled off her cross-slung satchel and laid that down too. Kumar indicated she should take the chair opposite the station chief's and she carefully settled into it.

She glanced around the room as Kumar brought up the briefing file on the table's built-in, hardwired display system. The chairs had the solid feel of metal frames under the generous padding that cushioned her aching butt. She suspected the blond wood paneling was veneer over more substantial soundproofing material, but the table was a solid block of engineered neoteak, or something like it. They'd probably fabbed everything in place back when the Consulate was built to ensure the Ileris, or one of the other powers, hadn't slipped listening or recording devices into the furnishings as they were printed.

"You scanned the media feeds on your way here?" Kumar said as faces appeared above the tabletop.

"The assassination is the top story," Meiko said. "I assumed that's why you brought me back."

"The murder of our Consul is an 'all hands to stations' moment, that's for sure," Kumar affirmed. "Even those under a cloud."

Meiko straightened slightly. "I've been certified free of nanoware contamination," she said carefully. "That's why I was assigned as a liaison with the Ileri scientists, wasn't it? Their lab was the best equipped to treat any lingering infection."

"That's one reason." Kumar leaned forward. "Even setting aside your target infecting you with Exile-grade coercion nanoware, your last mission was a disaster. You were supposed to confirm the wreckage on that ice moon was that of the cruiser *Fenghuang,* and recover the anti-matter conversion bombs if they still somehow existed so they didn't fall into the wrong hands."

Ah. Here it is. Meiko nodded. "The goal was achieved. The weapons were kept out of hostile hands, and we rescued the survivors in the emergency nanostasis pods once we dug them out of the ice." She took a deep breath. "But I concede many things went wrong."

"Some of which were due to poor decisions on your part."

She hesitated before nodding. "Much of that was clear at the time. I've recognized other mistakes in the time since."

"Good. To be clear, I don't blame you for the nanoware infection. Incorporating it into the stasis gel to ensure they got all of you was rather inspired, if horrifying."

"Not nearly as horrifying as knowing you've got nanoware in your brain able to convince you that your skin is on fire," Meiko retorted. "Which is what they did to our chief salvage engineer."

"So I recall, and your point is taken. But still." Kumar sat back. "The Service is not happy with you, Meiko. The heads suggested it might be time for you retire." She let that hang in the air.

The silence ticked on for a few seconds as Meiko considered her response. "Do you concur?" she asked, softly.

Kumar took a moment herself before giving her answer. "I think you've got a forty-year track record of largely independent action that consistently delivered results," she said at last. "And right now that record, combined with your long-standing contacts on this station, make you uniquely qualified to help find whomever killed the Consul. And potentially help keep Ileri on track to join the Commonwealth, to boot." She flipped her hand open and the display filled with headshots of the Consul, Minister Ita, and the other victims. "It would be senseless to set aside an asset like yourself at this juncture."

"Very utilitarian of you," Meiko said dryly.

"Meiko." Kumar leaned towards her, tension obvious in the cords in her neck, and she spoke with fierce intensity. "It's not just your career at stake here. There's more going on than you know, and I don't just mean Ileri joining the Commonwealth. Though that's a huge thing in itself."

"Things I'm not cleared for?" She couldn't keep *all* the frustration out of her voice.

"Not yet." Kumar stood, and wearily, Meiko climbed to her own feet. "But *if* you can manage to pull off a good result here, I *might* be able to read you in."

It was a slender lifeline Kumar had thrown her, and it might not bear the weight of the challenge she was saddling Meiko with. But, she thought as she trailed Kumar towards the transient quarters, a slim chance was better than none.

CHAPTER THREE

OUR LADY OF THE LEAP

"WE CAN'T TELL you how long the wormgate will stay open. *Zheng He* reports that, this time, it opens in the outer reaches of another star system, with at least three planets detected so far. There is no time for another cycle of the gate in hopes of finding a better system, even if we had the antimatter for another cycle, and we don't. Unity's vessels will be within range in seventy-two hours. You must go *now*. With our blessings, go. Carry our dreams with you, where Unity cannot pursue you. We'll make sure it cannot."

— *Dr. Vritika Chatterjee, PhD, "The Lady of the Leap," from the Sol system wormgate station, Day Zero of Exile*

Noo

KUTI PARK DISTRICT, ILERI STATION, TRAILING RING

DATAMANCY PARTNERS OCCUPIED a perfectly average office building in the trailing ring, across the street from Kuti Park with its lake. Noo could see the far edges of the greenspace rising ahead as she approached from the transit stop with her work partner. Fari Tahir was Noo's partner, Fathya's granddaughter, and Saed's sister, all rolled into one package. She was shorter than her brother but broader in the shoulder and hip, with a round face. The broken nose, courtesy of a training injury and left crooked by choice, transformed her features from 'handsome' to 'strong'.

You'd never know she spent time crying for her lost sib. Noo herself couldn't tell, and she knew that face as well as that of her own children.

Over in the park, a bunch of primary-school kids kicked a football around in time-honored tradition, deftly adjusting to the curling, Coriolis-charged arcs. Noo couldn't make out their chatter but recollection supplied its own soundtrack. Not so many years ago she'd shepherded first her kids and then the Tahirs on football outings.

Fari slowed. Noo turned and caught her watching the children, saw the tears welling, and fought back her own urge to weep. She was caught by a sudden vision of standing among the parents loitering beside the pitch, watching Fari or her own son Izu sliding across the grass to knock a ball free so Saed or Ifeyinwa could capture it and then race downfield.

She pushed the memories down.

Do the job. Catch the fuckers that killed him. Then we can mourn.

She tapped her partner on the arm. "Are you with me, girl?" Fari jerked and shook her head.

"Not entirely. Sorry, Auntie." She wiped her eyes and caught up to Noo.

Noo eyed her from head to toe and back again, before turning and taking the younger woman's arm. "I don't need you at full spin, girl, but present you must be," she growled. "Wits and body both. Clear?"

"Clear, Auntie," Fari said. "Are you going to tell me who we're seeing, anyway?"

"Some things are best not talked about in the open. Let's just say it's not someone your grandmother could meet with."

"But you can?"

"They're connected to the owners of the Second Landing Social Club," she said as she pushed the door open and stepped inside.

Fari's eyes widened, but only slightly, as she followed Noo into the building's lobby. *Wondering how your Auntie can just stroll into a Fingers stronghold, eh, girl?*

A human attendant seated behind a desk built to stop a breaching round greeted them. The alert-looking man had Fari's blocky build. Late twenties, Noo guessed. Her djinn scooped up his public profile while her digital agent swam through the firm's archives, matching their records with the public files. He was an arena-fighting prospect, turned Fingers muscle after failing to catch on with the fans, according to their intel. She watched Fari and the goon give each other the kind of reflexive once-over threat assessment that bruisers always did.

"M. Okereke and M. Tahir here to see M. Loh," Noo announced loftily as the door closed behind them. "Be a good boy and let us in, would you?"

A drawer slid noiselessly out from the wall to their left. "You'll need to deposit your hardware first, Auntie," the man said with a thin smile.

"Hrmph." Noo opened her jacket and pulled out her improbably large handgun, settled it into the drawer, then slipped her stunner from its holster and laid it alongside the much larger weapon.

"Very nice," the attendant said. "Twelve millimeter? Isn't that a little large for you, Auntie?" Fari laid her own weapons in the drawer; together they barely massed more than Noo's pistol.

"Size matters, young man, that's one thing I've learned in my years," Noo quipped back.

His smile broadened into a genuine grin. "That's what I tell my man."

"Enjoy it while it still works, dear," Noo said, and his face darkened slightly. "Buzz us up, please, your boss is waiting."

Noo

A RANGY MAN with straight steel-gray hair, a narrow face, and wary eyes, met them as they exited the lift. He wore an elegant collarless jacket in royal-blue silk, open to show a pale gray shirt beneath and loose black trousers. Noo closed on him and shook hands. "Good afternoon, Pericles." She turned to Fari. "Please meet my associate,

Fari Tahir." Politeness and manners remained important in these affairs even while one's djinn harvested someone's public profile, and in the case of everyone present, trawled their respective private databases for information about that person. Or would have, if this part of the building hadn't been signal-shielded.

If playing the game finds the goat-fucker who did this, then I'll play the game this way.

The man took Fari's hand in his own thin, long-fingered ones, and spoke in a warm, rich basso. "M. Tahir. I'm sorry to meet you under such circumstances. I'm Pericles Loh. Would you please come this way?" He guided them down a short hallway, through the sole open door and into his office. Loh guided them past a sleek, functional desk with modern projector units and utilitarian meeting chairs, settling his charges instead into a trio of comfortable armchairs arranged around a low circular table. Noo settled her broad hips into her seat as Loh offered them tea from the elegant service—handmade, she was sure, nothing from a fabber—as a woman near Fari's age rolled in a cart bearing a number of covered dishes. She uncovered them, revealing bowls of steaming noodles, sliced vegetables, and spiced shredded vat pork. She left and Loh served his guests himself.

Refreshment seen to, Loh settled deeply into his own chair and looked from one woman to the other. "My condolences on your loss, Ms. Tahir. Please convey my sympathies to your family."

Fari murmured her thanks as Noo cut in. "We appreciate that, sincerely, Pericles. Please extend ours to the families of your people." Loh inclined his head in gratitude. Noo pressed on. "Time is ticking on, so pardon me for being direct, and for talking business while we eat."

Loh smiled faintly. "When have you ever been anything else?"

Noo glared at him but pressed on. She sat perched on the edge of her seat. "Maybe I'm off-base, but I'm pretty sure no one in your organization is foolish enough to kill the Commonwealth Consul just to get a shot at Ita, especially in one of your own properties. Not that I think killing Ita is something your people would have done; open trade means more business for you."

Loh nodded. "All hypothetically speaking, of course."

Noo snorted. "Sure." She jabbed her chopsticks at him. "But there might be pressure on someone to make that *seem* like a logical course of action if answers aren't forthcoming. Toiwa's on your ass like a boil, yes?"

His smile dropped instantly. Loh laid down his fork and leaned back in his chair. "Indelicately phrased, but accurate. There's also the little matter of the gun, which has the Constabulary somewhat incensed," he said, crossing one leg over the other.

"Right," Noo said. "Violating the prohibition on firearms, especially one with enough lethality to kill everyone in a room in seconds, is pretty much a declaration of war against the yellowjackets. Only a fool or a grounder uses a weapon like that on a station. So they're going to run that all the way down. We don't believe your people are willing to risk that, even in whatever bizarre alternate universe where these killings serve your people's ends."

Loh kept his expression bland, but his voice was clipped. "Obvious facts, M. Okereke, that anyone with even a cursory interest in station affairs knows. What brings you to my door? Especially since, as you so colorfully put it, we have the Commissioner's full attention."

Fine, be that way. "I'm sure we'd both like to see the perpetrator sucking vacuum at the earliest possible moment. And I know about the service-ring passages, Pericles."

Loh's shoulders gave an elegant shrug. "The three tiers of decks below the station's surface level all contain such passages. How does it signify?"

"Do the yellowjackets know that's how the shooters got away? And perhaps how they got in?"

Any remaining amity vanished in a blink, though the only outward sign was a sudden chill in Loh's voice. "That would be significant, if it were true."

"Do you have another explanation for how the killers managed to carry a projectile weapon capable of killing nine people with eleven or twelve shots through the station without being flagged and tracked down? Or how they got out without being seen by the club's other employees, or witnesses outside?"

Frosty silence answered this.

<*Let me try,*> Fari sent Noo across their private channel. She laid down her own utensils, and Noo saw she'd polished off a substantial helping. "M. Loh," Fari said in a polite but firm tone, "I'm sure such a deductive leap is within the grasp of the Constabulary, or perhaps one of the other agencies involved?" Loh shrugged, then nodded. "And no doubt, in their zealousness to uncover the murderer, long-standing arrangements are being trampled upon. Everyday business disrupted, deliveries impeded, that sort of thing. Even more so than things have been lately, with Commissioner Toiwa up the cable

on a clear mission to sweep the station clean."

Loh shrugged. "And if all that is true, so?"

Fari pressed on, even and relentless as an assembler bot putting a structure together. "Perhaps, in their pursuit, they might care about finding *an* assassin, and less concerned with finding *the* assassin."

The man's eyebrows twitched slightly at that. He studied Fari for a moment, then tilted his head to look at Noo. "More insightful than I'd expect from a person her age. You've trained your protégé well."

Noo repressed her answering smile—mostly. "Fathya's as much as mine."

"Still." His gaze shifted back to Fari. "Let's say I concede the possibility your suppositions are accurate. I acknowledge your obvious motivations in resolving the matter. What can we do for each other here?"

Fari leaned forward, elbows resting on her knees. "We could provide an unofficial channel for information your organization might possess that directs the authorities in the proper direction, for one," she said. "Giving you a way to cooperate with the Constabulary without appearing to. Or we can run down leads which your own assets cannot easily pursue, due to the excessive attention you're under right now."

The fingers of Loh's left hand drummed atop his knee as he considered this. "That has possibilities, certainly," he said after a moment. "But by itself, that's not likely to sway my colleagues into cooperating with you."

Fari took a deep breath. "And, naturally, I would be *personally obliged* to you."

Both Noo and Loh sat upright in their seats. <*Do you know what you're doing, girl?*> Noo shot across their link. <*This isn't something you do casually. It's deadly fucking serious.*>

<I'm *deadly fucking serious.*>

Loh blinked several times, then settled back into his chair again, surprise evident on his face. When he finally spoke, the words came slowly, each selected as carefully as tiles in a mosaic. "I believe the prospect of a personal favor from the woman who will one day run the top private security firm on Ileri Station might persuade them, yes." He shifted forward, taking up his teacup. Fari followed suit, and they saluted each other, then drank. "I will have to consult with my colleagues. But I think you'll hear back from us quickly. As you say, it's in everyone's interest to see this settled as rapidly as possible." He finished off his tea and leaned back in his chair, his eyes never leaving the young woman.

Fari set her drink down as well but remained perched on the edge of her seat. "Rapidly or not, I want the bastards who killed my brother sucked dry of everything they know and sent to the recycler," she said in a voice suddenly tight. "And then I want the same done with every person up the fucking chain until I reach whoever put this into motion. That one, I might take my time with."

A smile touched the corners of his lips. "Fathya's blood indeed," he murmured.

<*Saints and spirits, Fari, you're committed now,*> Noo sent.

<*I was committed the moment they killed my brother,*> Fari shot back.

Shock and surprise finally gave way to the need for action, and Noo put herself back into the fray. *I'm not leaving here empty-handed after all that.* "Perhaps," she said, "you might toss a bone of consideration our way, a good-faith gesture while your lot talks this out?"

Loh gave a quick nod. "That seems reasonable." He rose smoothly from his seat, gesturing for them to keep theirs, and crossed the room to his desk, calling up a private AR window. Returning to stand before Fari, he opened one hand, offering her a data packet Noo could see but couldn't read. *Private encryption, djinn to djinn? Weeping Nana, Fathya's going to lose her shit when she finds out her girl has given even this much to the Fingers.*

Fari accepted the packet. "Thank you." If she opened the packet to read it, she gave no outward sign. She offered Loh her hand to shake, and just like that, the deal was sealed.

By this time Noo's appetite had fled completely. After the pro-forma exchange of regrets that they couldn't linger, Loh brought them to his office door. Outside they found the tough-looking young woman who'd served their lunch.

"Myra will see you out," Loh told them, "and she'll be your primary point of contact for routine communications with me. Her information is in the packet. M. Okereke"—he nodded in Noo's direction—"knows how to reach me if something urgent or high priority comes up."

Fari crossed her arms, balking at crossing the threshold. "And how long do you expect deliberations to take?" she asked.

Another shrug of those elegant shoulders. "A few hours, at most. As discussed, affairs are in disarray, so it will take a little time."

"By second shift, then?"

"I should hope so," Loh replied. "If for some reason there's a delay, I'll let you know."

That seemed to satisfy her. Myra escorted them to the lobby, and they retrieved their weapons under the watchful eyes of the guard. A few moments later they sat ensconced in a transit car bound for the south ring.

Noo snapped up a privacy field. "I hope you get something worthwhile from this, girl. You grandmother's going to be pissed when she finds out you've cut a deal with the Fingers," she said. Weariness crept into her voice; when had fatigue snuck up on her? The catnap she'd snatched at the office hadn't been enough, clearly.

Fari activated her own privacy functions, and popped open a private AR window, no doubt looking over the data Loh had given her. "What makes you think she's going to find out?" she asked, absently.

A snap of Noo's fingers got Fari's attention. "That's a foolish thought, to suppose she won't discover what you've done," she said, fatigue temporarily displaced by anger. "She's not a fucking imbecile, and she's got sources everywhere, for all that she's too fucking upright to deal with the Fingers herself." She shook her finger at the younger woman.

Fari's face hardened, an expression Noo was all too familiar with, a sign of genuine anger. *Shit, she really is just like the old woman.* "Of course not, Auntie. She's had you to do the dirty work all these years. But there will come a day when I won't have that luxury." She stared at Noo through the translucent panel of her AR window. Noo met the look, returned it with a stern one of her own. Finally, the two women relaxed. "How did you get connected with that old rascal, anyway? Did you sleep with him too?" She said it without any sense of mockery.

"Pericles? Oh, no, child. He fancies men." She chuckled. "It was his sister." Fari gave a wan smile and a small laugh of her own. "Long ago. Anyway. What did he give you?"

With a wave of her right hand Fari shared the AR window with her and flipped it round so Noo could read it. Noo's head jerked back in surprise. "Councilor Walla from the forward ring? How's she involved?"

The car surged, pressing them back into their seats. "According to Loh, she was on the guest list last night, but didn't show up," Fari said. "I thought we'd go pay her a visit."

CHAPTER FOUR

MEIKO

COMMONWEALTH CONSULATE QUARTERS BLOCK, ILERI STATION, SOUTH RING

MEIKO, MUCH REFRESHED after a nap and shower, sat cross-legged on her couch, hands wrapped around her coffee cup. It was good stuff, or at least the style she preferred, dark and strong. The kind of coffee you drank while minding the probe feeds during a survey run, or on an all-night stakeout. She took a fresh look at her quarters with the benefit of anti-inflammatories, caffeine, and a few hours of rest. It was a *nice* room—a suite really—with a dinette/work cubby, a comfortable bed big enough for three, even a kitchenette. The bathroom was fancier than her own back home on Novo Brasilia.

I guess Kumar isn't going to dump me in the organic recycling just yet.

She finished her coffee as she coded up smart agents to parse the available information about the killing.

She plumbed both the Commonwealth reports on the consulate systems and the public feeds, hunting for correlations and outlying bits of evidence. Kumar had provided surprisingly wide-ranging clearance to her files and Meiko spent another leisurely half-hour browsing for potentially useful items. High-resolution maps of the planet and station went straight to her djinn's storage, along with dossiers on the new governor and head of police, and the station's other leaders. She was about to close out her session when a backdoor into the planetary geophysical satellite network caught her eye. On a whim, she grabbed that too; junctions between her public and secret lives didn't come along often. After that, though, she shut down her workspace, leaned back, and stretched.

She wasn't going to crack this case sitting in quarters. Time for some legwork.

She had just finished dressing for her sortie when her djinn pinged with an incoming call from Kumar.

"You're still here?" the intel chief asked.

"I am about to go out, actually." Meiko assessed her clothing: loose black trousers, a yellow blouse over a black T-shirt, and a programmable jacket. "Is there an update?" She considered her limited footwear options; pathfinder boots were too conspicuous, so she settled on a pair of well-worn dock shoes with concealed steel undertips, with adaptive soles suitable for everything from streetgrass to steel grates.

"Nothing that's not the consulate files."

Meiko glanced in the mirror to check her hair. No time to fab a wig; she ought to have started one last night. *Missed chance. Have to hit one of the body shops.* She made a last check of her pockets—makeup wand, headscarf, a pack of breath mints, stylus. "I'll be going dark once I'm clear of the neighborhood, so the minions needed to be set up first." She flicked a command for her djinn to open the door and stepped out into the corridor.

"Do you have a check-in protocol logged?" she asked.

"Every six hours," Meiko said. "Authentication keys verified. Panic button verified, too."

"Good. Any estimate for how long you'll be out?"

Meiko paused in the corridor, considering. "I'm not sure. It depends on how much pressure the Ileris are putting on the Fingers. Making contact might take some time if they're laying low because of police attention. Getting to someone in their organization with both the authority to talk to me about the killings, and the willingness to do so, will take more."

"Very well. Good hunting." Kumar closed the link.

Meiko followed AR tags to the side entrance. The plain-clothes attendant inside let her out without comment, but the baby-faced troopers in uniform standing guard outside advised caution. "I don't advise going out alone, ma'am," one said. "Off-worlders have been targeted via their social profiles and singled out. A few beaten pretty badly. You should really have someone to watch your six."

"I could call one of the off-duty team to escort you," her partner offered.

"That won't be necessary. I've been to the station before." Meiko adjusted her jacket and looked both ways, up and down the side street linking the main pedestrian thoroughfare in front of the consulate and the service alley behind. An intermittent stream of tiny electric vehicles and a substantial number of autopallets zipped along the alley in both directions. "How are the attackers getting away with it? Don't the Constabulary track their djinns?"

The troopers looked grim. "The yellowjackets find them, all right," the short one said. "Not before the beatings, though."

"Hm. Good point. Well, I'll be careful." She thanked them, turned, and walked towards the front of the Consulate.

She could do something about her social profile, the basic identity information broadcast by her djinn, once she reached Eko, the south ring's primary market, and shook any physical tail the Ileris might put on her. One of the many negative outcomes of her last mission had been the blowing of her public cover to the Ileri authorities, though they hadn't outed her. The lack of a minder waiting for her in the Consulate lobby was curious; they had to know she was here to investigate the assassination. Were they were stretched too thin to assign someone full-time to shadow a partially-blown covert Commonwealth operative? Did they consider her an ally already, ahead of the imminent referendum? Or would they follow her discreetly?

She never had issues mixing with crowds here, at least visually. The station's populace wasn't as cosmopolitan a blend as one would find on, say, Singapore Baru, but it was diverse enough that Meiko blended in without notice. Some of her ancestors had fled up the Macapá elevator off the coast of Brazil; further back along that branch of her family tree lay the Japanese farmers who'd emigrated to South America in the early 20th century, before the Great Looting and the Melt, or so family legend said. Those already blended genes were further intermixed with East African and Malay blood, along with a dash of Vietnamese, in the two hundred and fifty years since Novo Brasilia's settlement. She didn't know which of her ancestors to thank for the thick, straight hair, still dark brown and currently trimmed to a pixie cut. Her skin was more golden-toned than usual here, but not noticeably so, and enough of Ileri's people had East Asian ancestry that her cheekbones didn't stand out either. Someone might notice that she moved like a spacer, but that, too, was pretty common on-station.

She reached the street and smoothly made her way into the passing throng before a disturbance cut her musing short. A knot of bodies coalesced before her eyes, as first three people, then six, then a dozen, then twenty or more, converged from several directions at the intersection between Meiko and her quickest route to the market. Then with a snapping noise and the smell of cheap fabber plastic, one of them pulled a banner from a backpack, and they began unrolling it, blocking the street in the process.

NO COMMONWEALTH — NO WAR — ONE WORLD, it read.

Oh, great leaping Mother, a protest perfectly timed to screw up her evasion plan.

Someone bumped her from behind and she glanced back to discover another line of protestors was gathering at the intersection closest to her. This new rank of activists deployed their own banner and cut off that end of the block. Those passers-by caught in between the lines, perhaps fifty or sixty people, began shouting at the activists. The impromptu blockaders, for their part, donned the flat caps that prompted the nickname 'buttonheads' and broadcast public AR signs proclaiming their allegiance to the One World party, along with anti-Commonwealth slogans.

The young man who'd stumbled into her apologized profusely. She nodded at him and turned to push her way through the crowd. A few people began taunting the One Worlders with shouts of "Buttonheads!" and "Dustbrain!" as the protestors answered with insults of their own.

Voices rose, heated and sharp. A quartet of women in hijabs began shoving some of the One Worlders, trying to push their way through the line. Suddenly both factions were exchanging shoves. A man in rigger's coveralls, two meters tall and built like a blast door, snarled as a One Worlder accosted him, jabbing a finger towards his face like an autopick. Meiko missed whatever the buttonhead said that finally put the rigger over his limit as she tried to slither between the knots of conflict starting to crystallize. But she, and everyone else, heard the howl of pain as the rigger's enormous hands wrapped around the buttonhead's arm at wrist and elbow and pushed. She wasn't sure how many recognized the sound that followed as the smaller man's arm breaking, but she'd heard it enough to know.

No slow fuse here; the One Worlders dropped their banners and went at the rigger and the others pushing against them with fists and feet. The crowd responded in kind, and just like that, the situation cycled from 'disturbance' to 'riot'.

A One Worlder made the mistake of taking a swing at Meiko. She swayed to avoid the blow, then twisted back upright and snapped a kick into his knee. A little bump of the shoulder was all it took to send him to the floor, right into the path of someone trying to rush forward to reinforce one faction or the other. As that person tumbled into the streetgrass, she stepped on their back and sprang into the momentarily clear spot they'd vacated. Hands grasped for her and she twisted free from clutching fingers. She drove the heel of her right hand into the handsy bastard's chin, felt the jolt of contact along her arm. Her would-be assailant reeled back into another combatant and she flowed into the gap.

There was no rhythm to this fracas, no dance to groove to. Meiko elbowed ribs, swept ankles, and tried to flow through the crowd. A woman wearing a One Worlder flat cap tried to grab her hair, but Meiko caught her by the wrist, spun, twisted, and ignored the woman's howl as she ruthlessly flipped her into another protestor, sending both face first into the ground.

That created the last opening she needed. Meiko found herself on the fringes of the crowd, among people who were trying to get away rather than to join in. She spotted a pack of buttonhead reinforcements closing in, though, and the whining turbines of Constabulary bots filled the air above. She pushed her way through the crowd, joining a group headed down a side street away from the fracas.

At least, she reflected as she touched the tiny spot on her jacket's collar, changing its color from orange to dark green, any physical tail Ileri intelligence might have assigned to her would have their hands full tracking her through *that* mess. She set out at a brisk pace for Eko Market.

TOIWA

CONSTABULARY HEADQUARTERS, ILERI STATION, FORWARD RING

SOMETHING ON THE main display caught Toiwa's attention as Detective Sergeant Imoke finished up his in-person report. "Nidal!" she snapped to the watch commander. She pointed at the screen. "Where is that happening?"

One of the analysts was already expanding the image to fill a full third of the video wall. On-screen, dozens of people brawled in the middle of a broad street. Toiwa stalked across the room to stand next to the watch commander, with Imoke and Valverdes in her wake.

"South ring, ma'am," the watch commander said as her deputy ordered the rapid response team dispatched from the hub. "Damn, it's the Commonwealth Consulate. Flashmob protest."

"That's not a protest, that's a riot in the making," Toiwa retorted. "What do we have on scene?"

"The usual courtesy patrol, two officers, and two aerial bots," an analyst called out. "More bots en route, you'll have a dozen in sixty seconds."

Toiwa called the south ring's watch commander. "Inspector Karungi. You're aware of the developing situation, I trust?" She raised her left hand, flicking her fingers open to send the audio to the overhead speakers.

Karungi was an old hand, pushing forty years' service, much like Sergeant Imoke. Given his rank, he had likely played ball with Toiwa's corrupt predecessor, though he'd been cagey enough to avoid being nailed in Toiwa's first anti-corruption sweep. "Yes, Commissioner," he said in his thin, reedy voice. "I'm assessing my response."

That was not the answer she expected to hear. She blinked, mouth working but not forming words for a few seconds. Her words came out sharp as razors. "Assessing. Your. Response." Her jaw tightened. "Inspector. That is the Commonwealth Consulate. There are at least"— she glanced up to read the still-climbing number on the screen—"sixty people involved in a developing riot. What do you intend to do?"

Karungi responded with a chutney of bureaucratic weasel-words. That annoyed her, but as soon as the word "deliberation" escaped his lips, she made her decision. Inspector Karungi would be the next notch in 'Toiwa's Axe'.

"Inspector Karungi, you are relieved of duty." The blustering man sputtered to a halt. "Is your second-in-command present?"

"I've got her on-line, ma'am," Nidal answered from her right.

"Patch them through." *Dammit, who is Karungi's second?*

<Deputy Inspector Tábara is Karungi's number two,> her aide Kala Valverdes sent over their private link, anticipating Toiwa's need.

"Deputy Inspector Tábara. Effective immediately, you are the first shift watch commander for South Ring. You have a rapidly developing riot outside a diplomatic facility of a friendly foreign government. Rapid response is en route from the hub. You are incident commander. How are you going to handle this?"

In a sober alto voice, Tábara assured Toiwa she was dispatching her entire on-duty force not required elsewhere, along with every available bot. She requested permission to summon her second shift team as reinforcements, which Toiwa granted immediately, as her overtime budget for the next reporting period sailed out of sight. Karungi raged in the background until one of the analysts cut him out of the circuit. Toiwa scarcely finished approving these measures when Valverdes signaled an urgent message coming in.

The governor. Not unexpected, but Ruhindi could have waited a few more minutes, surely. "The Head's calling," Toiwa told Nidal, who nodded and carried on assisting Tábara with managing the response teams. Toiwa shifted away from the command dais and popped open the call window, but didn't engage the privacy field. When shit like this went down, you wanted things on the record. And witnesses. "Governor. I assume you're calling about the situation in the south ring?"

If Ruhindi had looked frustrated this morning, she was positively dyspeptic now, nostrils flared, eyes narrowed, seeming to lean forward into the pickup as if getting right into Toiwa's face. "This is unacceptable, Nnenna," she snapped. "I told you this morning we can't afford open clashes like this. How did it happen?"

Toiwa frowned. *Really, this is her question?* "We're focusing on response rather than root-cause analysis just this moment, Governor, but initial indications are it was a flash mob. I'm sure you know those are virtually impossible to prevent." *At least without turning ourselves into a lockstep police state like the Saljuans.* The rule of law was one thing; domination by law was something else entirely.

"Dammit. All right, do you at least have it contained?"

Toiwa glanced over at the display wall. Perilously thin

lines of uniformed constables had formed on each of the streets leading to the fracas. A full two-dozen aerial bots reinforced the officers in the street. Someone clever had brought Transit into the loop and halted all traffic to the affected area except for the response units. The count of the crowd seemed stable, hovering around a hundred and twenty people. The Commonwealth guard detachment at the consulate entrance had grown from two to eight, she noted, but they seemed to confine their response to keeping the area around the doors clear with stun sticks. "Almost, Governor. No one new is joining the fray, at least. The Consulate remains secure. We should be ready to move in and secure the instigators within ten minutes or so, I think, as soon as the response force arrives from the hub."

"You've identified the instigators?" Ruhindi demanded. Toiwa could see the tendons standing out in her neck.

"One Worlders started the protest, but it appears a heckler initiated the violence," a low voice murmured from her left. Toiwa glanced over and saw Imoke standing nearby. Several AR windows replaying the first stages of the riot hovered around him. He flipped one around so she could clearly see a large man gripping the arm of a smaller person in a One World T-shirt. "There may have been incitement." That last word was key, legally speaking. Ileri law recognized incitement to violence as unprotected speech—a lesson, Toiwa knew from her legal studies, of one of the many missteps during the Great Looting back on Earth. If the One Worlders were found to have engaged in agitation with intent to draw a violent response, they bore ultimate responsibility for what followed.

"Thank you, Sergeant," Toiwa said. She turned back to face the governor. "Tentatively, it looks like we can lay this at the door of the One World party, ma'am, but there's some uncertainty."

Ruhindi sucked in a breath and grimaced. "Those dust-brained idiots," she said. "I don't doubt they brought this on themselves. Singling their faction out risks escalating the partisan feelings, though. That's only going to lead to further trouble."

"If One Worlders are the ones poking the anthill, Governor, surely we need to shut that line of action down." She made a sweeping gesture, as if to take in the whole station. "Just this morning, in fact, you were impressing on me the need to cut any violence off as quickly as possible."

The governor seemed to rock back and forth slightly. "Yes, yes, all that's true." Ruhindi shook her head, frowning deeply. "But sentiments are much more delicately balanced than I'd realized. As evidenced by this affair."

Toiwa could feel the tension in her own neck ratcheting up and frowned. "What are you suggesting?" she said in a clipped tone. "That I not apprehend the perpetrators?"

Ruhindi raised her hands in a placating gesture. "No, no, not at all," she said hurriedly. "But the government can't be seen to be favoring one side or the other."

"The Constabulary is not the government," Toiwa said.

She got a snort in response. "You don't seriously believe that, Commissioner, do you?" the governor said. "Not part of the elected government, certainly, but you can't be arguing that the planetary police force is not an arm of the state."

Imoke cleared his throat. "If I might offer a suggestion, Commissioner." He waved another AR window into existence, displaying a flight of large bots speeding through the air. "The heavy crowd-control bots will be in position within a minute," he said. "Carrying a full load of tangler rounds."

Toiwa's left eyebrow arched. "And you have a suggestion regarding their employment, Sergeant?"

Imoke nodded. "Clean sweep," he said. "At the very least, it defers the question of assigning culpability until a suitable determination can be made."

That course certainly possessed the brutal elegance of simplicity, and it would definitely put an end to the fighting. Let Ruhindi fault her for *that*. "Inspector Nidal," she called over her shoulder. Nidal acknowledged. "As soon as the crowd-control bots are in position, have them saturate the area with tangler rounds. Target everyone inside the zone except for Commonwealth personnel. I mean *everyone*. Is that clear?"

"That's hardly a better solution, Commissioner!" Ruhindi hissed at her. "You can't do this."

"You can take that up with the High Commissioner, ma'am." She nodded at Imoke before resuming her position beside Nidal, as the watch commander gave orders to her automated systems specialist. On her left, Toiwa heard Valverdes muttering annotations to the record for the inquiry that Toiwa no doubt had in her future. She watched the screens, seeing the bot's icons flip from amber to green as they reached their positions. "Fire," she ordered in a clear, ringing voice as the final icon changed color.

Above the mob, eight robots aimed the broad mouths

of their tangler guns down at the roiling crowd. Even over the muted audio Toiwa heard the *splatsplatsplat* as sticky projectiles rained down across the combatants, starting at the outskirts of the crowd and then, circling, working their way towards the middle. Balls of nano-motile adhesive, the tangler rounds burst just before impacting their targets, covering them and any nearby surfaces in blobs of gummy goo. These blobs flowed together even as they moved clear of nostrils, mouths, eyes, and other orifices. Within seconds the goo stiffened, immobilizing anyone caught within.

Thirty seconds later the barrage was over, and so was the riot. One Worlders, counter-protestors and innocent bystanders alike stood, knelt, or lay locked in place. Here and there Toiwa saw constables unlucky enough to be caught in the spillover. They had her sympathies; she'd experienced that indignity herself once as a rookie, after being called up to clear out a block party that got out of hand.

Well, she could handle a little grumbling from the beat officers. She suspected they'd appreciate decisive action that spared them having to wade in and subdue the belligerents by hand, after they'd thought about it. She had when she'd been in their shoes, at any rate.

Toiwa turned back to the governor's window. "The riot is now contained, ma'am."

"Thank you, Commissioner," Ruhindi answered, but there was no warmth in her voice. "I'll expect a full briefing about this incident this evening, along with an update on the assassination investigation."

"Absolutely, ma'am." The window blanked and Toiwa waved it closed. She turned to Imoke as Nidal and Tábara between them began coordinating the work of extracting those caught in the tangler goo, beginning with the injured. She gave the sergeant an appraising look. "Not many Detective Sergeants would put themselves in the middle of a spat between a couple of heads," she said.

He grinned. "I have been told many times that I'm not properly mindful of my station."

Toiwa found herself smiling back, if briefly. "It was a good call." She tilted her head towards the video wall. "It's still a mess, but a manageable one, now."

Imoke's grin widened to a full smile, and she noted the laugh lines. "But not my mess to clear up, fortunately," he said with a chuckle.

Toiwa sighed. She dismissed the detective with a wave and turned to Valverdes. "I'll need the paperwork for Karungi's dismissal ready as quickly as you can manage, Kala, but notify Detention to prep for a mass arrest first." Her aide nodded from zer workstation, AR windows popping open even as ze moved. Toiwa gave her attention to Nidal. "All right, Inspector, let's sort these people into their proper bins."

CHAPTER FIVE

Noo

Councilor Walla's Office, Ileri Station, Forward Ring

Walla's office was decorated in what Noo dubbed 'Intellectual of the People Retro' style. Images of the councilor meeting with scientists and engineers competed for wall space with shots of her among crowds of constituents, browsing the ring's market, or watching concerts in Pei Park. The furnishings were definitely all station-fabbed: all bright, tough synthetics built to withstand assault by a full creche's worth of children. Or, perhaps, for barricading the office against a restless mob.

The councilor actually came out from behind her desk to greet Fari and offer her condolences, though she retreated behind it immediately afterwards. Her assistant set a fresh pot of coffee on a low side table between the visitor's chairs and exited, closing the door behind her.

Walla looked first at Fari, then at Noo, then back to Fari again before asking, "Why have you young ladies come to visit me in this dark hour?"

Noo fought down the urge to laugh. Walla was scarcely four years her senior, an utterly insignificant distance at their ages. *She's let her hair go gray,* she realized. *Playing the venerable elder card, that's for sure.*

Fari, accustomed to dealing with elders, and de-sensitized to it by her close contact with Noo, kept her cool. She stuck to the play they'd hashed out on the way over. "We are concerned about you, Councilor."

Walla looked puzzled. "Whatever for? Mother of the Leap, child, your brother is dead." The councilor shifted uncomfortably in her chair. "I would think you and your auntie here would be dogging the Constabulary or knocking on doors yourselves to find who did it."

"We have been," Fari replied in her most earnest, serious voice. "And in the course of our inquiries, we've come to believe you might be a target yourself."

The posture change was subtle, but Noo, watching for it, caught the sudden stiffening in Walla's muscles as she straightened ever so slightly in her seat, hands tensing on the chair's arms, like a racer in the blocks poised to spring forth. "I don't understand," Walla said, a hint of tension creeping into her voice. "Why would someone want to attack me?"

"We don't know," Noo said, taking up the thread. Walla's head swiveled to face her. "But we've learned you were to be at last night's meeting and are concerned that perhaps the assassin intended you die along with the others."

This did nothing to relieve Walla's tension, but that

was the point, after all. *Find the button and press.* Walla leaned back in her chair, arms folded across her chest, and stared at the pair with narrowed eyes. "I don't see how that's possible, since I had no plans to meet with Minister Ita last night. You can check my schedule."

They had checked Walla's public schedule, of course, or rather an agency analyst had while they were in transit. "Your schedule shows you were attending a private engagement yesterday evening," Fari said evenly. "We understand that at least part of that time was to be spent with Minister Ita."

"Your understanding is incorrect," Walla said.

"Mazlan," Noo said in a soft tone, using the councilor's given name, drawing her eyes back to Noo. The firm had done work for Walla over the years, and Noo traded on that familiarity. "As you say, Fathya's grandson is dead. You've been a player on-station as long as she and I. Do you really think we would stint on any possible means to ferret out every conceivable lead?" It was a fine line she trod, with words that could signal either threat or concern. Which way would the quarry move?

The councilor uncoiled slightly, settling back into her chair and folding her hands in her lap. Her expression, though, remained hard as a pressure bulkhead. The silence stretched on for several seconds before she responded. "How did you come by this information?" Her voice carried not a hint of warmth.

"Our technical analysts have been working nonstop on this since last night," Fari said, which was true enough. "We've ascertained you were on Second Landing Club's guest list for the critical period." This was of course also true, if unconnected from her previous statement.

Since the councilor was certainly recording the interview and might run voice-stress analysis or some other forensics against the recording, they'd agreed to stick to facts as much as possible while still shielding their arrangement with Loh.

Behind her desk, Walla smacked her teeth. "*Fathya* wouldn't breach a privacy seal like that." She jabbed one finger, spear-like, at Noo. "*You* certainly would, though. Or"—she smiled, her voice taking on a false sweetness— "did you fuck one of the staff for it?"

Think you're going to shake me, wrapper? Tempting as it was to say "Yes", she stuck with misdirection. "Our young associate Haissani is a wizard system cracker," she said, continuing the factual-but-irrelevant line of patter.

Fari allowed the two older women to continue their stare-down for several more seconds before cutting in. "You were planning to visit the club last night, and to see the minister?" she asked, the picture of calm professionalism.

Walla cocked her head at Fari. "It's not something I'm at liberty to discuss. Sensitive government issues are involved."

"That's curious," Fari said, her own head tilting. "Something involving the Commonwealth vote, perhaps?"

"I cannot discuss it," Walla said flatly.

"I see." Fari hooked one ankle over her knee and leaned forward. "Whatever came up to prevent you from attending such an important meeting must have been significant."

The councilor's eyes flicked aside for a moment. "It was a family issue," she said. "Rather private." She glared at Noo. "Privacy which I hope you will respect."

Fari's response was smoother than a shot of Old Whistler rum. "I hope the situation is cleared up without undue complication. I would hate for another family to be in distress today."

"No, no, it was all settled last night," Walla said with a touch of haste. She paused. "I'm sure you and your grandmother must be reeling."

Fari dropped her foot to the floor, straightening in her chair. "We find work the best therapy."

"I would be honored if I could attend the funeral," Walla said.

Fari nodded. "Grandmother would be pleased," she replied. "I'll make sure you're notified once the time is set."

"It's not sorted, yet?"

Fari shook her head. "The Constabulary hasn't released his body yet. We hope they will in time for Maghrib."

After another round of expressions of mutual sympathy, they allowed Walla to chivvy them out of her office. At the doorway to the outer office, though, Noo turned. "I wonder, Councilor, what you think of the proposal to join the Commonwealth? Since you were to meet with the Commonwealth Consul last night."

Walla was too practiced a politician to freeze, but Noo caught another slight hesitation before the other woman answered. "I will defer to the will of the people on that," she said. "I think, on the whole, a healthy relationship with the Commonwealth that respects Ileri's traditions and standing is the best course," she said. Her response was smooth, practiced, a feed-nugget for media—and voter—consumption, but didn't commit her one way or the other. "It is my hope that these tragic events don't jeopardize that relationship, regardless of the referendum's outcome."

Nodding, Noo allowed herself to be guided out. The pair made their farewells and, wordlessly, made a beeline for the nearest transit stop. Once settled into their car they snapped a privacy field into place.

"She's lying about why she didn't go," Fari said without preamble.

"Caught that, did you? Good." Noo instructed the car to take them to the south ring, back to the firm's office. "That bit about government matters, hmm, that might be real. Your grandmother might have a hook on that. But in a Fingers-run venue? That doesn't scan true."

"Agreed." Fari flipped through her own AR fields. "How well known is Second Landing for being a Fingers place?"

Noo tapped her lips. "It's not like they have a sign over the door, but any serious player on-station would know. The Consul's people would have known for sure."

"Is Walla getting flash from them?"

"The Fingers? Not that I know of, or nothing significant. She's bought and paid for by the big family concerns, mainly the consortium that runs the outer-system station." Noo frowned; Fari's father had died in an accident building that station, but the mention didn't seem to disturb the younger woman. "That might be why she was supposed to attend, to represent some of the commercial families who weren't there." Three of the victims represented commercial concerns, family-run enterprises. She called up the list again. "Lim, they're biotech wetware, the Parma do environmental systems. Anwar, huh. They do a lot of provisioning for New Arm colonies, mixed manufacturing."

"That's an odd bunch," Fari said, flipping through her own AR windows as the car whizzed along through the transit tubes. "But it makes a sort of sense. If the referendum passes, markets are going to shift."

"Maybe." Fatigue, which had lurked for the last few hours like a caffeine addict waiting for the coffee shop to open, ambushed her at last. Noo closed her eyes and slumped in her seat. Her body might be hurtling through the bowels of the station, but she'd run out of energy to keep her own momentum up for the moment. The empty spot she'd been able to ignore since Daniel showed her Saed's body abruptly clamored for attention, riding the coattails of her exhaustion, trying to draw her down into the desolation of sorrow. She gasped at the onslaught, caught herself, and jammed her fists into her eyes, trying to drive it down with pain of another sort.

Fari swept her AR windows aside and looked hard at Noo, her own face drawn. "Are you all right, Auntie?"

"No, girl. Not hardly." Noo sucked in a breath, held it, blew it out. Then again. The emptiness retreated, just a bit, and she whispered a prayer: *I salute Oshoshi, master of himself, wise one who gives blessings...*

No presence filled her; none had for decades. But she said the words anyway, and felt a bit control return. She opened her eyes and saw Fari across from her, now crying silently. She reached forward and took the younger woman's hands, which gripped hers with fierce strength. "I'm not all right, but the hunt doesn't stop for tears. So, on I go." She leaned forward and Fari did the same, until their foreheads touched. "And you?"

The younger woman sniffed once. "As you say. We go on." She leaned back and slipped one hand free, rubbing the back against her eyes to clear them. "But it hurts, Auntie. It hurts *so much*."

"It do, child. That it do." Noo found herself slipping into her own mother's cant, a sure sign of distress, or exhaustion, or both. She gave Fari's hand a squeeze and sat back but kept hold. "But we find the one that did our boy, yes?"

"Inshallah," Fari said.

Noo tightened her grip. "Then we make ourselves His instruments."

TOIWA

COMMISSIONER'S OFFICE, CONSTABULARY HEADQUARTERS, ILERI STATION, FORWARD RING

VALVERDES' HEAD POPPED into Toiwa's workspace, displacing a window showing the latest collection of witness statements from the assassination case—at the present, interviews with the victims' next of kin. "Commissioner? Minister Miguna is calling. He's rather insistent."

Toiwa stifled a groan; the last thing she needed was another government busybody. But refusing to take the Treasury Minister's call wasn't an option, at least not without another riot as an excuse. "Thank you, Kala. Is the documentation for Karungi's dismissal in order?"

"Just waiting for Inspector Nidal to sign off on her attestation. She's reviewing it now."

"Very good. Let Miguna know I'll be right with him and put him in my queue." Valverdes' disembodied head nodded, and the AR window winked out.

Toiwa waved down the fields she'd been working in, poured herself a glass of water, and flipped open a mirror field to check her appearance. Finding nothing amiss, she squared her shoulders and waved the new window open. "Minister Miguna, good afternoon. My apologies for keeping you waiting." She fixed on her 'professionally helpful neutral' face.

Ajax Miguna had parlayed his leadership of the One World party into a sizable chunk of the vote in the last election, and thus secured his current position as Treasury Minister. Toiwa hadn't met him in person but had seen him at campaign events during her last posting, and he'd been a steady feature on the news feeds even before the election. He was a big man with the symmetrical features, glowing golden-brown skin, and slicked-back hair of a media drama star, and, she had to admit, the charisma to match. His public persona featured a lot of bombast and expansive statements, often running right up to the edge of truth, beyond which the Ministry of Information's fact checkers would begin assessing penalties. All this combined to give Toiwa a distinctly uneasy feeling whenever she listened to him. She wondered how he'd present himself to her in a private meeting.

"Commissioner!" he barked. "You're detaining members of my party illegally, and I demand you release them immediately."

Straight to domineering asshole it is, then. Toiwa locked her expression in place. "I'm not sure what supporters you mean, Minister. I can assure you the Station Constabulary has detained no one illegally. Could you please elaborate?"

"Don't play coy, Commissioner." Whether he was truly

peeved or not, Miguna certainly *looked* aggrieved at this supposed infringement of liberty. "I'm talking about the citizens exercising their lawful rights of assembly and speech who gathered outside the Commonwealth Consulate earlier today. Your officers scooped them up willy-nilly along with the violent instigators who assaulted them."

"I see," Toiwa said, feeling the muscles in her jaw tighten. She took a sip of water as she pondered which tack to take. 'Bureaucratic stonewalling' won out. "I'm afraid we're still assessing the video evidence and taking statements from all involved. It will take some time to complete those actions and ensure that due process is granted to everyone involved. I'm sure that once the proceedings of justice have run their course that your supporters will all receive the appropriate outcomes." Which, based on Inspector Tábara's initial report, would include at least a half-dozen charges of incitement to violence, which carried cumulative penalties based on how many violent acts followed the incitement. The presence of the reinforcing goon squads spoke to premeditation, which—if her people could prove it, and she thought they could—meant this particular bunch of buttonheads were looking at years of confinement and counseling, in addition to reparative damages.

"Preposterous. The video I've seen clearly shows my people were victims of the first assault, and simply acted to defend themselves." Miguna leaned forward into his pickup, as if to intrude into Toiwa's space. "I'm certain that as a senior officer of the Constabulary, you don't condone such vindictive personal violence."

Do these cartoonish intimidation tactics really work

for him? As a fresh young constable, Toiwa had faced off against drunken riggers down the cable for bone leave, angry football fans half again her mass, and on one memorable occasion, a five-hundred-kilo haexcat that had wandered in from the bush. One puffed-up demagogue thirty-six thousand kilometers away didn't worry her, at least where physical confrontation was concerned.

Political confrontation, on the other hand...

"I'll be sure to instruct the investigating officers to be especially diligent, Minister," she said, and did her best to inject a note of 'Just between us, wink wink, nod nod' as she ostentatiously made notes in her personal window. That the notes read 'Make certain case is airtight before sending to magistrates' and 'Send recording to the High Commissioner' was her little secret.

Whether this genuinely satisfied Miguna or not, she wasn't sure, but he smiled and relaxed. "Thank you, Commissioner. That's all I ask." He flashed her a toothy grin. "I'm sure your people are terribly busy, after last night's horrible events."

"The last few shifts have been eventful, yes."

"You must have developed some promising leads by now."

Toiwa smiled faintly, saying nothing.

Whatever his skills and virtues were, patience appeared to be absent from Miguna's kit. Or perhaps two decades of questioning subjects gave Toiwa superior ability at waiting for other people to open their mouths to fill the silence. The minister didn't make it to a full ten seconds before blurting, "Surely you've made headway apprehending the suspects?"

71

"It would be most improper for me to discuss an ongoing investigation of such sensitivity," Toiwa said primly.

"Of course, of course," he said, waving his hands as if to dismiss the faintest whiff of impropriety from the air. "Such a horrible act, an attack on a sitting minister."

"And the Commonwealth Consul, and seven other people, all shot dead," Toiwa said, and this time she couldn't keep a note of irritation out of her voice. "My people pursue justice for *all* the victims."

"That's all well and the proper way of things, Commissioner, and I'm glad your people all feel that way." Miguna folded his arms across his chest. "I am simply pointing out such a brazen attack on poor Ita, combined with today's violence, well, things must be very chaotic on the station."

Is that a dig, or maybe an attempt to goad me? She was considering her response when the icon signifying an urgent message from Zheng gave Toiwa release from his baited hook. She flicked her thumb, opening the message, eyes widening slightly as she skimmed it.

She focused back on Miguna. "My apologies, Minister, but there's been a development I must attend to right away."

"I'm sure it must be absolutely crucial," Miguna said. "I'll ask the High Commissioner for an update, then." The call snapped shut from his end.

"Be my guest, Minister," she said aloud to the open air. She wondered whether he'd actually make good on the implied threat, rather suspecting Miguna lacked the moral fiber to confront the HC, a seasoned veteran of the capital who'd outlasted a half-dozen changes in government. She felt a sudden urge to wash her hands, as if Miguna's oily personality had left some physical residue even over the virtual link. Shaking her head, she popped open her window to Valverdes. "Send Zheng and M. Okafor in please, Kala," she said, and stood up to greet her visitors.

OKAFOR

JOSEPHINE OKAFOR HEARD the constable with the slightly husky voice call her name even as her djinn picked up the officer's approach. "M. Okafor? Commissioner Toiwa is ready for you."

"Thank you, Lieutenant." She stood up, snapping her cane to its full extension. The lidar and radar beads in her clothing mapped the room and fed their data to her djinn, which in turn transmitted it to her elbow-length sensory-haptic gloves. These turned the information into tactile sensations she'd learned to read over many years' practice, aided by the array of detectors she'd had embedded in her forearms as soon as she'd been old enough to request them. But she'd used the cane almost from the time she'd learned to walk, and nobody knew better than she that electronics could be fooled.

"If you'll follow me?" Zheng said. Okafor followed, leaving enough room to sweep her cane before her, tap-tap-tap as the plastic tip met the floor. She slowed almost to a halt as Zheng opened the door for her, then passed into the Commissioner's office.

She marched confidently up to stand next to one of the chairs in front of Toiwa's desk, switched her cane to her left hand and extended her right one. "Josephine Okafor, Commissioner. The High Commissioner sent me up with the forensic team on the morning shuttle."

The pattern of tingles on her arms told her Toiwa leaned forward to shake hands. The Commissioner's hands were warm, smooth, and strong, with the faintest hints of callouses at the base of her fingers. She lifted weights, then, or perhaps played tennis. "Thank you for coming, please, sit down," Toiwa said, taking her own seat as Okafor did the same. She heard Lieutenant Zheng take the other chair. "We're grateful for all the assistance from planetside. You said you came *with* the forensic team. Does that mean you're not part of it?"

She collapsed her cane and tucked it into its holster, then placed her right hand on the edge of Toiwa's desk while the left remained in her lap. "I'm afraid not," she said. "I'm an infonet security specialist on the High Commissioner's staff. I've been investigating anomalies in the station's infonet."

"What sort of anomalies?" Toiwa asked. Okafor didn't need the biometric data her sensors were pulling in to detect the puzzlement in Toiwa's voice.

"It might be easier to show you," she said, raising both hands to chest level, palms up. "If I might use your projector?"

"Of course." Her djinn caught the authorization packet Toiwa sent, and her fingers began an intricate dance. The haptic sensors in her glove turned her motions into commands in concert with those sent by her neural implant, and she conjured her model into being.

"This is a real-time view of Ileri Station's infonet," Okafor said. She couldn't see the 3D mesh of light hanging in the air, but she'd traced each of those lines by hand over the past five months, adding colors to aid the sighted. She moved two fingers and the colors dimmed, leaving behind a faded gray tracery depicting the whole network. Three faint constellations remained, each spread throughout the visual filigree. To her, they consisted of thicker threads than the rest of the network, with jagged textures. "These are collections of compromised nodes within the station infonet. We became aware of this first network"—a slight flexing of one finger caused the smallest web to flash bright red—"about two months ago. It saw a major spike in activity yesterday evening, several hours prior to the attack, and then again in the immediate aftermath."

"Wait a moment." Toiwa sounded perplexed. "You're telling me there are *three* different sets of illegal subnetworks here in my infonet? And I'm just finding out *now*?"

"Yes," Okafor said, imperturbable. "The HC felt you should be notified in person, given the nature of the threat." She cocked her head at Toiwa, her hands rocksteady. "May I continue?"

"Yes, please."

"Thank you. I was about to say, this network seems very recent, active only for the last few months. It expanded rapidly and aggressively, and the techniques and tools aren't consistent with domestic infonet criminals."

"Implying off-worlders?" Toiwa interjected.

"Indeed. I'd guess one of the major powers: the Commonwealth or the Saljuans, maybe the Triumvirate, but I wouldn't entirely rule out another player yet. They've been very canny, despite their loud and fast tactics."

"And the other two?"

Another finger twitch suppressed the red network and a much more extensive yellow web shone among the tangle. "We believe this network belongs to the branch of the Fingers operating on the station," Okafor said. "It looks to be long-established and has a high correlation with the tools and techniques we see employed in Fingers infonet operations planetside. I'd been mapping this network for several months when the apparently foreign network appeared." Her fingers flexed again, and the yellow network was replaced by an orange lacework even larger and more complex than the putative Fingers network, but fuzzy in places. "Before the foreign attackers showed up, however, I discovered this other unauthorized network. Its origin is a mystery. It's highly interlaced polymorphic code, quite unlike anything we see used anywhere else. It's been in place for a long time."

"How long?" Toiwa asked. "Since the war?"

Okafor's lips twitched. "Much older than that, Commissioner. The Fingers network is at least a century old. I'd estimate this one being nearly the same age as the station."

"I'm not sure I understand the significance," Toiwa said. "I understood that the Exiles built the station and the elevator at the same time as they settled the surface. Wouldn't they have used some of the protocols they brought with them?"

"Yes," Okafor said, "I'm afraid so. This is the same kind of code used on some Earth networks before Exile."

Across the room, Zheng cleared her throat. "Excuse me," she said. "You mentioned highly interlaced polymorphic code. I'm not an infonet specialist like yourself, but I've had some intrusion training, and there's only one example of that I'm aware of."

"You're correct. I'm afraid this isn't innocent code," Okafor said. "It's not for running life-support systems, or the space elevator, or the station's mass-management system. It's a network designed to regulate and process communications between a massive number of distributed nodes, using protocols designed for biomechanical nanoware."

The horror in Toiwa's voice was unmistakable. "You mean…"

"Yes. The kind that, in the brain, can control human behavior, putting people under the control of puppet-masters. This is the kind of code that powered the Unity Plague."

CHAPTER SIX

MEIKO

EKO MARKET, ILERI STATION, SOUTH RING

MEIKO EXITED THE market's service passage just behind an older man who carried a small thermal bag that she guessed was his lunch. He held the door open for her with a polite nod. She nodded, her temporary and newly acquired tresses bobbing, and smiled back, then turned and set off for the closest transit station at a casual walk. She settled her weight back onto her hips and shortened her stride, dropping her shoulders. Her all-too-brief visit to a body shop on the market's third level had provided with her darkened skin, longer and lighter hair, and a fresh makeup job that would give most facial-recognition systems fits. It wouldn't trick a smart agent looking at her gross biometrics, but it would fool Ileri's routine crowd-scanning system, and any casual human analysts too, at least for a little while. Her djinn now identified her as Meriel Suzuki, native-born to Ileri—one of several seriously illegal modifications to her djinn—which ought to further obscure her trail. She hoped. She affected a confident air and sauntered down the ramp into the transit station to purchase a one-way ride to the station's hub.

No constables, or worse, intelligence operatives, accosted her when the bubble-car's doors opened into the riot of color, noise, and zero-gravity motion that was Maseko Circus, deep in the heart of the asteroid that anchored the space elevator and formed the station's core. She flowed into the crowd, grabbing hold of one of the towlines hauling people to the retail arcade. Meiko's decades as a spacer meant she could have joined the zero-g adepts who sailed along independently, but it seemed most people on Ileri weren't so skilled; better to stick with the masses and hold her capabilities in reserve. She reached the arcade, detached herself from the towline, and picked a cafe with a cluster of empty serving cubbies. She slipped her feet into the restraining loop and ordered a platter of spiced newt skewers. She watched the crowd while waiting for the bot to deliver her order. Nothing seemed out of place, and no one seemed to be paying any attention to her, so she finished her snack and placed a call.

Her call yielded a transit system routing code that resulted in a ten-minute, roundabout ride through the hub's tube network. No one else got off at her stop, a nondescript stretch of station corridor, unoccupied but for the ubiquitous maintenance and janitorial bots. Meiko had to give the Ileris credit; if there was a dingy spot on-station, she'd never found it. No public tow lines graced this sector but plenty of grip bars lined the walls, so it was a simple matter to shoot herself down the corridor to her destination, a blank ceramic-coated hatch that opened after she waved her djinn at the pickup. Showing off a little, she swung her body in through the hatchway with a half-twist to land lightly on the deck, hooking her feet beneath one of the ubiquitous grip bars and straightening in one graceful, flowing motion.

Her contact floated just beyond the antechamber, his meaty arms crossed and with one foot hooked under a grip bar, perpendicular to both Meiko and the hatch, proclaiming he was someone who wasn't about to cater to those unaccustomed to zero-g. His round face seemed caught between expressions of curiosity and wariness, settling on the latter as he took in her appearance. "Meriel?" he asked. "It has been a long time."

She smiled. "It's me under the new look, Kaki," she said. "Do you still take your tea with lemon?"

Kaki relaxed slightly. "Just so. Are you inviting me to tea, then? Or are you here to place an order?" Behind Kaki she could see into the room beyond the antechamber, racks upon racks of fabricators busy turning out goods not sanctioned by the planetary government, or just outside the normal channels of tracking.

Meiko chuckled. "If time and circumstances permit, I'd be happy to treat you to tea, at least. I don't have long to chat at the moment, but I was wondering if you could help me make a connection. I'm involved with some inquiries."

"What kind of inquiries?" Kaki asked, his tone shading back towards caution.

She took a deep breath in through her nose and let it

out slowly, focusing her full attention on him. "Matters related to the killings last night."

One doesn't *recoil* in zero gravity, but Kaki seemed to pull away from her just the same. "Those are very serious matters. And nothing I have any involvement with."

She nodded. "I understand, not your line of business at all." But even though he dealt in black market goods, he definitely knew players; he'd been the one to help arrange for her Meriel ID more than twenty years before, back during the Three-Planet War between Shenzen and Goa, a time when Ileri Station had been *the* intelligence hotspot in this part of the Cluster. "But I thought perhaps you might have heard something or know someone who might have."

"It's a runaway fire, that mess," he said. "I'm steering clear of it, but it's making a right shambles of things. Worse than that demon Toiwa coming up the cable." His frown deepened to full-on scowl. "Constables and spooks tramping round places they oughtn't, deliveries interrupted, key people yanked in for questioning."

She nodded in sympathy. "I'm sure it's quite disruptive. But do you know anyone who might be willing to talk to me?"

"Not likely," he said flatly. "I mean, I'd tell you if I thought anyone would. But everyone's locking down like a pressure barrier during a breach." He paused, one hand coming up to stroke his chin. "I can tell you this, though. It wasn't us. No one in our business is stupid enough to muck around with a political killing." He paused again, seeming to wrestle with a decision, then continued. "Another thing I'll share. Things have been a little strange for the last month or so."

"How do you mean?" she asked.

"A lot of strong-arm action lately," he answered. "Some rough operators started leaning on people. Unsanctioned disappearances, people yanked out of the corridors, held for a few days and dumped somewhere afterwards, with memories blanked but signs they'd been interrogated. Some of ours, some civs, some station admin people. And that's on top of the One Worlders losing their shit over the referendum."

Meiko wanted to lean forward, but zero-g prevented her. "Any idea who is behind that?" *Kumar, you didn't give me anything on this.* Did the station chief know about the disappearances, leaving Meiko to discover it— or not—as a test? Or had her people truly missed them? *Or is someone covering it up?*

Kaki's hands waved twice, making the spacer hand-sign for *don't know.* "No one has a clue, or if they do, they're not telling. Bounties offered, but no claims. Some new player, and that's got the heads worried."

Meiko tapped her lips. "I might be able to help your people with that, if they're willing to share what they know." *And if I can shake loose some intel from Kumar.* "Maybe we can work a trade? Could you at least pass my offer on?"

"Help in tracing who's behind the snatching in return for what we know about last night?" She held her left hand out flat at chest level and tapped her right fist up against it twice, spacer handsign for *yes.* Kaki shrugged. "I'll pass it on, but can't promise the heads will bite."

"Remind Pashun that I found the ones that did for her brother."

"Oh yeah, I'd forgotten about that. Goan muscle, tried

to move in on her business."

"That's right." They *had* been Goan muscle, but part of that world's military intelligence arm, not a separate criminal enterprise. Taking out some of the opposition while ingratiating herself with the locals all in one operation just happened to have been a fortuitously elegant solution, the kinds of successes that had marked her career.

Until the *Fenghuang* debacle, at least.

"Good, good, I will remind her. That should help." Kaki seemed more relaxed now. "Is there anything else?"

She thought for a few seconds. "The One Worlders staged a protest by the Commonwealth Consulate this morning that got out of hand."

"I heard. One of my cousins got rounded up by the yellowjackets along with everyone else for a block."

"Sorry to hear that." She adopted her most sympathetic expression. "Do you think the One Worlders are behind the new nastiness, though?"

"Don't think so." Kaki looked thoughtful. "I mean, it could be, and their people got tagged back in retaliation. But they aren't that subtle. Hitting people in the face, sure-sure. Snatching off the street to drain 'em, not so much."

"I see." She ran a hand through her hair and updated her mental model of the station's factions and players with this new information. "When I passed through a year ago, nothing like that was going on. I mean, there were rants in the media feeds, but nobody beating up off-worlders in the street. What happened?"

"That man Miguna made a bigger show in the elections than anyone expected," he said with a grimace, and his accent slipped from station-standard as his voice got heated. "A lotta people mad they don't get a seat at the table. Families that made it big during the war choking off the chances for everyone else, ya know? Man took that anger and spun it into hating on the off-worlders, instead of where it belongs."

That's a clearer and more concise summary than all the analysis memos Kumar gave me. Bet it's closer to the truth, too. "I thought the idea of joining the Commonwealth was pretty popular? The PM wouldn't have called for a referendum unless she thought it would pass, would she?"

Kaki chewed his lip for moment before replying. "I think most people like the idea, yeah," he said. "Most of the people I know, they're for it. Polls said so too. But there's a hard core, twenty, maybe twenty-five percent hard-set against it."

"Thanks, Kaki." She filed that away with a note to check the polling data. "Anything I can do for you, personally?"

He gave the hand-sign for *no*. "Unless you have a way to move five thousand kiloliters of medical aerosol to the south ring, no."

Meiko's eyebrows furrowed. "That's a pretty specific request. What's that about?"

Again, he flashed the *don't know* sign. "Heard it's some experimental treatment for one of the New Arm worlds, treatment for a local allergen. The inert carrier for it, anyway. Mostly legit job, just off the books." Kaki flipped both hands palm up. "What's a man to do when the yellowjackets go to war? Can't move it with them crawling all over the smuggler's ways." One of the

Fingers' most prized assets was their collection of hidden smuggling routes through the station's infrastructure. "We'll have to go with plan B. Will take longer, but it's off the yellowjackets' radar."

"What's plan B?" she asked innocently.

Kaki just grinned at her. "I like you, Meriel, but not that much." They shared a laugh at that.

Kaki recommended she use a different transit stop for her trip out and she took her leave, feeling the subtle change in the airflow as the massive hatch closed behind her. She toggled a set of AR wayfinder arrows into view and pushed off down the corridor in the opposite direction from which she'd arrived.

She was halfway back to the transit station when she spotted the person lying in wait, if one could be said to be lying in zero-g.

A large person-shaped bulk hung motionless about thirty meters down the corridor, where a cross-corridor intersected the passage from her upper left as she glided along. The big, blocky man stared directly at her—definitely not a good sign. Another corridor intersected hers between them, just ten meters away and to her right. Without missing a beat in her push-offs she changed course, angling for the closer junction. The watcher pushed off from the wall as if to intercept, but she easily reached the passage before him. She tucked her legs, rotating and spinning in mid-flight before straightening just in time to hit the wall of the cross-corridor feet first. She absorbed the impact with her legs and drove off at a new angle, sailing down the side passage.

She called up her djinn's route-finding and asked for an alternate path to the hub. The red arrows pointing back to her original course flipped around and turned green, leading down this passage for a few hundred meters. She glanced back and saw her pursuer keeping pace, though not gaining. She looked ahead.

A woman hung from a grip bar perhaps forty meters down the passage. She gestured in Meiko's direction with her free hand to her companion, who zeroed in on Meiko as well. Both pushed off in her direction.

SHIT. She was being herded. For a brief flash she considered fighting it out; chances are they wouldn't expect one skinny older woman to put up much resistance. But then she saw the newcomers pull stun buttons and she opted to evade, kicking hard against the corridor wall to somersault gracefully past the pair, just out of reach. Both cursed but didn't bother reaching for her—a sign of experience in zero-g. She hit the opposite wall, kicked off again, and shot down the side passage the pair had been guarding.

So much for a solo run. As she landed and pushed off again, the first pursuer close behind, she activated her panic button. Her djinn flipped back to her original ID and squirted a message to both the Consulate and directly to Kumar using her emergency code. She bounced off the opposite wall and pushed off even more strongly, angling to skim along the side of the corridor.

Did Kaki set me up? She didn't think so; if he wanted her out of the way, she'd be on ice in the back of his shop waiting for someone to come along and process her organs. On impulse, she shot Kaki a message about her pursuers too.

She looked ahead and saw two more people clutching objects in their off hands stationed near the next intersection, perhaps sixty meters further along.

FUCK. She readied herself to use the next push-off post to check her progress and reverse course. She'd have to take the first pursuer out quickly, then hope she could ambush the next two...

Five meters ahead, 'above' and to her left, a door slid open and a pair of six-legged maintenance bots emerged, pulling some kind of mechanical assembly out into the passage.

New plan. She hit the grip bar but instead of reversing course, she cast herself across the passage, aiming for the newly opened doorway. She missed but not by much, clipping the bot's cargo with her left shoulder. There was a tearing sound and pain flared along her triceps as a protruding bracket ripped a line of fire down her arm.

She smacked into wall next to the hatch and flung her good arm out desperately, hooked her fingers on the open door frame, and her body swung around the new pivot point as she rebounded off the wall. She heard shouting from both directions up and down the passage as she steadied herself, then pulled herself inside into the maintenance way.

Alarms flared as she crossed the threshold, sensors detecting her unauthorized entrance.

Some kind of spy I am, when tripping the alarm is a good thing.

CHAPTER SEVEN

Noo

Maseko Circus, Hub Transit Nexus, Ileri Station

Myra's call caught Noo and Fari in the hub, one bubble-car ride from the home of Parma, the slain environmental-systems builder, whose family had consented to an interview. Noo opened her side audio only; visual distractions and maneuvering in microgravity didn't mix as far as she was concerned. "M. Okereke. M. Loh asked me to pass on a new bit of information, and to ask a favor," Myra said.

"Let's hear it," Noo said as she gauged her transition to the next towline. Fari, younger, more fit, and possessed of better gravity-transition adaptation, glided ahead of her with a grace belying her rugby-player physique. The younger woman coasted to a near stop as she reached the towline and slipped one hand into the grab-loop.

"There's another party making inquiries outside

official channels," Myra said. Noo reached and grabbed for a pair of loops. Her legs kept traveling from the momentum of her initial push-off. "M. Loh believes it might be productive for you to meet her."

"Who is this person?" Fari said.

"Another person we do business with," Myra said smoothly, answering without answering. "She just left one of M. Loh's associates. Thus, the favor. He asks if you could escort this person to him."

"We're not nursemaids," Noo snapped as she wrestled her body into alignment with the towline.

Fari cut in smoothly. "What my colleague means to say, M. Obi, is that we'd be happy to act in a spirit of mutual assistance. But we expect our backs scratched in return."

"M. Loh said he assumed you'd say that, and that he'd offer compensation when you all met together," Myra said.

Fari glanced back at Noo and flashed a hand sign in the agency's private code, not station-talk or spacer hand-speak. *New plan.* Noo, still gripping the towline with both hands, frowned but nodded. "Ogun's tears, this gets more fucking messy as we go. Loh vouches for this person?"

"She's done business with our organization before." Again, answering without answering.

Noo glanced up at Fari again, and saw an arched eyebrow indicating her partner had caught the evasion too. "That's a pretty thin endorsement, coming from Pericles."

Myra's shrug came through even over audio. "It's what I can tell you at this time. Hopefully we can sort this out face to face shortly. Time is pressing. Are you willing?"

"All right. Send us the location." Her djinn blipped with the incoming packet and Noo carefully slipped her right hand free to wave up wayfinder arrows.

Fari beat her to it. "We need to drop the towline at the next platform and catch a transit car. Thank you, Myra." Noo finally wrangled the packet open and discovered the contact's name and likeness. The image of Meriel Suzuki revealed a thin woman, medium-brown skin, short straight hair. Her high cheekbones and the shape of her eyes hinted at some East Asian ancestors, but that was true of something like a third of the Cluster.

Moments later, they debarked into the sort of industrial district Noo didn't often visit, an area devoid of towlines. They were gliding along the path of their wayfinders when the infrastructure-compromise alarm went off nearby, three long rings followed by two short ones. Myra called at the same moment, and Noo accepted, once more audio only.

"Our mutual friend is in trouble," Myra said without preamble. "She's hit a panic button and reported that she's being herded by unknown assailants."

"Fuck." Reflexively, Noo checked her weapons in their holsters and saw Fari do the same. "We've got a station services alarm here. That can't be a coincidence." She blinked up an area map, seeking their target, spotted the green glyph adjacent to the flashing red station alarm. "Shit, that's her all right. How'd she break into a maintenance passage?"

"No data," Myra said with a traffic controller's calm. "She flashed a message that she was under attack. I have other assets en route but with the alarm I expect station people to beat mine."

"Got it." It was an even bet whether a rapid response team from Infrastructure would arrive before the Constabulary. Normally Noo found the inter-agency rivalry amusing, but she didn't relish getting in between the responders and the alarm. She and Fari shot down the passageway. Fari effortlessly bounced off the far wall and changed course to sail down the cross-corridor their wayfinders now pointed. Noo gritted her teeth and followed her partner's example with considerably more effort and less grace. The younger woman moved lightly, bounding from contact point to contact point with the strength and agility of youth and training. Noo trailed behind, struggling to keep up even as she drifted further back. "Not. Too. Old. For. Field. Work," she huffed as she pulled herself along the grip bars.

Fari reached the next intersection and flung herself down the new passageway, drawing her stunner as she went. A brilliant scarlet AR tag appeared above her head, announcing she bore a licensed weapon. Noo banged her way roughly through the course change and drew her own stunner.

Two people hovered near a maintenance doorway, arguing in the light of the alarm flashers. Nearby, two robots clung to the wall clutching a mechanical assembly. "Stand down!" Fari called out, snatching a grip bar to arrest her forward motion while she trained her weapon on the pair.

The man sprung at Fari with explosive force, hands extended. Calmly, Fari lined her weapon up with her target, slipped her finger over the trigger, and fired.

Her shot caught the man squarely center-of-mass. He convulsed, arms and legs jerking wildly, putting him into a tumble. Deftly, she pushed off to her left and snagged the next grip bar around the passage's circumference. Noo, still heading for the point Fari vacated, cursed as the burly man sailed into her track. She was going too fast to brake against the passage wall, but she twisted and got one hand down anyway. She pushed off as strongly as she could and missed the man by scant centimeters.

Her evasion came at the price of tumbling. This close to the wall, the usual starfish maneuver to stabilize herself in zero-g risked a broken limb, or at least a sprained joint. She managed to get a foot into contact with the wall and steadied herself just in time to hear Fari fire a second time.

"Dammit. She ducked inside," Fari said. She glanced back at Noo, then at the first attacker, now hung up on one of the grip bars and still paralyzed by the stun shot. The alarm rang out relentlessly, *woowoowoowahwah, woowoowoowahwah*. "We follow?"

Noo got her legs under her and launched towards the hatch. She caught herself on its lip as Fari did the same. "Hot pursuit," Noo said. The two women locked eyes, nodded at each other, and pulled themselves into the promise of danger.

MEIKO

MAINTENANCE ACCESSWAY 4976H, HUB ZONE, ILERI STATION

A CLUSTER OF maintenance bots surrounded the inner side of the doorway as Meiko sailed through, waiting their turn to exit, or perhaps their next set of orders. A row of conduits a good quarter-meter wide took up one wall of the hexagonal corridor. A large pump projected out from the wall about ten meters to her right. Red lights flashed in a slow rhythm, three flashes, a pause, then two more, then the cycle repeated. She heard an audible alarm from outside, and angry AR tags sprang to life everywhere she looked: RESTRICTED ZONE, AUTHORIZED PERSONNEL ONLY, ACCESS STRICTLY FORBIDDEN, VIOLATORS WILL BE VIGOROUSLY APPREHENDED. She hoped that help of some kind would be inbound double-quick given warnings that strident.

She hit the far wall feet first, spun, and pushed off to her left.

The service way ran at an oblique angle relative to the regular passage she'd come from; she wasn't sure where it led, but at this point, she didn't care. Without a map for this non-public space she had to rely on her djinn's inertial dead-reckoning system, which while certainly better than average, was hardly infallible. Still, she thought going left ought to take her to public spaces, if station people didn't intercept her and her pursuers first.

She pushed down the monkey-brain fear that threatened to bubble up at the thought of being caught in a dead end and sought the calm of rhythm.

Her maneuver shook free the blood welling up from where the machine had sliced into her triceps. The oblong scarlet blob sailed towards the entry and hit the first of her pursuers, the big man, across the face. Startled, he jerked and twisted, which put him into a tumble. He cursed in one of the local languages as he slammed into the far wall and ricocheted off it towards the pump assembly.

Almost without thought, she grasped the opportunity hanging before her like a shiny apple. Her thighs screamed as she hit the wall and drove off it with all her strength, changing course to arrow straight at her pursuer. She rotated through another 180 and came at him feet first. Hard.

The man managed to arrest his headlong spinning progress by grabbing onto the pump. This meant his hands were firmly wrapped around the rigid metal assembly when Meiko's feet slammed into them. She felt bones give way and heard a horrible crunching sound, which was immediately drowned out by his scream.

Contact made and damage done, it was time to make good her escape. She allowed her body to fold until her hands made contact with the pump housing and immediately launched herself from all fours, flying back down her original course before the man had drawn a second breath to continue screaming.

Her victim's partner sailed through the doorway just as Meiko passed it. The woman's outstretched hand bumped Meiko's left thigh, causing Meiko to spin round and tumble off course herself. She felt the woman's fingers scrabble in vain for a grip on her trousers but she scissored her legs, swinging them free. She tried to catch the attacker with a booted foot but missed.

The woman barked out to the screaming man to collect himself in that same local dialect. The linguistics module in Meiko's djinn caught up and identified it, and now provided her with a running translation. She ignored her pursuers for the moment and focused instead on trying to convert her imminent collision with the wall into something more productive. Her kick exacerbated her spin and she couldn't kill it in time. She hit the wall left arm first, gasping at the pain and leaving a bloody smear. She righted herself and pushed off with all fours again, skimming along the a few centimeters from the wall like an underwater swimmer gliding along the bottom of a pool.

She got herself moving forward, albeit much more slowly than she wished. Pain shot through her left arm with every reach for a grip bar, with every pull to send her body ever-faster down the passage, and the imbalance between her good and bad arms began to affect her course. She grunted as she wrestled herself back onto a straight path. She had no time to think or feel anything but the play of muscle, the bump of impact as she hit the grip bars.

The big man stopped screaming.

Kumar chose that moment to call. "Mother of the fucking Leap!" Meiko blurted out. A flick of thought opened the connection, audio only. But she gave Kumar access to her sensory inputs, letting the spymaster see what Meiko saw, hear what she heard.

"What the hell are you up to?" Kumar snapped as the link opened. "A restricted area? The locals are shitting themselves."

"Got made." She caught the next grip bar and flung herself forward. Slowly, she built up speed.

Something crashed into her back and she slammed into the wall, skidding down the passage. A hard object smacked her in the back and then pain ripped through her abdomen, every muscle spasming.

Fortunately for Kumar, the sensorium feed included

neither tactile sensation nor pain replicators, but the spymaster drew the correct conclusion from the way the tunnel suddenly whirled. "Are you under attack?"

Meiko tried to say 'Yes', but only managed a pained hiss.

"What's that?" asked a strange voice, as strong fingers slipped inside the waistband of her pants, yanking her to a stop.

Kumar's voice went flat as she went into crisis-management mode. "Hold on. Security is scrambling. How many hostiles?"

Meiko struggled to remember how many chased her, to find the breath to vocalize. She was about to twitch out a text message when hands grasped her left arm and slammed it backwards against the grip bar. She screamed as her elbow gave way.

The motion spun her around and she forced her eyes open so Kumar could see her attackers. The woman who'd chased her down didn't look like a typical bruiser, but then again, neither did Meiko. But her captor was wearing a shock palm, and that explained how she'd incapacitated Meiko with one hit. A man who she thought was the first one she'd spotted came flying up the passageway towards them. She heard shouting from the hatchway and saw two more people sail through it.

The woman grabbed Meiko by the collar with her left hand, and raised her right, palm open. The charging indicator on the shock palm flipped from red to green, the woman slammed her hand into Meiko's solar plexus, and the world went away for a time.

Noo

Maintenance Accessway 4976H, Hub Zone, Ileri Station

Noo and Fari came through together, stunners drawn, searching for targets. "Stun everything and let the constables sort them out afterwards," she growled.

They found themselves in a service passage and automatically rotated, one facing each way to cover both directions.

This brought Noo practically face to face with a heavily built man hanging curled in a ball like an infant, his hands tucked protectively against his stomach. Her djinn mapped a targeting reticle as soon as she'd drawn her weapon, and now it swung across him as she lined it up with her target. Noo's finger slipped over the trigger, squeezed once, and was rewarded with the sight of the man's body rippling as the charge took him. Finding no more targets she called out, "One down, clear this way." Her voice was steady and dispassionate as if she were describing the color of the wall. She pulled herself clear of her flailing quarry and turned in time to see her partner shoot the woman they'd chased inside.

"One down, three targets," Fari said, her own voice steady. "Twenty meters."

"Understood." Too long a shot for a hand stunner; they weren't terribly accurate past ten meters or so. *But they won't have guns, and we do.*

Or do they? An image of bloody corpses not even a full day dead flashed in her mind.

From ahead she heard the distinctive *SNAP* of a shock

palm discharging, and Noo decided they probably still had the advantage. *These people were out in public. Security would have caught unlicensed weapons.* She hoped that was true.

"Correction, two targets." Fari said, and pushed off hard to glide down the passageway, weapon trained on their quarry. "Stand down!" she shouted. "You're in a restricted area! Disarm yourselves and move away from the woman." Not that they really had authority here, but most people didn't realize anyone besides the Constabulary and the station Army garrison were authorized to carry weapons; barely two dozen, in fact, and half of them worked for Noo and Fathya.

Noo trained her own weapon on the pair and pushed off to follow her partner.

The man launched himself at Fari when she was perhaps ten meters away. Both Noo and Fari fired at the same time but he twisted and their shots both missed. He crashed into the younger woman and they bounced against the wall. Fari's stunner went flying as the pair grappled, and the fourth attacker sprang for it, hands outstretched.

Noo worked her way around the passage, away from where Fari and her opponent spun, and tracked the flying woman as she snatched the errant weapon, keeping her own stunner fixed squarely on target. The woman spun around to hit the passage wall with her feet, collapsing perfectly to absorb the shock of her landing. She pointed Fari's stunner at Noo and pulled the trigger. Nothing happened. A look of puzzlement came across her face as she tried to fire again.

"Biometric lock," Noo said, and fired twice herself.

Both shots hit and the woman spasmed like a snapped rubber band.

Noo spun in place to see how Fari was doing. Her opponent out-massed her slightly, but Fari trained regularly in zero-g combat. Both her legs wrapped around his, pinning them, which freed both her hands. The man clawed for her face, but she jerked her head back and jabbed a sword-strike into his left armpit with one hand while her other grasped his collar. Their spin brought her feet into contact with one of the grip bars and she hooked a foot under it, opening her legs to let the man swing free. His exultant cry was cut short as she clamped her free hand on his belt, spun him around, and slammed him head first into the passage wall once, twice, then a third time, before releasing him to float free.

Noo shot him anyway, just to be sure.

Fari, breathing just a little heavily, pulled a set of restraints from her jacket pocket and looped them around the man's arms and ankles without any visible consideration for his comfort. "You are hereby apprehended under the Covenants of the Ileri Republic," she intoned, yanking the ankle band tight. "In other words, you're clipped, son."

Noo swapped magazines before holstering her own weapon and tossing her own restraints to Fari, who went to work on the other attackers. She pushed over to the shock-palm victim who still floated where the goons had left her. She checked the image. "Meiko Ogawa," she said as her djinn grabbed the woman's ID and social profile. "Who was Meriel Suzuki just a few minutes ago, if this picture our mutual friend provided is any indicator." She could tell the pictures of Meiko and Meriel were of the same woman, but she had to look closely, beyond the differences in skin and hair color.

Ogawa/Suzuki's eyes fluttered, but she made no other response.

Noo examined her from head to toe, taking in the bloody shoulder, the left arm hanging limply and *wrong*. "Got in over your head," Noo murmured, as a pair of constables sailed through the hatchway from the main corridor, followed closely by a team of Infrastructure Services people in softsuits, and things became official.

CHAPTER EIGHT

TOIWA

CONSTABULARY HEADQUARTERS, ILERI STATION, FORWARD RING

TOIWA WATCHED THE meeting clock in her personal AR field roll into its second hour and stood abruptly, bringing the acrimonious debate between her second deputy and the representative from the Ministry of Defense to a halt even before she flung up one well-manicured hand. The unexpected break in that spirited argument caused some of the other sidebar conversations around the room to fall off as well. Toiwa pointed first at her deputy, then at the Ministry woman. "Sit. Down." Her staffer plopped into his chair with admirable speed. The Ministry rep hesitated for a moment but wilted under Toiwa's impassive glare and crumpled into her own seat. Around the table, the others participants—a mix of her own staff, representatives from the Intelligence Directorate, three other civilian agencies, a contingent from Defense, and a handful of Commonwealth officials—all turned to look at her. The lesser subordinates and ancillary attendees who formed the outer ring lining the wall adopted their most attentive poses.

Well, not Fathya Shariff, who sat straight as a sword, as she had this whole time. Shariff noticed Toiwa's glance and inclined her head slightly. Toiwa gave the barest of nods in return; Shariff, at least, wasn't on Toiwa's shit list. Yet. Toiwa wondered just how Shariff's operatives happened to be on top of the scene when the Commonwealth woman was assaulted; her police brain didn't believe in convenient coincidences. At least Shariff's motivations in the assassination case were clear, and considerably more righteous than the shifty weasels from the Directorate, just to name one example. Plus, and Toiwa hated to admit it, Shariff's people's competence was unquestioned. Unlike that of most of the parties represented.

Toiwa let her hand fall to the table and leaned forward. "If everyone's done marking their territory and performing their dominance displays, or making excuses why something that's happened in the last"—her eyes flicked to another timer, this one tracking elapsed time since the killing—"fourteen hours is not the fault of themselves or their organizations, I should very much like to focus on getting my constables back onto the matter of solving this most heinous crime. I exempt our honored guests, of course, from that criticism," she said with a nod towards the Commonwealth deputy consul and his colleague. She wondered again why the diplomat had brought his science attaché. A mystery for later, but she made note of the incongruity, knowing that Valverdes was probably also digging into the woman's files, and would probably have a ten-screen dossier ready by the time the meeting ended.

It was a little dicey, calling out the other government reps in front of the Commonwealth people, but the off-worlders had possessed front-row seats to this whole clusterfuck of a meeting. If the governor or anyone else gave her grief about it, she could simply replay recorded excerpts from the last hour and let the idiocy speak for itself.

The deputy consul cleared his throat and she nodded at him, inviting him to speak. "Thank you, Commissioner. We certainly want the Consul's murderer brought to justice. But there have been at least two other attacks against our citizens in the meantime, aside from the riot and the assault on M. Ogawa." Toiwa's face remained impassive; she'd expected him to bring this up. "We appreciate that the perpetrators have been so quickly apprehended. But the ambassador has expressed concerns, which I share, that we might be on the cusp of a period of truly serious disorder, and further assaults might be inflicted upon Commonwealth citizens here on the station, or planetside. It also calls into question the viability of the referendum. And with our vessel, *Amazonas*, due soon to observe the referendum, we're concerned about sentiments being further inflamed."

Her response came easily. "As you say, M. Wang, the assailants were immediately apprehended and are all in custody." Not in Constabulary custody, unfortunately. She longed to get the Directorate nullwits alone, preferably in the secure interrogation room, to find out what the dust they were about. Holding her suspects?

People over whom the Directorate had absolutely no jurisdiction? It burned her but would have to wait; she had to douse the first fire before lighting another.

"The Constabulary is on heightened alert, with additional personnel on duty in the areas most frequented by visitors, to help forestall any incidents. We have additional rapid-response teams standing by to deploy should anything occur, and a full complement of crowd control and other response bots are deployed across the station." Which meant her overtime budget for this period was irretrievably shot, with its own reckoning to come later. "I've requested additional resources from planetside, and I'm told teams are already preparing to come up." A first detachment would be on the morning shuttle, the HC had promised, in addition to the constables already on their way up the space elevator. While the new people wouldn't know the station, at least she'd have bodies to throw at any problem that tactic could solve, and that would let her people stay focused on the main investigations and on the ramped-up surveillance. "And I'm assigning one of my staff"—she pointed at the sacrificial aide, a holdover from her predecessor but a solid, dependable administrator nonetheless—"as a full-time liaison with your Consulate. I hope these measures ease your mind somewhat?" She raised her hands from the table, holding them out to encompass the whole room. "And I'm sure I speak for my fellow Ileris when I tell you we shall all do our utmost to ensure the referendum takes place without undue issues."

"Those sound like prudent measures," he said. "In the meantime, I'd like to ask that one of our security team be embedded with the incident command team overseeing the assassination investigation."

Her fingers drummed on the tabletop as she considered. "That seems quite reasonable," she said. She glanced down at Valverdes, seated to Toiwa's right, who was busily manipulating windows with zer sole hand. "See to it." Toiwa turned back to the the diplomat with a tight-lipped smile. "Is there anything else?" He shook his head and she straightened, sweeping the whole room with her gaze. "Very well, then. While I appreciate the cooperation and contributions of the other interested departments in this investigation"—*like a damned yeast infection*—"I believe our best course at the moment is to let the investigators follow their current leads. Teams will continue work through all shifts." She summed up the schedule of updates, status meetings, and public briefings planned for the next twelve hours. "If there is no new information, or further business, I suggest we adjourn." Her staff, well-trained, immediately rose from their seats and headed for the exits, prompting the other attendees to do the same. She pitched her voice to carry across the rising babble as side conversations blossomed around the room again, and pointed at one of the intelligence liaisons. "Captain Teng, a word, if you please." <*Imoke, attend please,*> she sent, and the Detective Sergeant—part of the perimeter cloud of minions—took his place behind her as the Directorate rep shouldered his way through the crowd.

She'd have taken the tall officer for a military man by his bearing, even dressed as he was in an orange civilian tunic and trousers. For a spy, he didn't look very covert, she thought; entirely too good-looking, too fit. Perhaps he blended in somewhere, but she couldn't conceive of what milieu that might be. She waited until the room had emptied except for herself, Teng, Imoke, and Valverdes. The man had the good grace not to stare at the stump at the end of Valverdes' left arm, which didn't take him up any notches, but perhaps set a higher floor for her expectations about him.

She noticed one last person hovering nearby, just outside the circle. "Yes, M. Shariff?"

"I wanted to thank you, Commissioner, for expediting the release of my grandson's remains." Shariff held herself erect, but she'd been awake as long as Toiwa, and it showed in her voice.

Toiwa nodded. Even without Governor Ruhindi's admonitions about Shariff's connections, pushing the release through was the sort of simple kindness she liked to make happen when she could. Shariff and her family, whatever else they were, were victims in this. "I'm glad we were able to. There was no cause to hold his remains any longer once the medical examiner completed the necessary work. I recall you're a person of faith, and that holding the service within a day is important to you."

"It is. The funeral will come after the Isha prayers. You are welcome to attend, of course, if your duties permit."

So much for home, a shower, and bed. She turned to Valverdes. "Kala, would you check my schedule and clear it if possible? And see that M. Shariff has whatever she needs?" Valverdes nodded and hustled off to escort Shariff out.

Toiwa would have preferred to have another witness present while she had it out with the spy, but a little show of respect to Shariff through the personal attention of Toiwa's principal aide couldn't hurt. Imoke could serve as her reliable witness here; she trusted him that far, at any rate. And he'd proved quite clever dealing with the riot—sweet Mother, that was just this morning.

Once the two women left, she stabbed a finger into the room's virtual controls with enough force to have put out an eye. The privacy field kicked into place and she dropped the facade of civility. "What in God's name are you dung-eaters doing, sweeping up all the perpetrators that attacked that Commonwealth woman? And who the hell is she?" She leaned forward into Captain Teng's personal space and jabbed her finger at him, driving each word home like a nail. "What. The. Hell. Are. You. People. Playing. At?" She kept him fixed in a glare that threatened to scorch the walls.

Teng stood unperturbed. "M. Ogawa is a consulting specialist," he said, ignoring her first question. "I am not at liberty to discuss her areas of expertise with uncleared personnel."

"Don't pull that 'matter of planetary security' nonsense with me," she snarled.

"It's the truth." Teng shrugged. "There are a number of collaborative efforts underway with the Commonwealth even before the referendum. They're a friendly power, after all. She is part of one such effort, and uniquely positioned to assist with certain aspects of this situation."

"And what aspects are those?" Imoke asked.

Teng sighed, and she ground her teeth. "Aspects involving planetary security," he said.

Dust take him, enough of this. "I want her off my station," Toiwa snapped, and the captain stiffened. "I'm serious," she rolled on, before he could object. "She dropped out of surveillance for several hours after the riot in front of the Consulate, evading both your people and mine. Then she attracted an attack by unknown assailants. *That* investigation is taking up resources I desperately need focused on keeping the good order here while a mass murderer roams my corridors, pro- and anti-Commonwealth sympathizers are knocking each other's heads in, and we have a major vote in less than two weeks." *Not to mention that I'm still cleaning up the mess of three decades' worth of corruption on the part of my predecessor and his pack of thieves in constables' clothing.*

She jabbed her finger at Teng's chest again. "I don't care how you do it, what pretext you come up with, or whose desk you have to prostrate yourself in front of, make it happen. Get her off my station."

She gave him credit; it took a full thirty seconds before he broke. "I'll have to clear it with my superiors," he said.

"You can *inform* your superiors. Do not mistake this for a suggestion, or a negotiation." He nodded, looking unhappy. "But *first* you're going to turn the suspects you swept off to God knows where over to Constabulary custody." Yanking criminals out of the corridors and hiding them from her on *her station*, probably in the military installation in the hub, was too brazen an act to let stand.

The captain started to open his mouth to object but she rolled right over him again. "I've got the attack on video record, and goddammit, I have jurisdiction here. My people need to be the ones interrogating them so that evidence can be put in front of the magistrates."

His resolve collapsed. "I'll make the necessary calls," he said.

"You have two hours," she snapped. "You will coordinate with Detective Sergeant Imoke for the custody transfer. Sergeant?" Imoke stood to attention. "You will escort the captain to a place from which he can contact whomever he needs to and remain with him until it is accomplished. M. Valverdes or Lieutenant Zheng will see to any support you require."

Imoke nodded. "Yes, ma'am."

"And if it isn't done in two hours," she said, eyes fixed on Teng, "you will arrest the captain for obstruction of justice and lock his ass in a shielded cell."

Imoke grinned and gave her an informal salute, two fingers to his right brow. "Yes, boss."

Teng bristled. "You're overreaching, Commissioner," he snapped.

"Maybe," she said, without moving. "But your superiors don't like to operate in the light. The media is already carrying stories about the brawls in the corridors, and rumors are already flying about the intrusion into the service passage being attempted sabotage. If word were to get out that this was a flubbed intelligence operation? Worse, if this jeopardizes the referendum?" She gave an elegant shrug. "The person on the scene and all that. Sacrifices have to be made sometimes, and we know who'll be the one on the pyre."

They glared at each other for a full ten seconds before he finally gave in. "Very well. I'll make the arrangements. But with your permission, I'll deal with Ogawa in the morning. Her injuries will keep her out of trouble until then. The Commonwealth people have taken her to the Consulate for the night to complete her recovery."

She considered that, then nodded. "That's acceptable.

Meanwhile, you and the Detective Sergeant can sort the matter of the prisoners out." She turned to Imoke. "And I expect you to get some rest once the prisoner transfer is complete."

Imoke cocked his head before responding. "I'd like to defer my rest period until after Saed Tahir's funeral," he said.

Oh, right. "Of course, Sergeant, that was thoughtless of me. I'd forgotten you knew M. Tahir. I will see you there, then."

Imoke saluted again. "Yes, boss." He took Teng by the elbow and escorted the spy from the room. Toiwa followed them out and turned for her office.

She was halfway there before it hit her. *That's the first time one of the old hands has called me 'boss'.* The epithet was a mark of respect from subordinate to superior among the Constabulary, of respect that had been earned, not simply respect for one's position.

Well, it's a start.

CHAPTER NINE

MEIKO

COMMONWEALTH CONSULATE,
ILERI STATION, SOUTH RING

MEIKO WOKE IN dim light, feeling warm and soft. She felt soft, warm air around her face and bare forearms, with a soft, warm blanket tucked round her body.

On the upside, she had experience with waking up in a treatment bed without precise memories of how she'd arrived there, or why. The downside, of course, was not knowing whether she was in friendly hands or not, and just what they were pumping into her. She felt no pain. That was good, although given the cast on her left arm and the fact she'd been hit with a shock palm—she remembered that much—she suspected that she ought to feel *something*.

Alone, maybe? Monitored? Definitely. She took a few slow, deep breaths to clear her lungs and help center herself, then opened her eyes to take stock of her situation.

She looked right and discovered an IV line attached to her hand. She traced the line as it snaked up her arm into the bag hanging next to her bed and read the AR tags identifying it as a standard mix of painkillers and nanosurgeon nutrient solution. *Wait, I can read the AR tags?* She glanced down at her left wrist, looking for the djinn which had to be somewhere on her body if she could access augmented reality, then realized it was snugged around her right arm with the IV line running over it in blatant disregard for standard medical procedure. She relaxed. Only friendlies would let her keep her djinn. But which friendlies?

She blinked rapidly three times and her ocular implants switched from passive to interactive mode. The first thing she checked was her location and discovered to her surprise that she was in the consulate's infirmary.

That was either very good or very bad, but it was certainly better than 'abducted by unknown assailants on foreign territory,' which had seemed likely when she was being pummeled by anonymous goons.

The door opened and a stocky, forty-something enbee with long frizzy hair, wearing a medical robe and brandishing a diagnostic wand, sauntered in. "Good evening, citizen," ze said, and busied zerself with the diagnostic wand. "I'm Doctor Tran. Lie still, please." Diagnostic scans and their interpretation occupied the next few minutes, followed by a brief rundown of Meiko's injuries and prognosis. Doctor Tran ticked off the issues one by one. "The arm is the worst. You'll need to keep the cast on for twenty-four hours, and keep your arm in a sling, while the nanosurgeons finish with the forearm fracture and the torn deltoid. The ribs aren't too bad, just bruised. Those and the intercostal muscle damage from the shock palm should be all right by morning."

Meiko nodded. "Thank you. I'm familiar with the recovery regimen."

Tran snorted. "I should think so. Your medical records are... illustrative." Ze peered down zer nose at Meiko. "Your musculature is overall in good condition, but you've been in microgravity for a long while, and at your age it's going to take you a bit longer to recover than you may be used to."

"Hmm."

"Light activity for two days. Local days, so fifty-four hours," Tran said in what Meiko thought of as 'Medical Imperative' voice. "Your file says you're a capoeirista?"

"That's my primary discipline. I train in some others."

"No weight-bearing moves, or strikes, or heavy blocks with the left arm for two days, but you can do stretching and such on the second day. As long as you take the supplements to keep the nanosurgeons fed, that is."

Meiko made the appropriate affirmative noises, and Tran affected to believe her before sauntering out. "If you're back in my infirmary before three days have passed, I'll pop you into a body brace," ze warned before exiting.

Tran's joking threat still hung in the air as Kumar entered, followed by a man in his early thirties. He looked like a young Menti Uwais, the famous martial arts vid star from Meiko's youth: the same wolfish smile and shock of black hair, the same broad chest and muscular arms. His walk told Meiko he, too, was a trained fighter, and she wondered what his style was.

His social profile provided a bare minimum of

information: Femi Teng, it read. An Ileri citizen, but no listing for his occupation or affiliation beyond that. That put her on guard; he almost certainly worked for Ileri intelligence in some way.

"Good evening, Meiko," Kumar said. "I'm glad you're awake. We have things to discuss." She came to the foot of the bed. "Are you feeling well enough to talk?"

"I believe so," Meiko said. She opened the AR window for the bed's controls and raised the back until she was sitting nearly vertical. "Who is our visitor?"

"Captain Femi Teng, Ileri Planetary Security Directorate," the man said in a lush baritone voice that under other circumstances—say, over drinks at a beachside bar—Meiko would have enjoyed listening to. For a while, anyway. "Your case has been assigned to me."

"My case?" Meiko asked, feigning ignorance.

"Your activities after leaving the Consulate," Teng said as Kumar pulled a chair up to her bedside and slid into it. Teng remained standing near the foot of the bed. "There's the physical assaults during the disturbance outside the Consulate—"

"Self-defense, during the *riot* outside the Consulate, which endangered Commonwealth citizens, as well as the station's populace," Kumar interjected.

"The riot, just so." Teng waved a hand nonchalantly. "I've watched the recordings. It's indeed all self-defense, but nearly all the other individuals involved were detained and statements taken. Most are still in custody, being processed. We'll have to get some kind of statement from you for the official record since Commissioner Toiwa"—his face twisted as he said the name—"is proceeding absolutely by the book where this is concerned."

"Sending a message," Kumar murmured.

Teng nodded. "Just so. She's putting the One Worlders and everyone else on notice that nobody gets to throw *that* kind of party on the station without consequence."

"A statement seems reasonable," Meiko said, and she felt muscles relax she hadn't realized were tense. "But I take it there's more."

Even the man's frown looked charming. *How the hell does he work in Intelligence? He's far too memorable.* Maybe the Ileris had him working the entertainment and media sectors?

"Unfortunately, when you took measures to evade the station security monitoring network, you violated a number of, shall we say, *arrangements*, between our governments," he said. "While the matter might normally be resolved amicably through informal channels"—*just between us spies*—"the attack on your person puts that out of the question. Since the Constabulary got involved, that is, making it a matter public record. There's also the matter of your incursion into the maintenance passage. The station services director is quite irate."

Meiko glanced at Kumar, trying to gauge her reaction. The intelligence chief, for her part, looked relaxed but alert. *She's heard this already.* Would Kumar back a wayward subordinate who triggered this kind of reaction from the Ileris?

"The incursion, as you put it, was hardly intentional," she said in the most persuasive tone she could muster. "I was fleeing from multiple armed assailants, in point of fact."

"Yes. Well, that's immaterial, at least in the eyes of station services," Teng said. He cleared his throat. "Or the Commissioner, who insists that you leave the station at the earliest opportunity. The services chief endorses this demand." His lips twitched into a ghost of a smile. "She went on about it at some length, in fact."

Wait, now I've pissed off the people who are responsible for my air? That's a first. She glanced at Kumar, who sat watching the pair, saying nothing. No clue from that sector, then. She considered various gambits and settled on the most direct. "Why?" she asked Teng.

"I tried to persuade her otherwise, that we could let you remain on-station with a permanent escort. But the pot is near to boiling, with the membership vote imminent, the Commonwealth warship *Amazonas* inbound, and the One World party gone sub-nova."

"But what does that have to do with me?" Meiko asked.

Teng spread his hands placatingly. "The Commissioner views you as a destabilizing influence." Kumar snorted. "She's worried you'll stir up trouble, and she needs her people on the cases they're already working or keeping the peace." She started to open her mouth, but he raised his hands. "I'm sorry, it's non-negotiable on her part," he said.

"Surely, M. Ogawa can be allowed some time to recover from her injuries?" Kumar asked, softly. "As long as she remains here in the Consulate?"

"Oh, yes, just so," Teng said with a nod. "In fact, as far as she knows I'm not delivering this news to you until the morning. I wanted to inform you as soon as possible, though. Professional courtesy and all that." He smiled, seeming so genuinely friendly and conciliatory that Meiko decided the Directorate kept him around for just these sorts of situations, smoothing things over with other organizations.

"Well, she certainly won't be going anywhere before then," Kumar said. "Thank you, Captain. You may consider the message delivered."

Teng took the hint, and after arranging a time to meet in the morning, slipped out the door. Meiko spotted one of the door guards from the morning waiting just outside her room to escort him out. The trooper nodded at Kumar before closing the door.

Kumar wagged her right index finger and the door frame shone green in AR. "Inconvenient, but not unexpected," she said. She dragged her chair around to face Meiko. "What did you get before you were jumped?"

Succinctly, Meiko related what she'd learned from Kaki. Kumar listened attentively, particularly when she reached the part about the mysterious attacks and kidnappings. "He seemed quite concerned about the incursions by the new players, whoever they are," she finished.

"Do you think that's who attacked you?" Kumar asked.

"No clue," she replied with a shrug. "The method definitely sounds similar."

"Hmm." Kumar tapped her lips. "I do have a source in the Constabulary. I'll see if they can find out anything after the prisoners are interrogated."

"Reinforcements arrived in time, I take it?" Meiko asked.

Kumar smirked. "By pure random happenstance, if one believed in such, a pair of private security people were nearby and heard the disturbance. In fact, they're two of the very small number of civilians authorized to carry weapons on the station. They caught your attackers in the rear and stunned them all before they could make off with you."

"Remind me to send them a thank-you note."

Her incoming message indicator blinked, but there was no return address code. *Anonymous routing? Through the consulate network? I didn't think that was possible here.* She scanned the header; the message had been sent to Meriel's box, but the smart agent on that account had forwarded it to her own, and the consulate infonet had passed it through Kumar's screen, which turned out to be set against outgoing signals. She raised her IV-plugged hand, forestalling Kumar's response, and blinked the message open.

Sorry you encountered such poor hospitality, she read. *My colleagues are still debating involvement, especially given the public splash, but offer the enclosed in the spirit of goodwill and wishes for a swift recovery. K.*

There was an attachment. "I need a sandbox," she said to Kumar, who raised an eyebrow but called one up from the consulate's internal infonet server. Meiko tossed the packet into the window Kumar conjured, and the two looked to see what Kaki had sent.

The packet turned out to be ten seconds' worth of 3D imaging, showing a short, tawny, wiry man with a heavy brow and flattened nose under thick black hair. Meiko recognized the scene immediately. "That's the passenger-shuttle terminal," she said. The clip ended with the man framed at the mouth of the boarding tube.

"Stop," she said, and the image froze. "Magnify." The image grew to nearly a quarter life-size, and they could read the flight number on the display beside the boarding tube.

Kumar murmured to herself for a few seconds, then turned to Meiko. "He boarded a surface-bound shuttle that departed fifty minutes after the attack," she said. She inclined her head at the image. "Is that what I think it is?"

Meiko nodded and read the message. "The Fingers think he's involved, at least, if not one of the assassins himself."

"Or want us to think so. But I think you're right. I'll call the station chief down the cable and pass this on. And get some analysts working on an ID." Kumar stood and patted Meiko's shoulder. "I hope this was worth getting kicked off the station for."

Inspiration flashed, and Meiko seized it. "You know... planetside is off the station."

Kumar withdrew her hand and stared at her subordinate, arms folded across her chest. "That's cheeky," she said.

Silence stretched on for nearly half a minute before Meiko cracked. "You need me on this," she said. "Do you have anyone else with contacts like mine?" She sat up as straight as she could manage. "This is a win for everyone. I leave the station to make the Commissioner happy. I keep working the case to keep us happy." Kumar cocked her head. "Fine. It keeps me happy. We can feed this to the Ileris through Teng to make the Directorate happy. We can find the actual killer, which ought to please everyone."

"Except the dead," Kumar said dryly.

"Well, no," Meiko said, feeling her face flush. A prick of guilt lanced her eagerness, guilt about being so focused on pursuing the case, on putting her career to rights, that she'd forgotten about the very real crime which had started this mess.

"I'm inclined to push for it, though," Kumar said. "It's one thing to play nice with the locals, but I think the ambassador can be persuaded that simply kicking you back into the box might let the Ileris think they can push us around. We can play up the riot as well, use that to push for a concession if we need to. Yes," she nodded. "This works. But first"—she reached out to tap Meiko's shoulder—"you sleep. Dr. Tran will come back to make sure of it."

"Understood, ma'am," Meiko said. Kumar left and, as promised, Dr. Tran returned a few moments later to fit Meiko with a set of trodes to help induce medical sleep.

We're behind, but you're stuck down the gravity well, she thought as she drifted off.

She dreamed of a falcon plunging towards its prey.

CHAPTER TEN

Noo

MASJID ALJISR ALNUJMAA, ILERI STATION, SOUTH RING

NOO HATED FUNERALS.

Since the station kept the same time as New Abuja below, prayer times for the station's Muslims followed suit. Since the Isha salat, the night prayer, began at 2036 hours on the surface, and so it did in the station above.

The architects had done something clever to give Masjid Aljisr Alnujmaa, the Star Bridge Mosque, a feeling of open airiness, Noo thought, but she couldn't quite put her finger on it. Perhaps it was the way the arching dome seemed to draw the eye ever-upwards, or the delicate latticework open columns that braced the dome and ceiling while still providing a view. And the ceiling was high, even from Noo's perspective in the Visitation Gallery lining the upper level. It was a delicate robin's-egg blue of the open sky Noo had seldom seen in person, the kind of blue that her station-born-and-raised brain usually gave her fits over. But here, it worked some magic on her, bringing a small measure of peace.

Most of the firm's employees were present, a few in the mosque proper, the rest in the Visitation Gallery. Two had been dispatched somewhere mysterious by Fathya on some errand she declined to discuss with Noo. Two others remained on duty back at the office, and a handful more worked assignments unrelated to the killings. A number of the young man's friends had come, some of whom Noo recognized by sight, though she couldn't have put names to any of them if her djinn hadn't pulled their IDs and helpfully displayed AR tags above their heads. As family, Noo and her daughter Yinwa claimed spots in the front row of the gallery. Fari's wife Ifedepo, nearly the physical opposite of Fari in every respect with willowy slender limbs and delicate features, sat with them. She and Yinwa worked together in biosphere maintenance; in fact, Yinwa had introduced the couple to each other.

Daniel Imoke, looking weary, slipped in shortly before prayers began, which wasn't a surprise. Commissioner Toiwa arrived on his heels, which was. Toiwa spotted Noo watching her, caught Noo's eye, and nodded crisply before taking a free spot in a back row.

Fari stood, resolute, next to her brother's coffin at the back of the mosque, with her grandmother Fathya beside her. Two cousins who didn't work for the firm hovered nearby, with several of Saed's friends rounding out the party of bearers. When the call to prayer came, all the bearers but Fari took their places among the prostrating worshippers. Ifedepo sucked in her breath, and Noo was surprised herself. A crisis of faith, maybe? Or was it something like a Christian being out of grace? She shot a glance at Yinwa, who shrugged; she and Fari were close as sisters, but either she didn't know the reason behind the behavior or was keeping it to herself. Noo felt her fragile sense of peace begin to crack, knowing that her work partner's soul was out of balance and that she hadn't known. Or was this a new development, just spawned today? *Later. Be the arm she can lean on when she asks for it.*

The service began but Noo paid scant attention to the rounds of prayers, prostration, standing, and yet more prostration that followed. Noo resisted the impulse to call up personal AR fields, and instead offered her own silent prayers. *Guide Saed to his rest. Peace unto his spirit, and to the spirits of his kin. Bring us light in our hour of darkness.* Her jaw tightened, and her hands curled into fists. *And grant strength to my limbs, cunning to my mind, and sharpness to my vision, that I might enact righteous justice.*

You weren't supposed to ask the orisha for vengeance, but Noo's personal faith had evolved into a more flexible creed over the years. Had she lost her sense of the spirits because of this, or had her attitude changed when her prayers began being met with silence? She frowned, not trusting her own memory. Still, the need to rationalize burned in her brain. *Not vengeance, but justice,* she told herself, as if thinking the words made it so.

And if what she truly sought was both? So be it, and fire take those in her path.

The imam read a chapter of the Quran in Arabic but, lost in her own thoughts, she turned down the translation her djinn helpfully offered. After another round of prayer, the faithful stood and at the imam's gesture, a path opened down the middle of the congregation. The pallbearers took up their burden, carrying it to the front of the worship room, and placed it upon a folding stand. The imam took his place and the faithful arrayed themselves in lines behind him. The squat man spread his arms wide and uttered the funeral prayer. The rhythm of his recitation drew her in, and despite herself, Noo followed along, this time accepting the audible translation.

"O God, forgive our living and our dead, those who are present among us and those who are absent, our young and our old, our folk of all genders. O God, whoever You keep alive, keep them alive in Islam, and whoever You cause to die, cause them to die with faith. O God, do not deprive us of the reward and do not cause us to go astray after this. O God, forgive them and have mercy on them, keep them safe and sound and forgive them, honor their rest and ease their entrance; wash them with water and snow and hail, and cleanse them of sin as a white garment is cleansed of dirt. O God, give them a home better than their home and a family greater than their family. O God, admit them to Paradise and protect them from the torment of the grave and the torment of Hell-fire, and fill their rest with light."

I guess they mean grave figuratively now, she thought. The van waiting outside would take the body and the immediate family to the Renewal Center, where Saed's body would be recycled, continuing the circle of life as had been the practice since the earliest days of Exile. The hard truths of the closed-loop life-support systems and terraforming of the First Fourteen had demanded all the Earth-based biomass available, Way Back When. Survival of the species—the uninfected part, anyway—drowned out the religious objections. *Or so the histories tell us.*

The imam gestured again, and once more the crowd parted. The bearers carried the coffin towards the entry. Noo turned to hug Ifedepo and spotted Daniel joining Toiwa, who now hunkered in a corner of the gallery with her chief of staff, Valverdes.

"Are you coming, Mamma?" Yinwa, arm in arm with Ifedepo, asked.

Noo glanced towards the entry but Fathya, Fari and the others had already moved outside. Her eyes flicked back to her daughter, and then over to the tight little knot of constables. "Afraid not, loves. Business." She jerked her head in Daniel's direction.

"Business always wins," Yinwa said, not bothering to hide the bitterness in her voice. But she yielded as Ifedepo shushed her and guided her to the steps.

Noo ached to explain, that it was all in service of finding Saed's killer, and that she could serve him best by doing this, instead of seeing his body handed over to the Reclaimers. She'd made that trip often enough. But the girls—she found it hard to think of them as women — were gone too fast, and the moment was lost.

She chewed her bottom lip and stalked over towards Daniel and Toiwa, pushing her way through the last of the departing visitors. *Let's see if we can dig some news out of the tight-ass.* Valverdes tried to intercept her but she shouldered the younger woman aside with a low grunt, feeling the buzz of a privacy field as she did so.

"I want our people in on this, Sergeant, there's no

way—" Toiwa cut off as Noo invaded their space, shooting the investigator a fierce look. "M. Okereke, we are discussing sensitive Constabulary business."

"Not discussing a break in the case, then?" Noo set her feet and planted her hands on her hips. "Since Daniel is the primary investigator, I assumed that's why you called him over so urgently."

"A *Constabulary* investigation." Toiwa locked eyes with Noo. "Please excuse us."

Valverdes made to tug at Noo's elbow but she side-stepped, staying just inside the privacy field's boundaries. "You understand that this is personal for me, for Fathya, for Fari? For our whole concern? That we'll keep digging and following every lead we find, wherever it takes us, until we find the killers?" Toiwa opened her mouth and Noo flung up her hands. "We can go places you can't, talk to people who won't talk to yours. But we don't have to work at cross purposes." She shrugged off Valverdes as the smaller woman tried once more to pull her away. "Read us in. We can work together on this and clip these fuckers."

The sound of Daniel clearing his throat drew both women's attention. "M. Okereke has a point, Commissioner," he said. "I can tell you from experience"—he grimaced—"*much* experience, decades worth, that M. Shariff and M. Okereke will pursue this to its conclusion. And," he said with a nod in Noo's direction, "she's also correct that their operatives can supplement our officers in, er, unconventional settings."

Toiwa glared like the sun through an unfiltered window. "You mean, she has criminal connections she can exploit." Her eyes flicked towards Daniel. "Just like—the other party we were discussing."

Daniel shrugged. "They're getting positive results. We've mostly got negative ones so far. As you say, speedy resolution is essential." He turned to look at Noo. "And at least in their case, we can be assured their motives and loyalties align with ours."

An impulse sidled up to Noo and she rode it. "Besides, we know some things you don't."

Toiwa fixed her with a glare that probably caused probationary constables to wither in place like they'd been hit with a flamethrower, but Noo stood her ground. At last she waved Valverdes off. "It's all right, Kala. Sergeant Imoke has a made the case on M. Okereke's behalf. And I'm curious to see what she's gleaned that our people haven't." She turned again to Noo, her face solemn. "If I read you in on this, well, it's a Secrets Act issue. Breach that and I'll hand you over to the Directorate so fast your clothes will scorch. Do you still want in?"

Noo hesitated for a few seconds. *The Secrets Act?* Penalties for violating that included lifetime imprisonment on a wind-blasted island in the far northern hemisphere the Army used as a winter training base. *Hot intel of some kind, has to be. What the hell is going on?* But the rewards seemed worth the risks. "I do," she said.

"All right. The Directorate has learned via a tip from the Commonwealth, and I have no idea where *they* got their information, that a potential suspect took a shuttle down to the planet shortly after the killing. We're sending a joint team down in a few hours."

"I want in." The words were out of her mouth before she'd consciously finished processing Toiwa's speech. The need to be on the trail of the killer burned, deep inside. "I'll want my partner, M. Tahir, along too."

Toiwa nodded, even as she frowned like she was sucking a lemon. "All right. In exchange, I'll want whatever information you've gathered today. Give that to Inspector Valverdes or Sergeant Imoke and we'll get you on the manifest."

"Agreed." Noo stuck out her hand and they shook on it.

At that moment every djinn in the room immediately flashed red, and priority message alerts screamed in Noo's ears. "Shit!" She waved it open. The messages were coded at the highest priority, reserved for major emergencies. *A hull breach? Catastrophic collision?*

She read the message. It was both better and worse.

ARRIVAL

FLASH FLASH FLASH AT 205051 NEW ABUJA TIME AN UNSCHEDULED STARSHIP EMERGENCE FROM ALCUBIERRE DRIVE WAS DETECTED INSIDE THE EXCLUSION ZONE. SYSTEM DEFENSE UNITS ARE RESPONDING. ALL SYSTEMS TO CONDITION RED ZED THREE.

-

FLASH FLASH FLASH 205126 NEW ABUJA TIME ENERGY PROFILE OF NEWLY ARRIVED STARSHIP CONSISTENT WITH MILITARY VESSEL.

-

FLASH FLASH FLASH 205147 VESSEL TENTATIVELY CLASSIFIED AS STAR REPUBLIC OF SALJU 'HAKIM' CLASS SPACE DOMINANCE

VEHICLE. NO SALJUAN MILITARY VESSEL SCHEDULED TO ARRIVE. EXCLUSION ZONE DEFENSE SYSTEMS HOLDING AT CONDITION RED ZED THREE.

FLASH FLASH FLASH 205418 EMERGING STARSHIP IDENTIFIED AS STAR REPUBLIC OF SALJU SPACE DOMINANCE VEHICLE IWAN GOLESLAW. COMMANDER HAS INVOKED RIGHTS OF VISITATION UNDER ACCORDS OF 83 PE. SDV IWAN GOLESLAW IS NOW BURNING AT ONE-POINT-TWO GRAVITIES FOR HIGH PLANETARY ORBIT ASSIGNED BY ILERI OTC. STAND DOWN FROM CONDITION RED ZED THREE TO RED ZED ONE.

CHAPTER ELEVEN

ANDINI

COMBAT INFORMATION CENTER, STAR REPUBLIC OF SALJU
SPACE DOMINANCE VEHICLE IWAN GOLESLAW, *ILERI ORBIT*

"EYES JUST UPLOADED their new assessment of the Ileri exclusion-zone defense systems, Captain."

Captain Nia Andini, commander of the SDV *Iwan Goleslaw*, looked up—which only had meaning as her vessel was under thrust—from the AR window from which she'd been reviewing the post-transition engineering status report. "And just how dead would we have been, XO?"

"They've identified two of their three railgun installations so far, one of which was only twenty-four thousand klicks from our emergence point, so very dead." Andini winced and the XO nodded. "They had us painted within thirty-five seconds and the gun was aimed only twelve degrees off our trajectory when we popped back into normal space. It was on target and ready to fire in under a minute. We're lucky they aren't as trigger-happy as Shenzen."

She cocked her head at her XO. "I assume they're not pointing it at us still?"

"No, but they've got two targeting radars on us at all times. And one squadron of heavies is burning to shadow our assigned orbit, unless I miss my guess."

"I expect you're right." She unbuckled her lap belt and stood to stretch, which barely brought her head to her XO's shoulder, even though he was short for spacer-born. Andini had flown attackers before switching to the command track. That she'd been able to take up gymnastics again and put some muscle back on after making the switch back had been a welcome change; every gram counted in those flying coffins.

"Keeping us painted is a rather aggressive step," the XO said.

"I warned the minister that emerging in their EZ was unnecessarily provocative." She rolled out her shoulders as she turned slowly, observing her combat information-center crew at work. The ship was at Condition Two, one step shy of full battle-readiness but fully able to defend itself, if not bare the full length of its claws. The CIC crew wore their soft suits at their stations, arrayed in front of her command dais like an orchestra's musicians before the conductor, though they all faced the giant display tank across the compartment instead of her on the dais. Crew murmured softly to each other, or to their comrades elsewhere on the ship. Andini had served with captains who kept their CICs dark, lit only by the glow of the fixed screens and open AR windows, but she favored light bright enough to read by. Darkness on a spacefaring vessel meant something had gone wrong, and things that went wrong in space could kill you with incredible swiftness.

"And speaking of the minister..." the XO said, just above a whisper, as the one person Andini had to answer to—here in Ileri space, at any rate—climbed the steps into the CIC.

Ping Dinata, Minister Plenipotentiary for Technology Constraint, filled the picture in Andini's mental dictionary for the word 'dour'. She was medium height with broad shoulders and hips, neither skinny nor fat, with light-brown skin and long, straight hair she wore in the traditional ministerial side-braid. Andini wondered if the woman's face was capable of smiling, then wondered how she'd react if the minister ever cracked one.

She checked her clock. "Conference time, number one. Tell Ears we'll take the call from the dais."

The XO acknowledged and hurried off to be Somewhere Else before Dinata reached the command dais steps.

"Good day, Captain," the minister said as she pulled herself up onto the dais. "Shall we shift to your briefing room to deliver our message to the Ileris?"

Andini shook her head. "I've instructed my communications team to route the message to us here on the command dais."

Dinata's brows drew down. "That seems unwise, given the sensitivity of the matters we're here to deal with."

"The crew has been fully briefed on our mission, including the contingency plans," Andini said as she waved the spare acceleration chair out from its normal stowage compartment. "I have complete confidence in their willingness to take whatever action is deemed appropriate." She settled herself into her own chair and gestured for the minister to do the same. "And in the event the *Iwan Goleslaw* needs to go to Condition One in the course of our—discussion—I'd prefer to be in my CIC."

Dinata tried to brush off the implied risk of violent action. "Surely the Ileris wouldn't dare fire on us. No one has ever dared fire on one of our SDVs before. That's why the Assembly chose to send this vessel."

"Ileri is one of the First Fourteen, Minister, with the military to match," Andini said. She related what the XO had passed on about their emergence. "My ship may mass as much as a sizable fraction of Ileri's navy, and we'd blood them badly if it came to a fight, but please do not doubt which side would win."

"Do you really think they'd risk starting a war?" Dinata asked. But she sat down in the spare seat, usually reserved for squadron commanders using the ship as their flag.

"Is it likely? No. Possible? Absolutely," Andini said. She opened a channel to her communications officer. *<Ears, we're ready. Patch us in, please. Holo to the dais display.>* Ears acknowledged and images of two conference rooms materialized between her and Dinata. Labels appeared seconds later identifying one as belonging to the Ileri Minister for Interstellar Affairs, while the other showed Government House on Ileri Station.

Interesting. Quite senior enough to not give offense or be dismissive, but not the very top of their government. The intelligence briefing on Ileri's Prime Minister had noted that she was known for being a skilled negotiator. Using Ngo, the Interstellar Affairs Minister, as a buffer between the head of state and the Saljuan minister struck

Andini as a savvy move. More immediately, she felt the knot of tension in her neck that had been present since just prior to emergence relax a bit; she'd half-expected to be dealing with Vega, the Defense Minister, which would have made for a *very* different conversation. Though Vega was on the call; she sat two seats away from Ngo, like a weapon close at hand, ready to be grasped.

She noted, though, that the Commonwealth ambassador sat next to Ngo, a likely indication the Star Republic's chief rival supported its prospective member. Andini silently offered thanks to the merciful Father that *Amazonas*, the Commonwealth warship she'd been told was en route to Ileri, hadn't yet arrived.

Once introductions were made, Ngo, a soft-featured woman with a melodious voice, came straight to the heart of the matter. "Minister Dinata. The message you broadcast after your *unconventional* arrival into Ileri space indicated you wish to conduct inspections as specified in the Accords of Year 83 Post Exile. Perhaps you would be so kind as to elaborate on that request?"

Even as Dinata drew breath to speak, Andini felt the knot of tension return.

"We are not making a request, Minister Ngo," Dinata said flatly. "That is a notification. A statement of intent."

There was a three-second delay as the signal and the return message bounced from ship to station and planet.

"Notification typically arrives ahead of the inspection team," Ngo said.

Dinata flicked the fingers of her right hand as if brushing off a fly. "It is the right of all signatories to the Accords to conduct unannounced inspections at any time. The Star Republic chooses to exercise that right at this time."

She fixed her gaze impassively on the video pickup as if she could bore through the intervening kilometers into Ngo.

A private message window popped up and Andini waved it open, down by her left knee as Ngo and Dinata continued to spar. <*Ears. What is it?*>

<*We just received an encoded burst transmission, Captain. We're decrypting it now, but the header codes are from Anomalous Cases.*>

A sick feeling in the pit of her stomach arrived to match the literal pain in her neck. <*How long to decrypt and verify? And where did it come from?*>

<*Should be ready in about a minute. It seems to have come from Ileri Station.*>

<*Tight beam?*> Please let it be a tight beam.

<*No, ma'am. They used a directional antenna but it's radio frequency, not laser.*>

Andini was grateful that gymnastics competitions in her youth had given her the ability to fix an expression on her face despite whatever she felt inside. <*What are the odds the Ileris intercepted the message and traced it?*>

Ears frowned. <*Very high they intercepted it, I'd think. Whether they filtered it out from the background chatter, that's harder to say, but if their traffic-anomaly detection is any good, they'll have it isolated shortly. As far as tracing it?*> Ears shrugged. <*To the station, certainly. Maybe to the specific antenna they used. Beyond that, I really couldn't say.*>

<*The Anomalous Cases team risked exposure to send this to us?*> Andini asked.

<*That seems possible.*> Ears glanced aside at another

AR window. <*It's decrypted. Eyes only to you, the Minister, and Major Nkruma.*> Nkruma commanded the four-hundred-person inspection and security team.

<*Send it.*> A new window popped up and Adina skimmed the précis with a sinking feeling. She saw Dinata tilt her head, no doubt reading the report in a private window of her own.

Vega, the Defense Minister, took over after the brief lag. "Minister Dinata," she said after the most recent lag gap. "I wish to formally deliver a protest from my government to yours regarding an espionage operation directed against the safety and good order of the Republic of Ileri." The protest document appeared in the main projection field over the table as it simultaneously hit Andini's inbox.

She was impressed by the Ileris' thoroughness, sending it to her personally as well as to the conference channel. Vega probably knew that messages to her personally would be logged, regardless of what Dinata chose. She popped open the message to see the Ileris had, indeed, intercepted the Anomalous Cases signal. That was a fast bit of work. She prayed they weren't able to crack the cipher.

Dinata's eyes returned to her vid pickup. "This is immaterial," she said impassively. "My government has received information that the government of Ileri, in conjunction with the government of the Commonwealth, has come into possession of Exile-grade mind-domination and reprogramming technology, in direct violation of the Accords of 83 PE."

Andini heard the gasps in the locals' conference rooms quite clearly. She didn't blame them; the specter of the

Unity Plague which had driven their ancestors not only off of Lost Earth, but out of the solar system, loomed large in the Saljuan consciousness. When the cabal of plutocrats and their religious fundamentalist allies had unleashed the nanoware agent that gave them control over the infected populace, her world's people had fled up Earth's space elevators with so many others. Unlike the Ileris, or the Novo Brasilians, her forebears hadn't ended up on a garden world.

She locked her face into full-bore commander mode. This was Dinata's operation to run, the Commandant had made that abundantly clear. She had her concerns about the ministers' methods, but not about their ultimate goal.

"The Republic of Ileri categorically denies this charge," Ngo, the Interstellar Affairs Minister, said.

Three more seconds ticked by.

Dinata shook her head. "It doesn't matter if you deny it or not," she said. "My mission is to determine whether or not this is true, and if so, to exercise our lawful rights to ensure any illegal material is destroyed." To Andini: <How long until we reach orbit?>

Andini glanced at the mission plot. <Two hundred twenty-seven minutes and change.>

"My government is not going to allow you to conduct a fishing expedition," Vega chimed in before Ngo could respond.

Dinata leaned forward. "Minister. Captain Andini informs me we will achieve our initial parking orbit in approximately four hours," she said. "We intend to dispatch an inspection team escorted by Major Nkruma's troops to Ileri station. We shall provide you with flight plan prior to launch. Please prepare to receive them and make arrangements for them to conduct their inspection. I expect full cooperation under the provisions of the Accords. If cooperation is not forthcoming, I will recommend immediate interdiction of the Ileri system."

Vega braced up, and Andini recalled the woman's combat record as a peacekeeping-force commander. "Minister, we have no intention of cooperating until the matter of the espionage team has been resolved. We believe they are involved with the kidnapping and assault of Ileri citizens."

The Commonwealth ambassador spoke up at last. "Speaking for the Commonwealth, Minister, while we respect your rights under the Accords, we advise you against precipitous action in exercising those rights. Enacting Interdiction without positive evidence of compromise is most emphatically *not* recognized under the Accords, and the Commonwealth will respond appropriately."

That finally broke Dinata's implacability, and she actually sneered. "Your people are just as complicit in this matter, Ambassador," she said. "And you've been skirting the abyss for decades. You'd see us all made the thralls of the force our ancestors fled." Her mask descended again. "We'll speak again once our vessel attains its orbit."

Dinata made a chopping motion with her left hand, below the pickup's view. *<Ears, cut the signal,>* Andini ordered.

"Captain Andini." She heard Dinata's voice as if it came from somewhere far away, instead of a little more than a meter to her right.

"Yes, Minister?" Her voice was steady, at least.

"How quickly will you be able to launch the inspection team's shuttle once we achieve orbit?"

"We can be ready to launch almost immediately, Minister, but there may be a delay until *Iwan Goleslaw* is in proper position relative to the station for rapid transit." Her hands moved to call up the navigation plots.

"Very well. I want Major Nkruma's team on the way to Ileri Station at the earliest practical opportunity." Dinata pulled herself to her feet and made for the steps. "Please tell Major Nkruma I'm on my way to brief him personally."

"At your direction, Minister," Andini said. She called her XO. "Keep the ship at Condition Two and prep a shuttle. The hunt is on."

CHAPTER TWELVE

MEIKO

JOINT BASE ADNAN,
NEW ABUJA, ILERI

MEIKO STOOD ON the grassy strip between the runway and shuttle hangar and faced the sun, arms at her side and eyes closed, feeling the warmth of the sun and the cool of the morning breeze off the bay at once. She caught the waxy scent of gardenias and the sweeter aroma of jasmine along with a sharper, crisper smell she couldn't identify.

Captain Teng stood next to her, his yellow kaftan trimmed with green piping rippling with the wind. "First time groundside in a while?"

"First in nearly four standard years. First time without needing an exosuit of some kind, that is." She had a flashback to her disastrous last mission, of bounding across the frozen, airless surface of Haem IV's third moon, racing to get one of her critically injured companions to their shuttle's nanostasis tank in hopes the doctor could stabilize him enough for stasis. She suppressed a shiver, not from memory of cold, but from the knowledge of how close they'd all come to dying in that remote, desolate place. She rubbed her injured left arm and turned back to face the sun again.

She and Teng stood a bit apart from the others. A pair of civilian investigators, one Meiko's age and the other in her early thirties, stood together a few meters away with a trim young Constabulary officer, clad like Teng in civilian dress. The constable displayed better taste, to Meiko's eye. The trio talked quietly between themselves, as if leery of standing too close to the spies.

Teng looked on expectantly, and she indulged him with an answer. "Not since I was home last, in fact."

"Have you been on Ileri before?"

She couldn't fault him asking, but only smiled faintly in response. Either he knew already, and was trying to catch her in a lie, or he *didn't* know, and was fishing for intel.

No freebies here, young man.

Teng didn't press and shifted topics, instead asking about her recovery. Truth be told, she felt pretty good; Dr. Tran's treatments were doing their job, and she'd scrupulously followed the supplements regimen to keep the nanosurgeons fed. She wasn't used to the weight of the cast on her forearm but, then again, she wouldn't have it on long enough for that to be a factor. Or so she hoped.

He relented and let her enjoy her brief communion with the relative novelty of an unregulated environment in silence. All too soon she heard the soft whir of an electric motor. She opened her eyes, scooped up her go-bag, and joined the others as they ambled towards the gray van come to deliver them on the next leg of their journey.

She found herself sitting next to Okereke, the older of the two civilian investigators, while Teng sat in the back next to the woman's partner, with the policewoman settled in up front next to the driver.

"It seems we have some mutual friends," Okereke said as the van's gentle surge of acceleration pushed them back into their seats.

"Excuse me?" Meiko asked, startled.

Her seat mate flicked a glance back at Teng, who was chatting with the younger woman, Tahir. Okereke leaned towards Meiko, speaking softly. "Fari and I are the ones that saved your ass yesterday."

Meiko laid her hand on Okereke's arm. "Thank you," she murmured. "That could have gone very badly if you hadn't come along." The rush of gratitude she felt was tempered with caution. The woman had connections with both the Fingers *and* the police. Interesting. *Whose side is she on?*

"Thank our friends. They're the ones who vectored us in." Okereke eyed the cast around Meiko's left arm. "You look pretty good considering how they were working you over."

"Timely rescue and a good doctor." Her fingers twitched and she called up Okereke's public profile, something she'd have done earlier if she hadn't slept through the flight down. "What's your involvement in the case?"

Okereke leaned away in surprise, her eyes widening. "You truly don't know?" She nodded towards her partner. "Fari's brother was Minister Ita's bodyguard on-station. He was one of the victims."

Meiko cursed silently as she flashed up the victim list. There was the name, Saed Tahir, along with a picture of a grinning young man. "I'm sorry, I didn't make the connection," she said aloud. "My condolences. You knew him well, then."

"He was family," Okereke affirmed.

"We both want the killers brought to justice," she said. "Trust me, I want this as much as you do."

Okereke nodded. "I'll take your word for it." She cocked her head and said, "Your social profile says you're a planetary surveyor from Novo Brasilia. Your other profile, the one our friends passed me, also claims you're a surveyor but that you're an Ileri." She looked Meiko straight in the eyes. "Is *any* of that true?"

Meiko hesitated, but Teng seemed caught up discussing some kind of fighting competition with Okereke's partner, seemingly uninterested in whatever Meiko might say to the civilian. "Let's just say my current profile is correct but not complete," she said at last.

Okereke nodded as if she expected an evasion, but she stayed relaxed. "I hear surveyors get around. You've been to a lot of worlds?"

"I've seen my share, yes." The van slowed as it pulled up to the canal-side quay where a Constabulary boat waited to carry them to the city center. "More than most. I've been lucky." She glanced at Okereke. "How about you?"

Okereke shook her head. "I've never been out-system," she said. "Born on the station. Hardly ever come planetside." The Ileri woman eyed the gently bobbing watercraft sitting quayside dubiously, and Meiko noticed the sheen of sweat on her forehead. *Nerves?*

Meiko wondered. *Afraid of open water?* Okereke caught her looking and grimaced. "Not a fan of unmanaged weather." She pulled a handkerchief from her pocket and wiped her face.

Transferring their scant luggage—it seemed they all traveled light—went quickly, and the team settled in to enjoy the early-morning view of Ileri's largest city from water level.

Meiko had caught a few overhead views of the city on her seat's vid panel during their landing approach, including the bright flashes of the canals which served as the city's arteries in the early-morning sun, a patchy web of silver between the districts. New Abuja sprawled across its island near the center of Lake Perpaduan, hugging the bay that cradled the lower terminus of the space elevator. She'd only glimpsed a few towers; the capital tended towards shorter buildings, four and five stories tall, arranged in blocks around central courts, many of which served as green spaces.

Now, from the water level, she looked up and saw the brightly colored facades of these buildings as they zipped past. Residents walked or rode bikes or the tramline on their way to school, or work, or wherever they were headed, but fewer than Meiko expected. It was hard to tell from some meters away, but she got a vague sense of nervousness, or even fear, among the people; they clustered together in packs, heads down, eyes scanning for... something. It had been nearly twenty years since she'd last come down the cable to the city, but she remembered the sounds of music, even in the morning hours, people singing as they walked, of buskers getting an early start. A major war had swept through the systems on their doorstep but that hadn't repressed the jaunty boisterousness of New Abuja's citizens.

Now, they looked as if they feared the demons which had haunted the streets of Shenzen's and Goa's cities were poised just outside of view, waiting to sweep in and wreak havoc.

Okereke, again seated next to her, noticed it too. "It's worse than on-station." She scanned the meager crowds and frowned. "Heard there were more disturbances here than we've had. Wonder how bad they've gotten."

"Bad enough," piped in Zheng, the stationside policewoman. She was taller than average, long-legged and built like a swimmer, with a round face framed with straight black hair bobbed short. Her comment earned her a disapproving look from Teng, which she blithely ignored. "No fatalities yet, but last night there was a pretty significant fight between One Worlders and the Harmonians, believe it or not." She stretched her long legs carefully as the boat slowed to negotiate an intersection of canals. "The Commonwealth ship coming for the referendum had them stirred up plenty, but the Saljuans popping up unannounced, inside the exclusion zone to boot, and shouting about the Accords? It's like poking a stick into a nest of flare ants."

"What about the inspection team?" Okereke asked.

Zheng got the distant look of someone reading a private AR window on their implants. "They've docked but they're still bottled up in the hub. Their commander wants them to be under arms in the station and our people are having none of that. Standoff, phase two." She focused back on her companions, and her eyes settled on Meiko. "We might need to do something about your social profile, broadcasting you're an off-worlder, when we reach HQ. We've got enough to do without needing to spend cycles keeping people from wanting to tear your face off."

"Hm." Meiko glanced at Teng, who shrugged. "I can handle myself, but that's a good idea."

"Even with one arm down?" Zheng pointed at Meiko's cast.

"More than you might think," she said, as the boat slowed again, rounding a corner onto a broader canal, one of the major thoroughfares.

"Shit," the driver said. A massive freight barge sat wedged across the canal a hundred meters ahead with One World banners draped across it. "They must have just blocked the channel. Call it in," he snapped to his assistant before heeling the craft over to the right, cutting across the broad canal, aiming for a narrower intersecting canal midway between themselves and the barge. "Hang on, this might get choppy." Meiko grabbed hold of a stanchion with her good hand.

"Pop the berry?" the assistant asked.

"Not yet," Zheng half-shouted over the now-brisk wind they all felt as the driver punched it. "Liable to set the buttonheads off if they see just one Constabulary boat by itself. Might think we're easy pickings." Zheng stood and faced forward, hands gripped tightly on the rail behind the driver's station, her knees slightly bent and flexing as the boat surged forward. Her jacket blew open, and Meiko could see Zheng's twinned shoulder holsters. With a start she realized that she was probably the only person on the boat without a weapon.

The boat bucked like an aerobraking shuttle as the

driver accelerated. That connection gave Meiko the framing she needed to reach for, and find, a relative sense of calm. *Just another ride.*

"Shit, someone's coming after us," Fari Tahir called out. The driver jerked his wheel to the right and the boat skipped sideways as he aimed to shoot straight up the intersecting canal. Meiko risked a glance at their pursuers and caught a glimpse of Okereke, who had a death-grip on the closest stanchion. The station-sider looked like she was about to heave up her breakfast then and there. Meiko twisted further and saw what Tahir had: two boats about the size of their own, cutting towards them at speed. Any chance the interlopers weren't after them was dashed by the person standing in the bow of the lead boat pointing directly at the Constabulary craft.

"Pull up the real-time feeds and find us a way around," the driver ordered their assistant.

"I'm trying, system's down," he said.

"That shouldn't be possible," Zheng said, nearly shouting now between the wind and the whine of the boat's motor. She let go with her left hand and swept it across each of them in turn, twisting to point at Meiko and Okereke. A fresh contact icon popped up in Meiko's personal field and she accepted it. Status icons appeared over the heads of each party member as if they were all part of an interactive game. She popped open a map window and saw everyone's location painted on it. *An ad hoc tactical net. She must expect trouble.*

They came upon the next concentric belt canal and the driver heeled the boat hard to the left. He'd no more gotten it pointed down the channel when Zheng shouted "STOP!"

Barges were wedged across the new canal in both directions. They were trapped.

Noo

CHATTERJEE CANAL, NEW ABUJA

THE DRIVER SPUN his wheel hard to the right and cut his speed at the same time. The boat slewed as if to turn down the intersecting canal, but the barge wedged firmly across the way blocked their path. The driver abruptly jerked the wheel to the left as the obstacle loomed dangerously close in front of them. The left side—port side, she remembered—slammed into the quayside wall with a sickening *crack*, followed by a horrible scraping sound. The impact threw her from her feet, and she found herself the middle layer in a human sandwich, with Fari on the bottom and Teng on top of her. The pressure proved the last straw for her queasy stomach and her plantain omelet wound up splatted across both Fari and the bottom of the boat. Water splashed over them all and added *cold and wet* to her inventory of discomfort.

The boat slammed to a stop with a second crash and more water cascaded over them. On the plus side, Teng was thrown off of her by the impact, and she herself slid off of Fari's back only to wind up on top of Teng. Her head slammed into one of the seats, hard enough to have her seeing stars. She heard screams and cries of distress, but they seemed to come from somewhere away and above.

A strong, thin hand grasped hers and pulled her

upright as her vision cleared. "Are you OK?" Ogawa, the Commonwealth woman, asked.

"Mostly." She gingerly probed the top of her head, finding a lump and wetness. She pulled her fingers back and examined them, finding water and vomit but no blood.

"EVERYONE UN-ASS THE BOAT!" Zheng's command voice hadn't suffered from their collision, at least.

"Why?" Noo asked as Ogawa bent to scoop up someone's bag, stood, and flung it onto the quay, narrowly missing a number of bystanders who'd rushed forward. Several of these crouched down, arms extended, reaching down for the beleaguered company.

"Because we're sinking," Ogawa said calmly. She bent for another bag, heaved it up, and passed it to one of their rescuers.

"Shit. I hate coming down the cable," Noo grumbled. She started to bend down but her head was having none of that.

"Climb out. I've got this," Ogawa said, scooping up another bag and tossing it to one of their rescuers. Noo realized she was doing this one-handed; the woman wasn't exactly skinny but though she lacked Fari's muscular bulk, she evidently was a lot stronger than she looked at first glance. She caught Noo staring at her and jerked her head towards the quay. "Go on."

Noo clambered awkwardly around the scattered bags towards Fari, who had just boosted the driver up onto the grasping hands of the quayside rescue crew. She realized with a shock that their craft was sinking more rapidly than she'd thought possible; the water was ankle-deep and rising fast. She glanced forward and discovered that the bow was a ruin, with water pouring in at an alarming rate.

With a mutter of "Come here, Auntie," Fari grabbed her and hoisted her halfway up to the quay. Her flailing hands were caught by a pair of men in paint-splattered smocks, who each grabbed one and pulled her up onto solid ground. Noo turned around in time to see the two pursuing boats slowing as they approached, one on either side of their beleaguered vessel. The people clustered at the bows of each glared at her, her companions, and the whole quayside crowd with what certainly looked like malicious intent.

She twisted her fingers and toggled the tactical network Zheng had presciently set up. "Incoming hostiles, right and left. At least twelve," she said hoarsely. Her djinn picked it up and rebroadcast it to the others.

Zheng, newly hoisted onto the quay, spun to see their pursuers closing in. She snapped her fingers and her Constabulary ID shone above her head. The AR tag's border turned red as she drew her stunner. The crowd pulled Ogawa and Teng, the last of their little band, onto the quay and the group closed ranks around Zheng, even the Directorate spy accepting the constable's leadership. Zheng turned to address the crowd, her djinn amplifying her voice so that it rang out and echoed off the buildings across the street. "Thank you, but please stand back while we sort this out." She waved at their rescuers and the other bystanders, most of whom took a few steps backwards, muttering. She turned back to face the canal. "Non-lethals," Zheng ordered.

"That's all I've got," the driver said, but Teng's hand shifted direction and he plucked a stunner out from under his tunic, instead of whatever he'd initially reached for. *Wonder what else he's carrying?* Noo drew her own stunner and stood, wet and sore, covered in her own puke, and waited for the trouble to start.

She didn't have long to wait. The hostiles, unhampered by things like an abrupt collision or sinking boats, scrambled up onto the quay.

Zheng held up her left hand, holding her stunner low by her right leg. "I'm Lieutenant Zheng of the Constabulary. Do you have something you'd like to discuss?" she called to their pursuers.

They answered her with silence, and as soon as everyone but the boat drivers had clambered onto solid ground, they rushed Noo's little party from both sides.

Noo braced her feet and swung her weapon up as the first stunner shot buzzed. She tried to sight around the driver, who found himself face to face with a pair of assailants. She stepped to the side as he was driven back and snapped a shot at the one closest to her. Her breath came hard and fast as she scrambled backwards, away from the rushing swarm, and she fired again and again. Even un-aimed, one her shots found a target and one of the attackers crumpled to the ground, tripping up the beefy woman following him.

She caught a flicker of movement on her right and spun, ready to fire, only to see Ogawa fly past *upside down*. She turned around further, heart pounding, thinking that perhaps their rescuers had joined the hostiles, but for the moment, the shocked crowd was holding back. She checked the others and saw Teng and Fari and Zheng each tangling with at least one opponent hand-to-hand, while the driver's assistant backed them up with his stunner.

She turned back and raised her own weapon, then lowered it in stunned surprise as Ogawa simply took the hostiles on their side apart all by herself.

Noo had cracked her share of heads in her day, and while she wasn't in Fari's class by any means, she could hold her own in a brawl. She'd watched her partner spar in training, cheered her in a few competitive matches; and they'd had to mix it up with miscreants on a few occasions. She'd seen Daniel fight too, though his style was nothing like Fari's. Where the younger woman fought like a lorry with a pair of whirling hammers attached, Daniel was like a mongoose, lightning-fast strikes and kicks coupled with sinuous motion.

Ogawa moved in a way Noo had never seen before, flowing and spinning, bouncing from left to right, never still. She looked more like a dancer or rhythmic gymnast than like someone engaged in combat. As Noo watched, dumbfounded, the Commonwealth woman spun on her head and one hand as her scything legs kicked a pair of attackers squarely in the head. Somehow, she turned her horizontal rotation into a sort of flowing cartwheel that brought her behind her opponents, a pair of bruisers each easily half again her mass. They staggered from the force of her kicks but remained upright.

Noo's senses returned in a rush. She jerked her stunner back up and fired twice, dropping them both.

Hot hands grabbed Noo's left sleeve and jerked her sideways. She spun, letting her assailant do the work of swinging her weapon to bear as she ducked a wild punch. She came face to face with a short, skinny man with shocking blue hair and a scraggly beard, so she shoved her stunner into his gut and pulled the trigger, then stepped back as he collapsed into a spasming heap.

She turned back and saw Ogawa spinning in a vertical circle as she executed a one-armed handstand. Her legs snaked around the neck of a stocky man and her momentum yanked him off his feet. Ogawa sprang free and landed lightly on her feet, swaying and bouncing side to side as her target tried to roll over to stand. Unceremoniously, Noo stepped forward and stunned him.

With a start, she realized that all the attackers on their side were down. So was the Constabulary boat driver, pinned beneath the two-meter, hundred-fifty-kilo woman who'd driven him to the ground before he stunned her. Ogawa bent down to roll the woman off of him. Noo realized that the attacker's boats were pulling away from the quayside, and she took a couple of potshots at the drivers, but they were out of stunner range too quickly for her to bag them.

"One thing the vids never get right," Noo wheezed between shots, "is how fast a fight is over if one side's playing for keeps."

"Got that right, Auntie." Fari's voice floated from behind her. Her partner came up on her right side, breathing a little heavily herself but otherwise seeming no worse for wear. Zheng appeared on Noo's left, missing the right sleeve of her jacket, her hair charmingly mussed. "What do we do now?"

"I've called for backup and an air extraction," Zheng said. "But it sounds like things are breaking out all over the city so it might be a while." There was a low growling sound to their east, perhaps a block or two away. The braver bystanders hovered nearby, goggling at the twitching bodies of the attackers.

As the adrenaline surge faded, the physical toll of the last few minutes came due in the form of muscle ache down her whole left side. Her head hurt too; she probed the lump again, but her fingers came back blood-free again, thank the Mother. At least her stomach wasn't bothering her anymore, or maybe it was just too far down the damage roster to be acknowledged.

"Where's the crews of these barges?" Fari asked.

"Good question." Zheng scanned the buildings fronting the canal as she slipped a fresh charge cartridge into her stunner. She turned to face the locals and passers-by who remained. "Did anyone see who jammed these barges in here?"

One of the painters took a cautious step forward. "No crew, konstebo," he said. "They bots."

That made Noo's headache worse. She made a note on her djinn to call the firm's senior tech analyst, Haissani, to see if he had any idea how hard that would be. She wasn't sure just how big a deal screwing up the city's canal network was, but if it was anything like the time a programming error had brought the station's transit system to a halt for two infuriating days, it was pretty bad.

The rumbling sound to the east grew louder. She glanced around nervously, looking for cover or concealment and finding both scarce. Aside from a few benches and the ubiquitous sycamore trees lining the quay, the street was bare of handy obstructions they could use as firing positions. Not that their tiny band would be able to hold off a crowd, stunners or no.

Fuck me, I hate coming down the cable.

Turbines whined overhead as a formation of bots

zoomed past, following the canal, their golden AR tags proclaiming them Constabulary bots. "Reinforcements?" Fari asked hopefully.

Zheng shook her head as they sped past in the direction of the ever-louder crowd. "No, or not directly. I think they're going to try to interdict the rioters, though." The officer seemed to come to a decision, nodded once to herself, and spun on her heel. "We should put some distance between us and that lot, though. Let's move." She began to stride briskly in the other direction, the others at her heels, only to be brought up short by the sight of a large apron-clad woman who looked Noo's age, her hair done up in the beehive style that hadn't been fashionable since their primary-school days.

"Auntie Chell!" cried the driver happily. "She runs a cafe a couple blocks from here," the driver explained. "A lot of the marine branch eats there on the regular."

Flanking Auntie Chell was a mixed crowd of people of all genders and ages, wearing everything from workout clothes to sharp business suits. They all were armed after a fashion, Noo realized with a start, bearing blunt objects of every description, from Chell's walking stick to cricket bats, with a couple of donga sticks for good measure. The cafe owner marched directly up to Zheng, who regarded the crowd warily. "The buttonheads give you trouble, konstebo?" Chell asked.

Zheng glanced back at the array of still-twitching bodies lining the quay and started to answer but caught herself. She turned fully and scanned their would-be assailants and Noo did the same, squinting through her headache. Auntie Chell tapped her stick on the pavement while she waited.

<*None of them have One Worlder regalia,*> Zheng sent.

<*Is that significant?*> Ogawa asked.

<*Every incident I can think of, they've worn their markings,*> Zheng replied. She turned back to Auntie Chell, whose crowd had been reinforced not just by the bystanders who'd been present all along, but by a steady stream of citizens who joined in ones and twos. "I'm not sure if that bunch are One Worlders or not," she said aloud. "But the pack making trouble two blocks east are, according to my colleagues."

Angry retorts from the crowd answered that news but quieted swiftly when Chell raised her hands above her head, her stick grasped firmly between them. The polished wood glinted in the morning sunlight. "Miguna's dust-touched thugs aren't welcome in Bluewater," she proclaimed, and the crowd at her back cheered.

Pleased as she was by the prospect of reinforcements, Noo felt anxious about being part of a much larger brawl than what they'd just been through. Zheng apparently felt the same. "I can't condone you breaching the peace," she said, using her djinn's voice amplifier just a touch, enough to make herself heard without seeming like she was shouting.

"Then you'd best see to keeping it, konstebo," Chell shot back.

Further discussion was cut short as a phalanx of Constabulary aircars, surrounded by crowd-control bots, came roaring up the course of the canal, screaming past them at just below rooftop height. One set down a short distance away while the others landed up the street, close to the ever-louder rumble of the riot. Constables in full riot-control gear piled out and deployed in double-ranks across the street as their bots took position overhead. The nearest car disgorged a stocky officer whose AR tag identified zem as Captain Thanh. Ze beckoned to Zheng, who trotted over to confer with her superior.

Noo and Chell exchanged glances. "It looks like you won't need that today, Auntie," Noo said, with a wave at Chell's stick.

"Oh, I don't know about that," Chell said, resting one end on the ground and clasping both hands atop it. Her eyes flicked towards the line of police. "But I think I be needing it another day soon, if not today. The yellowjackets can't be everywhere, all the time. And the pot's right boiling."

CHAPTER THIRTEEN

Toiwa

Commissioner's Quarters, Ileri Station, North Ring

Toiwa LINGERED OVER her coffee at the kitchen table while her husband, Eduardo, cleared away the breakfast dishes. Her dress-uniform tunic hung over the back of the chair next to her, and a tea towel covered her dress shirt to spare it from the perils of coffee spills or honey smears. They were alone in the apartment; their son and daughter had left for school in the company of some friends.

At least we got breakfast together. Mother only knows when I'll get home tonight.

"The Saljuans have backed off for now?" Eduardo asked. He wore his hospital scrubs, fabbed from smart fabric that repelled organic material—like all the body fluids a nurse came into contact with. The joke that his attire was armor for the kitchen and housework as well as his job was an old one between them.

"For now," she said. "*Amazonas* popped out of a-space before the *Iwan Goleslaw* made its orbit. I think Captain Andini wasn't ready to escalate things with the Commonwealth ship in the same system."

"Not the nannie minister?" Eduardo used the pejorative term for the Saljuan official.

Toiwa recalled Dinata's final words in the previous night's conference and felt a chill. "I think," she said slowly, "that if Minister Dinata had her way, her inspection teams would either be deployed by now, or the Navy would be exchanging fire with her ship."

Eduardo scraped the last of the food waste into the recycler, put the final dish into the sanitizer and switched it on before grabbing his own coffee cup from the counter and sitting across from her. His face always wore his feelings, and his feelings right now were clearly 'worried', judging from his frown. "Why wouldn't the PM allow the inspection? Surely we've got nothing to hide." He took a swallow of coffee. "Unless it's a matter of not looking weak in front of the Commonwealth?"

"I honestly don't know, love," she said, which was the literal truth, if only just. "That's above my pay grade."

"For now," her husband said, giving her a grin that made him look ten years younger.

She glanced at her time display. "Aren't you going to be late?" Eduardo was a pediatric nurse, which had come in handy when the children were small. He worked at the forward ring's hospital.

He took another drink and waved his other hand dismissively. "Pavan is covering for me until I get there. I figured this might be our last leisurely meal until things settle down." He waggled his eyebrows, making her

162

laugh. "How much time *do* you have, anyway?"

"Not that much, you lecher," she said, and he laughed back. "Besides, even if we had time for *that*, I wouldn't have time to climb back into this." She smoothed her hand over her uniform blouse.

"Why are you all dressed up?"

"*Amazonas'* lighter is docking shortly, and I've got to meet whomever they've sent."

Almost on cue, her message indicator lit with a call from Kala Valverdes. She waved it open. <*Ma'am? Constable Chijindu and I are in the corridor.*>

Toiwa signaled the door to unlock and open. <*Come on in,*> she sent.

Valverdes bustled in and Eduardo rose to greet her, swapping cheek kisses, as Toiwa donned her tunic. She left the damned collar undone for now, though. She glimpsed Chijindu's bulky form lurking outside the open doorway as Valverdes fended off Eduardo's offer of coffee to go. Eduardo kissed Toiwa goodbye and she swept out, her aide at her heels.

Chijindu, a towering man who looked like he regularly bench-pressed transit cars, murmured his greetings before turning to lead the way to the lifts. Toiwa's rank entitled her to a security escort, but she'd never used one before. With the heightened tensions the High Commissioner had made the sort of suggestion that was really an order that she do so. She'd decided to leverage her newfound rapport with Sergeant Imoke and asked for his recommendation; he'd named the mountainous corporal without hesitation. "We're in good time, ma'am," Valverdes said as they fell in behind him. "Change of plans at the 0730 briefing. Lighter's docking at the trailing-ring spindle instead of the hub. Colonel Carmagio's people are shuttling the Commonwealth arrivals straight to Government House and the welcome will be there at 0900."

"I won't say no to getting to avoid a morning in zero-g," Toiwa said. "Though I might have eaten a bigger breakfast if I'd known." She smiled at Kala, letting zer know it was a joke and not a rebuke.

Their second escort, a short, slight woman awaited them at the building's entrance. She radiated a 'don't cross me' aura just as potent as Chijindu's that Toiwa sensed from across the lobby. As they approached, she exchanged glances with Chijindu, then gracefully pivoted around towards the street exit. She ducked her head out and scanned the street, and held the door open for the rest of the party, letting Chijindu take the lead and falling in behind Toiwa and Kala. The pair of constables automatically created a bubble amongst the pedestrian traffic as they walked briskly to the transit station.

With shoptalk forestalled for the moment, Toiwa took the opportunity to gauge the mood on the street. She couldn't tell if people walked more quickly than normal, but to her relief, she saw few signs of obvious furtiveness or fear; no one hunched over as they walked, and the only tightly gathered group she could see was a bunch of pre-school children being herded by their caregivers. She spotted the rabbi of the Congregação Israelita headed the other direction and exchanged nods of greeting with her. Across the street, a neighbor she knew only from passing in their building's corridors whirred past in his power chair. The young sweet-bun vendor was in his usual spot, sporting his customary wide grin and clever sales patter—no, wait, he was actually chatting up a good-looking man his own age, dressed in a bright yellow baju melayu with a dark sarong wrapped around his hips.

"Are things like this in your neighborhood?" she asked Kala.

Her aide nodded. "For the most part. There was a shouting match on the floor above me overnight, but I think it was because Douala lost the football match. Nothing like what's going on in the capital."

Unease warred with relief before she decided to accept the small gift of peace on her own patch. "I expected a little more tension, or something, after yesterday."

"I expect it has something to do with them." Valverdes pointed at the cluster of officers in public-order gear posted near the transit station. They were mostly groundsiders, shuttled up overnight, with a pair of station constables attached. Toiwa noted with approval that her people interacted with the locals while their visiting reinforcements hung back. She stopped for a few minutes to chat with them, commending the sergeant in charge for disposition of their officers, and greeted her own by name until Valverdes quietly pinged her a reminder that they still needed to transit to the trailing ring. She broke off and moments later all four were ensconced in a car Chijindu summoned.

With their privacy fields snapped in place, her aide passed over the latest of the morning's reports. Toiwa quickly reviewed the search for the suspected Saljuan cell that had squirted out a message when *Iwan Goleslaw* arrived; two empty safe houses raided, search still ongoing— before bringing up another bit of last night's business.

"I've highlighted Inspector Li's report about the gang that assaulted the Commonwealth woman," Valverdes said. "There's definitely something odd with that."

Toiwa found the indicated report and popped it open to scan the summary. She frowned. "What does she mean, there's no connections between these people?"

"Exactly that. None of them are related or have any kind of personal association that we've been able to trace. No social connections closer than three degrees. Well, two of them appear to eat at the same cafe on the south ring occasionally, but never at the same time in the last six months."

"Some kind of flashgang?" Toiwa asked, rapidly skimming through the report, disturbed by the abnormality.

Valverdes shrugged. "That's Li's working theory." Chijindu grunted, and both Toiwa and Valverdes turned to look at him. "You have a thought, Corporal?"

The big man nodded crisply. "I do, ma'am, and my thought is that theory stinks. I've never seen a group coordinate like that without any prior contact. I watched the surveillance vids of the attack," he added. "They moved like a unit."

The corporal seemed to share Sergeant Imoke's disdain for deference to authority; perhaps, Toiwa reasoned, it's why they got along. She personally found it refreshing.

Toiwa called up one of the vids in question and watched it at high speed and found she was inclined to agree with Chijindu's assessment. "I see what you mean, Corporal. I agree things don't add up." She looked at Kala. "What do the techs say about their signals traffic?"

"Intelligence only released their djinns a few hours ago, so they're still working on them," Valverdes said. Toiwa felt cold anger rising. Her aide shrugged. "I don't know if Captain Teng got cute or if his superiors did, but they held onto the djinns when they released the prisoners. They fulfilled the letter of your demand to Teng but held the djinns, at least until Inspector Li realized what had happened and called them on it."

Over the years, Toiwa had learned to channel her anger into action. "Who's the Directorate chief on the station? Is that Kwame?" Valverdes flipped through zer AR fields for a moment and confirmed her guess. "I want a meeting with them at headquarters at"—she glanced at her schedule—"1030 hours."

"We won't be back from Government House before 1100 at best, ma'am," Kala objected.

Toiwa's smile showed teeth, but not in a nice way. "Indeed. They can wait in the secure conference suite until we get back." The signal-shielded conference suite was notably lacking in creature comforts. It would be a suitable venue in which to lay out for the Directorate just what Toiwa was prepared to do to people who interfered in Constabulary investigations. *And Kwame can stew in their own juices without infonet access until I get there.* "Find out who Kwame reports to in the Directorate, please. I may turn the HC loose on their boss."

They pulled into the transit station built under Government House just as Valverdes finished making those arrangements. They made their way up to the reception hall on the main level. With security well in hand between the Army and the governor's security detail, Chijindu and his partner faded back, hovering close enough to reach them in a few steps but otherwise leaving their charge free to work.

Toiwa found Major Biya, Colonel Carmagio's second-in-command. He was a dark-skinned man of medium height, solidly built, with broad shoulders and large hands. He looked far more comfortable in his dress uniform than she did in hers. The lack of a high stiff collar probably helped, she thought, quelling her urge to tug her own collar open by tucking her thumbs into her belt.

"Thank you for the loan of the breaching team," she said after they exchanged greetings. She'd asked for Army backup in case the suspected Saljuan team resisted forcefully. "We hope to be finished with them soon."

"Glad to assist," he said. "They don't get much opportunity to use their skills on-station. In fact, I'd like to talk with you about setting up some joint exercises when things are a little less hectic."

"And when do you think that might come to pass?" she said, one eyebrow arched.

He laughed softly. "After the referendum, perhaps."

Further discussion was cut off by the arrival of Colonel Carmagio and the Commonwealth delegation. Toiwa and Biya found their places in the reception line, and the ritual of handshakes and greetings got underway.

The third visitor introduced herself as Dr. Ngila. Toiwa's djinn fed her the details from the doctor's social profile. "I'm curious about the diversity of fields represented," she said. "I didn't expect scientists to be part of the delegation. You're a biochemist?"

"A molecular biochemist," Dr. Ngila corrected her gently. She was a short, thin, dark-skinned woman in her early seventies, with warm, fine-boned hands and a soft voice Toiwa strained to hear over the background chatter. "Though I've been dabbling in neuroscience for the last decade or so."

Her last statement set off a furious itching in Toiwa's brain as Dr. Ngila moved onto the next Ileri dignitary and Toiwa found herself fumbling her greeting to the next visitor. Pieces clicked together in her mind.

A long-hidden secret network running Exile-era code related to the Unity Plague.

A group of individuals with no known affiliation gathering together to commit an organized assault on a Commonwealth agent.

An agent who was working with the Directorate on unspecified matters of planetary security.

A Commonwealth scientific delegation that looked, now that she scanned the rest of their specialties with the possible connection in mind, as if it was tailored to look in nanoware.

Defense Minister Vega and the PM stonewalling the Saljuan inspection team, who were *definitely* geared up to look at nanoware.

Mother, there might be something going on here after all.

CHAPTER FOURTEEN

NOO

CANTEEN FOUR, CONSTABULARY PLANETARY HEADQUARTERS, NEW ABUJA

THE NERVE CENTER of the planetary police force was staffed around the clock, all twenty-seven hours of it, which meant its canteens were always open. But during emergencies few officers or civilian staff took breaks for meals, choosing to eat at their workstations instead. So Noo wasn't surprised that when she finally tracked down the Commonwealth woman in the canteen, she sat alone with the remains of a plate of groundnut vat-chicken over rice.

Noo grabbed herself a cup of coffee and a packet of cream and crossed the room to Ogawa's table, taking a seat across from the other woman. Ogawa looked up briefly from a private AR window and gave a small wave of welcome before turning back to her reading. Noo added cream to her coffee, sipped, and waited patiently.

Ogawa wrapped up her business, whatever it was, and closed the window with a downward swipe of her right hand. She looked as tired as Noo felt; they'd both taken their share of pounding over the last couple of days.

"All done reviewing the groundsiders' reports?" Ogawa asked.

"For now. They're still running smart agents against stored imagery." Noo took another sip of her coffee, which was surprisingly good. Or maybe not, since this canteen was up in department-head country. "Thought you might be resting in the transient quarters they assigned us."

"I got the notice, but needed to feed the nanosurgeons, and had things to check on first," Ogawa said. Noo looked at her quizzically, but Ogawa declined to elaborate, instead lifting another morsel of chicken to her lips.

Of course she's going to keep her secrets. Noo realized she couldn't expect the Commonwealth woman to behave the way Ileri investigators, Constabulary or private, did: everyone focused on the case, everyone sharing information. You didn't crack a case through solo efforts, no matter what the feed dramas said. Major crimes were solved by diligent work, by chasing down the leads and then feeding every data point into the big machine that was the investigation, then letting smart people and smart agents look for patterns. For correlations. For outliers.

But back on the station Ogawa had gone off by herself, pursuing whatever trail of crumbs she'd been following until she'd been caught, alone, and beaten bloody. Maybe spies worked differently.

Or maybe just this spy.

Noo tried a different tack. "That was quite a display

you put on this morning," she said. "How did that gang catch you last night?"

Ogawa swallowed, shrugged. "I was ambushed, though I still have no idea how I got made. I thought I could evade them long enough for reinforcements to arrive, or to get somewhere public with too many witnesses to be taken without someone seeing. If I could have dodged them for another couple of minutes, it might have worked." She gave Noo a small smile. "Thank you again for coming to the rescue, by the way."

Noo waved her hand. "You're welcome. Just sorry Fari and I didn't get there a little sooner." She sipped her coffee again. "Still, you fought brilliantly this morning. Even with a broken arm."

Ogawa glanced down at her cast. "It's a good thing a big part of capoeira is about kicking."

"Um hm. How is your arm, by the way?"

Ogawa grimaced. "Itchy. I can take the cast off tomorrow, though."

"Well, you seem to be in fighting trim otherwise."

"For short bursts, anyway." Ogawa rolled out her shoulders. "I've spent a long while in low-g and microgravity, so I'm a bit out of condition."

Noo filed that tidbit away, intending to follow up on it later, but decided she might try an oblique approach. "This morning, you said your cover was true but not complete. I'm guessing most surveyors don't train for close combat."

Ogawa leaned back and studied Noo. "What you call cover, we call 'legend'. It's our backstory, the public persona. A good one is built from as many verifiable facts as possible. In my case, my career as a planetary surveyor is a matter of public record. It let my work for the Service fly under the sensor horizon for a long time."

"What happened?"

Ogawa sighed. "I was part of the expedition that found the *Fenghuang* last year. There were... aspects of that case that required assistance from your Directorate and military to resolve."

Understanding bloomed. "And now the Directorate knows who you really work for."

"Something like that."

The rescue of the *Fenghuang's* long-lost survivors, trapped for nearly three decades in nanostasis, had been a major media event. Noo supposed that didn't help to keep a secret identity, well, *secret*. But where had Ogawa been in the system in the months since? Another item for later investigation, she decided. "That's why you have contact with, er, our mutual friends?"

Ogawa nodded. "My turn." Noo waved for her to go ahead. "This person we've followed down the cable, Rio Mizwar. What do you know about him?"

Digging for information, or cross-checking? If the information exchange was going to be a tit-for-tat affair, so be it. "Not terribly much. His ID claims he's from Singapore Baru, but even I know how common false IDs from there are. He arrived on a driveframe from S-B about ninety days ago, though, so he at least passed through the system."

"Huh." Ogawa rubbed her right hand over the cast absently and her eyes took on a faraway look; not that of someone viewing a private AR window, but rather of someone in thought. "What's his occupation supposed to be?"

"Logistics specialist."

Ogawa laughed softly. "Really? That's what they went with?"

Noo felt annoyed at missing what seemed like an obvious joke. "What's so funny?"

"Oh, sorry. It's just that Mizwar, or whomever he's working for, got sloppy. Or lazy. Or maybe they were rushed." Ogawa thought for a moment. "Is there some kind of common mistake stupidly naive criminals make?"

I think I see where this is going. "Oh, plenty. Usually forgetting that cameras are pretty much everywhere on-station." She found herself nodding. "So claiming to be a 'logistics specialist' is some kind of giveaway that someone's up to no good? Or not who they claim to be?"

"Hm, sort of. What I mean is, logistics specialist is one of those jobs that works really well as a legend for an operative, at first glance, anyway. It's such a vaguely defined role, and so ubiquitous, that you can travel almost anywhere without being questioned too deeply. It's so tailor-made for intelligence work that, well, it's *too* well-suited. Too obvious."

Noo cocked her head inquisitively. "And 'planetary surveyor' isn't?"

Ogawa shook her head. "Too small a community, really. We don't all know each other but chances are, I know someone who knows any other given person in the field. Well, perhaps there's two degrees of separation between me and some of the newer people in the discipline. And then there's the academic requirements." She shrugged. "There just aren't that many of us. But 'logistics specialist'—"

"Is something anyone who can bullshit well enough

can pass themselves off as," Noo interjected.

"Right. And because it's so obvious, it's one of the first search filters we use when hunting potential operatives."

Noo considered that. "Do you think Teng knows that?"

"Our ornamental captain? Probably." Ogawa shrugged again. "If he doesn't, someone in the Directorate will. Your people know what they're about."

The description of Teng as 'ornamental' caught Noo's attention. The man was clearly Ogawa's minder; in fact, Noo was surprised he wasn't hovering nearby. "He is a pretty one, isn't he?"

Ogawa smirked. "I don't understand how he wound up in Intelligence. He can't really work covertly. He's too good-looking, too memorable."

It was true, the man would hardly pass unnoticed, and likely attracted admirers of the male form from across the gender spectrum. "I'll take your word for it." Noo took another pull of her coffee. "He's not keeping you under close watch?"

A downward flick of the eyes. "I suppose he thinks I can't get into too much trouble in the middle of police headquarters. Too much monitoring for me to be able to go off on my own."

"Do you do that at lot? Work on your own?"

Ogawa paused before answering that. "I most usually operate solo, or with only one or two partners, perhaps some local support."

That made sense, Noo thought, given the woman's public job. She hitched herself up in her seat and gave the other woman a frank look. "Got a suggestion for you."

"Hm?"

She reached out and tapped one blunt finger on the table just in front of Ogawa's dish. "You're part of a team on this. A weird, slapdash team, I admit. But we got out of that situation this morning because we all worked together. The only reason your maneuver in the melee worked is because the rest of us had your back. I don't give a rat's scrotum who gets the credit for solving this. But I want this fucker Mizwar under the question, whether he was the trigger man or no." Her voice dropped to just above a whisper. "If you can work with the team, we all get what we want, eh?"

Ogawa chewed on her lower lip as she regarded Noo. It seemed an unconscious habit, and for just a moment made the Commonwealth woman look at least a decade younger. Noo schooled herself to wait patiently and studied Ogawa in turn.

At last, Ogawa nodded and reached her hand across the table. "As you say, we can all get what we want." They shook on it, then both sat back and relaxed.

"What's our next move?" Ogawa asked.

"First step is determining if he stayed here in New Abuja or headed somewhere else," Noo said. She pointed at the floor. "We'll let the Constabulary do the legwork. They've got a building full of analysts and smart systems to rip through the data. We've got a likeness and some biometrics from the video footage."

"He most likely had some kind of support network on the station. Does he have contacts down here? Accomplices?"

Noo shrugged. "I was hoping you'd have some insight into that. Did our friends not give you anything relevant?"

"Afraid not. They seem to be playing things close to their chests, considering how much pressure these people must be putting on them." Ogawa gave a little jerk of her head towards the Constabulary seal displayed on the video wall.

A high-priority group call alert flashed in her implant and they both waved open message windows. Lieutenant Zheng's youthful face appeared. "We've got a lead," she said. "We've got a probable biometric match for our subject boarding a flight to Kochi. Briefing in meeting room 2347A in ten minutes. Bring your things. We'll be leaving as soon as transport is ready."

They both acknowledged and wiped their message windows closed as wayfinder arrows appeared. "Guess it's a good thing I can sleep on planes," Ogawa said.

MEIKO

CONSTABULARY HQ, KOCHI, ILERI

KOCHI LAY SIX hours flight north and east of New Abuja. It was a waterfront city like the capital but possessed of a different character. Where the capital sprawled across the equatorial plain, Kochi sandwiched itself between Tempest Bay to the east and the Black Claw Mountains to the west. Many of its towers clung to the sharply rising slopes of the range's foothills. There were few blocks of low-rises here, Meiko discovered as she gazed out the window, cradling a mug of tea. Aside from the few blocks along the harbor proper and the industrial district south of downtown, Kochi tended to soaring towers, streamlined to allow the ever-present winds to flow around them. A network of connecting bridges, skywalks, cable cars, and elevated monorails meant citizens could go days or even weeks without descending to ground level.

The sky outside was dark gray, and low-hanging clouds shrouded the nearer peaks of the Black Claw Mountains rising to the west. Darker, more ominous clouds massed to the east, slowly pressing nearer to the city. The forecast called for a significant thunderstorm, which Meiko actually looked forward to; it had been too long since she'd last experienced nature's force. Not that she planned to go out in a storm like that, but the feel of rain on her face was tempting.

Someone joined her at the window, and she recognized Fari Tahir's broken-nosed face reflected in the glass.

"It's a pretty view," Tahir said. "Almost makes up for the weather."

Meiko half-turned towards her. "You're not a fan of temperate rainforest climates, then?"

Fari shivered. "Temperate? It's only fifteen degrees out there, colder with the sea breeze blowing in."

Meiko laughed softly. "You dislike unmanaged weather, like your partner, eh? I suppose you wouldn't like some of the places I've visited."

"Guess not," Fari said, bringing the cup up near her face, breathing in the steamy warmth. "You were part of the *Fenghuang* expedition, weren't you? All those months on that ice moon." She shivered again.

"That is one of the colder places I've been, true, but we kept things toasty warm inside the habitat. It was below negative one-sixty Celsius on a good day outside. No atmosphere to speak of, so no wind chill to worry about, though." She sipped her tea and watched the tiny people on the street far below going about their business. "I've done work on icy habitable worlds where you do feel the cold, and I've been to Salju once."

Fari's eyes widened a bit on hearing that. "Really? I didn't think they allowed many visitors."

"The Saljuans don't court visitors, but they're a major world," Meiko said. "One of the First Fourteen, just like Ileri or Novo Brasilia, if arguably the most marginally habitable of the lot. There's a certain amount of interstellar visitation. Most people live in the underground complexes, but a few people live on the surface. I was there for a scientific conference that had an excursion to one of their geothermal oases."

That seemed to pique Fari's interest. "An oasis? I thought that was a desert thing."

Despite herself, Meiko found herself slipping into teaching mode, something she'd discovered she had a knack for. "Salju—did you know that means 'snow' in their language?—is quite active, geologically speaking, so there are places where you have hot springs that create warm zones. They're intensely interesting microclimates."

"Were you there as a scientist, or in your other capacity?" Fari asked.

Meiko pursed her lips. "Let's just say I frequently find myself doing both jobs at once."

Fari nodded, and the two women fell silent for a moment. They contemplated the forested mountains challenging the sky as their companions chattered behind them. "What are they like, the Saljuans?" Fari asked. "As a people, a culture, I mean. We rarely see any of them out here in this part of the Cluster. I think that's one reason people are so spun up about the warship."

Meiko sipped her tea, pondering her answer. "Individually, I suppose, they're not that much different from people that I've met anywhere else," she said. "People who want to pursue callings that interest them, find companionship, perhaps raise a family." She paused, considering her words; what to say with the Saljuans making threats? "There is a certain, well, resentment, I think, that suffuses their society. Like most of our ancestors, they came from very warm places on Earth. They wound up stuck on a glacier-covered world because their arks couldn't make it any further and couldn't reach a more accommodating planet. Is it any wonder that they're so intent on keeping the mistakes that led to Exile, the abuse of nanotechnology and biotech and weaponized computing, from reoccurring?"

"I guess not," Fari said. "But that doesn't explain why they annexed Para and Rama by force." She pointed skyward. "Or come here courting a war with both us and the Commonwealth."

"They don't feel safe, I think," Meiko said. "They suffered greatly in those early decades, working to make the world they'd been handed into a place where they could do more than survive. The survival margins back then were thin. Not as bad as in space, or on a dead world, but still, they danced on a knife's edge of extinction for a while." She shrugged. "It explains their animosity towards the Commonwealth, since we're more welcoming of technologies they still blame for the Exile.

But we feel those genies are out of the bottle. Better to understand their nature if one wants to resist or control them."

"Like how djinns got their name," Fari said, waving hers. "To remind us of the way weaponized AI led humanity down the darker path towards our own destruction."

"I think that story is apocryphal, but yes, something like that," Meiko said with a chuckle. She drained her tea with a sigh. "I suppose we should get back to work. Looking at the mountains won't help find our target."

Fari nodded but stayed by the window. Meiko padded back to her work cubby, rolling out her shoulders to try and work the stiffness out. Her injured arm felt better; the nanosurgeons had done their work well. The itching in her forearm had subsided, finally, as the bones finished knitting. She looked forward to getting rid of the cast. At least the dose of Remex she'd taken before boarding the flight from New Abuja had let her sleep soundly. She hadn't felt this rested since she'd boarded the shuttle for Ileri Station.

She waved her djinn through the display field, feeding it the code key she'd been given. Windows popped open and she delved once more into the Constabulary system, or at least the little part carved off for her to access. Her djinn chimed and she popped open the message to find Okereke wanted the whole team to gather in the briefing suite.

The investigator grinned smugly as the station team, plus their local liaison, congregated around the big 3D model of the city. Meiko wondered what motivated that self-satisfied look. "Thought of a way to shortcut the brute-force approach to the sightings," Okereke said without preamble. "There weren't any obvious patterns to those partial biometric matches. But then I remembered the increase in assaults and kidnappings on-station, so I tried a little correlation for reports of violent or damaging incidents and got a hit almost immediately." Okereke waved her hand and the display transformed.

A column of gold light shone near a small cluster of potential sightings in a light industrial park in the southern suburbs. Text and images from incident reports flashed up in windows around the perimeter of the model, and the team gathered around whichever window was closest to them to read.

Zheng spoke up first. "A warehouse fire turned into a biological hazardous-material event is certainly unusual, but what makes you think it's linked to the assassin?"

"Why come down the cable?" Okereke said. "To escape? That doesn't make sense. If the assassination was the killers' only task, they'd either lay low on the station or catch a ride out-system. Or at least to the outer station, maybe a vessel heading out to the New Arm colonies. No, they're on a *mission*. They have *objectives*." She reached her hand into the model and tapped two fingers at the site of the fire. "And somehow, this ties into one of them."

Meiko chewed her lower lip as she considered Okereke's theory. The evidence supporting it was thin, but plausible.

"You think our assassin has turned saboteur?" Teng asked.

Okereke nodded. "At the very least, it seems worth looking into."

Meiko scrolled through the reports. "Do we know what was destroyed in the fire? Why it became a hazmat situation?"

"Here it is," Fari said. "Medical nanotech, a new kind of broad-spectrum antiphage treatment. Meant for use in the New Arm colonies."

Meiko felt a chill. "Medical nanotech? For off-world?" She pawed open a window and called up her files on the killing. "Wasn't one of the collateral victims of the assassination involved with that kind of thing?"

Zheng, Teng, and the liaison officer conferred briefly while Meiko zoomed in the display to examine the scene of the crime, freshly updated with imaging from the Constabulary and fire department investigations. She glanced over at Okereke, who wore a feral smile. "This is a solid lead," Meiko said.

"Damn straight," Okereke replied.

The discussion across the room took on a tone of excited agitation. "We've got something," Teng called across to them. They gathered around him as Zheng and the local liaison scurried off. "Another anomaly. The locals have been chasing down the producers of the biologicals destroyed in the fire. It's a small bespoke manufacturer, dealing mainly in custom wet-nanoware biotech." Teng stuck one finger into the model and another golden column sprang up. "Aye Tuntun Specialists. Guess who owns that?"

"The Lim family," Meiko and Okereke said simultaneously. They locked eyes across the model. A Lim family rep had been killed along with Ita, the consul, and Okereke's kin.

"Constabulary pay this manufactory a visit yet?"

Okereke asked.

"They're waiting for us before they move in. Zheng just went to arrange transportation."

"How quickly can we get there?" Meiko asked.

"Ten minutes by aircar. We'll check this out, scoop up the staff and bring them back here for interviews. The Kochi team can handle the forensics."

Zheng reappeared. "We've got rides," she said with a grin. "Two aircars. We'll drop into their lot and go in the front door while our people watch the back. Use the potty if you need to and gear up," she finished. "We move out of here in fifteen minutes."

CHAPTER FIFTEEN

Toiwa

Starfall District, Ileri Station, Northern Ring

"TELL ME THEY didn't have the whole building," Toiwa said as Valverdes and the rest of her entourage, including the infonet specialist Okafor, approached the six-story building. It was surrounded by constables, small teams of Army troopers in half-armor, and bots belonging to both services. AR warning signs promised dire consequences for anyone who breached the perimeter. The mid-shift crowd of onlookers and passers-by gave the warning signs all due respect, but the presence of soldiers bearing shock guns and goober launchers probably had a lot to do with that. Even the media bots kept a respectable distance away.

"Just the top floor, and an office suite on the ground level," Valverdes reassured her. "Sergeant Imoke says they were posing as a consulting firm advising groups headed for the New Arm colonies, but we've found no record of any actual clients."

"Not so far, at any rate," Okafor chimed in. She swept a white cane in front of her as she walked, the ferrule making scritching sounds on the turf as they walked across the street. She held her left arm across her chest, her gloved, open hand over her sternum. Her fingers moved continuously in slow, arrhythmic dance, her version of a sighted person interacting with a private AR field. An autopallet whisked along behind her, stacked with expensive-looking technical gear. The ever-present Constable Chijindu, head swiveling back and forth, led their little parade.

They passed through Imoke's cordon and into the building's foyer, now crowded with crime-scene technicians, Constabulary infonet specialists, and an idle pair of medics. It took Toiwa a moment to twig to what was wrong with the scene before she recognized it. The building's own bots were stilled, locked down, robbing the tableau of the ubiquitous background movement of the station's robotic population. Floor polishers, wall-climbing dusters, and a couple of courier bots all sat on the floor of the foyer or the central hallway leading to the ground-level office suites. The sound of Okafor's cane switched to a sharp *tick-tick-tick* as they left the pedgrass street behind for the tiled interior. Valverdes directed them past the lifts, also locked down for the duration of the op, to a stairwell guarded by a uniformed constable in tactical gear and a pair of Colonel Carmagio's troopers, these in full unpowered armor. After detailing the constables to pick up Okafor's gear from the autopallet and carry it wherever she told them to, they trudged up the stairs.

Upstairs they found the doors of all the apartments, neatly blown out by cutting charges, leaning against the hallway walls. A 'Follow Me' arrow provided by Sergeant Imoke led them to the living room of one of the apartments. Imoke himself stood in the middle of a crowded, partially furnished room nearly half the size of Toiwa's entire apartment, directing the assorted uniformed constables, plain-clothes detectives, forensic technicians, and the military breaching team he'd borrowed for the occasion. A pair of individuals—Toiwa couldn't make out anything other than that there were two people—slumped against the wall, surrounded by constables.

Imoke wrapped up his conversation with a Constabulary bot-wrangler and gave Toiwa a jaunty salute. "Fourth time was the charm, Commissioner." He twirled his index finger in a circle. "The first three locations the signals team located for us were quite small. But as soon as we realized they had the whole floor plus the office downstairs, I thought we might strike water. I'm pleased to say we did."

"You've secured their hardware?" Okafor asked.

"Indeed we have. Corporal?" Imoke flagged down one of the uniformed constables and sent Okafor and her temporary pack mules off to plunder the digital spoils.

"Have you identified them?" Toiwa asked.

He flashed the station sign for 'No'. "Just the high-quality fake IDs they used to rent this property. But the medics took assays. We'll have DNA traces and initial microbiome flora analysis in twenty-four hours. But if you'll come this way, Commissioner, you'll see why I asked you to come personally." He led them down a hallway past the bathroom to a still-closed door, guarded by one of the uniforms. "We spotted her with the microbots before we executed the breach. She's got a biomed feed into her djinn the medics were able to tap once they used the emergency overrides, so they determined she was just sedated. I had them pull her off the drugs. She woke up while you were en route." He tapped the door twice, then pushed it open.

Councilor Walla, dressed for a normal day in a green sari with teal trim, sat on the narrow bed set against the far wall with a standard-issue emergency blanket wrapped around her shoulders. The room was small, perhaps three and a half meters in each direction, painted a cheerful yellow. An emergency services medic in her high-vis orange jumpsuit hovered nearby, surrounded by a dizzying array of biomonitor feeds. Walla switched from scowling at the medic to scowling at Toiwa. "Nnena! Why am I being held here? And why won't they give me my djinn?" She shook her naked wrist in the medic's face.

Toiwa slipped in to stand in the tiny room, leaving Imoke, Kala, and Chijindu in the hallway, and leaned down over the councilor. "We just need to make sure you're all right after your ordeal," she said in her best 'soothing ruffled feathers' tone. "As for your djinn, I imagine it's evidence, and being scanned as part of the investigation. I'm sure it will be returned once the technicians have ensured it isn't compromised." And, no doubt, captured a gestalt for evidentiary purposes, but no need to trouble Walla with that little fact yet...

Walla pushed herself upright and stood, if not face to face with Toiwa, at least face to chin. Her anger was palpable. "You have no right to treat my djinn like that! I'm an elected councilor—"

"My people have every right to do so, this is a damned crime scene, madam," Toiwa said, shifting immediately to ice-queen mode. "These people are under arrest for cracking the station's infonet and your djinn likely was compromised. They kidnapped you so smoothly my people didn't know they had you until Imoke's team prepared to breach the door. We're not taking chances." She leaned in towards the politician and spoke softly but clearly. "And before you go off about sensitive political matters, I don't give a damn about what you've got in your storage unless there's evidence of a crime."

Walla's eyes blazed with a 'We're not finished yet' glare Toiwa found refreshing in a politician. *Why can't I have more adversaries who just clearly hate my guts, instead of ones that act like they're my friends while angling the knife?*

Toiwa glanced at the medic. "Is she fit to travel?" After affirming the councilor was, indeed, fit to travel, but that the biomonitor sensors on her forearms should remain in place for another hour, the medic began packing up her gear. Toiwa stepped aside and pointed at the doorway. "Why don't we get you to more comfortable surroundings, Célestine, where we can take your statement?"

"Already told them what I remember," Walla grumbled as she shouldered past Toiwa and out into the hall, letting the emergency blanket slip from her shoulders for Kala to snatch up. The little party reversed their earlier journey, Chijindu in the lead this time as they trekked back into the living room, followed by Kala and Imoke, with Walla and Toiwa bringing up the rear.

Once Walla entered the living room, though,

her behavior turned bizarre. Her head jerked down towards the prisoners, now laid out on the floor and in restraints, still dazed from the breach team's stunners. She stopped in her tracks abruptly. Toiwa turned to face the politician. "It's all right, Councilor, they're secure. They can't hurt you again," she said. Walla remained still, her jaw working furiously. Toiwa reached out one tentative hand, tapping the other woman on the shoulder. "Councilor?"

Walla suddenly twisted at the waist and smacked Toiwa's hand away. Toiwa was about to apologize but the woman continued twisting and drove her fist with the full force of her body into Toiwa's stomach.

Toiwa had taken her share of knocks as a uniform, and during training since, but no one had *ever* sucker-punched her like that. She folded over like an umbrella and staggered backwards, falling on her ass.

Walla spun around and kicked Valverdes precisely in the back of zer left knee, sending zer sprawling to the floor. Toiwa tried to right herself as Walla lunged towards one of the uniformed constables. She jerked his sidearm free from its holster and moved to straddle one of the prisoners. She aimed down at the supine figure's head as her finger slipped over the trigger—

Chijindu hit Walla like a runaway lorry. One meaty hand clamped down over her right wrist and wrenched the weapon up and off target even as his body slammed into her. The force drove the politician into the wall with a resounding *thud*. The big man kept her pinned against the wall with his left hip while he planted one enormous hand on her right elbow. She squirmed and tried to wriggle free as he stripped the weapon from her. He tossed it to a surprised Sergeant Imoke who just managed to catch the weapon. Chijindu proceeded to put Walla into a submission hold, rumbling, "Now now, settle down, ma'am." He arched, pulling her off her feet, and leaned his head back as the older woman tried to claw at his face. Failing to reach her target, she pounded ineffectually at his forearms.

The whole action was over in less than twenty seconds. Imoke blinked at the pistol in his hands, loaded with frangible anti-personnel rounds—the breaching team had expected armed resistance—before handing it to the clearly embarrassed constable who'd lost it. The sergeant helped Valverdes up before hurrying to assist Toiwa, an expression of concern on his face. "Are you all right, Commissioner?"

Toiwa flashed the 'OK' sign before taking his hand to pull herself upright. Well, mostly upright. She waved him off as she stood, or rather, hunched. "What the dust are you about, Célestine?" she wheezed at Walla, whose struggles grew more feeble by the second.

The councilor ignored Toiwa and instead did her utmost to elbow Chijindu in the ribs, but her arms moved like noodles left too long in the pot, loose and floppy. Her eyes opened wide and her face suddenly drew into a rictus of pure animus and she hissed loudly as she tried to pry his hands loose, but he resolutely maintained his vise-like grip.

"Enough," Toiwa said, a little less wheezily this time. "Where's that medic?"

Chijindu tightened his arm and Walla passed out before the medic arrived. At Toiwa's insistence they tranquilized her anyway, and loaded the councilor onto a gurney for transport to the north ring's trauma center.

"I didn't know she had close combat training," Imoke said with a shake of his head.

"She doesn't," Valverdes said. Ze'd suffered nothing worse than a bruised cheek and a bit of lost pride from zer trip to the floor. "I pulled her file when Sergeant Imoke told us she was here. Nothing like that at all in her history."

Imoke and Chijindu exchanged glances. "She moved like someone with expertise and experience," Chijindu said. "Just like..."

Toiwa cut him off with a raised hand. "I agree." She nodded at her aide. "I don't doubt your command of the official records. But the way she took us both down was too smooth for someone who'd never practiced. We need to know for sure."

With a glance around the crowded room, Valverdes opened a secure channel among the four of them. *<There's something very wrong here. I recommend we bring the military medical people in on this.>*

<What are you concerned about?>

<I'd like to await more evidence.>

<See to it, then.> With her breath back, Toiwa felt as good as she was going to without some analgesics, so she moved out into the hall. Okafor and her little troupe of porters joined them bearing armloads of EM-shielded bags. "Any problems, M. Okafor?"

"None, Commissioner. Your Constabulary specialists did an admirable job locking down the server during the operation. Data loss should be minimal."

"That's good to hear. How long until you have a preliminary analysis?"

"Impossible to say for certain until we get a good look. But we should have the scope of things mapped by sometime this evening."

"Very well. Let Inspector Valverdes, Sergeant Imoke, or myself know if you need anything."

The alert for an incoming call from the governor flashed in her optics. "Shit," Toiwa said, and opened the call, even as she tried to figure out how to tell Ruhindi that her main political supporter on the station was now a person of interest in the biggest investigation on Ileri Station since the war.

CHAPTER SIXTEEN

Noo

AYE TUNTUN SPECIALISTS MANUFACTORY,
KOCHI

DARK CLOUDS MASSED to the east, driving westward with uncanny speed as the team flew southward above the towers. "Roaring norther coming in," the pilot told them. A quick infonet search told Noo this was the local name for a variety of coastal storm system that in reality originated from the south. The spinning winds of the system, though, assailed the coastline from the northeast. 'Roaring' was the right adjective, she thought, with typical wind speeds in the eighty kilometers-per-hour range, and 'pockets of extreme turbulence'.

She tightened her straps and pulled an airsickness bag into her lap. *Ogun's balls, I hate coming down here.*

The team was split between the two large aircars. She rode with Fari and the Kochi liaison in one while Teng, Ogawa, and Zheng followed in the trailing craft.

Kochi constables piloted the cars and filled the remaining seats.

The high-rises gave way to low-level blocks reminiscent in overall form, if not architectural style, of New Abuja as they progressed southward. They descended, following the monorail line as they approached the industrial park. Noo spotted a column of vehicles she pegged as Constabulary reinforcements headed to reinforce the officers on the scene.

The manufactory proved to be a nondescript two-level building located near a major intersection. The pilots put them down relatively smoothly despite the increasing winds as scattered raindrops speckled the pavement. Noo ran a finger under her collar, freeing her jacket's hood, and pulled it over her head before ducking out of the aircar. The armor vest borrowed from the Constabulary tactical team made that a little trickier than it would have been unencumbered, but she welcomed the trade-off in mobility for the extra protection. She jogged across the street to join the rest of the team where they huddled at the rear of a Constabulary ground car which had pulled into the lot just as they landed.

"Surveillance got a probable hit on Mizwar about five minutes before the locals got here to set up the perimeter," Zheng said, flipping data packets to them all. Noo popped it open and watched a video clip of four hooded figures carrying duffel bags exiting a van, who then entered the building as the van pulled off. The locals would handle the vehicle. Another clip, from cameras across the street, showed the quartet in profile. One of the figures was captured face-on, and with a start she recognized Mizwar. She felt a flush of exultation. *Got you, you scum-sucking prick.*

"What's the plan?" Fari asked.

Zheng introduced Lieutenant Yazumi, the senior local officer, who ran down the situation. "We only got here a few minutes before you. I've got two teams covering the back and sides. The special operations squad is en route but they are about ten minutes away. District headquarters has rousted out all the standby teams and we'll have a full incident-response contingent in about twenty—"

The muffled sound of gunshots reached them from inside the building, and Noo's jubilant mood evaporated.

"Civilians inside?" Zheng asked.

Yazumi cursed, then nodded once. "Supposed to be five in there. Dammit. Duty of care. New plan. We go in now. Hue!" Ze shouted the name. A lean constable with a weathered face, bearing a shotgun, responded. "Breaching protocol! Entry team, stack up!" Hue sprinted across the lot, taking up position beside the door, his shotgun leveled against the knob. Another constable grabbed a ballistic shield from the trunk of the car and took up station along the wall next to the door, opposite Hue. Noo, Fari and the others from the station raced across the pavement with the locals, finding places in the line of bodies behind the lead constable. Yazumi pushed another shotgun-wielding constable into place behind the shield-bearer, took the third position for zerself, and drew zer sidearm. "Go!" ze shouted.

Hue blew the doorknob out, then shot away the hinges before stepping back smartly. The door fell outward with a crash, barely settling to the ground before the lead constable pushed into the building, shield raised high.

The rest of the breaching party snaked into the building behind him.

Noo felt a tap on her shoulder and glanced to see Ogawa, right behind her, flip a packet her way. She opened it to find a floor plan of the building. A wave of her hand and a mental command projected a wireframe diagram of the hallways, doors and rooms ahead of them, even as she wondered how Ogawa had obtained the plan.

The officers in the lead rushed down the hallway at Yazumi's command. Yazumi zerself remained in the foyer, directing the remainder in pairs to sweep through the manufactory. Teng pulled Ogawa out of the line, gesturing for her to remain in the foyer despite her brief but fruitless protest. Noo's heart beat a trip-hammer rhythm and she forced herself to breathe evenly as she and Fari padded down the hallway. Fari took up position next to their designated doorway and Noo slid up to the other side, next to the handle. *Huntress, watch over us and ours.*

Stunner in hand, Noo flipped the door open and Fari swept into the room, weapon up, Noo at her heels. They found themselves in a feedstock room, bins and tanks of chemicals and materials for the fabricators stacked and racked on shelves. Two doors led out of the room, one across from the way they'd come in and another to their left. They took up positions around the partially open door on the far side. Flipping it open they found another storeroom.

And a pair of bodies.

Fari guarded the door as Noo knelt down in what she already knew would be a fruitless check for life signs, judging from the wounds and spreading pools of blood. Both victims had been shot twice, once in the chest, once in the head. Noo informed Yazumi about the bodies. The lieutenant acknowledged and directed them to continue their sweep.

They took up positions next to the next door when a shotgun blast ripped through the quiet from somewhere deeper inside the building. Fari kicked the door open with a snap of booted foot as a staccato of pops answered the shotgun. Within seconds a full-blown firefight was underway.

Noo stood dumbstruck for precious seconds even as Fari dropped into a crouch and scuttled through the doorway. *That's an automatic weapon. How the fuck did they get those?* Hastily scrunching down herself, she patted the armor vest. Would it help against that kind of firepower? She took a deep breath, steadied herself, and duckwalked forward into what the floor plan claimed was the main hall of the manufactory.

Thighs screaming with the effort, she made her way around an idle pair of mover bots to where Fari crouched. The younger woman sheltered behind a large fabrication tank, the gleaming metal vessel festooned with pipes, hoses, and other feed mechanisms. Fari swapped her stunner for her flechette pistol. *<Are you sure you want to use that in here?>* Noo sent as she came up to kneel beside her partner.

<Lethal force all around,> Fari replied.

Noo tapped her on the shoulder, then pointed to a feedstock tank just a few feet away. Physical and AR signage announced CONTENTS UNDER EXTREME PRESSURE and FLAMMABLE. The other fabber vessels nearby displayed similarly dire warnings. *<Just because those dung-brains don't care if they blow themselves up*

doesn't mean we should follow them,> she sent. With a grimace, Fari switched weapons again. A new fusillade of automatic fire rang out.

After the initial shock of contact, Yazumi's people proved well-disciplined. The shooter's probable location was triangulated, and ze calmly directed zer officers into flanking positions, but ordered them to stay under cover. "We just need to keep them contained until the tacticals get here," ze ordered. "Keep them away from any surviving civilians but otherwise don't risk yourselves unnecessarily."

The gods of entropy had something to say about that, of course.

"Hold a moment," Ogawa said over the tactical link. "Aminu, turn back. No, left. There, hold. Shit. That's an explosive charge. Yazumi, they've rigged the place to blow up."

Three louder cracks followed by the crash of falling masonry drowned out the gunfire for a few seconds. They heard more shooting from a different direction, further away by the sound of it. Fari's head swiveled, looking for new targets while Noo covered her own sector.

"That's from outside," Teng said. "Shit, they blew a hole in the side wall."

"Yazumi, you need to get your people out *now!*" Ogawa's voice was insistent. "They're using classic insurgent tactics. We were lured in."

Yazumi cursed and ordered zer people to withdraw. "Closest exits," ze said. "Go go go! Exterior teams, try to contain them."

"Check the emergency exits for booby traps before you open them," Teng said. "I'm going outside."

Noo and Fari scurried back the way they'd come as fresh bursts of automatic fire, answered by shotgun blasts, echoed through the cavernous interior. They came across a constable struggling to drag her wounded partner down the main access hallway. Fari darted forward and helped hoist the injured officer into a chair carry while Noo covered their withdrawal. The shooting intensified, seeming to come from all directions now.

"Fuck, they're going for the aircars," Teng said. Noo cursed as her little party hurried down the corridor.

Automatic-weapon fire continued to rattle from inside. *A stay-behind?* Noo wondered as they burst into the foyer. Zheng, one hand clamping a bandage to her bleeding forehead, motioned them through the exterior door. "Move! We've got to get clear," she shouted, as they passed from one bundle of chaos into another.

Rain crashed down on them; big cold drops that hit like rubber bullets, stinging and chilling all at once. Noo was instantly soaked despite her rain jacket. The wind buffeted them, pushing them off course as they struggled towards the dubious safety of the closest aircar. She heard the steady popping of a single weapon and spotted Teng kneeling as he emptied his magazine at one of the aircars as it rose, slightly wobbling. The car steadied into a smooth, curving climb as Teng's rounds bounced ineffectually off the armor.

They're getting away. Sudden rage filled Noo. Her quarry was so close.

The other aircars sat there, beckoning.

Noo grabbed Fari's arm, tugging hard. "Come on!" She yanked with all her strength. "If we go *now*, we can follow them." Fari stopped to lower the wounded constable to the ground. They staggered and slipped, fighting both the wind and the rain-slicked concrete as they lurched across the parking lot to the second aircar.

Zheng seemed to have the same idea. She fumbled a fresh magazine into her pistol as she plunged through the howling storm, her forgotten bandage behind her on the pavement. Ogawa emerged from between the shelter of a ground car and raced towards them.

Rain blinded Noo as she fought the headwind. It seemed like all the wind in the world blasted her, sucking her breath away. Lightning flashed, rendering the world white-blue. Roaring thunder followed almost immediately, a deafening blast that she first mistook for the bombs in the manufactory going off. Hoarse, shocked voices echoed across the team link as Yazumi struggled to get a head count, trying to determine if all of zer people had gotten out.

Where the fuck are the reinforcements?

She must have said it aloud, or at least subvocalized it into the link. *<They're having to divert around an accident,>* Zheng sent across their link. *<A couple of auto-lorries crashed, and there's a chemical spill.>*

Noo's breath came in ragged gasps as she struggled across the last few meters to the car. Fari, a few meters ahead, banged on the door. It opened and Fari scrambled in. Noo's foot slipped on the rain-slicked concrete and she would have fallen, but someone grabbed the back of her jacket and arrested her descent. She glanced back and discovered that Ogawa had caught up with her, breathing hard but not nearly so much as Noo herself was. They made it to the car together and Fari's outstretched hands pulled them inside. Seconds later, Zheng arrived and scrambled in herself. Ogawa reached across the constable and closed the passenger compartment door.

The pilot goggled at them in his rearview mirror. "What are you waiting for?" Noo growled. "Get us up in the air and go after them."

"Are you out of your minds?" he said, and his copilot turned in her seat to frown at them. "In this?"

"I'm a licensed investigator in hot pursuit of a suspect," Noo said hotly. "I suggest you comply."

"They just shot up some of your colleagues," Fari shouted. "They planted bombs in the factory—"

"Yeah, we heard," the pilot snapped, cutting them off. "But I'm not taking off in this."

Hot rage washed over Noo, and she yanked out her hand cannon and leveled it at the pilot's head. "I'm not asking, constable."

The pilot's eyes widened in shock. "You're bloody insane. Dead now or dead when we crash, what's the difference?"

"I'll do it," the copilot blurted out. The pilot glared at her. "I'm serious. She's right, it's dangerous as hell, but we've got to go now."

The pilot cursed, hit the quick release on his harness, and slipped out of the aircar. The copilot spun the engine up as the door slammed closed. Someone banged on the passenger compartment door, and Noo turned to discover Teng hammering on it with his fist. Ogawa popped it open and he jammed himself inside as the copilot took off, spun around to the west, angling the car up between the tempest-lashed towers of Kochi towards the looming Black Claws.

CHAPTER SEVENTEEN

MEIKO

KOCHI AIRSPACE

"I DON'T SUPPOSE any of you know anything about sensor ops?" the pilot asked as she whipped their craft between the skyscrapers clinging to the lower slopes. Meiko glanced over at Zheng, who was arguing with the incredulous and profoundly outraged Yazumi over the link while Fari tried to bandage the lieutenant's head wound.

"I do," Meiko said. "Probably not the specific systems you carry, but I've done planetary survey work."

"You're hired," the pilot said. "I need to focus on the terrain-following systems and the other instruments. You'll need to take the pilot's seat for me to cut you into the system, though." The world suddenly tilted to the right as the pilot banked hard, sliding past a building that seemed to sprout directly in their path. The car hit an air pocket and lurched downward, then bucked sideways as they hit a shearing wind current, artifact of the city's complex aerodynamic landscape. Meiko closed her eyes, then opened them again as their flight steadied. She popped her harness release and began the perilous two-meter journey across the crowded passenger cabin to the cockpit. Okereke did her best to help, bracing her as the craft jerked and bounced in the turbulent air. Teng pulled himself into the seat Meiko abandoned.

"Tap my djinn," the pilot said once she'd strapped in. Meiko reached over and brushed her djinn against the pilot's. Augmented-reality windows and head's-up displays opened around her like tree leaves in the dawn. She queried for the help files, slurped them into her djinn along with a regional map file the system helpfully offered. She opened another AR window for the map as she tentatively probed the forward-looking radar controls.

"Shit," said Zheng behind her. "The bombs went off."

"Did Yazumi and the others get clear?" Fari asked.

"Yazumi did. Ze's getting a fresh head count. But it's going to be another toxic spill problem."

She heard a meaty thump and glanced at the mirror to see Okereke pounding her left fist into her thigh. "This entire operation is a clusterfuck," Okereke said. "We're stumbling around blind, chasing this turd, and he's making us look *stupid*."

"That's one view," Teng said, snapping the last buckle into place.

"Well, we're on his tail now," the pilot said. "Or will be if you can get a lock on him."

Meiko located the interface for the search systems. "Do these craft have transponders?" she asked as she warmed up the search radar. "It would be easiest to track them that way."

The pilot gave her the other craft's ID and she located the air-traffic display. There was no result when she fed the information to the system. "They must have disabled it somehow," Meiko said.

"That shouldn't be possible," the pilot said, as the aircar dropped a good twenty meters without warning. Her stomach lurched and Meiko was glad for her long experience with abrupt acceleration changes. Behind her came the sounds of retching and a scramble for airsickness bags.

She pushed aside the fear, focusing on her tasks as they screamed through the ever-darkening sky scant meters from the concrete-and-steel towers, chasing a group of heavily armed killers who'd shown no hesitation when it came to cold-blooded murder. This was the key, for her: find something to do, then do it. The shakes would come later.

The aircar hit an air pocket and bucked upwards, then dropped precipitously again. She hung the interface windows right in front of her face to minimize how much she needed to move her head. She heard someone new throwing up in the back.

She got the search radar online, and the infrared detectors as well, and Meiko had a fleeting sense of pleasure for having solved the puzzle of the controls. Their car flew through a gray world now, up among the clouds. The craft bucked again as the pilot worked to keep them aloft and pointed in what Meiko hoped was the proper direction. Finally, they cleared the towers and put the first ridge of the Black Claws between their aircar and the city proper. Somewhere below lay a narrow, steep-walled valley. The reverse slope of the ridge appeared to be too steep to build on, though radar showed clusters of low-rise structures lining the narrow river along the valley floor.

She adjusted the search radar to sweep ahead in a wide arc. She got an airborne return almost immediately, far off to their south, running fast along the river's course. "Contact," she said, and fumbled again with the interface as she hunted for a way to share data with the pilot. "Bearing one hundred and sixty-three degrees, range one-five kilometers."

The pilot cursed and swung the aircar onto the given bearing and put the nose down. "I think they're going for Moonstrider Gorge," she said. "It's the first gap in the range from here."

"I wonder why the hell they're running this way," Fari said. "They couldn't have known we'd come or have aircars they could steal."

"Catch the goat-fuckers first," Noo wheezed, "and you can ask them while I tickle their balls with a fucking torch."

Strong winds buffeted the aircar, shaking it like a child's rattle. The pilot put on as much speed as she dared. Once they reached the center of the valley, she dropped them down below the level of the towering ridges, and the ride smoothed out fractionally. Meiko managed to confirm that their quarry was the correct model of aircar, indexing the infrared emission patterns of the engines with the radar return off the fuselage, and comparing that to another helpful file the craft's system offered. She reported her findings aloud. "There's nothing else in the air at the moment, anyway," the pilot said, which Meiko's air-traffic display corroborated. "No one else is mad enough to fly in this."

Lightning struck them at that moment. The world turned brilliantly blue-white, dazzling Meiko's eyes before the canopy polarization kicked in. She smelled ozone and a hint of burnt composites, but the engines roared on steadily. The sensor systems all reset and rebooted, though, and the car dropped abruptly, losing a good fifty meters of altitude.

Meiko glanced over at the pilot, her face taut with fearsome concentration as she fought to maintain control. They steadied out and began climbing. The pilot shot her a look, grinning fiercely. "Like I was saying."

Someone in the passenger compartment retched again. "Why *are* you doing this?" Meiko asked the pilot. "They could cashier you for this. You might never fly again."

The pilot didn't answer that immediately, and Meiko took the opportunity to get the search systems looking for their target again. It had vanished, and the pilot grunted. "They must have turned west, up the gorge like I thought." Another bout of turbulence interrupted her as she fought the winds for a moment. "You're after the people who shot the minister," she continued at last. Meiko acknowledged this was true. "Ita was from my district," the pilot said. "My family has known his for generations. Hell, we're probably cousins of some sort." *Were cousins,* Meiko thought. Shearing winds rocked the car as they approached the gorge which kept the pilot busy for a moment. Their flight steadied and she continued. "I even met him twice, once when I graduated from flight school, then again when I got a commendation for a rescue operation." She began banking the aircar into a turn to the east, lining up to follow the river that carved out the gorge. "They killed one of my people. If there's a chance to catch them, I want in."

Zheng spoke from the backseat. "Constable, if your command gives you any shit for this, let me know. I'll have Commissioner Toiwa give them a piece of her mind."

"I'd pay to see that," Fari quipped.

They entered the gorge, and the ride actually became worse.

Moonstrider Gorge wasn't especially narrow, but it did wind more tightly than Meiko would have expected. The planetary-surveyor part of her brain started to model the effects of the clashing air masses involved, but she shook off that impulse and refocused her attention on the sensors. The overlay painted the river's course below as it snaked between the high rocky walls to either side.

Clouds still enveloped them, though the ground gradually rose as they fought their way up the gorge. The pilot had no time for chatter as she battled still more eddies and pockets of turbulence; keeping them aloft required her full attention.

They rounded a tight bend, coming onto a comparatively long, straight stretch, and the search systems pinged. "Got them!" Meiko exclaimed. The blip abruptly disappeared again as their quarry darted left, ducking into a branching valley about five kilometers ahead. Meiko flagged the point for the pilot, who gritted her teeth as she gunned her engines before swooping into a banking turn into the new valley.

They roared along their new heading when Meiko

realized that they had overshot their prey. The other car had turned around, hovering just above the treetops a few hundred meters up the valley. "There!" she cried as they screamed overhead.

"Shit!" the pilot said, and slewed the aircar around to the right, trying to reverse course without dumping too much speed. They swung seriously close to the right-hand wall of the valley, a nearly sheer cliff of dark basalt, so close Meiko thought she could have reached out to touch the stone. They swung around, leveled out—

Suddenly they were falling. No, not falling, being *pushed* towards the ground. Alarms sounded. "Downdraft!" the pilot said as they plunged, spinning, slewing sideways, left and then right as she fought to regain control.

Now the fear came. Meiko's whole body tensed and she clenched her armrests.

The pitch of the port-side engines dropped abruptly as indicators across the cockpit flashed red.

"Shit! Lost thrust—"The pilot's words were cut off as they smacked the cliff.

Metal shrieked and tore and there came a horrible ripping sound. Meiko's left side slammed against the inside of the compartment and she yelped as fresh pain stabbed through her still-healing arm. The car tilted to the right and the pilot tried to compensate, but that put them into a counter-clockwise spin. The front of the aircar hit the cliff and they bounced backwards. Someone, Teng from the sound of it, screamed, while the others, including the pilot, cursed.

Meiko was too stricken to do either, or even to take the crash position as the car's system implored them to do in three languages. The car tipped right, the right-side engines cut out, and they plunged ground-ward.

Everything went white, then red, then black, and then there was no sound but the rain, the wind, and the rushing river below.

CHAPTER EIGHTEEN

OKAFOR

TRANSIENT QUARTERS, GOVERNMENT HOUSE COMPLEX, ILERI STATION, TRAILING RING

OKAFOR SIMULTANEOUSLY HUNG suspended in virtual space and sprawled upon the couch of her tiny suite across the street from the massive Government House complex.

She'd spent a frustrating evening working on the material captured from the Saljuan team in the lab at Constabulary headquarters. Resigning herself to needing to allow the decryption routines time to work, she'd ridden the transit system back to the trailing ring, wishing the High Commissioner's office had been able to find her quarters closer to Constabulary HQ. Still, the bandwidth available at Government House was equal— if not superior—to what she could get at Toiwa's office. The Constabulary had better coffee, though.

Too keyed up to sleep, she had returned to her long-term project: probing the oldest and strangest of the illicit networks buried in the station's infonet. Calling her map a work in progress was something of an understatement. She suspected that all the work to date had barely sketched the shadowy outlines of the hidden web. The fact that peripheral nodes continually came and went as the polymorphic code bounced from system to system didn't help. Still, concealed beneath the ever-shifting layers lurked a central core of nodes that made up the heart of the secret grid. She was sure of it.

A slender fiber-optic cable linked her torc-like djinn to an auxiliary processing unit resting across her legs. Her VR trodes were likewise physically connected rather than wirelessly, the way most would. In part that was due to the increased bandwidth Okafor used, but in large measure it was because she fundamentally didn't trust any network she didn't control herself.

If her djinn was her workaday toolbox, the aux unit was like an entire machine shop, foundry, and fabber facility rolled into one. She arrayed the input fuzzers, packet analyzers, decryption toolkits, stack smashers, and all the rest of the tools of her trade about her virtual form as she contemplated her target. One of her smart agents had identified a potentially long-time compromised node, part of the command apparatus for the station's dynamic trim system, the physical infrastructure that maintained the balance of the massive conglomeration of rock and metal and composites. She didn't plan a full-scale assault on the node, not tonight anyway. Confident as she was in her skills and code, tampering with something so fundamental to the station's operations without backup, or without expert assessment of the potential for causing problems, was far beyond her personal risk threshold.

But that didn't mean she couldn't poke around a bit, and perhaps see about mapping and tapping the node's links to the rest of the dark net.

She felt the buzz of her physical-anomaly alarm against her neck and shifted her perceptions of her sensorium partially from virtual space to physical space. Finding nothing amiss in her quarters—no temperature flares, no chemical traces, no sudden movements of the objects around her—she realized the signal came from the smart agent she'd tasked to monitoring the hallway feeds outside her rooms. After she'd cracked them, of course. She'd send the local sysadmin a debrief memo detailing how she'd suborned the cameras when she moved out...

Cameras that at the moment showed four bulky figures, one in power armor, arrayed outside her door. She immediately fired off digital probes at each and got hits consistent with the same family of polymorphic code as the compromised node, just as her virtual form was cast out of the station network like a vase knocked off a high shelf.

Dumpshock threatened to overwhelm her sensorium, but this wasn't her first experience with rapid exit from VR. Still, her pulse raced and her hands threatened to twitch from the adrenaline dump. Discipline and long practice helped her still her hands, to breathe deeply, to ride out the physical reaction while responding to the situation, which became immediately kinetic as the soldier in power armor—and it had to be a soldier, only the Army had any armor on the station—kicked in her door.

Physically, Okafor was no match for two hundred-fifty kilos of armored soldier. But they were well within the ten-meter peer-to-peer range the aux unit gave her djinn—

Time seemed to slow as she went into full virtual-engagement mode, aiming every scanner in her collection at the armored form. She ran her virtual fingers across it, feeling the warmth of the IR hotspots and sensors, the chill of the blacklight, and *there* it was, a buzzing sensation under her fingertips as she located the communications array. The door sailed across the room and the soldier took the first step across the threshold, right arm with its integral mini-gun raised to sweep across the space. One of Okafor's agents counted the signal streams passing in and out of the suit, while she grasped her RF fuzzer and spammed the inputs, seeking a way in. The door crashed into the far wall as the trooper stepped fully inside, turning towards her supine form.

Aha! A diagnostic input. Her body remained still but for her hands as her fingers trembled, echoes of her virtual motion she couldn't fully suppress. She launched another agent with orders to brute-force the diagnostic mode, cycling first through her painstakingly compiled dictionary of default login credentials used by manufacturers over the years.

Success came almost immediately—pure luck really. No time for triumphant crowing, though, as the trooper took another step forward even as the diagnostic menus opened before her like popcorn kernels. Damn, it was read-only access. She called forth a cavalcade of stack smashers to hammer the diagnostic system, each one pumping volleys of code, trying to find a sequence that would crack open the memory space she needed...

"Josephine Okafor?" The voice projected from the

suit's speakers was surprisingly high-pitched. "Wake up, please. You will come with us. Resistance will be suppressed." The other three, two constables and another soldier, all dressed in their services' tactical gear and light armor, stepped into the room and fanned out on either side of the armored trooper. Her forearms buzzed as her sensorium mapped their positions.

Moving slowly to buy time, Okafor rolled to a sitting position, taking care not to dislodge her aux unit. "Why are you here?" she asked, trying to make her voice sound fuzzy, as if she'd just woken up.

"Disconnect the electronics and stand up," the soldier ordered, ignoring her question.

"Whose authority are you operating under?" she asked.

"Acting Prime Minister Miguna," one of the constables said in a flat voice.

SCORE. One of her stack smashers caused the diagnostic system to fail, opening the memory space to her arsenal of malware, which flowed into the space like spilled water, and *there* was the mobility-control module, and *there* were the weapon systems, and *there* the suit's built-in medical kit. Her agents seized control of these systems and *now* she let herself feel the exultant rush.

"I don't think I will," she said, and took over the suit like a puppeteer.

A flick of thought sent a massive dose of sedative into the trooper's veins. She punched right with one armored fist, knocking the intruder on the left into the wall with a bone-crunching thud. She raised her right hand and the suit mirrored her action, then swung it sideways and triggered the mini-gun. The tactical armor was no match for the armor-piercing rounds, and her first burst simply cut the next intruder in half. Blood and viscera sprayed everywhere, and the room flooded with a coppery smell. She felt the warm splatter of it across her face and almost lost control.

The fourth attacker screamed and ducked before fleeing into the hallway. Okafor gathered herself, doing her best to ignore the horrible smell, and walked the armor out of the room in time to register an additional three people in the hallway. She raised the suit's right arm again, only to lower it in surprise when one of the newcomers shot the fleeing intruder in the head.

One of the interlopers raised a rocket launcher to their shoulder before the one in the center smacked their arm. "Don't be an idiot," the center figure hissed, as Okafor realized that the suit was 'seeing' them on radar, not in the visible spectrum. "Backblast will fry us all indoors."

She found the external audio controls, cracked them, and spoke. "Who are you, and what the hell is going on?"

One of the figures stepped forward and reached up to pull a phototropic stealth hood up and away from their face. "Are you Josephine Okafor? My name is Myra. Pericles Loh asked me to watch over you." Myra pointed at the armored trooper standing before her. "We didn't expect this, though."

Pericles Loh? The rumored head of the Fingers on-station? What did he want with her? The post-combat crash started to take its toll, and she felt her control slipping away. "You only answered one of my questions," she snapped.

"Apologies." Myra took a tentative step forward.

"The Treasury Minister has launched a coup. His people are attacking Government House now."

Her control, already fragile in the wake of dumpshock, nearly gave way at the news. *A coup?* She knew the High Commissioner had her suspicions about Miguna, and rumors—low-voiced, one person to another—of probes into his dealings and the One World party had circulated for months. To launch a coup, though—Miguna clearly had backing in the military, and the Constabulary. Her breath caught and her body trembled as she fought to maintain a semblance of composure.

A quick check of the suit's comm systems seemed to confirm Myra's second assertion, at least. She identified ten suits of power armor—half the garrison's complement—as they crashed through the Government House complex across the street, accompanied by perhaps forty or fifty more combatants. The sounds of gunfire were audible now, and people were starting to stir about in the quarters block around her. "Damn," she said. "We can't fight our way through that."

"We don't have to," Myra said. "If you come with us, *right now,* we can get you somewhere safe."

"I need to get to Constabulary HQ," she said stubbornly.

Myra threw up her hands in exasperation. "If we're not out of here in the next sixty seconds, madam, the only place you're going is wherever Miguna wants to take you. Even if you're in a suit of power armor. However the hell that happened."

Okafor took a shuddering breath, returned her primary attention to her physical body, and sat up. She was reluctant to put her fate in the hands of criminals whose colleagues she'd chased for years, but they *had* shot one of her attackers. *Enemy of my... worse enemy.* Making her decision, she dropped her full arsenal of destructive malware into the suit's systems and carefully stood up. An armorer would have to completely rip out and replace the control systems before that suit would be functional again. Popping the emergency medical releases to retrieve the drugged soldier inside wouldn't help the rebel cause either. *Scratch one enemy asset.*

"I'm not in the suit," she said. "I'm in the apartment." With care, she undid the cables connecting her gear as the Fingers team hustled forward. "Let me grab my cane and we can go."

CHAPTER NINETEEN

TOIWA

CONSTABULARY HEADQUARTERS, ILERI STATION, FORWARD RING

A KNOCK ON the door of the tiny sleeping cubicle attached to her office roused Toiwa from her nap. Chijindu's voice rumbled through the partition. "Commissioner? Wake up, please. Inspector Zinsou needs you."

She rubbed her eyes and checked the time to find she'd been asleep for nearly a half-hour, then slid open the door. "What's going on?"

"Someone's attacked Government House."

"Shit!" The space behind her eyeballs still felt grainy but her brain cleared rapidly. She popped open a window to Zinsou, audio only, as she shrugged into an old fatigue shirt. "Toiwa here. Situation report." She tied in Chijindu and tried to loop Valverdes in as well, but her aide didn't respond.

"Multiple reports of gunfire at Government House,"

the third-shift watch commander reported. A row of side windows popped up displaying video feeds, some fixed, some from aerial bots. Armored figures fired into the complex as sporadic return fire lanced out. Wriggling into her pants, she watched as other armored figures swarmed the residence block across the street.

"Get Chakraborty on," she ordered. Chakraborty was the Trailing Ring third-shift commander.

"I've tried. We've lost contact with the Trailing Ring precinct."

"Open a call now with all the precincts and get Colonel Carmagio or Major Biya on the line too." She slid open the partition of her sleeping cubby to find Constable Chijindu in full tactical armor busy laying out her own gear. He paused to set a bottle of water next to her as she pulled on her boots.

Zinsou's voice was strained. "I'm trying, ma'am, but only North Ring HQ is responding." He paused. "We're pulling direct feeds from around the station. There's fighting in the Hub that looks like Army units fighting each other."

Toiwa's body jerked as the adrenaline hit. Chijindu, spotting the motion, turned, concern written across his craggy face, but she waved him off. He studied her for a few seconds before nodding and ducking out to the outer office.

Army units fighting each other.

"Commissioner?" Zinsou asked, hesitantly.

"I'm here." She took a deep breath. At that moment, her priority-message indicator lit; Miguna was calling her. "The Treasury Minister is calling me. I'm going to loop you in. But first..." She opened the contingency-plan file for the second time in two days and swiped through until she found the one she was looking for: *Mutiny*. "Initiate Red Tango Five immediately on my authorization."

"Contingency Red Tango Five, confirmed," Zinsou said.

Toiwa took another deep breath before answering Miguna's call. She tried to tie Zinsou in, but the minister had privacy-locked it. She found her override but it only let her record the call. She gritted her teeth. "Toiwa here. Why are you calling, Minister Miguna?"

"That's Prime Minister Miguna," Miguna said, the smugness in his voice thick enough to cut with a knife.

Perhaps she'd been desensitized by the rapid succession of shocks, as Toiwa barely twitched at his pronouncement. "What's happened to Prime Minister Dabiri?" In a side window, she messaged Zinsou to contact Constabulary headquarters and the High Commissioner.

"Dabiri's pathetic cozying up to the Commonwealth, and her cowardly response to this Saljuan incursion, demonstrated conclusively that she's not fit to lead Ileri at this critical moment. At the urging of my party, and with the support of right-thinking members of the armed forces and the Constabulary, I've assumed the role of Prime Minister."

Chijindu returned with a bulb of tea which he placed in her hands with surprising gentleness. She sucked down a welcome swallow and set it down, holding her arms out as he helped her into her armored vest. "That's outside the Covenants of the Republic," she said.

"Extraordinary times, extraordinary measures."

More side windows popped up displaying fighting at Government House in New Abuja and at other key points. *<Where's Vega?>* she messaged. She couldn't believe the Defense Minister had any part in Miguna's grab; she'd been a serving officer before switching to politics, and her disdain for the One Worlders was well-known.

"I'll ask again, *Minister*, why are you calling me?"

"I'm offering you an opportunity to do the right thing," Miguna said. "You have the chance to help make this transition smooth and minimally disruptive."

"By going along with an illegal coup?" she retorted, as Chijindu slipped her tactical harness, loaded down with the necessities a constable might need during an operation, over her shoulders and moved around front to buckle it in place while her fingers danced, messaging instructions to Zinsou.

"Nnenna, Nnenna, be sensible. This is the only rational course, the one that maintains our sovereignty, that honors our heritage and our place as one of the First Fourteen. My supporters are already in control of the essential points planetside and our comrades in the Navy will soon have orbital space under control." She actually heard him lick his lips across the circuit. "There can be a high place for you in my government."

She might have ambitions, but she'd be damned if she'd ride in this bastard's wake. "With all due respect, I must decline," she said.

Miguna's voice took on a menacing rumble. "You can save many lives if you play along, Nnenna."

That gave her pause. She could sense the seductive pull of his argument, saw how it might be true. How if she went along with Miguna, put the resources under her command towards his purpose, that the fighting taking place right now would be the last on the station—if Miguna won in the end. And that by giving him the keys to the planet's gateway, she'd greatly improve his chances of victory.

All she had to do was turn her back on her oaths, on her beliefs, on everything she stood for. To let her children grow up on a world where this fool set the tone. Assuming he didn't get them into a war with the Star Republic, or the Commonwealth—or both.

There was never a question about her answer, not really.

"I'll see you on the dock for this, you vile, traitorous fuckwit," she said.

"So be it," Miguna snapped, and closed the call.

"Zinsou, we're on our way—" she began, as every window but those local to her djinn blanked and went dead.

The station network—or at least their part of it—was down.

"Chijindu. Command center. *Now*," she hissed through clenched teeth, drawing her pistol and disengaging the safety.

The big constable nodded. Shotgun held at the high ready, he moved down the corridor with remarkable grace for a large man so heavily equipped. Their carpet-muffled footfalls sounded like a cavalcade in Toiwa's ears. Abruptly, she realized she was still carrying her helmet in her left hand. Chijindu reached the first corridor juncture and she tapped his elbow before he peeked around it. <Hold,> she sent across their private link, now running on near-field peer-to-peer communication between their djinns. She holstered her pistol to don and secure her helmet, leaving the visor open for now. She drew her weapon again and readied it. <Go.>

Chijindu was about to turn the corner when the first shots boomed from the direction of the command center. With a wordless curse, Toiwa flipped her visor down. The tactical overlay it displayed lacked the data feeds it should have pulled from an operational network, but her own audio pickups worked perfectly well, and her djinn had the building's floor plan in local storage. The shots were coming from the command center entrance, twenty meters down the corridor to their left. Her djinn plotted two likely targets based on the audio, and she tagged the target icons 'Hostile'.

Chijindu peeked his head around the corner, just a second's glance to give his helmet's cameras a look. The data streamed across their link and she counted the dark shapes huddled behind riot shields arrayed around the command center door. Constabulary uniforms and gear, she noted with shock. Her people were fighting each other.

She clamped down the sudden rush of fear. *Deal with that later. First get control.*

More shots echoed from the direction of the command center, and she could hear gunfire from other parts of the building as well. Shots were being returned and she could hear the *splat* as frangible rounds, meant to minimize damage to equipment like life support or electronic controls, impacted the attackers' riot shields. No one but the Constabulary or the military wore armor, so why would her people need to carry anything heavier? From the sound of it, the attackers were limited to frangible rounds too. A small favor, at least.

Their djinns counted the targets. <*Only ten. Good,*> she sent. <*None facing our way?*> Chijindu peeked around the corner again and her display updated. They were in luck; the attackers were all still focused on the command center door. She realized there were two bodies lying in the doorway, propping the doors open. Someone inside had been on the ball and dropped some of the attackers.

<*First bound, to the first cross-corridor,*> she ordered. <*You cross and take the right side. I'll stay on this side. Hold fire until we reach cover, then we unload on them.*>

<*Flashbang first?*> Chijindu asked.

<*You've got one?*> she asked, surprised. He raised two fingers. *If we live through this, I'm promoting this man.* <*All right. Use one to cover our first bound. Hold onto the other. Fire on the move.*>

Chijindu's gloved hand moved with the smoothness born from long practice. He plucked the grenade free, pivoted on his left foot to step into the corridor, planted his right, and tossed the grenade underhand. It was textbook-perfect, like a scene from a training vid. He pivoted back around the corner as bullets whined past; someone in the command center must have mistaken him for an attacker.

The tactical routines on Toiwa's djinn recognized the grenade and started the countdown timer. She watched the digits tick down.

Four.

Three. With a flick of thought she marked her targets on the overlay, the five to the right of the command center entrance.

Two. She placed her finger over her trigger.

One. Her body tensed, ready to spring.

BOOM.

Light and noise flooded the corridor. Toiwa's visor polarized briefly but the overlay laid the corridor out for her in wireframe. Chijindu leaped across the hall, reaching the other side in a single bound. Toiwa followed, her weapon up. Her target reticle flashed green as it crossed the target and she fired twice, hitting her target in the back of their legs. With scuttling steps, she moved up along the wall, crouched as low as she could manage. Chijindu's shotgun boomed. Hostile icons flashed red as he hit them. She swept her pistol left and she fired twice more as the reticle flashed green, recoil kicking the weapon up and her hands bringing it back down without conscious thought.

Chijindu fired again and again as he advanced up his side to the next corner, and each time a foe collapsed. Toiwa reached the intersection just behind him and snapped off two more shots before sidestepping behind cover.

Six down. There had to be more than ten hostiles in the headquarters. How many more were there? She shook her head. *One problem at a time.*

Chijindu leaned out into the hall and fired again. Another hostile icon went dark. Only three left here, and she and Chijindu had them neatly trapped in a crossfire. If the attackers turned to engage threat to their rear, they'd expose themselves to fire from within the command center. They could do this. She could secure her command center and get proper control of things.

She leaned out to line up her next shot and a hammer blow struck her chest, staggering her as it drove the breath from her lungs. Fierce pain radiated out from the point of impact as she stumbled backwards, falling hard on her ass. She flopped onto her back and struggled to breathe in despite the torment in her ribs. She heard the boom of Chijindu's shotgun again and again, the rattle of more pistol shots, voices shouting.

At last, the spasming muscles unlocked and she could inhale. Her left hand groped its way up across her body. Her overlay updated but she couldn't make sense of it; the fire in her chest consumed all her attention. She gasped shallow, frantic breaths as her fingers probed her chest, then yanked them away as they brushed against something searing hot.

The glare of the overhead lights was blotted out as Chijindu knelt over her, his visor open. His big hands were gentle as they moved hers aside. "Boss? Commissioner? Stay with me, ma'am." With exquisite care he unsealed her fatigue shirt and flipped it open. "You've been shot, boss, but the vest caught it. Probably broke some ribs though. And you might have lung damage. Medic's on the way."

She tried to nod but only managed to twitch her head. "Zinsou?" she gasped out. Damn, did it hurt.

"Here, ma'am," said one of the shadows over her.

With an effort, she forced herself to focus despite the pain. *One step at a time.* "Rally our people," she said. "Secure this floor, then work down." Several shadows detached themselves to turn her will into action. Her chest still hurt, but breath came a little more easily each time.

She looked up at Chijindu. "Get me into the command center," she ordered. "This is our patch. No one's taking it away on my watch."

CHAPTER TWENTY

Noo

Moonstrider Gorge,
Ileri

Noo hurt all over. Well, maybe not *all* over; but it damn sure felt like it. As she climbed the long, shaky ladder back to consciousness, she became aware of something even more wrong: she was very, very wet.

Light flashed up front and washed out the dim red glow of the emergency lighting. The darkness outside deepened, and the rear compartment where she sat—hung, really as the car was tipped over onto its right side—was cast into shadow. She could make out Teng, strapped to the seat in front of her, and the dark forms of Zheng and Fari below, to her right. Something hammered incessantly at the car's body and what remained of the windows on the left, now upper, side. *Rain,* she realized, as drops splattered onto her face. She smelled blood and fried electronics and a few scents she couldn't recognize, sharp and musty at the same time. A loud, rushing sound came from behind her. Water, moving fast, and lots of it.

The car jerked suddenly, the tail shifting position a few centimeters, and a fresh spray of water coursed across Noo's face. She hawked and spit and with a groan raised her dangling hands to wipe her eyes.

"Someone awake back there?" called Ogawa from the front.

"Me," Noo said, trying to project over the cacophony from outside.

"Me too," Zheng said. Noo saw movement beneath her and heard splashing noises. "Shit, I'm lying in water."

Fari groaned, then cried out sharply.

"The pilot's injured," Ogawa said from up front. Noo reached out and poked Teng, who began to stir, eyes flickering. "I think we landed on some rocks. They smashed the windows on that side of the car. I think she banged her head on one."

"Are you in water up there?" Zheng shouted. Noo heard more splashes and then metallic clicks, and suddenly Zheng stood beside her. "Grab onto me and I'll undo your harness," Zheng said, and Noo wrapped her arms around the younger woman. Zheng was just as wet as she was. Noo pulled her close and felt the warmth of Zheng's breath against her cheek as she smacked the quick-release on Noo's chest. Her feet dropped to the floor and into several centimeters of water.

"No, not really—wait." She heard splashing. "There's a little, towards the back. Makes sense since the rear is lower."

Noo shook out her arms and hugged herself for warmth as Zheng squatted down to deal with Fari's harness. Fari cried out again and Zheng cursed softly. "Okereke, give me a hand here." Noo crouched down and Zheng looped Fari's arm over Noo's shoulder. "We need to get her up. The water is rising."

Fari moaned as they heaved her upright. Her arms clenched around their shoulders as she snapped fully conscious. Teng roused and asked what was going on in a bleary voice. Noo held Fari up, bracing her against the rear wall of the compartment while Zheng unbuckled Teng.

With a loud thump, the car jerked a few centimeters sideways, accompanied by a dreadful scraping sound. Noo almost dropped Fari but her partner grabbed hold of a dangling strap. Fari teetered on her left leg. "What's wrong with your right leg?" Noo asked.

"Fucking hurts," Fari hissed back through clenched teeth.

"She had a bloody great splinter of rock through her thigh," Zheng said. "I pulled it out." She looked at Noo, then at the still-blinking Teng, then back at Noo. "I think we crashed right on the riverbank. We need to get out of this thing before it fills with water or it gets swept away."

Noo wiped her eyes clear again. "Why would it fill up with water?"

"Storms like this cause flash flooding," Ogawa said. "Narrow river gorges are prone to them."

The sense of dazed numbness Noo had felt since coming to vanished in a sudden flash of rage, and she stood straighter, hauling Fari another centimeter higher. "I fucking *hate* coming down the cable," she spat.

Fari barked out a hoarse laugh, and Zheng's teeth

shone in the darkness as she grinned. "Can you grab Tahir's other arm?" Zheng asked Teng. He nodded and scooted under Fari's right, taking the bulk of her weight in the process. Zheng cupped her hands in front of Noo. "If I boost you up, can you push the door open and climb out?"

"One way to find out." Noo slipped out from under her partner's clutch and put her hands on Zheng's shoulders. She could feel Zheng's muscles bunch and tense as she took Noo's weight. The constable dropped her hips as Noo pressed her hands against the door. Noo's hands fumbled for the release, found it, and popped the door mechanism, Zheng straightened her legs with a grunt and Noo pressed as hard as she could.

The door popped free and Noo was glad whatever mechanism held the gull-wing doors open on the ground still functioned. She got her hands onto the door frame, then scootched her ass onto it as rain lashed her face. She looked right, towards the rear of the car, and gasped. "What is it?" Zheng demanded. The constable squatted down again, fumbling with something under the bench seat.

"You were right. The back of the car's in the water," Noo shouted back down. She couldn't see the riverbank well, but she got an impression that it was made up of stones and gravel, sloped at perhaps fifteen or twenty degrees down towards the water. Even in the darkness she could see how the torrent swirled angrily as it flowed past the car. She looked forward and saw trees, perhaps ten or fifteen meters away.

<There's a winch in the front,> Ogawa sent, peer-to-peer. No signal coverage out here in the backcountry

without a satellite link. *<I think I can get it working. Can you find something to secure us to?>*

<Good idea,> Zheng sent. She rose and put something heavy into Noo's free hand. *<Torch,>* she sent. *<Get up front and see what you can do about anchoring us, will you?>*

<Right.> She glanced down but decided the rushing water was too close to risk alighting from where she sat. *Well, fuck dignity.* She slid on her ass along the frame until she reached a point from where she felt safe to dismount. With a grunt, she pushed her legs around until they hung over the side and then shoved herself off.

It wasn't the most graceful landing and she nearly face-planted on the rock-strewn riverbank. She remembered her long-ago fight training, though, or at least the part about never trying to break one's fall by sticking out your arms. Instead she twisted and her right shoulder slammed into the gravel. She yelped at the impact, tasted blood, and realized that she'd bitten her lip when she hit. She spat blood, scrambled to her feet, and half-staggered to the front of the car.

At least she'd managed to hold onto the torch. She flipped it on and played it over the front of the aircar, locating the winch under a bit of aerodynamic fairing that would have concealed it had the car not been laying on its side. *<I've found the winch,>* she sent, her eyes tracking over a confusing array of cable, gears, and machinery. *<What should I do?>*

<If Ogawa can't get the automated control working, there's a manual release lever for the drum on the right side looking from the front,> Zheng sent.

Noo spotted the lever and was reaching for it when she

heard a BANG from the car's rear, and the whole vehicle seemed to fly away from her by a good quarter-meter. She heard the cries of her companions even through the relentlessly pounding rain and the constant rushing of the river. <*What the fuck was that?*> Zheng sent.

<*No idea. The car just jerked backwards,*> Noo replied.

<*I think I know,*> Ogawa sent. <*The storm is knocking debris into the river, or the rising water is freeing trapped debris.*>

Noo got the picture. She scooted forward and wrapped her cold, shaking hands around the lever, and leaned back. Nothing happened. <*What the hell, it's broken,*> she sent.

<*Are you pulling or pushing? You have to push it from the front,*> Zheng sent.

"Oh for fuck's sake," Noo said aloud, and pushed the lever. The tightly wound cable relaxed as the drum unlocked. She found the heavy metal tow hook and unclipped it. Zheng snapped orders to the others over the team circuit as she organized their evacuation from the car. Noo clutched the tow hook in both hands and pulled.

Fuck, this is hard. Her breath came in ragged gasps as she drove backwards with her legs, her whole body shaking with the effort. One step. Two steps. Slowly, slowly, the cable uncoiled from the drum. The muscles in her thighs screamed with the effort. Somewhere, as if from a great distance, she heard Teng shouting, but her world narrowed, just Noo and the damned cable and the never-ending rain. Another step backwards and her shoulders ached. Another and her elbows answered with sharp, bright pains of their own. She felt hands, large hands, wrap over her own and heard Teng's voice in her ears, close as a lover's. "Together now. Heave. Heave. Heave." Her left foot slipped off of a water-smoothed rock and she stumbled, caught herself before Teng could assist. "Heave." Perhaps it was her imagination, but the cable seemed to move more easily now. Was that because Teng was helping her? Because of something Ogawa had done?

It didn't matter. Step by step, every muscle in her body seemingly on fire, she drove herself back, her hands locked around the tow hook as if her own life depended on it. Not that she thought about it; there was no room for thought, for reflection, nothing but the tension in her arms, her shoulders, the treacherous footing beneath her feet, the fire in her legs and hips and back and really, her whole body, as she pulled the damned cable up the stone-covered riverbank as rain pounded against her head and shoulders, against every part Teng's body didn't cover.

Her right foot slipped across the top of some rain-slicked stone again and this time she didn't recover, her foot flying high as if she was kicking a game-winning goal. Off-balance, she fell, and she felt the new pains of every river stone beneath her biting into her muscles like hungry rats. Her breath whooshed out and she struggled to breathe, panic rushing up from wherever she'd banished it as fire rose from the back of her head, from her back, her ass, from every part in contact with these thrice-damned rocks scattered across this shore. Rain pelted her face and her eyes closed instinctively. Distantly she heard Teng grunting as he took up her load, somehow keeping his own grip on the cable as she'd fallen.

The fury of the rain's assault on her face lessened, and she opened her eyes. "Are you hurt?" Ogawa asked.

Noo found she could breathe again. "I'm OK," she tried to say, but in her depleted state she couldn't voice the words. With a herculean effort she lifted her right hand up over her body and gave Ogawa a thumb's up. Ogawa reached down and took Noo's hands in her own. She pulled back and Noo felt the fire in her whole body as the spy pulled her into a sitting position.

Ogawa crouched down. "We're all out," she said. "Teng is securing the cable around a tree but I don't know if that's going to matter. The car's filling with water and I wouldn't be surprised if it pulled the tree out with it when the river finally claims it."

"Fuck," Noo said. "Fari. She out?"

"Everyone's out of the car," Ogawa repeated. "We've got Fari and the pilot up by the treeline. Seems reasonable that the river won't flood that high, at least not before we can move. Zheng's scouting for shelter." Ogawa crouched down and Noo could tell she was being scrutinized. "Can you move? We should get to higher ground with the others."

Noo tried to take stock of her condition but the combination of fatigue, pain, and what some distant, rational part of her brain recognized as shock, conspired to overwhelm her. She finally managed to nod, and Ogawa hauled her upright. The Commonwealth woman was her age, near enough; how did she still have the reserve of strength to pull Noo up like that? Ogawa slipped under Noo's arm, wrapped her own around Noo. "It's all right. Just one step at a time."

CHAPTER TWENTY-ONE

Toiwa

Constabulary Headquarters, Ileri Station, Forward Ring

"Commissioner, the hardline is up!" Zinsou called from his watch position in the command center.

"Finally." Toiwa started to lean forward but was brought up short by a twinge from her bruised chest.

The bullet had indeed fractured two ribs and likely bruised her lung, the medic told her. The medic wanted to take an X-ray but Toiwa waved a trip to the infirmary off. After receiving an analgesic patch and a blood-oxygen sensor, Toiwa took command back from Zinsou. The medic departed to treat other wounded, of which there was no shortage.

Kala Valverdes was one of those. Ze'd taken a grazing wound to the head but was fine aside from a potential concussion. The medics insisted ze remain off duty until morning, however, until they could evaluate zer for a possible traumatic brain injury. Toiwa missed having her chief of staff, but Zinsou proved a reasonable substitute.

Maddeningly, she'd had no word about Eduardo or the children. She guessed that he'd taken them to the medical center, so he could do his job while ensuring the kids were looked after. But the center was in one of the rebel-held parts of the north ring.

The best way you can help them is to restore order across the station. Getting in touch with the government is part of that.

She forced herself to relax, physically at least, and leaned back into her chair. "See if you can get Colonel Carmagio, or the High Commissioner on."

"It's someone at Fort Ali, ma'am," said a technician with her right arm in a sling. That made sense; the hardline communications system ran through the station's hub down the space elevator cable to its terminus on the surface. Fort Ali was part of the downside complex. It connected with but did not pass through the military headquarters in the station's hub. Still, she was glad to have a link to *someone* in authority.

Maybe that person would know what the fuck was going on.

Less than a minute later, the head and shoulders of Defense Minister Vega materialized in the command center's main display field. Toiwa straightened involuntarily in her seat, grimacing from her injury. Vega had been career Army before her shift to civilian life and politics and was well-known for her military bearing. "Minister Vega. It's good to reach you, ma'am," Toiwa said. "I was afraid Miguna had gotten to you."

"Good to see you too, Toiwa. I heard you'd been shot."

How did she hear that? Toiwa wondered. "In the armor, Minister," she said, patting her side gingerly. "Broken ribs though."

"The rebels left that bit out of their claims," Vega said. "They claim you were killed when they took over your headquarters."

"Not on my watch," Toiwa said in a firm voice.

Vega nodded. "Very good. As far as Miguna getting me, well, he missed that shot too. What's your situation up there?"

"Confused," Toiwa admitted. "The station network is down, at least in every part my people have access to, so our information is patchy. We're stringing repeaters and using peer-to-peer in the meantime. The transit system is down too, though the cars seem to have reached safe zones and disgorged their passengers before shutting down. There's been fighting in the hub and in all the rings. I've secured my headquarters and most critical points in the forward ring, at least for now, but the rebels hold the med center, one of the airplants, and a few other less crucial locations. A runner from the north ring made it through the hub. My people have secured their precinct house and the north spoke, or at least the part near the ring. They report rebel military units hold the rest of the spoke and the hub, and rebel constables have occupied two of the north ring's airplants and the med center there. No word from the south or trailing ring, or from the hub proper." She paused for breath. "No word from Colonel Carmagio or her staff, or any non-rebel military units, but a few individual troopers have reported in and the senior NCO is getting them organized."

"Carmagio's dead," Vega said flatly. "Her aide-de-camp shot her. Major Biya, her executive officer, saw it happen. He and a few troops escaped the HQ complex at Government House and made it to the armory in the hub, only to find it largely stripped. They've got access to the hardline system but are otherwise cut off."

"Damn," Toiwa said. She'd liked Carmagio; the woman could be a little pompous at times, but she'd been a competent officer and a good partner in managing the station's security. "Any word on the rest of the forces here on the station, Minister?"

"Not much," Vega admitted with a frown. "Our people hold the main shuttle bays, the military side anyway. The *Amazonas*, the Commonwealth cruiser, undocked shortly after the fighting started. I've been in touch with Captain Gupta, her commander. Ze told me that their scientific delegation and a handful of zer marines were cut off somewhere in the trailing ring near Government House. Don't suppose you have any word of them?"

Toiwa had forgotten about the Commonwealth naval vessel, and the Saljuan one too for that matter. She shook her head. "I'm afraid not, Minister. I know military troops attacked Government House and the residential block, but I've had no intelligence since the infonet went down. We've not yet re-established contact with anyone in the trailing ring. Or the south ring, for that matter." She flicked a glance at Zinsou, who nodded, making a note. "We'll look into it. Sorry I don't have more news, or better news. What can you tell me about the bigger situation?"

Vega rubbed one hand across her eyes. "My news is as confused as yours, though I've got better data. The Prime Minister is dead, along with about half the cabinet. I was on the conference in telepresence when Miguna and his lackeys came in and shot them."

Toiwa ignored the gasps around her in the command center. "That's unfortunate," she said, and reviewed the casualty list that accompanied Vega's statement. She thought about the rules of succession. "Miguna is after you in the line of succession. Is he just ignoring that?"

"So it appears," Vega said. The other woman's gaze seemed to sharpen as she looked at Toiwa. "Do you recognize him as the legitimate head of the government?"

Toiwa didn't say anything for a few seconds. Then she flexed her left hand, grabbing control of the video pickup, and panned it around the room, pausing to show the scorch marks, bullet holes, and bloodstains, the constables and staff hard at work, some of them in bandages. She resettled the camera on herself. "He called me and asked me to go along even while his lackeys were shooting their former comrades. After I turned him down, his people did this to my headquarters, Minister, and shot *my people*. Hell, they shot *me* and who knows how many others, including Carmagio. No, I do not recognize the slimy little toad's illegitimate grab for power. As far as I'm concerned, you're the head of government under the Covenants, sworn in yet or no."

Vega's shoulders dropped a little, and Toiwa realized the other woman was just as tense as she was. "Thank you, Commissioner."

"My pleasure, Prime Minister."

Vega shook her head. "Just Minister for now, but the swearing in will come as soon as we can rig a broadcast. We've got infonet troubles too, though not as bad as yours."

"As you will. Can you put me in touch with my superiors in the Constabulary? Or in the station government?"

"I'm not sure you have any superiors anymore," Vega said.

That rocked Toiwa back, and she sat, stunned, for a few seconds before responding. "What do you mean, Minister?"

Vega turned to her left. "Carmen, send up the pictures from the Ministry of Justice, please." She turned back to Toiwa as the packet arrived and Zinsou threw it up on the display.

The Ministry of Justice building was simply *gone*. In its place was a burning pile of rubble covered by inky black smoke shot through with orange flames. More gasps sounded around the room. Toiwa felt like she'd passed to somewhere beyond shock. "How?" she asked.

"Kinetic energy weapon deployed from orbit," Vega said, her face taking on a grim cast. "Miguna's got some of the Navy in his pocket, too."

"But not all?" Toiwa asked.

"No, thank the Mother. Looks like the split is something like sixty-forty in our favor, but that's in total number of ships. The match in combat capability is a lot closer than I'd like," Vega said. "There's been three close-action engagements between opposing vessels that were in proximity to each other when this all started. We won two of those fights, lost the third. Now both sides are trying to gather ships into combat formations, or using them to support ground actions, while also trying to keep individual ships or weaker groups from getting picked off. The orbital control people are having ulcers."

Toiwa was suddenly aware of the vulnerability of the

station, feeling the weight of all the souls that suddenly were her responsibility. Or were they? "What about the governor and the station civilian government?"

"I'm sorry. I should have led with that," Vega said. "You're the first person in the station civilian government we've been able to reach. The rebels claim they've killed Ruhindi with video evidence we believe genuine. Indications are that while they failed to take you out they were successful with the rest of the station government."

The room seemed to recede from Toiwa as she processed this. Distantly, she sensed the eyes of all the command center staff on her. Slowly, slowly, she looked around, taking in the expressions of shock, surprise, fear, and determination on her staff's faces. Often two or more emotions warred across the same face.

She realized one person wasn't looking at her: Chijindu. Instead, the constable's eyes roved across the room, returning to the doorway every few seconds. He stood between her and the door, left thumb hooked into his equipment belt, his shotgun resting atop one of the consoles with his right hand on the stock, ready to swing it into action.

He was doing his job.

So would she.

She worked her mouth once, swallowed, and found the words.

"I understand, Minister." She opened the all-hands channel on the improvised local network her people had cobbled together. "Attention. In the absence of superior civilian authority, I, Commissioner Nnenna Toiwa, Chief of Constables on Ileri Station, hereby assume the position of Acting Governor, as of 2541 hours station time, pending the restoration of competent civilian authority, in accordance with the Covenants of the Republic of Ileri. Deputy Commissioner Zinsou, would you please witness?"

Zinsou licked his lips, nodded, and added his affirmation to the record.

Vega's head nodded in the display field. "Noted and logged on this end, Governor Toiwa. My staff is reviewing the status report your team's transmitted," she said. Toiwa realized that Zinsou, or one of his command center people, must have taken care of that while she and Vega had been talking. "In the meantime, is there anything you need?"

"Protection from space-borne attack," Toiwa said immediately.

"Already on the way," Vega said. She raised her left hand and twisted, bringing a holographic field up in the command center display. An image of Ileri and the station occupied the center, an ever-shifting constellation of brightly colored dots swirling around both station and planet. *Ships*, Toiwa realized. "We obviously can't establish a static screen powerful enough to deflect any attack, and static defense is useless in space warfare anyway. Except for point defenses, that is. Your point-defense system should be automated according to my staff. It's tied into the systems protecting the station from random orbital debris."

"Does your staff know if they'll function with the infonet down?" Toiwa asked.

There was a short pause as Vega consulted her staff. "We think so," she said. "Each cluster has fail-safe mechanisms to let it operate on local control."

Toiwa nodded. She didn't understand military ordnance, but she could follow Vega so far. Her mouth was suddenly dry, and she took a sip of water before continuing. "Good to know. I'll try to get contact with someone on the military side who can verify the system." Something clicked in her mind, pieces of data coming together. "Wait, you said you have a link to Major Biya. Can you relay communications between his people and mine?"

"That should be possible," Vega said with a nod. "In any case, we're sending a patrol frigate to help with local space control near the station, but that's the only vessel that will be nearby for a while. The *Lomba*, Commander Habila's ship, should be there in two hours. We'll have to relay communications with her, too, until you can get your infonet back up, or rig a tight-beam. But other ships are taking orbits which should discourage the rebels from making a run at you. They can provide interdictory fire against any ordnance launched your way as well."

"Thank you, ma'am." Toiwa studied the seemingly chaotic dance of the tiny lights in her display. She noticed one, brilliant purple not matching any other vessel, in a high orbit all by itself. She pointed at it. "Is that the Saljuan vessel? What have they been up to while this has been going on?"

Someone on Vega's end manipulated the display, shifting and zooming to focus on the *Iwan Goleslaw*, the big Saljuan warship. "They've deployed what look like autonomous weapons platforms, but their radiators are still deployed," Vega said. "They have asked if we know the status of their inspection team. Were they still in the hub when rebels attacked?"

Toiwa glanced at Zinsou, who shrugged before detailing an analyst to check. "I believe so," she said. "We'll try to confirm. But until you told me about Major Biya, we thought the whole hub was under rebel control." She grimaced. "I'm a little surprised Minister Dinata isn't calling for sanctions on the whole damn planet by now."

The minister sighed. "Oh, she's threatening that all right. But they aren't shooting anyone yet, so I can ignore them for now."

"Fair enough."

"Is there anything else we can do for you, Governor?" Vega said.

Toiwa glanced around the room at her staff. No one indicated they had any ideas to bring up. "Not at the moment, Prime Minister," she said finally. "It sounds like you've got your hands full down there anyway."

Vega offered a thin-lipped smile. "Indeed. My staff will coordinate with yours to keep the communications line open. We'll let you know if there's any significant developments. Otherwise, I suggest we talk again in the morning, say 0800 hours?"

"Very good, Minister," Toiwa said. "Until then." Vega nodded and her image disappeared.

Toiwa closed her eyes for a few seconds, then opened them and looked around the room again. "All right, people. I need a point of contact for every department on the station that you can lay your hands on. I don't care if they're the third assistant deputy or a damned rookie on their first day on the job. Find the most senior person you can lay hands on and tell them they're in charge now, at least where we have control. Okoye." A short, slender woman stood up. "You're liaison with the military. As soon as Major Biya gets on the line, find out about the point defenses, and find out what forces are actually under his control. And put that Army sergeant who's wrangling our stray troopers in touch with him."

She leaned forward, slowly, hands on her chair's armrests, and carefully pressed herself upright. "I'm going back to my office to open the contingency files in the secure station there." And maybe to have a moment of clandestine freak-out in her private bathroom. "I'll hold a staff meeting in the conference center downstairs with whatever station operations people you round up at 0300 hours. Any questions?"

Zinsou looked around the room and Toiwa's eyes followed his, taking stock of her people: determination, anger, a few tears, an overlay of fatigue and shock; but every single person was at their post, working in spite of whatever their emotions, or physical condition. She felt a surge of pride. *This* was the Constabulary she knew, the one she belonged to, and the one she'd fought to preserve as she'd climbed the ranks.

Zinsou turned back to her and saluted. "No, Governor. The Constabulary is ready for duty."

"All right, then. Let's get on it."

CHAPTER TWENTY-TWO

MEIKO

MOONSTRIDER GORGE, ILERI

"I THINK THE storm is finally dying down," Meiko said, peering around the tarp's edge towards the cave opening.

"About fucking time," Okereke muttered from her seat near the fire.

Zheng had found the cave along the bluff in which the bedraggled party now huddled. It was thankfully free of creatures, or at least free of anything that felt like contesting their presence. The hike down the canyon had been hellish despite being short. Meiko and Okereke had supported Fari as she hobbled one-legged, while Teng had carried the pilot slung over his shoulders.

"I haven't been this tired since I birthed my daughter," Okereke said.

"Was it a hard labor?" Meiko asked.

Okereke grunted. "She massed nearly five kilos, and

the doctor took his time before giving me an epidural."

Meiko made sympathetic noises. Childless, she could only imagine that level of pain. She'd give a lot for a few painkiller tablets right that moment herself.

The cave ran back into the bluff some unknown distance, but they'd found a space to the right of the entrance that they'd partly closed off with the tarp— well, a stout emergency blanket anyway—that Zheng had scavenged from the aircar's emergency supplies. It was the kind of thing first responders carried to cover accident victims. They tacked it to the walls with strips from a roll of Everseal tape Meiko had scrounged from the pilot's compartment.

She chuckled softly, recalling the relief she'd felt at seeing the face of Grippy, the cartoon seal-in-a-spacesuit mascot of the brand. You could find Everseal tape everywhere in the Cluster, manufactured under license on just about every world. Sure, there were reverse-engineered knock-offs anywhere people had fabbers; but every spacer Meiko had ever met swore by the 'real' stuff. She'd used it herself to do everything from securing pieces of survey equipment to rover bodies to patching leaky habitats to tying up prisoners. When Zheng's eyes lit up on seeing Meiko produce the roll, she knew she'd found a kindred spirit.

Their teeth were chattering nearly nonstop by the time they constructed their dubious shelter. Meiko was about to start explaining how one treated hypothermia when Zheng produced another miracle from the emergency kit, a thermal bar. Zheng snapped off a portion of the bar along a pre-scored line, placed it in the center of the pile of wood scrounged from outside the cave mouth, and stroked the igniter wand across it after warning them to avert their eyes.

Even through firmly shut eyes the initial flare was impressive. When she dared to open them, she found the wood steaming and beginning to burn. Zheng put her in charge of arranging additional wood around the fire to dry and keeping it fed while the constable and Teng tended to the injured. Okereke, wiped out from her efforts with the cable, slumped nearby.

They split a pair of protein bars Zheng produced from one of her many pockets between the five of them before Fari dozed off, followed by Teng and then Zheng. The storm continued to lash the world beyond their little haven.

Meiko settled in beside Okereke, stretching her hands out to warm them by the fire. "I could use a spa visit after this," she said, and they shared a quiet chuckle. Their companions, all in something that passed for sleep, were silent but for their breathing.

"When we're back on the station I'll take you to my favorite," Okereke said. "We'll bill it to Toiwa." Meiko smiled.

"You don't get along with the Commissioner, I take it?" she asked.

Okereke shook her head. "Woman's got a stick up her ass," she said. "She's a crusader. Came up the cable eight months ago after supposedly cleaning up Kochi." She smacked her teeth. "Well, the Fingers are still there all right, at least according to my contacts. But she did go through the Constabulary like a fucking avenging angel, sacking department heads and career constables who'd been on the dash for so long they'd forgotten they weren't supposed to be."

"And she's doing the same on the station?"

Okereke nodded. "Got started, anyway. Old Ketti's stooges are dug in pretty deep."

"Like ticks," Meiko said. Okereke looked at her questioningly. "That's right, you don't have them here," Meiko said. "Parasitic insects that burrow their heads into their targets."

"Ewww."

"Yes, not my favorite creatures either," Meiko said.

"Well, something like that, maybe," Okereke said. "Ketti was rotten, that's damn certain. Fathya, my business partner, hated dealing with him. I think she had something to do with getting Toiwa assigned to the station, but she denies it."

Meiko scrunched her butt around, trying to find a more comfortable position. "Does your firm work with the Constabulary often, then?"

Okereke laughed at this. "Before Toiwa? Not directly. Not often, anyway. Hell, half our business came to us because people on the station couldn't trust most of the Constabulary. At least we quote our prices up front and you have recourse to a contract court if we fuck up, instead of a sergeant making vague hints about *donations*."

"But there are some you can trust?" Meiko said with a nod towards Zheng, who dozed a few meters away.

Okereke nodded again. "I didn't know her before the trip down, but someone I do trust vouched for her."

"That Detective Sergeant?" Meiko asked, remembering the tall, slim man who'd pulled both Okereke and Fari aside before they'd all boarded the shuttle down.

"Daniel is good people," Okereke said with a smile. "We've known each other for more than thirty years."

"I see," Meiko said. She thought she caught a wistful note in the other woman's voice and called up the sergeant's image. "He's certainly fit for his age."

"He is." The conversation lagged for several moments, finally broken when Okereke stirred the fire, causing a brief eruption of sparks. Okereke looked around. The others were all still asleep or otherwise unconscious. "Can I ask you a question?" she said, softly.

Meiko shrugged, studying the other woman. She was curious. "You can certainly ask," she said. "I might not answer."

"Fair enough." Okereke chewed on her lip a moment, as if choosing her words carefully. "We're in deep shit here. Not *here*," she said, waving one hand to indicate the cave. "Though this isn't exactly a resort. At least as long as they pick us up soon. But this whole situation. Assassinations, riots, fucking spies with bombs and super-hackers. My partner getting a piece of fucking *rock* through her leg," she said with a nod in Fari's direction. "So we're stuck together, working together, for a while longer. Until this is over, anyway."

Meiko smiled wryly. "Assuming my boss doesn't stuff me into a closet in the embassy to keep me out of further trouble."

Okereke snorted. "OK, sure, that might happen. Until then, though, you're part of this team." She looked the other woman in the eye. "And we're going to need to trust each other."

Meiko cocked her head. "You don't trust me now?"

"Not entirely, no."

That bothered Meiko and she sat up straight, her shoulders squared back. "I think I've proved my worth any number of times."

"I'm not talking about your abilities." Okereke tapped her chest. "I'm talking about what's in here."

What the hell? She was tired and sore and her left arm still hurt. She'd fought rioters off this woman and helped carry her partner to safety, and she still wasn't trusted? She forced herself to speak calmly. "I don't understand what you're asking."

Okereke blew out a breath, frustrated. "What makes you do what you do, woman? Why are you here? Are you really in this to the end?"

The intensity of her words rocked Meiko back, and she looked away for a moment. Understanding crept in, slowly. "Your motive is personal, clear-cut. But this isn't my world, my fight, so you don't know why I care? Is that what you mean?"

"Something like that," Okereke said. "And whether you want the *real* answers about what's going on, or just *an* answer," she added. "Are you just here to make sure the vote comes off and Ileri joins the Commonwealth?"

"Ah. I see. I think." Meiko thought for a moment. "For myself, I want the real answer. Not just because I abhor untruths."

"That's a strange sentiment for a spy."

"Most of my job is really about finding the truth." Meiko poked the fire herself, but no sparks burst forth. "These people are trying to break the peace. Keeping that peace has been my life's work. What's happening here is the kind of situation that could spark a conflict like we haven't seen since the Second Colonial War."

"Why are the Saljuans spun up so hard? Because they think that if Ileri joins the Commonwealth, the power shifts too far in your favor?"

Meiko shrugged. "Maybe. I don't know. But we've tried space wars. They're hard and expensive, and the example of Goa and Shenzen wrecking themselves for several generations ought to be pretty fresh in people's minds."

Okereke snorted. "Not everyone's minds. There's seventy million people on this planet, and nearly a quarter of them are under the age of thirty. They're too young to remember the war. I bet it's the same elsewhere."

"Huh." Meiko thought about that. She remembered background briefings mentioning the burgeoning demographic changes as the population-growth curve on the Cluster's established worlds shot ever-higher. There were a *lot* of young people, and despite the best efforts of educators—and the free press, where it existed—she knew first-hand that people often forgot the lessons of the past.

But none of that got to Okereke's question. And if she wanted to succeed, to clear her reputation and make whatever happened next in her career her own choice, and not that of Kumar or the legion of bureaucrats back home, she needed to work with this woman. And Zheng, and Fari, and even Teng.

How much do I need to tell her before she believes me?

"My last mission," she said at last. "The *Fenghuang* recovery." Okereke nodded but kept quiet. "It was a mess. I have—well, I *had*—a good bit of freedom to pursue opportunistic leads. A colleague let me know someone was hunting for a war wreck out in the wild space between Novo Brasilia and Shenzen. I signed on, and, well." She paused as memories of desperate hours on the ice came to the fore, memories of blood and burning and of watching a young man twitching on the floor as hostile signals fired along his synapses and nerves.

She took a deep, shuddering breath, and the tension flowed out of her. She could see the future after this affair clearly now. Even if she pulled it all off and Kumar gave her a glowing report, she *knew* this was her last hurrah.

She turned to face Okereke, and her eyes burned into the other woman's.

"For the first time in forty years, people died because I didn't trust them, and because they didn't trust me," she said. "I was running solo, and we were twelve light years from the nearest settled system. Our ship had left for repairs after encountering a leftover munition from *Fenghuang's* last battle, the one in which it was supposedly destroyed. If I'd only been dealing with the prick who wanted... who wanted something the *Fenghuang* was carrying, I might have been able to work with the allies I made after he showed his hand." She swallowed again. "But there was someone else along who wanted to keep secrets buried forever, and they damn near killed us all to make that happen. If I'd trusted some of my companions earlier, we might have figured things out, and some of the innocent might not have died. And yes, we rescued those survivors in the stasis capsules, people who everyone had thought dead for more than twenty years, but only just. It was a bloody mess in every way, and I fucked up, badly, for the first time in my career.

"You asked why I'm doing this. I need you to trust me, trust my motives." She took a deep breath. "I'm done after this mission, I know that now. They'll never let me operate in the field again. But I can still do good here. We can find the killer, save lives, and keep the peace. And if this is my last chance to do that work, then I don't mean to fail. And I need your help."

For a moment, the only sounds within the cave were the crackling of the fire. Meiko thought about the career of forty years that she knew was over, turned to ashes like the wood burning beside them.

But even as it burned, it gave light, and warmth, and saved lives.

Okereke reached out with her right hand. Meiko stared at it for a few seconds, then reached out to clasp it.

"Call me Noo."

CHAPTER TWENTY-THREE

TOIWA

CONSTABULARY HQ, ILERI STATION, FORWARD RING

"WE CAN SUSTAIN the loss of one airplant to the rebels, ma'am. We only need one operational per ring. The others are primarily for redundancy."

The Infrastructure supervisor for the forward ring was a lighter-skinned woman with tired, narrow eyes set in a thin, angular face. Toiwa's constables, backed by an Army fire team, had located her at her post in the forward spindle. A fiber-optic line had been strung posthaste between the control station and Constabulary HQ, where Toiwa still maintained her base of operations. The technical services people had every fabber they could re-task running full out to make more cable.

"So taking back the plant they hold in this ring needn't be top priority?" Toiwa asked.

The Infrastructure woman began to answer but Kala

Valverdes, back on duty, broke into the call. "Governor? Sorry to interrupt, but there's a group here that Inspector Zinsou said you'd want to see right away."

She glanced at the identities of the new arrivals and hastened to finish the call. "Send them in, please. We'll speak later," Toiwa promised the station manager, and closed the connection as her office door opened. Chijindu, now sporting sergeant's tabs on his shoulders, levered himself to his feet as the newcomers entered.

This looks like a good sign for a change. Toiwa carefully rose and made her way around her desk to greet her visitors. "M. Okafor, M. Shariff, I'm very glad to see you're all right," she said as she motioned for them to take seats at her briefing table. "I hadn't realized you were both in this ring when the rebels attacked."

"We weren't," Shariff said. "Pericles Loh brought us. He's waiting in your outer office."

Surprise rooted Toiwa where she stood, and her brain raced. *What the hell is one of the leaders of the Fingers doing here?* She knew who Loh was from intelligence reports, but of course she'd never met him. For a few seconds she wished Shariff's partner, Okereke, was here rather than planetside; rumor had it she knew Loh well.

The three women seated themselves in her conversation nook as a commissary bot rumbled in bearing a tray of wrappers filled with coconut rice, strips of newt meat, crisp cucumber and boiled eggs. Chijindu transferred the tray's contents to the table, set two wrappers in front of Toiwa, and shot her a look akin to the ones Eduardo gave her when she'd neglected to eat while studying for her lieutenant's exam. Her heart ached at the memory.

Still, he was right. Food was fuel, and her body needed

fuel to keep going. Chijindu placed spoons at each place and set the tea things on the table before fading into the background. She picked up her spoon and gestured to the women. "First things first. A senior leader of the Fingers brought you here himself?"

"Yes," Okafor said. "Actually, his people saved me from death or capture." Her fingers traced the edges of the paper around her serving, then peeled it open. She spooned a generous helping into her mouth.

"Could you elaborate on that, please?" Toiwa asked.

Okafor finished chewing and swallowed. "My apologies. I've missed several meals." She laid her spoon down, freeing both her hands to manipulate her AR windows. She briefly related the story of her near-capture.

Toiwa heard Chijindu start to say something, then cut himself off. She turned to him. "Something to add, Sergeant?"

"Just that, well, that's hard to believe, ma'am," he said. "Military armor's hardened against malware attacks."

"I did not say it was *easy*," Okafor said mildly.

"I'm sure it wasn't." Toiwa waved her spoon at Chijindu. "Sergeant, let's stipulate that M. Okafor is as good at her job as you are at yours." The big man nodded. "The Fingers rescued you. Why?"

"If Loh is to be believed, I attracted the Fingers' attention some time ago," Okafor said. "He knows about the ancient dark net and knew I was investigating it. He claims he received warnings about the coup just before it happened, and dispatched people to ensure my safety."

Shariff took up the tale, and Okafor went back to her

food. "In my case, he appeared at my offices in the south ring a couple hours ago with Okafor here in tow," she said, waving her spoon at the infonet specialist. "He asked, for the sake of his long-term acquaintance with my partner, for me to broker an audience with you."

"What does he want with me?"

"To propose an alliance for the purpose of retaking the station from Miguna's goons," Shariff said.

Stunned with surprise, Toiwa sank back into her chair, thoughts racing. The idea that the Fingers would take an active role in the conflict, on the side of Toiwa and the government, was incredible. She tried to reorient herself. "What is he offering?"

"You'll have to get the details from him, but he said his assistance would be threefold," Shariff said. "First, as he demonstrated by bringing Okafor from the trailing ring and me from the south ring, he's got ways to bypass the rebels. No, he didn't let me get a good look at it," she said, waving off Toiwa's unasked question. "Had to put my djinn in a Faraday wrapper and made me wear a blindfold."

"You weren't worried for your safety?" Toiwa couldn't help but ask.

Fathya Shariff's laugh at that was loud and ringing. "Not from anything *his* people might try," she said. "He knows Noo would neuter him if he betrayed me. And if she didn't, my granddaughter would." Shariff sipped her tea before continuing. "As for the rest, he says bringing us here is a sign of good faith. He wants to make the rest of his pitch in person."

"I see." Toiwa thought furiously. With communications down, and some the bulk of the military's arsenal in rebel hands, even the limited control her forces had over parts of the station was tenuous at best. But to deal with the Fingers, with their centuries-old legacy of extortion, smuggling, and occasional murder? Was that a bridge she was willing to cross?

Would that actually be better than capitulating to Miguna?

Maybe. If the deal is good enough.

She glanced at Sergeant Chijindu's implacable face. *Would I betray the trust of this man, and all the others putting their lives on the line, by making some kind of deal?*

Could she afford to not at least hear Loh out?

Stalling for time, she turned back to Shariff. "What's it like out there?"

The businesswoman frowned as she set down her teacup. "Not good," she said. "With transit and the infonet down, and most fabbers and bots offline, people are stuck wherever they are with only what provisions they've got. Folks are taking care of each other, from what I've seen, helping out their neighbors, people stuck away from their home rings. No one's going to go badly hungry for a few days, though a few might miss some meals." She squared her shoulders and faced Toiwa directly. "But people are scared. They've seen soldiers and constables shooting other constables, and seizing airplants and med centers, and the university in the south ring. There's a lot of rumors. Everyone seems to know about Miguna's claim that he's the new PM, but I didn't even know you were alive until Loh told us. And"—her eyes dropped to the floor—"some of the regular people? They're on his side. Some agree with him. Or at least the Saljuans showing up and throwing their weight around has scared them into agreeing with him on that point. There's pockets held by One Worlders and their sympathizers."

"That sounds like what we hear from down the cable," Toiwa said. She explained the overall situation to her guests. She turned to the infonet specialist. "M. Okafor, you witnessed, at least partially, the fighting at Government House. Can you confirm whether the rebel claims the governor's been killed are true?" *Since they lied about killing me...*

"While I had access to the suit, I tracked the force attacking the complex," Okafor replied. "Loh's people offered me video evidence confirming the governor's death, and I verified the imagery they gave me isn't adulterated, but a sighted person will need to view it. Loh had another data point, though, a more hopeful one. The Commonwealth delegation that arrived on *Amazonas* was taken with no deaths and only minimal injuries and moved to another location. His people managed to track them."

Thank the Mother. "Give all that to Inspector Valverdes, please."

"Already done."

"Good."

"It would seem, then," Shariff interjected carefully, "that an option that might help resolve the situation quickly is worth considering."

Right. That crystallized her thinking. "It can't hurt to hear his proposal, I suppose." She called Valverdes. "Show M. Loh in, please."

For someone who by all accounts had trekked through

the bowels of the station, Loh looked surprisingly dapper. He greeted Toiwa with warm politeness, and even graced Chijindu with an acknowledging nod. Toiwa cut short the niceties once he was seated. "You have a proposal. I'd like to hear it."

"Very well." He settled himself comfortably in his chair. "I take it the first capability I can offer has been demonstrated by bringing these two notables into your care?"

"You're offering us access to the smuggler's ways, or part of them," Toiwa said more hotly than she'd intended. Fatigue had caught up with her, making her irritable. "That's one item. M. Shariff mentioned you have two additional things to offer."

Loh seemed unfazed by her attitude. He held up two fingers. "Material support. My organization possesses our own unrestricted fabbers. We have no programmatic limits on what we can build, no restrictions but for what our fabbers can physically create from available feed-stock. I can offer you armor and weapons to put your people on equal footing with the rebels."

"Very interesting," Toiwa said. The gear disparity was a serious issue; one she could resolve on her own, in time, with the Constabulary's own fabbers. But not quickly. "And the third thing?"

"Bodies," Loh said, ticking off a third finger. "We can augment your forces, in addition to helping you reunify the loyalist groups on-station."

Just like that. Loh offered Toiwa exactly the tools she needed to push back the rebels and regain control of the station. *Of the planet's gateway*, she thought, recalling Ruhindi's words.

She locked eyes with the criminal. "And what does your organization ask in return for all of this largesse?"

Loh folded his arms against his chest. "Amnesty."

She felt her guts fall away, as if a giant void had opened inside her body. The word hung in the air for a moment before she pressed for more. "What kind of amnesty?"

His answer came in the mildest of tones, as if what he sought were completely reasonable. "Absolute forgiveness and immunity from prosecution for all acts prior to the beginning of the coup, and for anything done in defense of the station or anyone on it during the coup. No forfeiture of assets or funds. Clean slates for all my people." He tilted his head as he finished.

Toiwa sat back, stunned at the effrontery, the sheer brazenness of Loh's demands. "You want forgiveness for *every criminal act*? All the theft, the extortion, the assaults, the killings? Going back how far?"

Loh didn't even blink. "I believe thirty years is reasonable."

The faint sense of gratitude Toiwa had felt towards the man for saving Okafor and bringing her in was burned away by her sudden anger at his demands. "Out of the question. You ask too much. And besides, I'd have to run that through the Ministry of Justice, which at the moment is a bombed-out shell."

"Really, Governor?" he said, his voice soft. "These are exceptional times. And Prime Minister Vega has a reputation for pragmatism. I'm sure when you communicate your offer—"

Her right hand snapped up, palm open, and he stopped abruptly.

Toiwa fumed inwardly. For a brief moment, she'd

thought the tools she required were within her grasp. But Loh wanted decades of transgressions, thousands of acts, wiped away without consequence as if they'd never happened. She'd been police too long to acquiesce to such a deal.

"Governor?" Shariff asked.

She did *not* say 'Over my dead body', as much as she wanted to. "I'm going to have to decline your generous offer at this time," she said, trying to keep the anger out of her voice. "Sergeant?"

Loh, sensing the discussion was over for now, simply nodded, slowly, as Chijindu loomed beside him. "Should you change your mind, I would be happy to speak at greater length," he said as he rose. The room was silent but for footsteps as Chijindu escorted him from the room, before returning to hover discreetly in the corner.

Toiwa sighed and turned to Shariff. "I can't take those terms. But he was right about one thing—I find myself desperately short of trained people. I'd like to hire your firm for the duration of the emergency. Name your fee and I'll see it paid."

Shariff studied Toiwa's face. Whatever she was looking for, she seemed to find it. "I see." Shariff wiped her hand and extended it to Toiwa. "My people are at your disposal, Governor."

"Good." Toiwa rose and shook her hand. "Let's get Valverdes and my staff in here and figure out our next step."

CHAPTER TWENTY-FOUR

Noo

Moonstrider Gorge,
Ileri

THE RAIN FINALLY stopped mid-morning, and the clouds thinned, though they didn't clear out entirely. The pilot awoke, groggy but capable of understanding their situation. Zheng and Meiko ventured out to see if anything further could be recovered from the aircar, but returned moments later shaking their heads.

"It's just gone," Zheng said. So was the tree they'd anchored the car to.

The river had risen halfway to the treeline from where they'd left it. They picked their way carefully among the rocks along the new shoreline in a vain search for salvageable gear, finding nothing human-made.

"We were broadcasting our location up until the crash, so search parties ought to come looking for us soon. I'm surprised no one's overflying the valley already,"

Zheng said. She looked at her djinn wistfully. "No signal."

Meiko got a thoughtful expression on her face. "Perhaps not through the Ileri system," she said. "But there's another option."

"What do you mean?" Noo, applying a fresh bandage to Fari's wound, looked up. Her partner was running a slight fever, but they had nothing to treat the deep puncture to prevent infection, and she was worried.

"I might be able to contact *Amazonas*," Meiko said, raising her own djinn. "If it's overhead, that is."

"You've got satellite-comm capability in that?" Teng asked, astonished. "In that small a package?"

"Under good conditions, yes," Meiko replied. "If I can't raise *Amazonas*, there ought to be *something* overhead I can talk to, though it might take a while to get someone to answer."

"Why didn't you try this last night?" Noo demanded.

"Too much cloud cover and interference from the storm," Meiko said. "I still might only be able to receive. My transmitter's not that strong."

Zheng nodded decisively. "Let's try it. You need high ground with a wide horizon?" Meiko nodded. "Right. Teng, you go with her. Between the two of you, I expect you can find someone who will respond to one of you." She pointed at Noo. "Okereke, you and I will put together a distress signal. Someone's going to come looking for us eventually and we need to be easy to find."

Two hours later, a boom echoed down the valley and startled the birds nested in the trees lining the river. The air exploded with wings and bodies, a sudden burst of brown and black occluding the morning sky. In Noo's brain, the color of the sky was always blue of some shade; today was a hazy gray, and it just looked *wrong*...

"Right on time," Meiko said beside her, one hand shading her eyes as she watched the clouds.

Zheng emerged from the cave and ambled through the trees towards them. She looked up and down the valley, then across, then raised her djinn, pointing it first across the river, then both up- and downstream. Noo watched her, one eyebrow raised inquisitively. "Laser rangefinder," the lieutenant said, tapping her djinn with her right index finger. "Checking the LZ clearance. Old drop-trooper habit."

"Didn't you do that already?" Noo asked.

"It never hurts to be certain," Zheng said.

Noo spotted their target first. It appeared through a break in the clouds, a swift black shape too large and moving too quickly to be anything natural. She pointed. "There." The others turned and she saw relief on both their faces. The shape disappeared behind the clouds again, but then reappeared, larger and closer.

Zheng lit a flare from the emergency kit and tossed it onto the rock-strewn bank. "We should all move back up to the cave mouth," she said, and they scurried back to shelter.

The heavens roared, and all three of them ducked inside the cave as the descending shuttle fired its landing jets. "Told you I could find us a ride," Meiko said with a grin.

The whole craft was colored bright yellow, which struck Noo as odd. Then it settled in to fully land, its belly meeting the water, and steam exploded from the water's surface with such violence Noo took several stumbling steps backwards, only to be brought up short when she backed into the cave wall. Within the cloud of steam the shuttle disappeared. She brought her hand up to her mouth, wondering if it had exploded, even though she knew she'd be dead if that had happened. As the shuttle cooled and the steam blew away, Noo saw the shuttle change color, the yellow fading as it seemed to disappear within the cloud. Squinting, she realized she could still make out the outline, aided by the roiling water that surged around the lower fuselage and wing roots. *Chameleon coating,* she realized.

Her djinn pinged to her audio implants with the message that a new network connection was available, though her djinn couldn't access it. She looked over to Meiko who, it seemed, could, judging by the attention she seemed to be giving to a private AR window.

Five minutes after it touched down, a long hatch half the length of the fuselage popped out from the shuttle's side and quickly swung up. A pair of troopers in fatigues, light armor, and combat exoskeletons bounded out, crossed the wing in great, leaping strides, and splashed into the shallows. They bounded out to take up security positions, weapons pods protruding from their exoskeleton arms.

Perimeter thus secured, the rescue team surged out and soon surrounded their little party on the bank. They were all young, fit people, none of them over the age of thirty, if she was any judge. A slender young woman whose wide, flat face poked out from under her helmet came to a halt in front of Meiko. "M. Ogawa? I'm Lieutenant Lac," she said, in a lilting accent Noo didn't recognize. "I understand you have wounded?"

"Two, in the cave," Meiko said. "This way." Meiko turned to lead the little party back through the trees to their erstwhile shelter. Lac's medics stepped out of their exoskeletons and ducked inside. Meanwhile, Lieutenant Lac filled them in on all the news they'd missed. Perhaps she'd just absorbed one shock too many, but Noo could only listen numbly as Lac told them about the assassination of the Prime Minister, Miguna's coup, Vega's response, and the continued fighting in space and on the ground.

"Captain Gupta decided it was better to ask forgiveness than permission and ordered us to drop, said ze'd notify both sides ze was launching a humanitarian mission," Lac said.

"Anyone take a poke at you on the way in?" Zheng asked.

"Nothing more serious than a couple of sweeps by targeting radar," Lac said with a shrug. "More worried about the trip up, frankly. Our launch window opens in"—her eyes unfocused slightly as she checked her implants—"twenty-five minutes." She turned and leaned over to shout up into the cave. "What's the word, Sanjay?"

"Gonna need to put the pilot into stasis, ma'am," came the reply. "Hematoma and a bad TBI, don't want to overstress her with take-off acceleration."

"Can you move her to the shuttle and do it there, or do you need the pod brought here?"

"Stretcher to the shuttle will be fine," the lead medic answered. "I'd rather do the stasis prep in the bay there anyway."

The lieutenant turned to her lead sergeant, a lanky woman older than the rest of the squad but still not even half Noo's age. "Let's get the ambulatory aboard, Sergeant, then double back with the stretchers."

The sergeant murmured her orders over their tactical

comm net and Noo found herself scooped up by a trooper. The young man cradled her gently and her brief ride was surprisingly comfortable despite the exoskeleton's metal struts. He deposited her on the shuttle's deck with care before springing back out again.

The shuttle was all business. The acceleration couches had the blocky, robust look Noo associated with military gear. It lacked the friendly hues of a passenger craft; the paint was a mix of pale green and dark gray, relieved by colorful labels everywhere the eye looked. There wasn't a single loose object anywhere in the cabin; everything was tied, fastened, or bolted down.

"Are any of you prone to motion sickness, space sickness, or zero-gravity-adaptation syndrome?" one of the ratings asked them.

"Blessed Mother of the Rivers, yes," Noo said. The others shook their heads.

"Would you like a sedative before we launch, or just anti-nausea meds?" the rating asked, as he guided her towards one of the acceleration couches.

The prospect of sleeping through the launch was briefly attractive. Noo considered it but shook her head. "Just the nausea meds please. And a barf bag."

The rating helped Noo into the couch and helped fasten her harness. "One of the medics will be round in a few to administer the meds," she said. She turned, opened a compartment on the nearby bulkhead, and extracted several airsickness bags. She tucked one under each of Noo's chest straps, within easy reach, and two more alongside her legs. "Just in case," she said.

There came a clattering sound from the rear of the compartment as the rest of the squad returned with Fari and the pilot. They hustled the latter off to the rear of the compartment. Noo hadn't traveled in nanostasis herself, nor had she seen the prep procedure, but she gathered from the clipped voices just on the far side of unintelligible that they were rushing things a little bit.

The third medic squatted by her couch and requested access to her medical records. Noo bumped her djinn to his, transferring them. He examined them briefly, then ducked back to the triage bay. He returned with a pair of medication patches which he applied to her neck. "Those should hold you until we dock with *Amazonas*," he said. "Let me know right away if you feel sudden tongue swelling, or itching feet."

She gave him a weak smile. "And what happens if someone takes a shot at us?"

"In that case," he said, "things might get rather interesting. Have you ever been on a roller coaster?"

"A what?" she asked. The medic grinned, then sent her some video footage. "It's an amusement ride. We have them back on New Mumbai, and I've seen them on other worlds. Never been here before, though, so don't know if you have them."

Noo watched the footage with growing horror. "You people do this for fun? I'll never understand groundsiders."

Noo

Ileri Airspace

THEY ENJOYED A smooth take-off and easy flying as the

shuttle climbed to scramjet altitude. The crew chief supplied the Ileris with limited access to the shuttle's network, just enough to hook them into comms. She found she had access to at least some of the external cameras, too. She spent the first ten minutes watching the surface drop away below them as their spiraling climb took them ever higher.

Suddenly, the cabin lights all turned red.

"What's going on?" she asked the sergeant, seated in the couch next to hers.

The sergeant frowned. "We're being painted by someone's radar. Not just a brush, they're probably trying for a weapons lock." She settled her body deeper into her couch, rolled her neck once, and pressed her head firmly back into the molded headrest. "Best get ready for a rough patch, ma'am."

Noo tried to imitate the sergeant's actions and had just settled her head between the flanges that sprouted on either side when she heard a series of thumps from below and beneath. "Countermeasures deployed," said the sergeant.

"Why aren't we evading?" Noo asked.

"We've got to hit the right patch of sky before we kick on the big motor," replied the sergeant. "We need to be at the right altitude, bearing, and position in order to make our orbit insertion."

"What happens if we aren't there?"

"We'll still make orbit, most likely," the pilot said. "We'll just be in the wrong orbit to rendezvous with *Amazonas*."

They continued their spiraling climb. Another thump came from below and behind. The shuttle straightened abruptly, nose still angled to climb, no longer turning.

The sergeant cursed as the cabin lights flicked twice. "ALL HANDS, BRACE FOR ACCELERATION," sounded across the comm net.

"Too early," the sergeant said, and then the rocket fired and a giant's fist slammed into Noo for the second time in less than a day.

The pressure seemed to come all at once and she felt her body sinking into the gel-filled cushion of the acceleration couch. The sides of the headrest did indeed come up to cradle her head and neck protectively. She did her best to breathe and found it difficult but bearable. The worst part was the way her face felt, like her cheeks were being pulled off from behind.

Without warning, the rocket cut off and Noo's body surged forward against her straps. Her relief was short-lived as the shuttle rolled over, belly to the heavens, and the nose pitched down. Her stomach rebelled at this and her hands scrabbled for one of the airsickness bags. Someone whooped from the compartment's rear, and she heard the sergeant's answering bellow of "Secure that!" Another thump from behind and below, only now it was behind and *above*, and she filled the bag with last night's protein bar.

The shuttle rolled again, coming back into proper orientation at least as far as up and down went. She heard the roar of the atmosphere jets again and the nose pitched upwards. Noo managed to seal the barf bag and shoved it into a slot in the bulkhead, indicated by a friendly AR tag that popped up. Distantly, she heard a ripping noise, and the deck beneath her feet vibrated. "What's that?" she said, surprised at how steady her voice seemed.

"Point-defense cannon," the sergeant called back, and then the rocket fired again and stole her breath for a moment.

This time, the rocket fired for a solid six minutes and change, according to her djinn. In the AR window she'd linked to the external camera she watched the sky go from blue to violet to black as they climbed.

The rocket cut out again, and this time they were in zero-g. Noo's stomach was still unsettled and she gulped air but managed to avoid vomiting again. The cabin lighting returned to normal.

<How are you doing up there?> Meiko asked.

<Wishing I'd taken the damn sedative,> Noo admitted. <Will we make the rendezvous with Amazonas?>

<I don't think so, not the one they'd planned,> Meiko sent. <But we're in a good orbit, I believe. Lieutenant Lac doesn't look concerned.>

"Flight deck here," came across the all-hands channel. "As you probably noticed, we attracted some unwanted attention on the way up. Amazonas is preparing to maneuver for a new rendezvous, but we'll need to make a couple orbits before we can mate up. New rendezvous in one hundred fifty minutes and change."

<See?> Meiko sent. <Before long we'll be docked and have Fari in a med bay.>

<Can't come soon enough,> Noo replied, fingering her Eshu charm.

She tried to relax and pretend that she was just on a trip to the hub. The medic who'd ministered to her earlier came up to check on her. "She's solid," the sergeant told him, and Noo gave her best affirmative nod. Her discomfort eased and she engaged the sergeant in conversation for a while. The sergeant hailed from Jakarta, one of the First Fourteen worlds like Ileri, and a founding member of the Commonwealth.

Five tense minutes passed. Noo tried to see if she could spot the incoming craft and thought a particular bit of silver in her view field might be one of them.

The pilot fired the rocket again, and the thrust pressure actually made Noo feel better physically even as she realized this was bad news. Damn, but she hated being strapped down in this metal and composite can in the sky. She was tired of nameless, faceless enemies coming at her and her family. She was pissed off at Miguna and his faction for breaching the peace. She wanted, needed, to be free to operate, to chase down leads, to find the shit-lickers who'd shot Saed and killed Ita and all those others, to snap restraints on them and tell them they'd been clipped.

The motor cut out while she was trying to organize her thoughts, anger fueling her despite the exhaustion and her body's rebellion. "New hostiles, a pair of cutters, launched on us," the pilot said. "Be prepared for sudden changes in acceleration."

She saw the planet swing through her view as the pilot spun the ship onto a new heading. The giant stood on her chest again for a few seconds as the rocket fired once more.

Then, suddenly, a pair of brilliant flashes lit her window, and whoops once again filled the passenger compartment. The sergeant joined them this time, and a series of smaller flashes appeared, closer by.

<What happened?> Noo asked Meiko.

<Amazonas,> came the answer. <*They changed course*

to match ours, took out the cutters, and now they're clearing the missiles.>

<So we're going to make it?> Noo sent.

<It appears so,> Meiko replied.

<Good.> Relief had to be there somewhere, but for now, anger was her fuel. <We need to make a plan. We still need to track down those turds we came for.>

CHAPTER TWENTY-FIVE

TOIWA

SECURE INTERVIEW SUITE #3, CONSTABULARY HQ,
ILERI STATION, FORWARD RING

TOIWA STEPPED BRISKLY into the interview suite's observation room. "What did you need me for?" she said, a bit more harshly than she intended to Valverdes and Imoke, who sat inside. She'd managed a short, chemically induced nap, but Remex always left her feeling irritable despite supposedly being free of side effects. She waved her subordinates back into their seats as Chijindu slipped in behind her and secured the door. "Sorry. Fatigue's no excuse for discourtesy. You had something to show me?"

Valverdes walked to the one-way glass separating the observation room from the interview room proper. The subject, a solidly built middle-aged man in a prisoner's jumpsuit, sat restrained to his chair, which was itself bolted to the floor. A medic hovered nearby, scanning feeds from the biomonitor patches attached to the subject's neck, arms, and temples. "Who authorized a medically assisted interview?" Toiwa snapped, this time with genuine anger. They might be on a war footing, and might yet have to resort to such measures, but she'd be damned if it wasn't going to be done by the book and only on her say-so.

"Those are for treatment, not interrogation," Valverdes said. "The prisoner began exhibiting distressing physical symptoms, so Sergeant Imoke halted the interview and called for someone to check him out."

"What kind of symptoms?"

"The man looked like he was going to have a seizure episode," Imoke said. "Face flushed, his breathing became rapid and irregular, and his limbs alternated between twitching and locking up."

"So why call me?" Her initial flash of anger had subsided but being called away for such a relatively trivial matter, given everything else going on, seemed like a waste of her time.

Valverdes, sensing zer boss' mood, jumped in. "Because this is one of the people who attacked the Commonwealth agent. And the third one in a row to exhibit these symptoms when their interrogator began asking certain types of questions."

That certainly got her attention and set her police brain in motion. "Once is chance, twice is coincidence, three times is deliberate action," Toiwa said, and the others nodded. "What kinds of questions brought the episodes on?"

"Three things," Imoke said. "First, what led them to attack M. Ogawa. Second, what they intended to do with her after incapacitating and capturing her. And third, if they had any connection to Councilor Walla."

That was a left turn that left her tired brain behind. "Why ask about Walla?"

"We never found any sign she'd had martial arts training," Imoke said. "The same for these suspects."

Toiwa sat down, still confused. "Sergeant, this is all quite fascinating, but why are you pursuing this now with everything else going on?"

Imoke and Valverdes exchanged glances before he tossed her a data packet. "On a hunch, I asked M. Okafor to look for correlations between unusual activity on the illegal networks she's been probing and the incidents preceding the coup." He flipped open the table's projector field and a table with several columns appeared: dates, times, locations, and three columns color-coded for each of the illegal networks. "The patterns are obvious once you know to look for them. The Saljuan cell shows activity before and during the outbreak of assaults and disappearances over the last three months. I'll speak to them in a moment." He highlighted a different portion of the chart. "This is more relevant to these people. What Okafor calls the 'dark net', *that* one shows a spike in activity during the attack on M. Ogawa, as well as bursts during a number of the One Worlder protests." He scrolled down to a huge spike at the bottom. "This traffic came right before the coup, and the attacks here on-station."

"Sweet leaping Mother," Toiwa breathed. She stood and paced the room. Exile-era computer code; the Saljuan accusations that Ileri was dabbling in the forbidden tech; the sudden surge of Miguna and his followers.

Sweet Mother, what if we were playing with this? What if it got out?

"Bundle all of this up and shoot it to the Prime Minister's people down the cable," she said. "Ask if they've got prisoners with similar symptoms, and if they're seeing any of the same kinds of infonet anomalies we are."

Toiwa's djinn buzzed with a message bearing a military priority code. She flashed the tactical hand sign for *hold* and popped open the message window. "Toiwa here."

The head and shoulders of a dark-skinned woman with a fine-boned face and close-cropped hair appeared in her window. "This is Commander Habila of the frigate *Lomba*, on picket duty by the station. We've gotten a flash notice from Naval Operations that I'm to relay to you. The Saljuans are making a broadcast."

Toiwa swept her hand through the field, making it viewable to everyone in the room. "I'm sharing with some of my staff. Go ahead, Commander."

"Coming through." The window blanked before switching to the faces of Minister Dinata and Captain Andini.

Dinata spoke, her tone haughty as her expression. "We have waited patiently for the people of Ileri to bring their world into order so that we can conduct our lawfully permitted inspection to follow up on evidence the Star Republic of Salju has received concerning the development and experimentation with technologies forbidden under the Accords of 83 PE. Sadly, the government of Ileri has proved incapable of doing so."

"Sweet Mother, are they going to retaliate for their lost inspection team?" Imoke said. Toiwa waved him into silence.

"—find it necessary to act on the information we have received. I have directed Captain Andini to maneuver the

Iwan Goleslaw to rendezvous with a newly identified objective."

Andini took over, her tone strictly businesslike, that of a professional doing her job. "We will maneuver to close proximity and match orbits with orbital manufactory designated Albert Therese Five Seven Bolo. When we achieve stable orbit approximately fifty kilometers from the objective, our inspection team will launch via boarding craft to conduct their activities. Any interference with the transit of the *Iwan Goleslaw* will be met with lethal force. Any interference with the inspection team at any point of their mission will be met with lethal force. I will commence maneuvering at 1355 New Abuja time."

Dinata spoke up again. "The Star Republic of Salju will regard any acts taken against this vessel as an act of war. Any party that gets in our way will be dealt with harshly."

The Saljuans' window cut out.

"Those incredibly arrogant bastards," Toiwa said. She had a vague notion that ships would have to move to avoid potentially being regarded as threats to the *Iwan Goleslaw*, but for the most part, that wasn't her problem. "Thank you, Commander Habila. Will you have to leave us?"

"No, Governor," Habila said. "We're tucked in close enough to the station, astrographically speaking, so unless they come to dock here, we're well out of their way. And if they *do* try to dock here, I'll be reinforced. We're to deny them access."

"I see. Does the PM or your command have any other information or guidance for us?"

"Not yet, ma'am. We'll pass any developments onto you immediately."

"Thank you." She looked at her subordinates. "Any questions for the Commander?" Both shook their heads. "Very well then. Toiwa out."

"I'll notify the department heads," Valverdes said, rising.

Toiwa signaled for zer to remain. "In a moment." She turned to Imoke. "You mentioned there was more to say about the Saljuans. With them taking action, I'd better hear it."

"Yes, Governor. First of all, microbiome analysis has confirmed all the prisoners we captured in the raid where we found Councilor Walla are all Salju natives." It was technically possible to alter one's microbiome to disguise the world of one's upbringing, but it was a difficult feat, with potentially unpleasant side effects. "Second, the technical forensics team tells me they've found signs two of the fabbers from their safe house were used to construct projectile weapons with performance characteristics consistent with those used in the assassination."

"Dammit." Toiwa leaned back and rubbed her eyes. "We'll have to let the PM know about this too. Who else knows about this?"

"Just us and a pair of forensic techs. I let them know that if word leaked, they'd be cleaning organic waste tanks by hand for the rest of their lives. They told me, I told Inspector Valverdes, and ze put the records under your seal."

"Good." Links between the Star Republic and the assassinations were a serious matter beyond her pay grade, even as governor; they rose to the level of foreign policy, which was expressly not her charge. But what did that mean in terms of finding out the truth?

What it meant, she decided, was that until someone told her otherwise, pursuing the case was still her patch. What to do with that information, on the other hand, was manifestly not. That hadn't changed, when she'd gone from simply Commissioner to Governor. But why did it *feel* different?

She opened her eyes and saw her people watching her; Valverdes attentive, Imoke concerned. "All right. Anything else about the Saljuans we took?"

"No, ma'am. They've remained mute and declined to answer questions, or even to ask for counsel."

"Keep them secured, then, until we've got something more to go on." She looked at Valverdes. "We need to play things defensively overall, but we need some kind of small win, soon. Something to encourage the people holding out, but also to start reclaiming the initiative."

"You have something in mind, Governor?" Imoke asked.

"I'm thinking about the airplant in rebel hands here in the forward ring."

Imoke looked grave. "That seems like it might be the most vulnerable point we've got access to," he conceded. "But it will still be a tough nut. When do you want to move?"

"As soon as it can be put together," Toiwa replied. "I want Miguna's people taken down a notch. And I want them out of my damned ring."

CHAPTER TWENTY-SIX

MEIKO

CPC AMAZONAS,
ILERI ORBIT

AMAZONAS WASN'T THE smallest starship Meiko had ever shipped in, nor was it the most confined. The countless lighters carried by the great driveframes, used in every part of the Cluster but the New Arm, were all smaller. And she'd spent one memorable trip during the war in an overloaded Second Wave-era battlerider, converted into an independent starship. There'd scarcely been room for two people to pass in the corridors of that flying relic.

But *Amazonas* was a close second where feeling confined was concerned. Commonwealth patrol cruisers were meant for extended-duration, independent missions. Extended duration meant lots of room for stores, which meant less room for *people*. Meiko imagined a team of psychologists, naval architects, and logistics specialists cloistered within a design suite somewhere in the great

Novo Brasilia shipyard complex, running simulations on just how tightly you could pack humans together, and for how long, before the crew succumbed to behavioral sink conditions. After the designers backed off five percent for a little safety margin, bam, you had a patrol cruiser.

Captain Gupta had the crew quarter modules tucked in next to the cylindrical main hull rather than out on their extensible booms for spin. This kept *Amazonas* ready for action on short notice but meant the vessel remained in zero-g. This was no problem for Meiko and even Zheng got her space head back quickly. Noo and Teng, however, fared less well.

Meiko pulled herself into the four-person bunk space they'd been allocated and found Noo tucked into her acceleration bunk but still awake, while their companions dozed. She thought Noo looked somewhat better, or at least less likely to need a barf bag every fifteen minutes. "I thought you might be napping like the others," she said quietly, coming to rest against the wall of their tiny common area. Her fingers wrapped around the handhold automatically and she swung into the same up-and-down orientation as the other woman. She didn't think Noo was quite ready for conversation with a person floating at a ninety-degree angle to herself yet.

Noo grimaced. "I tried. Maybe later." She gingerly undid her safety straps and swung herself into a sitting position with care. Meiko had seen this in zero-gravity rookies before; old habits of what *should* be vertical stuck with the brain. "What's the word?" Noo asked.

"Fari's going to be all right," Meiko said. "She did pick up an infection but the surgeon's got her started on a cleaning regimen and is putting a regeneration matrix in place. She'll be on light duty for a time but ought to recover fully."

Noo's lips twitched with the hint of a smile. "She's a tough one, my girl."

Meiko smiled back. "She certainly is. I wonder who she takes after?"

"Spirits help her, that child—Saed too—got stuck with Fathya and me as role models. It's a wonder she turned out as well as she did." She licked her lips. "How's the pilot?"

"She'll be all right too," Meiko said. "The surgeon has a lot of experience with this sort of thing. Not too surprising for a military doctor, I suppose."

"They've revived her?"

"Not yet. She'll be easier and safer to transport in stasis, so they're keeping her in for now."

"I see." Noo's eyes took on a distant look, but not quite that of someone with a private AR window. "What's going on out there?"

"You haven't looked at the feeds?"

"Your people cut us off when the shuttle docked, so we can't access the network," Noo said. "Not that I blame them, given the clusterfuck going on."

"Huh. Well, I'll see if I can persuade someone to at least let you get the news feeds," Meiko said. Her face went grim. "It's not good." She popped open an AR window and began plucking out news items, bundling them into a packet as she filled Noo in. She explained about the relative standoff in space, the assassination of the Prime Minister and the fighting across the planet and on the station. "Given the number of coordinated attacks, Miguna's following is bigger than anyone realized.

And he's trying to claim both that he's simply taking action to quell the unrest caused by the attacks, and that the attacks against what he calls the corrupt prior government were totally justified."

Noo looked like she wanted to spit. "Miguna's a weasel," she said. "There was talk about him moving up to the station and running for governor, serious enough that Fathya and I had to discuss contingency plans in case he actually came and won. Any word from the station?"

Meiko finished assembling the news packet and tossed it over. "The rebels claim they control it, but Captain Gupta is in touch with Minister Vega, who says it's still contested." Meiko frowned. "The governor is definitely dead, but they missed Toiwa, who's acting governor now. That's not good for the rebels, I think. I'd want to take her out if I was trying to seize control of Ileri Station."

"Toiwa's a pain in my ass, but I'm with you," Noo said with a nod. "If there's enough people left in the Constabulary who give a shit about what they're supposed to do, instead of being pissed off at the dash going away."

"I think you'll find the Commissioner has a knack for inspiring loyalty in her people," Zheng said. Meiko glanced over and discovered the lieutenant and Teng were awake. Meiko flipped her news packet to each of them. Teng began browsing it as Zheng pulled herself from her bunk with languid ease. "It seems to me the question is, how can we best help?"

"What do you mean?" Noo asked.

"I see three, maybe four options," Zheng said, holding up four fingers. "One, we stay here aboard *Amazonas* until the situation sorts itself out. I'm not inclined to that course," she said.

"Me either," Noo said immediately. "No time for a holiday."

"Right." Zheng tucked one finger away. "Two, we beg a ride to the station, or maybe groundside, and pitch in to help put down the coup."

Meiko chose her words carefully. "Distasteful as Miguna seems to be, that's your fight, not mine," she said. "Not that I want to see him win, of course, but I think having a known Commonwealth operative working against him would be problematic." She motioned to indicate the ship around them. "Captain Gupta had no problem with mounting a rescue, the Spacer's Covenant gave zer plenty of cover for that. But actively providing assistance to one side in an Ileri internal conflict, even if that's just reuniting you with the government forces? I'm not sure ze will go for that."

Teng looked up from the news window. "What are you proposing, Zheng? That we continue the investigation?"

The constable tucked down two more fingers, leaving her index finger alone pointing at the forward bulkhead, which under thrust would be the ceiling. "Exactly. We still have suspects at large and a case to solve. A case," her eyes turning to Meiko, "that includes the assassination of a Commonwealth diplomat, so definitely still in your purview."

"I'm not done until those dust-sucking turds are clipped," Noo said heatedly.

In Meiko's heart there was only one answer. *I'm in this to the finish.* "I'm in," she said.

Zheng looked at Teng, still tucked into his bunk. "What about you, Captain?"

Teng shrugged. "M. Ogawa is my charge. Until I'm

relieved, wherever she goes, I follow. Unless it becomes necessary to keep her out of somewhere she's not supposed to be." He wiped the news window closed. "I have one question, though. How do you propose we continue the investigation from here? We've got no equipment, and no access to our organizations, who are all busy with the coup. We don't even have infonet access."

Meiko opened a shared AR window and set it for whiteboard mode. "Why don't we start by listing the investigative threads." She put *Trace aircar* first, followed by *Aye Tuntun*. Zheng added *Kochi safe house* to the list. Noo contributed *Explosives source*. They spent a few more minutes brainstorming potential avenues of investigation.

Zheng circled the first three. "These seem like the most promising." She frowned. "Teng's right that our resources are limited."

Something niggled in the back of Meiko's brain, and she tried talking it through. She tapped the window and highlighted *Trace aircar*. "We're talking about tracking it after we crashed, right?"

Teng snorted. "Hardly makes sense to track it before, from the Constabulary garage," he said.

Noo waved him down. "I know that kind of look," she said. "You've got something."

"Maybe." Meiko chewed her bottom lip in frustration. Exhaustion clouded her thinking and made it hard to pull things from memory. "What's the best way to track a flying vehicle?"

"The transponder," Zheng said immediately. "But you said they'd disabled it."

"Or eyes on it," Noo said. "Visual surveillance, or

radar, or something like that. Those Constabulary cars aren't stealthed, are they Zheng?"

Zheng confirmed they weren't. "No one to see it in the backcountry, though," she said. "Though maybe from orbit..."

The memory surged forth in Meiko's head like a breaching leviathan. "That's it," she said, her voice tight with excitement. "Satellites. Scientific ones." She trawled through her djinn's storage until she found it. "I might have a way to tap into some."

Teng opened his mouth, then closed it. "I don't suppose you'd care to disclose how you came by that information?"

"My public career provides me with a great number of interesting contacts," she said, the evasion as smooth as if she'd practiced it. "Let me talk to the signals officer." She ducked into the corridor to make the call while Zheng fetched drinks and snacks from the wardroom.

The cruiser's communications chief was intrigued at the prospect of tapping into the Ileri landsat array and authorized the link on her own authority. She even coughed up a set of hand terminals for the others to which Meiko could download the data, along with access to the public media feeds *Amazonas* intercepted.

Meiko returned to the bunk room, activated the backdoor into the satellite network, and began pulling data. The team pounced on it.

It was Noo that spotted the anomaly in an infrared scan of the region a dozen kilometers up the main gorge. "What's this?" she asked, highlighting a cluster of hotspots, bigger than anything natural.

Zheng checked the map but found nothing. The four of them pored over the image. "It looks like a trekker's base camp," Teng said after a moment. "I went a few times in university. There're bivouacs like this scattered around the backcountry, some run by clubs, others by individuals or family concerns. People fly in and then spend a few days hiking, or exploring, or sometimes just spending time in camp, away from the infonet."

Meiko hunted through the available data and pulled the records from the last several days. "Here," Noo said. "There were only two cars there at sundown yesterday, but three this morning." She checked the most updated image. "Still three there now."

"You think they landed there? And are still hanging around?" Meiko asked, feeling rising excitement.

"It's certainly possible," Zheng said. "I'm certain our people hit some of them during the firefight. They might be holed up, recovering." She jabbed one finger at the image. "We haven't found any other sign of a vehicle entering the area during the storm or leaving afterwards."

"What can we do with this information?" Teng asked. "I don't expect the Kochi Constabulary can spare the resources to check it out. I've checked the feeds, and the fighting there is only a little less chaotic than the capitol."

Noo swept them all up by eye. "I propose we pay them a visit." She locked eyes with Meiko. "I think it's time we met with the captain."

Noo

CPC AMAZONAS,
ILERI ORBIT

CAPTAIN GUPTA MET them in the forward wardroom

as zer executive officer guarded the hatchway. It was a wide, low-ceilinged space, filled with tables and chairs bolted to the deck that became the floor when *Amazonas'* engines fired. The walls were painted with bright colors in a scheme Noo found a bit jarring; coral, bright yellow, and sky blue that shaded to green towards the deck predominated. She smelled coffee and realized the beverage dispensers were running. She snagged an insulated bulb and cradled its warmth in her left hand as she made her way clumsily to a seat.

Gupta was shorter than Noo, broad of hip and shoulder, dark skinned with a wide face, a hawk nose, and short dark hair shaved on the sides and a military buzz cut on top. "I understand you have information about the assassins you've been pursuing," ze said in a crisp voice that resonated throughout the room.

Meiko accessed the room's projector and threw up the imagery of the trekker camp. She told Gupta how they'd accessed the Ileri satellites and how they'd traced the probable trail of their quarry. Noo let the Commonwealth agent carry the message and studied the captain with care.

Gupta's face was hard to read, but Noo didn't like the body language she saw. The captain sat still, even hunched over slightly despite the lack of gravity. Ze listened attentively, zer eyes ranging across the images Meiko projected, but gave no sign of eagerness. Gupta seemed much more reserved than zer Ileri counterparts Noo had met. Maybe it was the detachment required of someone in independent command. She'd hoped for some sign of enthusiasm.

Meiko wrapped up her briefing and Noo caught

Gupta's glance at zer XO. "As evidence goes, this seems rather thin," ze said. Ze reached forward to zoom in the video imagery of the camp, focusing on the new aircar which had appeared since the previous sunset. "None of your information confirms that this aircar is the one you pursued."

"The absence of any other vehicles makes it highly probable," Zheng said.

Gupta shook zer head. "I concede the point, but that's not even circumstantial evidence. It's plausible, I grant you, but not proof."

Noo felt her heart sinking even as Meiko projected the tracking data from last night's flight that she'd captured on her djinn, and explained their deductions and reasoning, but Gupta refused to budge. "You're asking me to act on the basis of absence of evidence," ze said. "Not positive identification and tracking." Ze locked eyes with Zheng. "I'm familiar with Ileri law. Would this be sufficient evidence from which to launch an operation?"

We're losing this.

Heat flared in Noo's face as imminent despair gave way to anger. "Don't you give a damn about truth?" she snapped.

Everyone turned to look at her with looks ranging from surprise to horror, except for Gupta, whose cool regard didn't shift one iota. "I care a great deal about truth, M. Okereke," ze said in the same calm yet penetrating voice. "I have no problem passing this information onto the Ileri authorities, and to my diplomatic counterparts. They can investigate and obtain confirmation, or perhaps refutation, of your findings."

"You know they can't do that right now," Noo shot back. She'd accessed the media feeds while Meiko arranged this meeting. "The Army and Constabulary are trying to keep the rebels contained and get civilians out of the way. They can't spare the people to check this out."

"What do you propose that I do?" Gupta said.

Noo found herself on her feet, hands clenching the edge of the table before her, the bulb of coffee forgotten. She felt a sense of pressure in her body, something like the surge when an express transit car shot up one of the station's spokes. *Momentum. Have to keep the momentum.* "You sent a shuttle to pick us up," she said. "Let us take one down."

The XO spoke from the doorway. "As you just pointed out, M. Okereke, Ileri is in a state of conflict. Your air and orbital space are being actively contested."

"You swatted those rebel cutters that tried to intercept us," Noo said.

Gupta sighed. "Rescuing you was a humanitarian mission, easily justified to all sides, even the damned Saljuans," ze said. "But they've escalated things by insisting on pressing forward with the inspection."

Her mind raced and she scrambled to find an argument that might persuade the captain. "Assume for the moment that we're correct," Noo said. "That parties linked to the assassination of our minister and your consul, that blew up a manufactory and killed who knows how many civilians, who've probably killed whomever was in that camp when they arrived—that they're here, holed up in this remote location, away from any of the zones of conflict. Away from any civilians or other collateral damage. There's not likely to be a better chance to scoop them up."

She held up a hand to forestall whatever response Gupta intended, took a deep breath, and continued. "Say we're right, and this is them. Now, the referendum on Ileri joining the Commonwealth may not happen on schedule. But if the rebels don't win, it's going to happen at some point." Her eyes drilled into Gupta's and she strained to keep her voice from rising. "What's going to make people more inclined to vote to join: that when the chance came to snap up the murderers who killed so many came along, that a joint Commonwealth and Ileri team swooped in to take 'em? Or that in the hour of need, the Commonwealth let the killers remain at bay?"

One couldn't drop a pin in zero gravity, but if one could, it would have been heard. Noo's anger was still there, burning in her chest, but she'd made a good case, a damned good case, and she knew it, and she felt a spark of hope.

Captain Gupta exchanged glances with zer XO. "You make a persuasive argument, M. Okereke." Then ze shook zer head and Noo's hope crashed and shattered. "But I can't risk my people on such thin evidence, even with such a potential payoff."

"Then don't," Meiko said. "Let us go by ourselves."

Gupta cocked zer head at Meiko. "What do you mean?"

"As M. Okereke pointed out, we constitute a duly authorized joint investigative team, with both Ileri and the Commonwealth represented." She gestured at the team in their scattered seats. "Let us use the shuttle. The drop and return can be pre-programmed. The five of us can land, apprehend the suspects, and then return with them to orbit."

"Five?" Gupta asked, puzzled. "There's only four of you."

Noo spoke up. "Fari will insist on coming with us."

"I don't think M. Tahir is fit for that kind of operation," the XO said.

"Loan us a combat exoskeleton," Zheng said. "I've seen troopers wounded far more severely use them."

"Hm." Gupta's eyes swept Meiko up and down. "And if the assassins are there? I've read your report. They're heavily armed."

Zheng cleared her throat. "I have an idea about that," she said, and explained her idea.

At last, Gupta nodded to the XO. "All right. In for a kilo, in for a ton. Might as well do this properly if it's to be done at all." Ze rose, and everyone still seated rose as well. "Number One, set them up with what they need. I'll be in the CIC plotting the drop window. This may be a fool's errand, but even fools can be right sometimes."

CHAPTER TWENTY-SEVEN

IMOKE

AIRPLANT 2, ILERI STATION,
FORWARD RING

IT WAS THE quiet that made Daniel Imoke's skin crawl.

No matter what shift, no matter what part of the station one was in, you could *always* hear other people bustling about on Ileri Station. Music was always in the background, solarfunk or fēiwǔ or Second Weave jazz on speakers; sometimes just a busker with a guitar or drums. Conversations between people, friendly or heated or simply the neutral acts of buying and selling. The whir of electric vans zipping down the alleys. The shuffle of feet on the grass or tiles, sandaled or shoed or booted, the rustle of neosilk or the swish of fabber-made linen. People moving, people doing business, people living their lives.

It wasn't silent, really, where he crouched a block away from the airplant's entrance, but it was still too quiet for his nerves. Imoke heard the people around him, a mixed squad of constables and troopers, as they checked their equipment and cracked the sort of bad jokes one told at these moments. But the civilians had been carefully, quietly evacuated to shelters blocks away, leaving the area around the airplant quiet as a grave.

Something else was missing: bots. Not entirely, of course; some bots performed basic maintenance and cleaning tasks, picked up refuse, inspected seals on the great quartz-crystal windows that let reflected sunlight in, or sampled the air to check for anomalous chemical traces. Okafor told him that life support and many infrastructure systems ran on a separate hardened network that seemed to be operational even while the primary infonet was down. When he asked why they couldn't piggyback Constabulary traffic on that net she responded with a load of jargon about special-use protocols and air gaps and a dozen other terms he didn't follow. 'Incompatible systems' seemed the heart of it, though.

At least the rebels couldn't use it against them. He hoped.

"All teams ready, Inspector," said the sergeant assigned as his deputy. It took him a moment to realize that 'Inspector' meant himself. Toiwa had elevated him a few hours earlier, just before handing him command of one-third of the force now set to retake the airplant. Another Constabulary officer led a second assault team, while an Army lieutenant led the third, and commanded the entire ad hoc unit.

"Very good, Sergeant." He toggled his squad's status to green and hoped the portable network repeaters worked as advertised.

"All set, boss?" the sergeant asked. His eyes ran over Imoke's equipment, one last visual check. 'Check your gear, check your partner's gear', was a mantra drilled into every constable from the first weeks of training.

Imoke flashed the hand sign for *ready*. He was as prepared as it was possible to be. He'd even broken down and sent Noo a message, though who knew when she'd receive it. Word of her planetary escapades and dramatic rescue had filtered through amidst the other reports, so he'd chased his temporary roommate out of the tiny cubby they shared in headquarters, taken a deep breath, and composed a message to the person who meant most to him in the world. Because that's the sort of thing you did when you got ready to launch a frontal assault on a fortified position.

The last squad's indicator flipped green. Imoke brought his shotgun up to port carry position. Ahead of him, his four Army troopers, hulking forms in their heavy body armor, snapped down their visors and hefted their carbines. Behind him, the rest of his team did the same.

The Go indicator lit and he heard the distinctive *chuff* of a pneumatic grenade launcher from their tiny fire support element atop a three-story apartment building across the street. The laser-guided projectile burst squarely in front of the airplant's entrance and dense gray smoke billowed forth. Without prompting, the soldiers at the head of his column took off at a dead sprint, and he followed.

Keeping pace with the soldiers turned out to be harder than he'd expected. He was fit, still put in his time on the football pitch when he could, and ran in the park regularly. But running in a pair of shorts and a jersey, in proper shoes, was one thing; running with fifteen kilos of body armor, weapons, and gear, with a tactical visor over one's face, was quite another. Still, only two of his people managed to pass him before they reached the far side of the street and stacked up beside the entry.

The airplant, one of three in the ring, rose above them, a cylinder thirty meters wide and sixty tall. Unlike the majority of the station's structures, its walls were substantial, nearly a meter thick here at the base. There were two entrances at ground level, on opposite sides of the cylinder. Imoke's team had this entrance, while the Army lieutenant took the other. Surya's team remained in reserve.

Imoke's troopers wasted no time in slapping cutting tape around the door frame. One soldier snapped the igniter and Imoke's visor briefly polarized as the entire rectangle flared with eye-searing brilliance. He felt the quick wash of heat and the harsh smell of burnt metal flooded his nostrils. That reminded him to pull up his collar and fix the chemical seal. It trapped the scent in, but was far better that than succumbing to any chemical surprises the rebels might have for them.

The door fell outward and one of the soldiers lobbed in a flash-bang. He must have set it to go off on contact because it burst two seconds after he'd thrown it. The soldiers rushed through in the explosion's wake and Imoke followed, his officers behind him.

A sharp bang from the far side announced the other team's entry. Weapons and sensors swept across the room, a large workshop occupying a good third of the tower's base. He was relieved to see that its dimensions matched the blueprints he'd been given. He toggled a wireframe view of the layout and set his wayfinder to mark the path to the stairs. Imoke detached two constables, one carrying their portable network repeater, to remain by the entrance, and signaled the soldier on point to lead them out on their prearranged path. They cleared the ground floor and found it unoccupied. Seconds later they made contact with the second team.

"Nothing so far," he told the infantry officer, who reported the same. The reserve squad moved in to secure the ground floor. Imoke collected his door guards and flashed the hand sign for *up* to the soldier on point, while the Army squad took the stairs down to the sub-levels.

After passing through chambers filled with gleaming tanks, mechanical valves, and a truly astonishing variety of gauges, the team found themselves at the bottom of a large open space, twenty meters from floor to ceiling according to his rangefinder. A dull gray column, five meters wide, rose through the middle of the chamber. A strong, steady current of air pushed outward from the center towards the outer walls, which in this part of the tower consisted of engineered fullerene mesh designed to trap particulates. So the overlay claimed, at any rate. A wide ramp spiraled around the circumference of the chamber leading to the intake pumps above. Imoke signaled to his scouts to lead the way up the ramp.

The rebels made their move.

Automatic fire lashed out from the top of the ramp. The rebel gunner ignored the well-armored troopers in front, instead pouring rounds into the constables in the middle of the column. Even with their ballistic ceramic inserts, Constabulary tactical armor couldn't stop the high-powered projectiles. Rounds punched through the vests of two officers who went down screaming. Imoke dropped prone as the line of tracers roamed across the space where his column had been.

His constables dropped in place, some scattering before hitting the deck, and began to return fire. The soldiers instead charged up the ramp, spraying suppressive fire from their autorifles. "Use the grenade launcher!" the fire team leader called as the hidden gunner switched targets, turning their fire onto the onrushing troopers.

"Wei's down!" came the call. Imoke looked over his shoulder and saw Wei's body a few meters behind him, the precious launcher a meter beyond her outstretched hand.

"On it." He flipped his shotgun's safety on, and crawled on hands and knees over to Wei, grabbed the launcher and snatched the bandolier from her body. He didn't need the status display to tell him she was dead; she'd taken three rounds to the torso and one to the head. There was blood, so much blood, like he'd never seen except for the charnel house inside the Second Landing Social Club, and bile rose his throat. Above him, the fire from the troopers' rifles quieted and he had a fleeting hope that they'd silenced the opposition, but that hope was dashed as the rebels' heavy weapon opened up again.

Something large and dark and not at all human-shaped fell past him as he raised the grenade launcher. His djinn synched with the weapon and he checked the load: an antipersonnel flechette round. He came to his knees and raised the launcher, sighting in on whatever had dropped from the ceiling. His heart raced and he fought to steady his hands as his aiming reticle tracked across his target.

Fuck, it's a combat bot. It was two meters tall and as many wide when one took the full breadth of its six insectile legs into account. The armored central carapace was much smaller but sported two turrets. Tongues of fire leapt forth as the bot turned its weapons onto Imoke's people.

"Focus on the enemy bot!" he called across the all-hands channel. No need for radio discipline now; the enemy knew exactly where they were. He fired the antipersonnel round at the bot, knowing the flechettes were virtually useless against the armor but hoping for a lucky hit anyway. His left hand swept along the bandolier in vain; they'd carried no explosives into the airplant for fear of damaging the infrastructure. He grabbed a ballistic rubber riot-control round and loaded it. "Fall back to the second level," he ordered. "Grab the wounded and pull back!"

He was sighting on one of the bot's legs, hoping to knock it off balance, when something lifted him and threw him into the central column.

Toiwa

Constabulary Command Post, Ileri Station, Forward Ring

Toiwa heard the rebel machine gun open up, the sharp rattle distinct even from two blocks away. Her stomach fell with the knowledge that her people were in deep trouble.

The personal feeds from the assault team became virtually impossible to follow as the soldiers and police scrambled to respond to the onslaught. Both Imoke's team on the upper floors and the Army-heavy team sent to clear the lower levels were caught in a devastating ambush.

"Sweet Mother, that's power armor," someone said. Toiwa glanced over to see the Army sergeant, wounded during the midnight coup but ambulatory enough to run overwatch for her comrades. The expression of horror on the woman's face matched the yawning pit that suddenly opened in Toiwa's gut.

"Combat bots engaging the top team," Shariff said. "Dammit, Daniel, get out of there."

"Cut the chatter!" Toiwa snapped. "Surya, get your people up to support Imoke's team. Sergeant Mohammed!" The Army sergeant turned to her. "What have we got that can take out the power armor and the bots?"

"Not much, ma'am," came the reply. "The fire support team has the only armor-piercing ammunition."

"Get them in the fight *now*," she ordered. The sergeant relayed commands as Toiwa scanned the status windows. So many red icons, so quickly...

She heard Valverdes call her name and turned to see zer at the doorway. Pericles Loh stood beside zer, hands clasped before him, a somber expression on his face. "Ma'am, Mr. Loh was quite insistent."

She locked eyes with Loh. *He knew what we'd run into. He knew it was more than we could handle.* She was certain of it, knew it in her bones. Anger and frustration welled up, but she took a deep breath and shunted them inside. "You have something to say, Loh?"

"I can help," he said. He held her gaze. There was nothing gloating or triumphant about his tone, or his expression. He affected the role of supplicant, even as he held people's lives—*her people's lives,* the people who'd placed their trust in her, the people who were now bleeding and dying because she'd refused to make a deal with the devil.

And if we can't even take a single airplant without these kinds of casualties because the rebels are armed to the teeth, how can we take back the station?

She knew she couldn't.

This was the choice, then: capitulate to Miguna and let him remake her world; spill gallons of blood and kill dozens, if not hundreds, in a doomed attempt to take it with the resources she had; or climb into bed with the biggest criminal on the station, if not in the system.

The hook was in. She knew it. Loh knew it. They both knew what she'd choose. But she'd be damned if he'd reel her in without a fight.

"Can you save my people in the airplant?" Her face was hot, her chest felt tight. The gunfire rattled on, punctuated now by the thumps of grenade launchers.

"I can," Loh said. "My people can hit the sub-levels from the maintenance passages."

Waving him forward into the room was the hardest thing she'd ever done. "I won't forgive violent crimes," she said. "No murders, no assaults, no sexual violence of any kind."

Loh moved to stand before her. Fathya Shariff came up to stand at her left. "It's the right decision," Shariff said.

Loh's eyes never left hers. "We can agree to that," he said.

"And any evidence of those kinds of crimes we might uncover is outside the scope of immunity," Toiwa said.

Her throat was tight and she swallowed to try and loosen it. She heard, as if from a great distance, her staff directing reinforcements to aid her beleaguered forces, the breathless calls for focus fire on one of the enemy bots, the curses as the enemy troops relentlessly ground forward.

Loh hesitated, then nodded. "We accept that as well. Do you have any other stipulations?"

She leaned forward until they were practically close enough to kiss. "You'll give me *everything* you know about the rebels, and you'll do it immediately after we rescue my people, and if you hold *anything* back, I'll cut your balls off myself and wear them as earrings," she hissed.

That seemed to catch him by surprise. Loh's eyes widened and he actually shuffled a half-step back. He started to say something, then seemed to think the better of it. At last he nodded. "Message received, Governor."

"It had better be." She turned to Valverdes and Shariff. "Inspector, M. Shariff, I ask you to witness my offer of conditional amnesty to M. Loh and associates he will designate, in exchange for the *complete and total* cooperation of he and his associates in suppressing the rebellion."

The two women gave their affirmations for the record. Loh extended his hand and she took it.

He reached his left to his chest and tapped twice. "Myra, it's done. Execute." The floor shook, and she heard a series of muffled thumps. "Shaped charges to breach the sub-level walls," Loh said. "My people are going in."

She felt detached from her body, moving as if controlled

by some distant puppeteer as she turned back to the displays. She forced herself to witness the results of her mistakes and prayed this wasn't another.

Is this the first step to becoming like Ketti?

She looked again at the swath of red icons as Loh ordered his people, who were poised in even deeper sublevels than the rebels, into the fray. If she had to pay that price so those beneath her didn't, it would be worth it.

It would have to be.

CHAPTER TWENTY-EIGHT

Noo

DROP SHUTTLE AMAZONAS BANDEIRA,
ILERI ORBIT

THE SHUTTLE BUCKED as it pierced the upper reaches of
Ileri's atmosphere. Noo clutched the airsickness bag in
her lap and kept her eyes closed. That didn't banish the
growing roar as a ball of plasma enveloped their ride.

She'd done this twice in four days, which was two
times too many.

To keep her mind off the terror, she replayed Daniel's
message once again. The Commonwealth signals officer
had relayed it to her right before they boarded the
shuttle, and she'd watched it twice already as the shuttle
detached from *Amazonas* and made its initial de-orbiting
burn.

He looked so serious, for all that he tried to keep his
voice casual as he relayed news of her family. Her relief
that those she loved most on the station were safe was

tempered by the situation report Gupta shared with them about just how much of Ileri Station was in rebel hands. Nevertheless, she took comfort knowing that for now, at least, they were free and unharmed.

And then came the part where he paused and licked his lips before continuing. "I don't know how to say this sweetly. You know I'm not that sort of man, not smooth in that way. So, I'll just say it. We've known each other a long time, loved each other a long time." He paused again. "Yes, love. I know sometimes it's been hard, and our corners rub up against each other and we fight, and we pull away because staying close hurts too much. But I find myself thinking about what matters to me the most. And what matters most is that I want to spend the rest of my life with you, however we can make that work." He smiled, and it touched his eyes, and once again she felt an ache in her chest. "And I'm sorry it took this for me to see it. I promise to try and be less dense in the future. Whether you'll have me or not, Noo Okereke. Stay safe if you can, but if you can't, remember what I always tell the rookies."

"Do it fast, do it dirty, and do it first," she murmured along with him, and closed the message window.

She sensed Meiko's eyes on her and turned her head to look at the other woman. "What?"

"If that was a prayer, well, we could certainly use whatever benevolence the universe has to spare," Meiko said.

"Not exactly," Noo said, and repeated Daniel's aphorism aloud.

Meiko chuckled. "I like it," she said. She looked around the cabin. "It's the best way to win a fight."

"Fair fights are for suckers," Noo agreed.

Nobody shot at them as they plummeted ground-ward, Saljuans, rebels, or anyone else for that matter. The shuttle passed through the fiery-brick-of-death phase of entry without incident and Noo considered her prayers well answered.

They began the long, banking turn that would bring them to their landing zone. Meiko sat on Noo's right, seemingly relaxed. She kept her helmet visor clear and Noo watched the other woman's eyes as they danced through whatever feeds or private windows she had called up. Meiko saw her watching and turned to flash Noo a grin. "You're becoming a pro at this," she told Noo. "And at least this time, we *mean* to be landing somewhere that people are going to be shooting at us."

Noo laughed at that despite her discomfort. "Our track record for travel is pretty bad, isn't it? The riot, the botched raid, the crash, the cutters on the way up, and now this?"

Meiko pointed to the space to Noo's left. "This time, we're coming properly equipped," she said.

Noo twisted her head that way and eyed Zheng. "For a change," she conceded.

She hoped Zheng's idea gave them the edge they needed. "I have to admit, there have been times I've wished I could wear a full rig on police duty," she said when they made the plan. She wore such a rig now: one of *Amazonas'* spare suits of powered combat armor, its chameleon coating hastily programmed with Ileri Constabulary colors.

Zheng didn't respond to their quips. "Is she sleeping?" Noo asked incredulously.

"I expect so," Meiko said. "It's a soldier thing. They can sleep any time they're not moving for more than a few minutes. I guess she's reverted."

"Wish I could do that," Noo said.

Fari stood braced in the cradle next to Zheng's, though her rig was one of the combat exoskeletons, rather than full power armor. The rest of them had settled for hard-shelled ballistic torso armor and padded, half-armored trousers along with helmets, all likewise borrowed from *Amazonas'* stores. Fortunately, one of the Commonwealth troops was close enough to her size that the set Noo wore didn't quite feel like she was wearing a sausage casing.

At least she carried her own guns. Zheng had her suit's built-in weapons, so she'd loaned her personal arms to Meiko, who bore a goober gun crowd-control launcher along with the pistols.

"Do you know how to use that?" Noo asked.

"I fired one on a virtual range once," Meiko replied, which didn't exactly fill Noo with confidence.

The mission timer flashed red, and the ship's system announced they were three minutes from touchdown. Zheng woke up and locked her arms into landing position. At two minutes out, the cabin lights switched to red. Noo fastened her face mask into place with hands that were suddenly steady and sure, the motion similar to what she'd practiced in numerous emergency drills at home on the station. She felt the calm of what Fari called her 'mission mind' settle upon her, cloaking her in cold purpose.

With less than thirty seconds to touchdown the autopilot slammed on the thrust reversers, throwing

Noo against her safety harness. It wasn't as painful as she expected, the force distributed across her body by the armor. Once again, the smart headrest clamped down automatically on the sides of her helmet, keeping her head from snapping forward. The lights cut out, the assault doors slammed open, and suddenly they were part of the backcountry night sky. Her audio implants kicked in to muffle the roar of the jets, filtering them out, leaving the rushing wind of their passage. It seemed like all the air in the world was blowing through the doors, making the cloth of her trousers ripple.

The headrest released its grip on her helmet and Noo looked out to get her bearings. Her borrowed visor shifted to night vision mode and she could make out the shapes of the cabins in the gray-green false color images.

The shuttle settled down onto the open space between the buildings and the river with a thump and she hit her harness' quick release. Pulling herself upright she saw Zheng spring forward like something from a nature vid, a gazelle perhaps, as the lieutenant launched herself out the door the moment the landing gear touched ground. A trio of airborne security bots whizzed past Noo to establish a perimeter around the shuttle. She trotted out onto the wing, Meiko right behind her, as the solider-turned-policeman bounded towards the buildings.

The largest didn't look like Noo's idea of a cabin, though she supposed it might pass for a 'lodge'. It was two stories tall, with single-story wings to the right and left of the main structure. The infrared scans showed it to be the only occupied building in the camp, so for now they ignored the others.

"Rio Mizwar and associates, you are hereby

apprehended under the Covenants of the Ileri Republic!" Zheng called out on her armor's external speakers.

Her words were still booming off the building's front as she blew the front door open with a breaching rocket fired on the run.

Noo ducked instinctively at the blast, even though she'd expected it, which allowed Meiko to surge past her with the goober gun. Fari crunched along in her exoskeletons, arm-mounted mini-guns already powered up. Noo cursed, waved off Teng's offer of assistance, and trotted behind her comrades.

The left-wing door crashed open. Noo's pistol was in her hand and she snapped off two rounds without conscious thought, the weapon bucking against her gloved palm. One round hit the door frame and *spanged* away. Someone inside fired back but she couldn't tell who they were shooting at. An autorifle cut loose from inside the main door, answered by the stuttering *rrrrrriiiippppp* of Zheng's mini-gun. Zheng slowed down to a brisk walk as she crossed the threshold, bullets ricocheting off her armor.

A defender fired again from the left door and she saw Meiko spin on one heel. Noo feared her partner had been hit, but instead Meiko planted her left foot, raised the goober gun to her shoulder, and fired a round into the doorway. The grenade burst on contact and then boiling foam filled the entry way, hardening even as Noo jogged up to the smoking ruin of the front door. She saw Teng lope around to cover the building's rear while Fari held position between the lodge and their shuttle, ready to offer fire support.

Once inside the smoldering doorway, they found

themselves in a large foyer with stairs rising to the second floor, from where they heard Zheng's amplified voice calling again for surrender. A fusillade of shots answered her demand. A body lay next to the stairs in a spreading pool of blood. Splotches of blood and bullet holes marked the wall. Meiko slung her goober gun and they passed the stairs, pistols drawn, and entered a large room furnished with couches, chairs, and a massive stone structure Noo realized was for burning wood.

Since they'd taken fire from the left side of the house, they pivoted that direction from the great room, finding two doors. "Get the back door, I've got the front," Meiko said, as she holstered her pistol and unslung her goober gun. Noo ran to take up position, feet thudding on the floor. She heard the *thonk* and *pop* behind her, and more gunfire from upstairs.

Noo studied the door in front of her, wondering how she could yank it open without the benefit of power armor, or at least a combat exoskeleton, as Meiko sauntered up next to her. "Try the handle," Meiko said, stunner in her left hand, pistol in her right. Noo licked her lips, nodded, and grabbed the handle. She twisted it and was surprised to find that it was, indeed, unlocked. With a jerk, she pulled it open and ducked inside.

And found herself looking at her quarry, who looked like he'd been about to push the door open himself.

Mizwar's eyes widened in surprise, but he still managed to step back, swung his rifle to bear, and fired from the hip as she desperately twisted away.

The three-round burst slammed into Noo's chest and belly, but the Commonwealth hard-shell armor was good kit; angled as she was, his bullets couldn't penetrate.

Even so, she staggered with the impact as the air was driven out of her lungs. But her djinn marked her target and she brought her pistol in line and fired, once.

Mizwar screamed as the bullet smashed his right hand, turning it to a bloody ruin. The rifle clattered to the floor as blood splashed across the wall and onto her visor. Noo careened to her left and crashed into the wall. It took everything she had not to double over and rip off her face mask as her body insisted that she ought to. Mizar dropped to his knees, his right wrist cradled in his left hand, as she put her pistol against the top of his head.

Her vision narrowed, like she was looking through a tube. Had she been hit after all? Was she dying, as Saed had, at this man's hands?

It would be so easy. Just one pull of the trigger.

Meiko reached forward and gently pushed Noo's gun up and away from Mizwar's head, then neatly kicked the rifle down the hall, firmly out of reach, and holstered her pistols.

When Noo could stand upright again she saw Meiko had Mizwar on the floor, face down, as she knelt on his back and yanked a plastic restraint band tight around his wrists. They ignored his cry of pain.

"Are you all right?" Meiko asked, after glancing at Noo's armor.

"Yeah," Noo said in the sudden quiet. The shooting had stopped upstairs.

"Would you like to do the honors?" Meiko said. "I understand there's proper form to be observed."

"There is, and I will." She set her weapon to safe, holstered it, and then slumped down against the wall. She braced herself with a weary arm and leaned over to look into Mizwar's face.

"You're clipped, you bastard."

MEIKO

ILERI BACKCOUNTRY

MEIKO FINISHED RESTRAINING her prisoner and eyed her partner up and down. "Are you sure you're all right?" she asked.

"Got the wind knocked out of me, that's all," Noo said. "I'll have some fucking spectacular bruises and I feel like I've been hit by a damned car, but I've been worse."

"Lucky he didn't go for a headshot," Meiko said. That brought a wheezing laugh from their prisoner.

They both stared at him. "Do you have something to say?" Meiko asked.

"Not really," he said. His voice was deep but ragged with suppressed pain. She groped at her harness and found the first aid kit. She gave him a carefully considered half-dose of painkiller. Not that Mizwar's comfort was her true concern, but at some point, she'd have to answer officially for his treatment. If the sedative lowered inhibitions and made him less resistant to interrogation, well, that was a side benefit.

She glanced up at Noo from where she squatted beside their quarry. "I believe there's a mandated warning about his rights?"

"Yeah," Noo said, and pulled herself a little straighter from where she slumped against the wall. She recited the caution. "You are hereby apprehended under the

Covenants of the Ileri Republic. You may choose to remain silent, but failure to disclose information you later rely on in court will be viewed with prejudice. Anything you do say can and will be considered as evidence in any and all proceedings. You have the right to a court-appointed advocate, and an interpreter if you require one. Do you understand these rights as they have been explained to you?"

"You're not police," Mizwar said, and Meiko repressed a sudden urge to kick him.

"I'm properly deputized," Noo said, "and my partner is providing mutual aid sanctioned by both our governments. It was a constable who blew in your door, though, so it's all nice and legal. Now, do you understand these rights as they have been explained to you?"

"I do," he said. Meiko felt the tension in her shoulders ease a little bit. She rose and offered Noo a hand up, and then the two of them yanked Mizwar to his feet. She then keyed the comm net. "We've got him. Minor wound but otherwise intact."

"What about my people?" Mizwar asked through teeth still clenched against the pain.

"Let's find out," Meiko said. "One dead for sure."

Zheng asked for assistance with two prisoners and Teng clomped in, since Fari's exoskeleton wouldn't fit through the doorway even after the rocket-based remodeling. Teng grinned as he recognized Mizwar, flashed them the hand sign for *mission complete,* and headed up the stairs.

They hauled Mizwar past the body of his fallen teammate and out under the wide-open sky. Fari clomped over, the arms of her exoskeleton raised high. She stared at Mizwar, and Meiko could see her hands flex. "You give him the caution already?" Noo affirmed that she had. "Pity," Fari said, and stomped away to stand near the shuttle.

The voice of *Amaonzas'* signal officer on their comm net came as a surprise. "Ogawa. You need to get your people moving. The orbital situation is evolving rapidly."

"What's going on?" she said as Zheng and Teng appeared in the doorway with the survivors of Mizwar's team.

Suddenly, the night sky turned to day.

They stared, all of them, as a new sun appeared, its brilliant white light casting harsh, sharp-edged shadows. It proved ephemeral, though, and over the course of a minute it faded away to nothing.

"What in the name of the Mother was that?" Noo asked.

"Someone just used a nuclear weapon in orbit," Zheng said.

"No," said Mizwar, and there was a note of triumph in his voice. Meiko saw with shock the most beatific expression on his face she'd ever come across. "True purification."

"What do you mean by that?" Meiko asked, her own voice shaking. Mizwar didn't respond; he simply stood, his face turned skyward, his face almost rapturous. She keyed the net to call *Amazonas* but there was no response. "Shit. I've lost contact with topside."

They gathered by the shuttle. Zheng carried one of Mizwar's companions, wounded during the firefight, to the triage bay. Teng, the closest thing they had to a trained medic, fired up the shuttle's expert system and did his best to stabilize the patient while Meiko and the others secured Mizwar and his unwounded compatriot in acceleration couches. Zheng grabbed two body bags and returned to the house for the last casualties.

"If it wasn't a nuke, what was it?" Fari asked.

"The only other weapon I know of with that kind of effect would be an antimatter conversion bomb," Meiko said. Noo and Fari stared at her. "It seems the Saljuans brought some along. I expect they'll claim to have found forbidden Exile technology somewhere in orbit."

"Do you think that's what *Amazonas* was trying to warn us about?" Noo asked as she finished securing Mizwar to his couch.

"Maybe. Or a conventional space battle might be starting up and they had to maneuver. Or both things. I'll see if I can raise the ship." Meiko made her way to the pilot's compartment and waved her djinn to open the hatch. She'd ridden in the copilot's seat of shuttles before, but never a military craft like this. Surprisingly, though, the shuttle's controls responded to her djinn, and her incoming message indicator flashed.

She opened the message and discovered it was from Captain Gupta. The captain had zer combat suit on, but zer helmet off, indicating action topside was imminent. "Ogawa. The situation is deteriorating rapidly. The Saljuans have announced they've found signs of Exile-grade nanoware being manufactured in orbit and are broadcasting their findings. I'll append the packet to this message. They're going to destroy the facility with an antimatter weapon." Gupta's eyes flicked to another window and ze spat out a curse Meiko's grandmother once used. "It looks like the rebel forces are moving to engage. We're going to have to change orbits or we'll get caught up in that mess. The pilot's sending you two course packages for the autopilot. One will take you to New Abuja. The other is for Ileri Station. I authorize you to exercise your own judgement and pick whichever destination best allows you to complete your mission. Gupta out."

Meiko sat back in the pilot's couch and closed her eyes. Weariness mixed with dread overtook her. Both the Commonwealth and the Star Republic had possessed antimatter weapons for many decades, but they'd never been used before. As far as she knew, anyway.

The veil is torn now. There's no going back.

Noo awkwardly clambered into the copilot's couch. "Have you reached anyone yet?"

"Kind of." Meiko forwarded the message to the rest of the team. No one spoke as they digested the news.

She heard Zheng clomping about as she stepped to the door and looked up. "I can see flashes of light in the sky," she reported. "I think they're going at it up there in orbit."

"So where do we go?" Meiko asked. "New Abuja, or the station?"

"Is there any question?" Noo said, gently. She laid her hand on Meiko's arm. "Take us home."

CHAPTER TWENTY-NINE

ANDINI

SDV IWAN GOLESLAW,
ILERI ORBIT

ANDINI PEERED CLOSELY into the main tactical display tank, her tactician's mind racing the expert systems, busy analyzing any changes in Ileri space following the destruction of the orbital manufactory. It made a great excuse to not have to look at Dinata's smug face; the minister had been practically euphoric when the inspection teams reported they'd positively verified a store of nanoware containing a Unity Plague variant. Andini and her tactical officer had unlocked the special ordnance store under Dinata's beatific gaze. The expression on Dinata's face as they watched the imagery relayed by recon probe, before radiation fried the optical pickups... Andini thought she'd have nightmares about that for weeks. Not that she didn't believe in their mission, or in the necessity of preventing Unity from appearing in the Exile Cluster; far from it.

But Dinata's low moan as matter's annihilation washed across the screen had sounded positively *orgasmic*. Andini realized that the woman took pleasure in destruction. The minister was part of that faction driving the Star Republic towards not just ever more extreme enforcement of the Accords, but to the imposition of Saljuan technology-constraint policies in unaffiliated systems. Her party had pushed for the annexation of Indra, which had been easy, and of Para, where insurgents still resisted the annexation, twenty years later. "We must maintain the safety of the Cluster!" Dinata had thundered during one of their early mission briefings. Andini had no doubt the minister would direct her to use the special ordinance against Ileri itself if she felt necessary, because to one of the alat pembersih, the purifiers, there was only one way to guarantee that safety.

Andini swallowed anxiously, wondering how she'd respond to that order if it came. The question no longer seemed to be purely hypothetical.

She noticed the change in the orbital situation almost the same instant the tactical expert system did. "Eyes, confirm vector change and energy profile of target cluster London Kilo four-five-seven," she ordered.

"Don't let them concern you, Captain." Dinata's voice rolled languorously. "They have seen our power and won't dare challenge us now."

If Andini had believed that was true, Eyes' response dashed that hope. "Vector change confirmed, Captain. They're no longer maneuvering to intercept that formation of loyalist cutters burning in from the outer-system station. They're bearing for us instead. Radiators are still deployed."

Her belly felt tight. "Still the same composition?"

"Confirmed. One *Solewa*-class cruiser, three *Protagonist*-class frigates, and six cutters—stand by. Update, formation is pulling in their radiators."

So much for not daring to challenge us. "Time to engagement envelope?"

"They'll be in our missile range in thirty-seven minutes, fifty-six seconds. Best estimate is thirty-three minutes, forty-two seconds for us to be in their missile envelope."

Andini grasped the handrail that ran around the command dais and pulled herself upright. "Fist, launch weapons bus waves one and two, set for defensive fire. Ears, record the following for broadcast." She took a deep breath, exhaled slowly, then took another breath. "This is Captain Andini commanding the SDV *Iwan Goleslaw* to all vessels in Ileri space. Our sensors indicate Ileri warships maneuvering with apparent hostile intent against my vessel. Any attempt to interfere with my vessel or our mission will be met with lethal force. Any attack on the *Iwan Goleslaw* will be met with lethal force. There will be no warning shots. Andini out."

As she finished speaking, she felt the vibration and fancied she could hear the distant clatter and rumble of the weapons busses being launched, each basically a miniature automated warship packed full of missiles, coil guns, or laser pods.

Dinata rose to stand beside the captain, her face now a mask of confused fury. *"They dare?"* she hissed.

Her belly still felt tight, but Andini reached for the calm of routine. Her vessel was already at Condition One, battle-ready but for pulling in her radiators so they wouldn't be shot away in the coming fight. Time to deal with that. "Hands, keep the radiators deployed for"—she checked the countdown until the rebel vessels would be in range of her weapons—"fifteen minutes." It would take seven minutes to tuck the radiators back within *Iwan Goleslaw's* armored hull. Dinata still raged beside her, pounding on the handrail, but Andini ignored her for the moment. "Ears, message for all crew." She paused until the communications officer signaled the channel was ready. "Attention, my children," using the traditional mode of address from captain to crew. "Rogue elements of the Ileri forces appear to be set on engaging us. We shall meet them, and if they persist on their foolish course, I have no doubt we shall prevail. The eyes of our people are upon us all. We bear the torch."

Across the CIC, and across the ship, *Iwan Goleslaw's* crew murmured, or spoke, or shouted the response. "We hold it high!"

She nodded at Ears, who cut the signal, before she turned to face Dinata, who still ranted. "Minister, it's time for you to relocate to auxiliary control," she said, as calmly as she could manage.

Dinata spun to face her, fists clenched. "You must chastise these people, Captain. They have violated the Accords, brought the taint of Lost Earth back from the brink!"

Andini chose her words with care. "With respect, Minister, we cannot say for certain that the Ileri government is involved in this." She gestured at the display, which now showed a second rebel formation maneuvering to engage them. "We do not yet have evidence of anyone's involvement besides the owners of the manufactory, which appears to be a legitimate Ileri business."

Dinata snorted. "Legitimate is hardly the word for those who traffic in proscribed technology. And besides, their ships are attacking us."

"I apologize, I worded that poorly." Andini shrugged. "But we don't yet have evidence of any link between the rebel faction those ships belong to and the nanoware."

"Why else would they react like this?"

"Perhaps," Andini said carefully, "a political faction notorious for their xenophobic worldview objected to the use of an antimatter bomb within their system." She squared her shoulders. "And now, I really must insist you follow protocol and relocate to aux control."

Dinata allowed herself to be escorted off by the executive officer, whose unfortunate mission would be to babysit the minister during the course of the engagement. Andini took advantage of the brief respite to use the head before settling in to begin the largest space battle since the end of the Three-Planet War between Goa and Shenzen two decades past.

By the time she returned from the head, the crew had just about finished securing the radiators. She strapped herself into her command couch and brought up her personal tactical plot. A second rebel force had changed vector to engage her ship. The sum of both rebel battle groups converging would be a challenging fight even for a SDV. But if she could defeat them in detail... Seizing the initiative was called for. "We're not going to just sit here," she said over the CIC net. "Fist, you and Legs give me a plot that closes with the first formation and lets us give them a proper paddling before that second squadron gets in range."

A bright orange line appeared, knifing right through the middle of the first rebel squadron. "Already plotted, Captain, and Chen gets to do my laundry for a week," 'Fist', her tactical officer, said.

"Chen, what course did you think I'd pick?"

A purple trace leading away from both squadrons joined the display. "I thought you'd draw them into a running duel, Captain. Let them waste their misses against our point defense," Chen, the maneuver officer— 'Legs'—said.

"There's a lot more of them than there are of us, Chen, and the closest depot to resupply our PDCs is eight weeks a-space travel away." She thumbed the authorization. "Execute."

Iwan Goleslaw rotated through two axes until its nose aligned with the new course while the acceleration warning blared. Then the main engines kicked into life, and the ship slammed forward from free fall to three and a half gs, its surrounding halo of weapon busses keeping pace like ducklings following their mother. The rebel formation shifted, adopting a computer-calculated, semi-chaotic dance as the ships executed the corkscrew-spiraling courses that made their exact positions more uncertain. Andini's ship came at them like a knight atop a destrier riding into a mass of footmen.

When the engagement timer reached zero, she thumbed the authorization tab again. "Weapons free," she ordered, and death leapt forth.

The opening rounds of the Battle of Ileri followed the course of most space engagements, with both sides pumping missiles at the other as their countermeasures tried to fool their opponent's weapons. Brilliant lances shot out from laser-equipped ships, and counter-missiles rocketed out into the engagement volume. As the range closed, *Iwan Goleslaw* and the Ileri cruiser brought their particle beams into play, and then, at last, both sides resorted to their last lines of defense. Short-ranged point-defense cannons saturated the probability cones through which the incoming missiles had to pass with thousands of dumb slugs. They didn't need to destroy the missiles, not entirely, just wreck their warheads, or their guidance systems, or their engines, letting the V-squared of the kinetic energy equation do the work.

Andini's first barrage took out half the Ileri cutters and one of the frigates, and then her first wave of weapon busses joined the fray. "Focus fire on the cruiser, Fist," she ordered, and a half-dozen mass drivers opened up on the unlucky ship at virtually 'can't miss' range for a space engagement. The Ileri ship cracked open like an egg smashed onto a countertop under the concentrated fire.

The surviving frigates and cutters began to scatter before *Iwan Goleslaw* closed to effective range for its shipboard mass drivers. "All right, let's deal with player two," she said as her CIC crew cheered. The destruction seemed to satisfy even Dinata, who texted a congratulatory message.

"We haven't won yet," she said to the tactical officer as they burned at a relatively sedate one-and-a-half gravities towards the second formation, which had prudently begun decelerating to allow additional rebel ships to join before engaging *Iwan Goleslaw*. "We caught the first group napping and it still cost seven percent of our ordnance."

"At that rate, Captain, we can take all the Ileri forces in

the system and have three percent left over. And our beam weapons don't need ammunition," Fist said hopefully.

Andini snorted. "You're forgetting about the three rail guns." The tactical officer had the good grace to look abashed. "We're lucky they're still under Vega's control, though I wonder why she hasn't used them on the rebels yet."

"Maybe she hopes some of the rebels will surrender, and she won't have to destroy their ships?"

"Perhaps."

The second stage of the engagement opened much as the first with missiles roaring forth. The results this time were somewhat less one-sided, though, and the SDV sustained several hits in exchange for smashing two Ileri frigates and several cutters. By this time, the rebels had committed nearly a third of their space force to attacking *Iwan Goleslaw* in what, in simulation at least, was something approaching an even fight.

One truism of space combat is that everyone can see what's going on, but very few can understand what's happening. Tactical plots on every warship around Ileri displayed the known trajectories and probable maneuver cones of the now thousands of missiles, weapons busses, ships, and major pieces of debris. Expert systems kept watch on more distant objects because even well-trained and experienced human minds tend to focus on the near and immediate. The problem with that is that distant and fast-moving can become near and immediate before one realizes it.

Andini angled her vessel away from the rebel flotilla, but that brought her track back into range of the surviving frigates from the first encounter. Those vessels, small and battered as they were, still had teeth. One of them had soft-launched a nuclear-tipped missile that drifted, engine stilled after its initial burst. The commander detonated the nuke in the middle of a pack of Saljuan weapon busses. This didn't clear them out; nuclear weapons in space don't inflict much damage to targets they aren't in contact with, not in terms of blast anyway.

But the radiation burst had the effect of blinding sensors, which allowed a mass-driver-armed rebel bus to approach undetected and fire on the SDV.

Even this wouldn't have been so bad except that *Iwan Goleslaw* was launching a fresh wave of weapons busses at that very moment. Two rounds struck an open launch port at four thousand meters per second, each five-kilogram projectile striking with forty million joules' worth of energy—*inside* the Saljuan ship's armor.

The projectiles drilled a path of destruction nearly two meters in diameter through the ship. Fragmentation and secondary explosions extended the damage along the path even as every weapon in the launcher's magazine detonated.

SDVs are tough ships, though. Internal baffles and blow-out panels in the hull over the magazine contained the devastation to an extent. What might have been a killing shot on any lesser craft became, instead, "merely" a critical wound. In a flash, Andini lost one-fifth of her crew dead and another fifth to injuries. Fortunately for Andini and her crew, the remaining supply of conversion bombs weren't in the affected areas, so the Saljuans weren't converted into MC^2 as the manufactory had been.

Helmet sealed against the vacuum now engulfing her CIC, her damage-control board awash in red, Andini belted out an order. "Fist! Option Zed! Execute!" The battered ship shuddered as the remaining launchers spat the rest of their weapon busses into space, followed by the onboard missile launchers, which fired half their magazines. Waves of death poured forth from the stricken warship.

Wounded, battered, *Iwan Goleslaw* cut its way free of the rebel flotilla. Behind it, the second Ileri cruiser fought for its own life as its escorting ships died. Andini took scant pleasure in noting the death of the frigate that had gutted her ship as a fireball consumed it.

Her comm pinged with an urgent message. Seeing it was from the surgeon and not, thankfully, Dinata, she answered. "What do you need, Bones?"

The surgeon, a sour-faced man at the best of times, relayed the initial casualty reports based on the feeds from the crew's djinns. Andini winced to hear the numbers. "Get the worst into stasis," she ordered.

"I can't," the surgeon said. "Bays six through ten were destroyed, and Gears tells me we don't have power for the functioning bays, not enough, anyway. Both main *and* secondary heat exchangers are down, and tertiary is only running at thirty percent capacity."

"Shit." Her heart sank into her stomach. Until the engineers could repair the heat exchangers, her ability to maneuver and fight was severely curtailed. Without cooking the remaining crew and systems, that was.

"I can't treat them all, Captain," the man said plaintively. "We need to evacuate them."

Guns cut into the call. "Captain, the loyalist ships are maneuvering. It looks like they're going to engage the rebels."

Andini switched her attention to the tactical plot, studying it intensely. *What is Vega doing?* Depending on which way the Fox of Tyngar turned her claws, the question of what to do with her wounded might be moot...

The vectors took the shapes she hoped for, and her belly unclenched the slightest bit. "I'll have to call Vega and ask for succor under the Accords," she said. "But she owes us a favor. We just gave her the opening to go after the rebels."

CHAPTER THIRTY

Toiwa

*Thanh Victor Medical Center, Ileri Station,
Forward Ring*

"Will he recover?" Toiwa practically pinned the doctor against the office wall.

The man, clearly exhausted, flung up his hands. "He'll survive, yes. He should recover fully from the shrapnel and gunshot wounds. But the spinal damage from being thrown into the pillar..." He shook his head. "We can do a lot, but it's doubtful he'll ever walk again without a medical exoskeleton."

"But you're doing everything you can for him?"

Her poking must have triggered something; the doctor straightened and squared his shoulders. "Governor, we are doing everything we can for *all* the casualties. Even the damned Saljuans you've foisted on us, and they're a tremendous drain on our resources. We'll be able to do more once our fabbers get back online to replenish our stocks. But there is some damage we simply can't repair."

Kala Valverdes seemed to materialize by her elbow. "Governor, there's an urgent personal call for you," ze said.

Her anger melted into fear like butter in a skillet. A personal call... <*Eduardo...*> she sent, not trusting herself to speak.

<*He's fine, and so are the children. They're waiting to speak with you.*>

Relief washed over her, and she suddenly felt both incredibly light, and as if the weight of her responsibilities would crush her.

I will not *fall apart in public.* She breathed deeply before turning back to the doctor. "My apologies. I'm sure you and your staff are just as dedicated to your patients as my spouse is to his."

That seemed to mollify him, and after asking if there was anything else her office could do for him, she asked if there was some place she could take a private call. "Use my office," he said, and left to continue managing the chaos. Valverdes followed him out, closing the door. She glimpsed Chijindu's bulk as he placed himself squarely in front of it.

She opened the link to see all three of them, Eduardo and the kids, packed into a smaller version of her borrowed office in the north ring med center. Eduardo cried openly as he told her about seeing one of his co-workers gunned down by rebels as they cut off the med center. Her daughter, her arm thrown protectively over her little brother's shoulder, related the hair-raising tale of their flight through the station's streets, just steps ahead of the rebels, in a matter-of-fact tone, as if she was summarizing the contents of a vid she'd watched for class. Toiwa's heart threatened to burst; she'd failed to protect not just the citizens in her care, but the people she loved most in the world.

She asked her son for his version of events, and he just grinned at her. "We knew you'd kick their asses, Mom," he said, and then the tightness in her chest gave way and she cried at last, and they all cried and laughed until Chijindu knocked circumspectly on her office door. Both he and Valverdes let her collect herself on the trip back to HQ.

They arrived to find Zheng overseeing the preparations for the medically enhanced interrogation of the prisoners from her daring raid. Toiwa's misgivings about crossing that threshold had faded as the stakes escalated exponentially. Antimatter weapons had that sort of effect, she supposed. But deep inside, she knew she was trading away a piece of her soul she'd never get back. She didn't know if learning what Mizwar knew would balance that, but it was her job to follow this path wherever it went. She stared at a projection of the man himself, stripped down to a medical undergarment, tubes inserted at half a dozen points of his body, and tried to fathom how this man's acts had been the match to set her world aflame.

Not that we weren't primed to go off on our own. We just didn't know it.

She watched from the observation suite down the hall as the medtechs fit a close-fitting cap over the prisoner's newly shaved head while others slipped mesh booties over bare feet. Fathya Shariff stood beside her, eyes fixed on the monitors, her gaze unrelenting. "You want justice for your grandson," Toiwa said softly.

"I want truth," Shariff said.

Toiwa hoped they found some. She touched Shariff's elbow. "I'm glad our people were able to fulfill my promise to find your grandson's killer."

"It was Daniel's promise, as I recall," Shariff said, her voice pitched low. "Though you did promise to devote every resource." She nodded at the screen. "You and yours have certainly done all I could ask."

Zheng called from her post beside the prisoner's gurney. "Governor? We're ready to begin."

"One moment, Lieutenant." She turned to the others in the observation suite. Ogawa, the Commonwealth operative, sat next to Okereke, talking in low voices to each other as they watched the proceedings. Teng, the Directorate Captain, hovered nearby. The missing member of their team, Fari Tahir, was ensconced in a treatment room down the hall. Kala Valverdes sat unobtrusively in the corner, while Chijindu warded the doorway. "They're ready to begin in there," she said. "What we learn here will be covered under the Secrets Act. Are you all prepared for that?"

"Damned straight," said Okereke, as the others murmured their affirmations.

"Please proceed, Lieutenant," she said, and turned to watch the screen.

Mizwar's supine form filled the middle display. Windows around it displayed data feeds: voice stress analysis, brain-activity readings, facial-expression analysis, pupillary-dilation scans, and a transcript of the questions and responses. Everything by the book, logged and auditable should the day come this testimony ever appeared before a magistrate. Assuming Vega didn't throw the man and his fellows into an oubliette somewhere.

The medtechs adjusted the flow of medication into Mizwar's system, a cocktail of inhibition-reducing drugs, relaxants, and gods knew what else along with the nanosurgeons at work repairing his hand. After a moment, the lead medic gave Zheng the go signal and she began her gentle questioning.

Normally one started with things you could verify to be true or false, and Maria Zheng kept to that protocol. She was hampered by the limited amount of genuine facts they had about Mizwar and his activities, causing her to run through their scant supply of known truths rather quickly. But the medtech signaled when they adequately established a baseline, and Zheng began to dig in earnest.

"Why did you kill Minister Ita and the Commonwealth Consul?" she asked.

"Collateral damage," Mizwar said. "Though he was likely already tainted."

"So, someone else was your target?"

Mizwar's head bobbed slightly. "Akindele and Wiwei were my primary targets," he said.

"Who were they?"

"Two of the businesspeople Ita and the Consul met with at the Second Landing Social Club."

"Why did you target them?" Zheng asked.

"Because my team discovered that they were infected," he said.

"Infected with what?"

"The Unity Plague."

That stopped Zheng dead in her tracks, and Toiwa felt her stomach drop, the way she'd felt when Vega told her she was the senior government official left on Ileri Station.

"I was afraid of that," Valverdes said. Toiwa's head jerked around.

"Hold on a moment, Lieutenant," she ordered. She eyed Kala warily. "Yes?"

Kala swallowed visibly before continuing. "Governor, I had the staff do a workup on Councilor Walla and the other prisoners who consented to testing." Ze stopped, looking nervous, and seemed to have trouble meeting Toiwa's eyes for a moment. "I also... Hm. I, well, used your authorizations to request analysis from a special lab once we got the forward-spindle comm array working."

Seems I'm not the only one who's compromised their values over this. Toiwa turned, slowly, and looked Valverdes in the eye. "What special lab?"

Kala seemed to find zer resolve. "The one M. Ogawa was posted to before she came to the station, after the murders. On asteroid 351 Juliette."

From Ogawa's sharply indrawn breath, Toiwa gathered Kala was treading some very dangerous ground. Her eyes flicked to the Commonwealth woman. "And the nature of that facility?"

Ogawa glanced at Teng, who shrugged as if to say, "Why not?"

"It investigates specialized bioactive nanoware," Ogawa said. She stood preternaturally still.

Fuck. Puzzle pieces began slotting together in Toiwa's mind. Walla's behavior, sudden martial prowess, hell, the fact that she'd tried to kill the Saljuan team that had kidnapped her in the first place, Okafor's dark net, the mysteriously coordinated actions by strangers to attack Ogawa. The presence of the illegal nanoware on Ileri in the first place. The reason the Commonwealth had sent a delegation of experts in this kind of nanoware.

We have this tech, we've always had it, and Miguna got it, and here we are.

She voiced her conclusions aloud.

"It appears we do," Valverdes said. "Well, not the plague itself. But something akin to it, according to the lab. Confirmation came in while you were at the med center." Ze tossed Toiwa a data packet.

Toiwa popped the bundle open, called up the précis, and began skimming. She reached the third sentence, stopped, and backed up to read it from the beginning, word by word. Her stomach dropped as she read on. "These findings are conclusive?"

Kala nodded. "Yes, Governor. Councilor Walla and the persons who attacked M. Ogawa all carry variants of the nanotechnological agent found in a prisoner M. Ogawa captured during the *Fenghuang* affair last year. Director Sadiq's researchers have definitively shown that it's related to the Unity Plague that sent our ancestors into Exile."

The Unity Plague. Her world, her children, all could be infected, all heartbeats away from forming a new pack of near automatons, bent to the service of—whom? Back on Lost Earth, the Plague had been the tool used by an unholy union of kleptocrats and religious fundamentalists to bring the world's unruly people under control for good. As the Unity began to blanket the Earth, as dissent died away to be replaced with blissful submission, the peoples closest to the space elevators had fled to join with those already in space, taking the first great jump that led to Chatterjee's one-way wormhole stargate and Exile.

But those people were more than two centuries and countless light years away. Who would pull the puppets' strings now?

Miguna and his cabal, it seemed.

But did it matter? If word got out a pocket of infection had come with them, and lived again on Ileri...

"Sweet Mother of the Leap," Toiwa breathed. "The Saljuans *have cause*."

"Only a minority of the newer prisoners are infected, though," Valverdes said, but Toiwa didn't hear it the first time and, embarrassed, asked zer to repeat it.

"It seems likely that only a relatively small number of the rebels carry the infection," her aide repeated. "The leaders all do, and some small teams like those who attacked M. Ogawa before the coup do as well. But most of the rebels we've captured since show no signs of contamination."

"Do we know why?" Toiwa asked.

"It seems this variant doesn't spread via the aerosolized vectors the original plague on Earth is believed to have used. We're not sure precisely how it's transmitted yet, but that means it can't spread like wildfire, the way it did on Earth."

"Well, that's a comfort," Toiwa said bitterly. "I'm sure the conversion bombs won't hurt so much." She looked hard at Ogawa, her eyes narrowed. "Do your superiors know about this?"

The Commonwealth agent glanced about the room, as if looking for cover, or perhaps escape. "I can only speak to what I know, and there are some things I can't say here," she said cautiously.

Toiwa leaned into the other woman's space. "Out. With. It."

Ogawa licked her lips, then squared her shoulders. "We know for sure that the person who led the expedition to recover the *Fenghuang* is indeed infected with a nanoware agent that is derived from the Exile-era Unity Plague. He also had access to a different strain of nanoware which could only be used to coerce those infected with it into following his orders by stimulating the victim's pain receptors." She glanced at Teng, lurking in his corner. "Your Directorate scientists are capable of removing the torture nano. The *Fenghuang* expedition leader is detained for study."

Toiwa turned to stare at Teng, who shrugged and nodded. "He's held in a secure facility elsewhere in the system. She"—he pointed at Ogawa—"was there as Commonwealth liaison."

"Is your prisoner one of Miguna's people?" Toiwa asked.

The spies looked at each other. Ogawa shrugged, but Teng shook his head. "If he is, I haven't been told."

"But both the Commonwealth and our governments know about this?" Both agents nodded.

So killing you won't keep this secret, Toiwa thought, and was surprised to realize she felt no shame at casually considering murder. *Gods, what's happening to me?* She pushed that line of thought down for later.

Ogawa spoke up. "Your scientists requested assistance from the Commonwealth to help investigate that nanotech. The team *Amazonas* delivered is full of specialists in this sort of thing. My government clearly wants to help."

Toiwa barked out a laugh. "The delegation was taken in the first hour of the coup." She shook her head and tried to push back the despair that threatened to claw its way to the surface. *The fools have brought this down on us.* "This is a death sentence for our world under the Accords. Every planet in the Cluster will be clamoring to scour Ileri with fire."

Ogawa didn't flinch. "It's not a monolithic set of phages. Some can be treated." She looked back up at Toiwa. "Your people already have some capability to do this. I've seen it work."

It was a lifeline, however insubstantial. Toiwa swept her eyes across the room. Shariff was aghast, her expression mirroring the dread Toiwa felt. Okereke looked angry, but that was her norm, based on her previous encounters with the woman. Valverdes looked grave, but Ogawa seemed... guardedly hopeful, Toiwa thought. Only Teng remained impassive as he skulked watchfully.

Toiwa's despair subsided, just a bit, and her resolve reasserted itself. *Maybe we're still doomed. But it won't be because we didn't try to dig our way out of this.*

She pointed at Valverdes. "Get the Prime Minister's people on the line now. This has to be handled at the highest level." Within moments, they had Vega's chief-of-staff looped in. Toiwa forced her jaw to relax before she started grinding her teeth. "Lieutenant Zheng, please continue the interrogation."

Over the next hour, Zheng drew the story out from her subject. They learned that Mizwar had been dispatched along with his team of special operatives not long after word reached Salju about the discovery of the lost warship *Fenghuang.* ("Someone must have leaked the information about my prisoner," Ogawa said. "Your intel people have a mole." Toiwa noted that for follow-up.)

Mizwar and his team were an advance guard, charged to investigate the extent of any incidence of the Unity Plague or other Exile-level technology. They had hacked the infonet just as Okafor had surmised and begun sampling potential candidates they identified via some kind of sophisticated algorithmic engine.

That led the Saljuans to what they were looking for, a cell of infected victims like the group which attacked Ogawa. They then traced that cell by following chains of anomalous contacts up to the businessmen Ita met with. "When we discovered their meeting, it seemed a perfect opportunity for a limited decapitation strike," Mizwar said in the singsong voice of someone doped to the gills. "We could observe the behavior of other potentially infected individuals and trace the extent of the contamination."

"You mentioned you were an advance guard," Zheng said. "You knew *Iwan Goleslaw* was en route?"

"Not that ship specifically. But I knew a warship would follow carrying a Technology Constraint Minister."

"And did you make contact with them?" she asked.

"My team on the station did when the ship arrived. I was planetside by then."

"And why did you go downside?" she asked. "I thought you were going to observe and trace the infected?"

"Because we discovered something new when we investigated the other people at the meeting with Ita," he replied. "One of them owned a biotech plant in Kochi. I went to investigate and discovered what they'd been making there."

"And what were they making in Kochi?" Zheng said.

"An aerosolized version of their variant of the Unity

Plague, like the original on Earth," he said.

Consternation drowned out his next words. "Quiet!" she snapped, and everyone fell silent. "Lieutenant, ask him to repeat that, please."

"We destroyed what we found," Mizwar said, and Toiwa nearly buckled in relief. "We cracked their server, found the inventory. About ninety percent of it was in the warehouse we torched. All but about one hundred liters' worth. But we discovered they were making more, in bulk, in orbit. We had just notified *Iwan Goleslaw* when the Constabulary blanked communications around the building, when your team landed."

"Do you know where the missing hundred liters is?" Zheng pressed.

"We figured it out when we reviewed the data later, after we slipped your people tailing us. It was shipped up to the station a few days ago," Mizwar said. A blissful smile stole over his face. "When Minister Dinata finds out, she's going to burn you all."

CHAPTER
THIRTY-ONE

Noo

CONSTABULARY HQ, ILERI STATION, FORWARD RING

"WHEN MINISTER DINATA finds out, she's going to burn you all."

Noo had passed into that state somewhere beyond both mental and physical exhaustion hours back. A nap aboard *Amazonas,* and another as they'd climbed back through the embattled skies to the station, hadn't come close to restoring her energy. The shocks encountered once they'd docked with the station—the scenes of destruction, limited though they were, Fathya pulling her aside to give her the news about Daniel's condition, and now Mizwar's revelations—it was simply too much to try to take in.

So don't, came the whisper. *You are a daughter of the Huntress. Do what you do best.*

"When Minister Dinata finds out..."

"Waitaminute," Noo croaked. Faces turned her way and she cleared her throat. "Zheng. Follow up. He said 'when Dinata finds out'. Does that mean he didn't tell her that last bit yet?"

Zheng probed, and Mizwar confirmed that their surprise raid had prevented his team from communicating their latest finding up to *Iwan Goleslaw*. The maneuvers that kept the warship away from the orbital forces of either Ileri faction had kept it out of position for Mizwar to share what he'd learned.

It was as if someone had swept a curtain away, and the fogginess in her mind she'd grown so used to over the last day blew away like atmo from a compartment venting into space. For a few seconds she felt like she was outside her own body, observing herself while someone else ran the program that was Noo, and then there was a sudden rushing sensation, a feeling of being carried along, and then she was back looking out from her eyes again.

Some part of her wondered if she was having an adverse reaction to the pharmaceutical cocktail the medics had dosed her with. She pushed that thought aside in favor of a death-grip on her newfound clarity.

"Then we can still stop them." Her voice rang out clearly this time.

"Which them?" Fathya asked. Noo looked at her partner, and that detached portion of her brain noted that Fathya Shariff suddenly looked *old*.

"All of them. Well, that goat-fucker Miguna and his pals, the plague-ridden, and those Saljuan shit stains." She raised a finger. "The nanoware is on the station. We find it and destroy it, and it doesn't matter what this turd-brain knows." She pointed at the monitor from which Mizwar grinned nonsensically at them. "We can show the Saljuans that Ileri's not a fucking nano-plagued shithole and if your people," she jabbed her finger at Meiko, "show a little backbone, then we can probably keep those dustbrains from starting the Third Cluster War."

"About that." Meiko hopped up from her chair, pawing through personal AR windows. "About the plague agent on the station, I mean. I came across something the other day." She found what she was looking for, and her eyes slid across the text. "One of my contacts mentioned that he was trying to get a shipment of medical aerosol moved to the south ring." She glanced at Toiwa. "It was the day after the assassination. The Constabulary was all over the Fingers, and all their illicit goods shipments were disrupted."

"Why does that matter?" Teng asked.

"Because I think the conspirators were using the Fingers to move their goods," she said.

Toiwa frowned. "That's quite a leap."

"Ask them," Okereke said. "They can tell us about the shipment. If it matches, we'll know."

"Did I just hear correctly that you wish to involve the Fingers in this?" a new voice Noo didn't recognize interjected.

There was a few seconds' silence. Fathya caught Noo's eyes and then jerked her head at Toiwa. The message was clear: *Let her handle this.*

"Prime Minister, I didn't realize you'd joined the link," Toiwa said.

Oh shit.

"Just in time to hear the last comment, though my

staff has given me an overview of the situation," Vega's disembodied voice said. "And I've just now seen the memo you sent earlier today, sketching out your agreement with M. Loh."

Noo darted a look at Toiwa. "You cut a deal with Pericles?"

Toiwa squared her shoulders. "It is an extraordinary move, I grant you. But in my judgment, it will be impossible to retake the station without their help." Noo saw the tendons in Toiwa's neck standing out. "We can't match the rebel's capability without substantial assistance that's not available from any other source."

"Perhaps we should discuss that later, Governor," Vega said.

Wherever her surge of energy was coming from, Noo was strapped in for the ride. She seized control of the conversation back. "We need to find and destroy the nano and rescue the Commonwealth scientists, so they can help us deal with the people who are already infected."

It seemed the Prime Minister was already up to speed on that aspect. "I concur with your overall assessment, M. Okereke," Vega said. "Retrieving the Commonwealth scientists might also help influence Captain Gupta to provide more open support, which would simplify operational matters in orbit."

"We'll need to retake the infonet if we're going to mount an operation of that scale," Ogawa cautioned.

"Noted," Toiwa said.

"I have M. Loh standing by," Valverdes said, somehow not managing to sound smug about it.

"Put him on," Toiwa said crisply. Noo saw the look

Fathya shot at the governor, recognized as one her partner had given her countless times over the years.

You resent that you're stuck relying on people with dirty hands. I love you like a sister, but if you pull your righteousness act here, I'm going to smack you.

Fortunately, everyone present, in person and virtually, maintained the veneer of civility. Toiwa briskly summed up the key points of discussion for Loh, keeping the momentum going. "What support can you offer in support of these objectives?" she said.

"Some aspects are easier than others," Loh replied. "Getting a strike team to a data junction so you can retake the infonet is straightforward enough, if dangerous. Getting to the Commonwealth delegation is a bit trickier. We believe they're held at a location that's not particularly convenient to one of our ingress/egress points. That team will require substantial firepower."

Noo was still riding her wave of energy. "What about the nanoware, Pericles?"

"I will need to confirm it, but if I'm correct, it's taking a roundabout route."

"Spit it out, Pericles," Noo said, as she hunched forward. Loh hesitated, and Noo could almost picture his expression. *This is something he doesn't want to give up.* "Come on. Your shorts are already on the floor, time to get it wet." Someone choked back a giggle at her vulgarity.

"Calliope always said you were pushy," he complained. "But as you crudely put it, we are intimately engaged—"

"Cut the shit. Where is it?"

"Traversing the outer surface of the station," he said, sounding peeved. "More specifically, being hauled by a bot across the outside of the hub to the southern spindle. Which is, unfortunately, very firmly in rebel control."

There was silence while everyone processed this. "If it's on the surface, can the Navy hit it?" Noo asked.

"Not without damaging the station," Vega said. "I'm sure they can target it, but the collateral damage would be huge. That might be a measure of last resort, though."

Zheng had left Mizwar to the medics and slipped into the observation suite. "I've done EVA combat ops before." She grinned. "And I've got the right party wear for it, thanks to Captain Gupta."

"I have experience with free-fall combat as well," Meiko said, nodding at Zheng. "If any of your maintenance people have an engineering hardsuit I can borrow." Major Biya chimed in that he could support them with a team from his tiny force in the hub.

"That leaves the data junction and rescuing the Commonwealth team," Noo said.

"I can send Okafor and a team, if Loh's people can guide them," Toiwa said, and Loh agreed.

"That leaves the boffins for me, then," Noo said. Teng volunteered to join her, and both Toiwa and Loh committed to support them.

Fathya put her hands up. "Out of the question. You're played out. And you've done your part."

Noo popped up out of her chair to confront her oldest friend. "We're not done yet, Fathya," she said. "Not while these turds can turn us all into zombies. Or give the Saljuans a chance to use the rest of their bombs." She pointed at the screen where Mizwar's face still loomed. "You heard him, heard Dinata. They'll burn our world down to the mantle if they have to, if that's what it takes to quiet their fears." She lowered her hand. "And besides, I need to pay these shits back for Daniel."

Fathya opened her mouth to say more, but Toiwa cut her off. "Your service is accepted, pending clearance from the medics." She gathered them all by eye, then spoke to the room. "We have our operational concept. Time is short. Let's turn this into an actual plan."

CHAPTER THIRTY-TWO

MEIKO

*READY ROOM B, CONSTABULARY HQ,
ILERI STATION, FORWARD RING*

MEIKO STEPPED THROUGH the door Zheng held open for her. She saw Fari sitting on the floor among her neatly ordered kit, legs stretched out before her in a medical exoframe. She didn't bother looking up from the belt in her lap, into which she was loading spare magazines for the wicked-looking autocarbine on the floor beside her. Meiko's djinn pegged them as armor piercing rounds.

"I'm through discussing this, Grandmother," Fari said.

"But what about Ifedapo?" Fathya Shariff, standing over her granddaughter, pressed.

<Ifedapo?> Meiko messaged Noo, who sat on a bench across the room, watching quietly, her own gear spread nearby.

<Fari's wife.>

"We've talked." Fari thumbed the ammunition pouch

closed, picked up a fragmentation grenade—Meiko didn't need her djinn's help recognizing *that*—and hefted it. "She understands why I need to do this."

"I don't."

"I can't help you there." Fari carefully slid the grenade into the carry loop and stroked her thumb across it, activating the gecko fibers that held it in place.

Meiko carefully stepped aside to let Zheng slip in behind her and they hovered near the doorway, unwilling to intrude. She thought of her own leave-takings, back when she'd been young enough that leaving her parents had been an event worth marking. *When did that change?* She couldn't remember. With a start, she realized that it had been a long, long time since she'd had anyone in her life close enough to make saying goodbye as hard as what she was witnessing.

Shariff ignored the newcomers, turning to harangue Noo instead. "And what about you? Even for you, this is daft. Who do you think you are, an action hero like Ming-Tse?" She stalked over to loom over her partner. "Do you want to end up like Daniel? Or worse?"

Noo slid a magazine into her sidearm, the massive twelve-millimeter hand cannon that made Meiko's wrists ache just looking at it. She double-checked the mechanical safety and slid the pistol into the tie-down holster strapped to her right leg, then finally looked up to meet Fathya's eyes. "No. I'm trying to make sure no one else winds up like Daniel. Or worse. And so that cunt Dinata doesn't have any excuse to use a conversion bomb against the station, or on New Abuja, and kill the people I love." She grabbed the arms of her chair and pulled herself upright. "There was a time you would have understood that without someone needing to explain it to you."

That rocked Shariff back on her heels. Finally, she spoke, so softly that Meiko would have missed it if her aural implants and djinn hadn't noticed her focus and boosted the gain accordingly. "I can't lose the rest of you, too," she said. Her hands twitched forward into the space between the two.

Noo reached out and took her old friend's hands firmly. "And if we do nothing, that's just what might happen. This is all hands to damage stations, no drill." Her voice was still pitched low, but loud enough to carry. "You've seen those constables and soldiers. They're as played out as we are. Everyone's been on duty since Miguna's buttonheads made their move, snatching a few hours' sleep, a bite to eat when they can." She glanced around the room. "But that means the other side has got to be worn down too. We're about evenly split, they've just got the heavier gear. Or did, until Pericles came through."

She let go of Fathya's hands and stepped back. "Let us go do what we have to. You keep Toiwa safe and give her good counsel." Shariff nodded and raised her hand to her eyes. Probably to wipe away tears, Meiko thought, but she couldn't see.

They embraced. Fari stood and walked over and took Noo's place in her grandmother's arms. Shariff turned to go, but Noo called out to her. "Fathya?"

The old woman stopped, and half-turned. "Yes?"

"If things go poorly, give this to Daniel, please." Noo tossed her a data packet.

Shariff nodded. "I pray the merciful Father watches over you both, but should his eye wander, I'll see it done."

"I know you will." Noo sat down again and Shariff headed for the door. Meiko and Zheng stood aside quietly.

Fari cocked her head at the newcomers. "I thought you'd be gearing up yourselves."

"Soon. You have further to go than we do." Zheng stepped over to inspect the array of lethal implements and gave a low whistle. "Borer AP rounds? The Fingers have these? What the hell for? Do they regularly need to shoot through bulkheads or something?"

"Sales to colonies in the New Arm, mostly," Noo said.

"Shit," Zheng said. "You're telling me someone probably shot at me with weapons and ammo from here, back when I was in the peacekeepers?"

"Wouldn't surprise me," Noo said.

The Ileri woman looked as tired as Meiko felt; the tale of the last few days was evident in the way they all moved. Meiko put her left hand on Noo's shoulder and as if on cue felt a twinge from her barely healed wrist. "You have enough in the tank to do this?"

The ghost of a smile flickered across Noo's face. "Not really. But that's what this is for." She pulled an autoinjector from the left cargo pocket of her newly fabbed battledress.

Meiko read the label and nodded. "That's potent stuff, all right. Just don't use more than one dose."

"Why not?"

"Because a second dose can cause organ damage bad enough to require freshly cultured replacements," Toiwa said from the doorway. She was alone but for her hulking bodyguard, who Meiko glimpsed a few meters away down the corridor. Toiwa came into the ready room and closed the door, scanning each of the women. "And the old ones will hurt the entire time."

"Well, that's a motivational anecdote if I've ever heard one," Noo said, and turned back to her preparations.

Meiko realized that the governor was running on fumes as much as she and her companions were. "It's what the doctor told me when I asked for more," Toiwa said. Leaving Noo to her own devices, she approached the others and put her hands onto Zheng's shoulders. "I wanted to see you off, Maria, and this is the only chance I've got."

Zheng flashed her a grin. "It's all right." She shared the grin with her... boss? Mentor? Surrogate older sister? Some combination of those, Meiko thought. "Thank you, Governor. It means a lot."

"You have everything you need?" Toiwa asked.

Zheng nodded. "The armorers were able to top off the stores in the Commonwealth marine suit I borrowed, and we've got another armored trooper kitted out." She tilted her head towards Meiko. "Ogawa and the others have non-powered hard-shell suits. Your watchdog frigates spotted the robot and the cannister with their passive optics, and it's right where Loh's people think it should be. We'd have the easiest run of the three if it wasn't for being an EVA."

Toiwa held her underling's gaze for a moment longer, then nodded, dropping her hands to her sides. "All right then." She looked at Meiko. "You've got experience with this sort of operation, M. Ogawa?"

"Things like this, yes." Twenty years ago, but that didn't seem worth bringing up.

"Watch yourselves out there, then." Toiwa turned to Fari. "I understand you're escorting M. Okafor?"

The young woman nodded. "I might not be fit for the assault element with this," she said, slapping the hip cradle of her medical exoframe. "But I'll get your tech wizard where she needs to go."

"Good. We're counting on you, and her." They shook hands, and Meiko saw Toiwa start towards Noo, only to stop after a tentative half-step. "M. Okereke?"

"Hmm?" Noo looked up from her preparations, her hands full of spare magazines.

"May the Huntress guide your steps."

The two looked at each other for a long moment, and Noo gave a slow nod. "Thank you."

I guess that's as close to a peace treaty as those two are going to reach.

Toiwa stepped back, swept them with her eyes. "Good hunting, ladies," she said, and backed out the door, closing it behind her.

Noo finished packing her ammo and stood back up. "Shit, that almost makes me want to like her," she said.

"It's all right, Auntie," Fari chimed in. "She's a politician now. She just wants your vote," and the room rocked with their laughter.

Zheng and Meiko couldn't help but join in. They stood there, the four of them, and whether it was the exhaustion or just the sheer absurdity of it all, the laughter consumed them. It took several minutes before they regained their composure, wiping tears from their eyes.

Fari reached up, putting her arms around Noo on one side and Zheng on the other, and then Noo and Zheng had theirs around Meiko. She put hers around them in turn, and felt a tightness in her chest, coupled with warmth. It had been years—decades, really, if she was honest—since she'd felt this way. Operating solo for so long, one forgot the joys—and pains—of being part of a team. She dipped her head in towards the others, who followed suit, and for a moment they just stood there, breathing each other's breath. She felt the sleek tautness of Zheng's shoulder muscles, the relative softness of Noo's, the heat of Fari's head where it met her own, and fancied she could hear the beating of their hearts.

"It's been quite a ride, ladies," she said, and was surprised to find herself choked up.

"It's not over yet," Noo said, her own voice thick. She pulled back, and Meiko and the others did the same.

"See you when it's all done," Zheng said.

Fari nodded. "Let's clip the bastards."

CHAPTER THIRTY-THREE

OKAFOR

SERVICE PASSAGEWAY 928-F, ILERI STATION, FORWARD RING

THE ARMORED GLOVE on Josephine Okafor's elbow gently guided her to the right. "Low pipe," Fari Tahir whispered into her ear. They picked their way forward for several more minutes before Tahir pressed gently on her shoulder. "Here. Last bulkhead before the junction. We're under cover."

"Will we be here long?" she whispered back. Tahir affirmed it would be a few minutes at least so she parked her butt on the floor. She tugged at her ballistic jacket, trying to shift it to ride more comfortably. As a civilian analyst, her duties had never required her to wear body armor before. She found the weight uncomfortable, and despite having been made to her measurements, it felt painfully tight in the chest, and constricted her movement, limiting her ability to twist and bend.

She felt the warm presence of Tahir as the other woman took a knee beside her, the subtle change of pressure, heard the woman's slightly labored breathing and the soft hiss of the pneumatics of her exoframe. If things were going according to plan, their assault element should be taking up their final positions before popping the hidden access panel leading from their secret passage— she wanted to chuckle, just thinking of that phrase—into the data junction. She and Tahir formed part of the tiny technical group, along with a Shariff infonet specialist and a Constabulary hardware technician. They were supposed to be holding position five meters behind the lead element. A few meters behind her group lurked the operation's second-in-command and the rearguard. She was safe, or at least as safe as anyone could be on Ileri station right now.

But she resented her dependence on Tahir, was irritable at having to be guided. Between her cane and her gauntlets, she was used to moving about independently. But her cane was impractical in the tight spaces they'd traversed, and they couldn't risk the emissions from the ladar, millimeter wave radar, and ultrasonic sensors of her sensorium, at least during this phase of the operation.

That would change once the shooting started.

These smuggler's ways were deliberately uncharted and fitted, Loh had told them, into something he called 'squinches'. "Think of the spaces on either side of an arch supporting a bridge," Loh said. "Our passages fit into spaces like that. The intersections can be confusing to people who don't know them." His analogy hadn't made any sense to her; blind since birth, she couldn't visualize the shapes he described, and their relationships to each other. Tahir, grasping the reason for her lack of comprehension, had formed the shapes with a couple of foam-covered cable ties and guided Okafor's fingers across them, allowing her to understand Loh's meaning.

The ready signal came, and she started to rise, but the insistent pressure of Tahir's hand on her shoulder kept her down. She shifted back into a kneeling position.

She felt the flash of heat and the mild pressure wave against her skin as the cutting charges went off. The sharp smell of burnt metal seemed to bite somewhere deep in her nostrils as the door clanged to the deck. A brief rush of air blew past her as the flow within the passage suddenly changed, spilling out into the data-node chamber beyond. The mixed force of constables, soldiers, and Fingers people surged forth.

"Up now," Tahir said. Okafor grasped her hand and came to her feet as the bark of weapons sounded in the room beyond. She activated her sensors, but Tahir hustled her forward before they came online. Her left shoulder pressed against the wall, and she heard the sharp, staccato bursts of weapons, commands across their comm net, and the cries of those hit. The harsh, acrid smell was strong here, close to the breach.

They huddled there by the opening for three minutes and seven seconds according to her timer. By then her sensorium was fully operational, and she carefully swept the space around them, building up her 'picture' of the area.

At last the assault commander called them forward. There were new smells, blood and ozone, piss and burnt flesh. She and the other two technical specialists hurried up to the node junction. Okafor heard the assault team bustling around them, rounding up the prisoners they'd taken and establishing a perimeter. The computer tech cursed as he fumbled with his tools and then she heard the sound of an access panel being slid aside. "Got it," he said, and then he pressed the familiar shape of a fiber-optic connector into her hand. She smiled and snapped it into her djinn. Then she sat down, leaned her back against the node's housing, and slipped into virtual reality.

Unlike most people, Josephine Okafor couldn't visualize VR, because she couldn't visualize *anything*. But the tactile sensor net had been part of her since she was five years old; she'd grown up with it, expanded it as years went on, learning to distinguish the finest gradations of sensation. At the same time, she grew to live with code. Her virtual experience was unlike anyone else's she'd ever heard of; but time had shown that for whatever reason, she was remarkably effective in VR.

The difference between this node and a normal, unadulterated one struck her immediately. Instead of one multifaceted junction in the sphere's center, there were two, one much smaller. That was the piggyback bridge to the Fingers' private network. She reached out with her right hand, touched it, and felt the connection spring into place. Good; Loh's access codes worked as advertised.

Haissani, the Shariff datarat who accompanied them, followed suit. He copied her motion, joining the Fingers infonet as she spun digital agents to seize control of this connection point, with orders to replicate and follow the myriad threads of the criminal network to its limits. She wouldn't cut them out of it, not yet, but the agents carried instructions to copy the data they uncovered, preserving it for later examination. It wasn't part of Loh's agreement with Toiwa, but Okafor felt the opportunity was too good to pass up.

"Securing our flank?" Haissani asked.

"Something like that," she said, and turned her attention to the main node. Okafor spun more agents into being around them as she and Haissani scanned the main node's input channels. She perceived a loose cloud of packets. Her virtual fingers sifted through them, like through a fall of sand, and discovered they were inbound access requests from djinns, sensors, bots, and the host of smart devices that filled the station. The rebels had locked them out from the infonet, but they continued to seek access.

There. One of her questing agents discovered a series of requests that *weren't* being rejected. *Interesting.* She followed the trace and discovered that the rebels didn't seem to be using the dark net after all! Instead, they had found a way to lock everyone but themselves from the regular station infonet. Her digital agent harvested data from the stream, and Okafor shunted the computation-heavy tasks of decrypting it over to the Fingers' network, saving her own onboard processing power.

It was like the difference between trying to pick a lock and simply cutting it out of the door frame with a plasma torch. Within seconds she had the keys she needed. She flipped a set of keys to Haissani and together, they spoofed access requests and fired them to the central node.

And then they were in.

The lockout program hung before her, a soft, amorphous, ever-shifting membrane just inside the outer layer of the node. She called up another agent and set it to trying the supervisory access credentials from the Ministry of Information against the chance the rebels hadn't managed to change all of them. Another pulsed a message out via the Fingers network, sharing the skeleton key she'd fashioned. Elsewhere in the station, loyalist and Fingers hackers launched their own attacks, hoping to divert attention away from her effort. Hopefully they, too, would be able to slip inside and take the fight to the enemy.

"Shit! Countermeasures!" Haissani said, and a trio of sharp, angry forms sprang into life and began gnawing on Okafor's avatar, like sharp pins stabbing her in the arms. She could feel the probing spikes of code seeking a way into her virtual form like a series of soft pulses. A flick of her hand brought attack agents of her own into play and she cast them into the fray.

She discovered an unexpected advantage now; she was intimately familiar with the defensive code used within the Ileri infonet, and aside from the access lockout, the rebels hadn't changed it yet. A mistake on their part; she'd make them pay for that.

Her guardian programs ignored the hostile agents trying to breach her defenses, instead targeting the virtual processors executing the attacking code. One by one, her digital minions seized control, shutting down the hostile programs even as the node tried to spin up new ones. She opened another link to the Fingers network, found her agents there had secured that first node, and ruthlessly slaved part of its processing over to her defensive agents. That, she thought, should give her a little breathing room.

Two options lay before her. One was taking control of the lockout program, freeing up the infonet for the loyalists, and everyone else trapped, while simultaneously locking the rebels out. The other was to push deeper into the infonet, tracing down and in to locate the rebel's point of control. Fortunately, she wasn't alone. She reached across the virtual space to ask Haissani to deal with the lockout program—

Only he wasn't there. The countermeasure programs had forced his avatar out of the system. Unless he could ride dumpshock as well as she, and few could, she was on her own for now. Given time, he'd be back. She hoped. But his absence made her decision easy. She rolled her shoulders out, felt the ghostly sensation of her body echoing the motion. Then she pulled another set of agents from her djinn's local store. One hand reached out, grabbed hold of the cluster of processing power she'd seized from the attacking programs, and slaved that power to her new programs. It was like going from hand tools to heavy machinery, from pick and shovel to a fusion-powered excavator. And even though she didn't know just how the lockout program worked, she *did* know how the system it was corrupting needed to work, knew intimately the potential points of vulnerability.

She slammed her code into the lockout program like an avenging goddess, plunged her virtual hands into it, found the dark heart of its kernel, and crushed it like an overripe grape.

The lockout program disintegrated, and the quality of the virtual pressure inside the sphere changed, from stagnant stuffiness to a breeze, and then to a growing wind, as all the questing systems once again connected to the station infonet.

She sent messages to Toiwa, to the assault team commander, and to the other hackers trying to break through elsewhere, passing on what she'd done, providing each of them with the means to undo the rebels' work. One of her analysis programs flashed an alert and she laughed as she hoisted out the new keys to the junction. *Amateurs. Left a copy in executable space for me. Might as well have used ROT13 encryption on it.*

An unseen blow struck her avatar from behind and spun her sideways. In real space her body lurched with a spasm.

She righted herself as her virtual sensorium reported that another avatar hovered before her, and she 'felt' heat radiating from the attack code it clutched like a physical weapon. "You won the first round, asshole," the rebel hacker said. It was a male voice, deep and booming. "Care to go two out of three?"

Josephine Okafor laughed as she flung her imaginary hands wide. Thick channels of data streamed across the infonet as she wielded her master keys and commandeered processing power from not just this junction node, but from the Station Constabulary's main data center. She reached one hand over her shoulder and drew power from the Fingers network as well. Her avatar swelled, growing in size until it dwarfed the rebel hacker. Her own hands sprouted bundles of attack code that she shaped into massive chains.

"This is *my* dojo, *asshole*," she said, and her voice rolled out across the infonet like a rushing tide. "And I think I'm going two for two." She flung the chains at her attacker, bound him, plunged her hands into his avatar's center, and ripped the operating kernel from within it. The avatar collapsed.

She sensed a new avatar in the node and readied her attack code again, but it turned out to be Tahir. "Aren't you on physical overwatch?" Okafor asked.

"Haissani's down. We're taking fire out here, and the rebels are counter-attacking. I wanted to check on you," Tahir said.

"Almost done," Okafor said, triumph in her voice. "Infonet access is back, and I've locked the rebels out. I just need to deal with the Fingers network."

"Right, about that," Tahir said, and her avatar disappeared from the node.

Okafor reached out to trigger the worm she'd planted in the Fingers network—

Pain slammed into her, and the virtual world disappeared. She gasped, or tried to, as what felt like every muscle in her body triggered at once, felt her bladder and bowels release as the stunner scrambled her nervous system. She could hear, distantly, the sounds of gunfire, and stunner shots, and in the distance, a muffled explosion.

"Sorry about that," Tahir breathed into her ear. "Don't worry. I'll hit you with some Pacifine in a moment. Standard treatment for stunner-shot victims. Has an amnesiac agent too, you won't remember any of this."

"Why?" Okafor managed to croak.

She felt a sharp, stabbing pain in her thigh, different from the ripping pulses of fire consuming her. She felt herself falling, as if down a deep, soft shaft.

"Because I'm personally obliged to someone," she heard Tahir say, and then things went black.

CHAPTER THIRTY-FOUR

Noo

TAKAMANDA DISTRICT, ILERI STATION, SOUTH RING

FOUR SHOTS CRACKED out at once, as near to simultaneous as Noo could tell, and just like that the four rebels guarding the spinward side of the apartment building dropped, dead before they hit the street grass. "Gogogo!" called the team leader, and one of the three power armor-equipped troopers in the raid force bounded across the street to secure the side door.

Myra, Loh's musclewoman, tapped Noo on the shoulder before scuttling towards the door of their building. Noo smacked Teng's arm in turn and followed the Fingers heavy as best she could. She'd used her dose of stimulant while still slogging through the smuggler's ways of the station or else she'd never have made it this far. It was still working; she could summon strength at need, and no longer felt like she'd been rolled in a rug and beaten with pipes. But she still wasn't used to the heavy load of gear and weapons and armor, still felt off balance, as fat and ungainly as one of the Goya's Swans that swam in the forward ring's lake. Stealth was not an option in her case.

Judging from the level of gunfire being exchanged, stealth was no longer required.

They hustled out across the first street between their shelter and the makeshift prison. Myra trotted at a pace Noo had trouble keeping up with, even with her biochemical assistance. Smoke billowed from one of the third-floor windows of the block-sized building, but she couldn't tell if that was from fire or a smoke grenade launched by the attackers. She heard the sharp rattle of an automatic weapon from somewhere off to her left, answered almost immediately by the harsh ripping sound of one of the armored trooper's mini-guns. Her little trio crossed the narrow strip of park between the two lanes of street grass, never slowing their pace until they bumped up against the building.

Noo struggled to catch her breath as Myra led them past one of the fallen guards to the doorway, smashed open apparently with the battering ram that now lay beside the portal. She glanced down at the guard and regretted it almost instantly. Taking the four sentries out had looked surgical enough, from a distance; but their snipers had made headshots with armor-piercing rounds. Half the woman's skull had been blown off and the rest was bloody ruin. She tried not to think about what she was stepping in.

They passed into the foyer and she saw a medic working on a fallen figure, one of Myra's compatriots in

the Fingers' nondescript gray body armor. The foyer ran
from the street door they'd come through to an opening,
through which Noo could see the central courtyard.
Looking that way, Noo saw more bodies. None of those
wore armor, though, so they weren't part of the strike
force. She supposed they could be hostages, hoped they
weren't, then remembered that her visor had an IFF
display. She blinked it on and was relieved when the AR
tags showed they were hostiles.

Myra led them up four flights of stairs to the third
floor, following the wayfinder path passed to her by
the strike team commander, a young Army captain just
about Noo's daughter's age. The captain remained across
the street for now with a couple of comms techs and
two constables for close security. She directed her heavy
hitters, the Army troops and some of the Fingers muscle,
many of them Army vets, against the knots of rebel
resistance. Other groups without the heavy weapons and
training for first-line combat swept the complex, looking
for the prisoners.

They passed by opened doors and empty rooms, some
furnished and some not. Myra squatted down when
they reached the corner, where the building turned to
follow the main street, and fished out a handful of flitter
drones. She tossed them into the air, and they whisked
off on delicate wings, like so many lethal butterflies.
Noo tugged at the tube of her camelback canteen and
took a drink while Myra studied the feeds from her tiny
flock, before leading them down a hallway into which
none of the strike team had yet passed.

They had barely traveled three meters, just shy of the
first apartment doors, when Myra snapped her weapon

to her shoulder and took a slantwise step into the middle of the hallway. Noo's adrenaline surged and her own weapon came up, her sighting reticle popping into life. She heard Teng moving behind her and laid her finger beside the trigger.

Doors on either side of the hallway, fifteen meters down, slammed open, and nightmares clattered out. Six-legged combat bots skittered towards them as weapon pods swiveled, and targeting lasers tracked across their chests.

Noo cut loose with a burst of armor-piercing rounds, saw them strike the carapace of the left-most bot. She kept firing as the bot's mini-gun opened up on them, but the impact knocked the bot offline enough that the return fire missed her. Teng engaged the other bot, firing burst after burst.

"Fuck this." Myra braced her rifle to her shoulder and used her grenade launcher. It coughed once, twice, and then the rocket motors of the grenades kicked in as their guidance packages locked onto their targets. Noo dropped to her knees and ducked her head. The grenades slammed into the bot's central carapaces and detonated, sending jets of plasma through the ceramic composite armor and into the sensitive internal components.

And, it turned out, the ammo bins.

Noo felt herself lifted by a giant flaming hand that slammed her against the wall. A blast of searing air washed over her, heat she felt even through the body armor, fire-rated battledress, and gloves. Bits of flaming debris pinged off her and she felt the wall shudder as a jagged hunk of what used to be robot embedded itself in the fiberboard between her and Myra, who'd been deposited next to her.

"Okereke, you all right?"

It took Noo a few seconds to realize that someone was talking to *her*, and a few seconds more to respond. She flashed the tactical hand sign for *I'm OK*, not trusting herself to speak yet. Myra, still standing, paused sweeping smoking debris from her shoulders and offered her a hand up. Noo got to her feet and bent to retrieve her weapon while Myra hoisted Teng to his feet. The hallway was a ruin of scorch marks and scattered bot parts.

"Look sharp," Myra said. "You just don't stick bots to guard an empty hallway." After reassuring herself that her team was functional, the Fingers hitter took point again. She activated her vocal projector. "Dr. Ngila? Dr. Lac? Is there anyone here? We're here to rescue you."

A head poked out from the left-hand doorway, about knee height. "We're here. Are you from the Ileri government?"

"Something like that," Myra said, and they hurried down the hallway. Noo followed Myra in and slung her weapon.

The door opened into the living room of a spacious three-bedroom flat that Noo pegged as properly belonging to a group of roommates in their twenties or early thirties rather than a family, judging from the odd mishmash of furnishings, a neoleather couch flanked by mismatched armchairs in two completely different styles. Windows on the far wall overlooked the central courtyard, or would have if the blinds were open. Six people waited inside the room, two on the couch, one in each of the armchairs, the last two on their feet near the doorway.

Myra crossed to the center of the room and Noo came up beside her, eyes darting across the prisoners. Her djinn matched their faces to images of the Commonwealth delegation, and AR tags identifying them sprang into life above their heads...

"The infonet's back up!" Noo exclaimed. She turned towards Teng, grinning—

And saw Teng aiming his weapon at Myra's back, finger on the trigger.

He was too far away for her to reach, and her weapon was still slung, so she lurched backwards and to her right, bent forward at the waist, and hip checked Myra as brutally as she had that smug bitch Indira on the football pitch back in her school days. Myra stumbled and pitched over as Teng's burst cut through the air she'd occupied a split second before. Noo lost her balance too, thrown off by the added mass of her gear and the inconvenient presence of a side table.

She took the fall properly this time, on the fleshy parts of the body, thigh then ass then shoulder. Her weapon was trapped beneath her and her right arm was tangled up in the sling. She watched in horror as Teng pivoted, weapon raised, and shot one of the Commonwealth scientists. A single shot, this time, but that was all he needed. The armor-piercing round punched through the scientist's chest and through the wall behind them, the bullet hole centered in the crimson spray that exploded from the exit wound. Myra spat curses as she tried to sit up and recover her own weapon, which she'd dropped when Noo slammed into her. Two of the remaining scientists froze in place, two dropped to the floor, Dr. Ngila lunged for Teng, who nimbly sidestepped. The scientist missed their grab for Teng's arm, stumbled into one of the armchairs, and tumbled over it.

Noo realized she'd never get her rifle free in time. Her hand closed around the butt of her hand cannon and yanked it out of the holster. The targeting reticle popped up and she discovered the sling, still wrapped around her forearm, kept her from angling high enough for a headshot.

She shot his knees out instead.

Teng dropped his weapon and collapsed to the floor, his screams adding to those of the scientists and Myra's stream of invective. His hands clutched at his ruined legs as Dr. Ngila righted herself, scooping up the fallen man's weapon.

"It won't work," Noo said as she rolled left, freeing her arm and keeping her pistol trained on Teng's head. "It's djinn-locked to him. But keep it away from him."

"What the hell is going on?" Ngila snapped. Despite Noo's admonition she kept the battle rifle's muzzle pointed at Teng.

"We *are* a rescue party," Myra said. Her voice sounded raw. Once again, she reached down and hauled Noo to her feet. "Supposed to be. Constabulary, Army, and other local assets." Which, Noo supposed, was a perfectly valid descriptor of Myra and Noo's roles. She pointed at Teng with her weapon. "He's Directorate, intelligence op, or supposed to be. Okereke, you have any idea what the fuck got into him?"

"Oh yeah." There was only one thing he could be. Noo holstered her pistol and took up her battle rifle again. "He's one of Miguna's moles. Maybe even one of the infected."

<Sort that out later,> sent the raid commander, who'd watched the whole thing unfold remotely via their cams. *<Heavy enemy reinforcements incoming, including power armor. Exfiltrate now.>*

<Right.> Myra began herding the scientists to the door. "Sorry about your colleague, but there's no time. We've got to *move,* people."

"What about him?" Dr. Ngila asked, still clutching the rifle.

"I'll take care of him," Noo said. She jerked her head at the doorway. "Go. I'll bring up the rear." She transferred her rifle to her left hand and drew her pistol once again as the others filed out of the room.

"So, what is it? Infected, or just a traitor?" she asked him, but got only ragged panting in response. Teng's eyes were fixed on her, his face a rictus of pain.

And then, suddenly, his body relaxed, arms falling to his sides, and his face took on a blissful look. "Belonging is *everything,*" Teng said in his gloriously melodious baritone. His voice showed no trace of the agony that should be consuming him. "Join us and your wounds shall be wiped away."

"Fuck that," she said, and fired two rounds into his face.

<Move your ass, Okereke,> Myra sent.

Noo holstered her pistol and set off down the hall in the best imitation of a trot she could manage. Dimly, she was aware of her body's protests at the accumulated abuse. Her back was killing her, and her thighs were just this side of screaming, and her right elbow felt funny. The gunfire had died down somewhat after the initial fusillades, but came more frequently now, as the muffled thump of grenades joined the rattle and rip of automatic fire.

She stumbled down the final flight of stairs but was caught at the bottom by a young Army trooper and his partner, a constable Noo recognized as one of Daniel's trusted cadre. "We're the tail," the constable said. "Time to haul ass." She set off at a run for the far side of the street. Noo did her best to keep up but her stimulant dose was wearing off. The soldier hooked one hand around her belt, both holding her up and pulling her along. Covering fire swept out as their comrades tried to suppress the oncoming rebel reinforcements.

They were five meters shy of safety when the rocket exploded in front of them.

Noo found herself on the ground again, on her back this time. Dazed, she sat up and tried to focus. Her vision swam, and her hearing was shot. Her legs hurt, so she looked down at them—

—and discovered that from the knees down, she didn't have legs anymore.

"Oh," she said, and flopped onto her back.

She felt herself continuing to fall even after hitting the soft grass. Or maybe *sinking* was the better term. The world around her grew less substantial.

I wish I'd given Daniel my answer, she thought before the darkness came.

CHAPTER THIRTY-FIVE

MEIKO

HUB EXTERIOR, ILERI STATION

THEY WERE TWENTY seconds from the intercept point when an annoying chirping sounded in Meiko's ears. "Fuck," one of the troopers next to her on the little maintenance cart said. "Targeting ladar."

"Loh said the drone didn't have anything like that. Javier, stop," Zheng said, and their driver hit the brakes. "Everyone off!"

Meiko unclipped her tether and swung herself over the rail, her eyes questing for a new tether point. Operating in microgravity meant that they could easily turn themselves into accidental and temporary satellites of Ileri, and easy targets if they went flying free in the wrong place.

The chirping ceased, for Meiko anyway, as she pulled herself across the surface to her chosen tether point. She checked her HUD for the positions of her teammates as she clipped in. Her tether was thirty meters long, which had sounded like a lot. But out here on the surface of an asteroid five klicks wide, it seemed pitifully small.

"Emission source pinpointed." One of the troopers, ten meters ahead of Meiko in the direction they'd been traveling, held a sensor wand out from behind the girder he sheltered behind. "Looks like a Hunter-class combat bot."

"Shit. Rebels must be coming for the nano too." Zheng had her right arm extended in firing position. "OK. Bounding overwatch, successive bounds. Ahmed"— the other armored trooper—"and I are trailing element and base of fire. Got it?" Everyone signaled assent, even Meiko; she hadn't practiced these kinds of tactics in decades, but the old lessons had stuck. "Haruman, Bakshi, you lead. Ogawa, you and Achide follow, then me and Ahmed. Go."

Meiko raised her assault laser and searched for targets but found none. When her turn came, she unclipped her tether and pulled herself to a position online with the first two soldiers, took cover, and clipped in again. Zheng and her armored companion then moved up to join the line, and they repeated the cycle. They didn't catch sight of the enemy, but twice more they caught splashes of ladar, confirming something was out there.

Things went to shit on the fourth bound.

She was just clipping in when Bakshi, one of the lead element, called out. "I can see the objective. It's about sixty meters ahe—"

High-velocity slugs punched through the radiator return line Bakshi lurked behind and through their armored suit like it was rice paper. Meiko watched in horror as the spray of blood and gas and tissue that vented out of the exit holes briefly sparkled as it flash-froze, then dissipated. Liquid coolant under high pressure spurted from the punctured radiator and flung Bakshi's corpse out to the limit of their tether, whereupon the combat bot shot them again.

"Counter-battery!" Zheng called. Achide pulled a tube from their chest pack and stuck their arm out from behind one of the radiator's support pillars. Sparkles briefly winked into existence at both ends of the tube as the compressed gas inside kicked the missile out of the launcher. Meiko, knowing what came next, ducked, so she missed the blinding flash as the missile locked onto its target and lit its engine. The trooper was already moving to a new position before the missile struck home.

She poked her assault laser out from around her cover and swept the camera across the area in front of them. She could see the drone now, and her IR sensor picked up the rapidly cooling hotspot that marked where the bot had crouched. Her djinn found a possible target, a human-shaped form on the ground next to the now-stationary drone. She lined up her target reticle and fired three pulses.

At least one of her pulses hit and she was rewarded with the sight of outgassing; she'd breached something under pressure, at least, though whether she'd hurt the person inside the suit wasn't clear. She pulled her weapon back behind cover and unclipped her tether, hunting for her next firing position.

That's when she saw the second bot. "We're flanked! Target bot, nine o'clock from my position, range eighty meters!" She brought up her legs, got her feet onto the stanchion, and pushed off hard. She skimmed along the surface to the next stanchion even as the bot, anchored into the rocky surface of the hub asteroid, fired another burst of slugs, catching Ahmed in the side. Even power armor wasn't proof against the bot's weapon and Ahmed screamed as the rounds penetrated. His screams cut off, whether from the severity of his wounds, loss of pressure in his suit, or the armor's internal medical system pumping him full of sedatives to try and stabilize him, she didn't know.

She reached cover, grabbed on to arrest her motion, and clipped in. She fumbled her laser into firing position and triggered a full ten-pulse burst, the most the weapon could handle before overheating. The bot moved forward and she pivoted towards the other side of her stanchion, anxiously watching the cool indicator. Something flashed between her and Zheng, who had moved forward to engage hostiles up by the drone, and Achide's status indicator went dark. That was bad; only Achide carried missiles, and only those or Zheng's weapons were likely to hurt the bots.

Meiko rolled right, sighted again, and triggered another ten-pulse burst to no evident effect. "Zheng! Can you deal with the bot on our flank? I can't hurt it."

"Busy," Zheng said. Meiko looked and saw her crouched over Haruman's body, realized she was slapping an emergency patch onto the trooper's suit. *Fuck*. Four down in less than a minute, and two of their heaviest weapons out of action to boot.

She rolled left, poked the weapon out again, and swept it across the space between her and the combat bot. *There*, another coolant return line, right between her and the bot, which was now only forty meters away.

"Keep it busy, Meiko," Zheng said. "Just need a few seconds."

"Trying." She unclipped her tether, took a breath and triggered her music. The volume was low, but she sang the ancient Porto song, older than the journey to Exile, as she lined up another ten-round burst into the pipe:

Long live my god
Long live my master
Who taught me
Capoeira...

Coolant sprayed from the holes she'd made, spraying across the space between her and her antagonist. It wasn't much of a screen, but she saw some of the streams hit the bot. Maybe it would help. Just a little... She launched herself across the rocky surface towards Achide's body, sure the bot would kill her before she reached it.

It is water for drinking
It is iron for striking
It is from the sacred drums...

"GOT IT!" Zheng cried out. Meiko blinked up her feed and saw the pressurized canister rupture under the hail of armor-piercing slugs from Zheng's mini-guns. Her djinn, scanning the debris, flashed highlights around a piece bearing a biohazard symbol. From the data dump they'd captured from Mizwar, she knew the nanoware couldn't survive the combination of vacuum and radiation. The station was saved—

The bot fired, but not at Meiko.

Zheng cried out, once, and then her body was sailing out into the dark as the bot fired again, and again, each burst hitting her, each bullet pushing her further out into the dark.

Zheng hadn't clipped her tether.

Meiko blinked back both tears and Zheng's feed, now showing a pinwheeling view of the stars. She grabbed hold of the girder to which Achide's body was tethered and wrapped her legs around it like a lover. Her grasping hands pulled at Achide's chest pack, found the missile. She leaned back, pointed it at the bot and twisted the firing collar. She released the tube and snatched up her laser, sighted in, and fired.

Golden light seared her vision as the missile's engine lit, and a lance of fire hit the combat bot, blowing it to pieces.

Then it was silent, except for the ragged heave of her own breathing.

Her nemesis dead, she carefully eased down to the surface, then scanned the battlefield. Nothing moved, and all the IR traces were dying out, cooling rapidly.

She looked up in the direction her djinn told her Zheng's body must be but couldn't find it. She checked the status indicators again and found that Haruman, indeed, was still alive. She checked the integrity of the emergency patch Zheng had applied, then carefully gathered the trooper into her arms for the short trek back to the cart.

Mission accomplished. But God, what a price.

CHAPTER THIRTY-SIX

SSV Iwan Goleslaw, *Ileri High Orbit*

"Incoming message from the Ileri escort commander."

Andini snapped awake and rubbed a hand across her eyes. She glanced at the time display, grimaced, and reluctantly peeled her sleep sack open. "Put it through, audio only." With pressure restored in perhaps half of *Iwan Goleslaw's* undamaged compartments, she'd felt secure enough to sleep without even a softsuit. A T-shirt and workout shorts were hardly fitting attire for a call with the watchdogs Vega had insisted shadow her ship, though she suspected her counterpart would understand. "Andini here." She didn't croak, exactly, but she grabbed an energy-drink pouch from the stash she kept by her bunk and took a drink to clear her throat.

"Captain Andini, this is Commander Langiri. The rebels appear to be making a push. They've launched a number of shuttles from the surface and all their craft in orbit are maneuvering. We're going to action stations and respectfully suggest you consider doing so as well."

She'd wondered when the next phase of the battle would light off. "Thank you, Commander. I'll do so. Do I have clearance to relaunch my remaining weapon busses?"

"Not at this time, Captain. Please maintain your connections to the task-group tactical net so we can coordinate defensive fires and keep clear from each other's firing solutions."

It was the answer she'd expected, but figured it was worth a try. "Absolutely, Commander. Do you advise securing my radiators?"

Langiri hesitated. "Perhaps not immediately. The analysis teams are still working out the rebels' likely deployment. But we're well within the probability cone."

Damn. The damage to her ship's heat-management systems had turned out to be too severe for her crew to repair, and the lost coolant and phase-change material had to be replaced anyway. If she had to pull in the radiators, her combat power would be limited to point-defense guns and whatever weapons the Ileris permitted her to launch. But if she kept them deployed to keep the lasers and particle cannon operational without cooking the ship, she risked losing all her last good way to dump heat. She'd have no alternative but to beg the Ileris to let her dock, and the thought of that was unbearable. "Understood, Commander. *Iwan Goleslaw* will come to Condition Two and await further information." After the briefest of pauses, she added a codicil. "Be aware that I intend to exercise my discretion in defending my vessel."

Langiri sounded bemused. "I understand completely, Captain. We'll keep you informed as things develop. Langiri out."

Andini drained her drink pouch and fancied she could feel the chemical kick-start already working. Imaginary or not, she felt her fatigue recede just a bit. She snapped open a command window. "Attention, my children. Action stations. Bring the ship to Condition Two. Execute." She heard her slightly muffled voice through her cabin door, along with the alarm buzzer, followed by the sounds of her crew hurrying to their stations. She sighed, grabbed a nutrient bar from her stash, tore it open with her teeth, and started the process of shucking her clothes so she could don her suit as she chewed.

With her yeoman's assistance, fifteen minutes later she was able to pull herself, fully suited, into the combat center. "Status report!" she barked after the watch officer transferred the con. The news was mixed. Casualties had been fully offloaded at last, and two of her three shuttles were snugged into their bays. The third remained on Ileri Station. Point defense was still completely down on the damaged side of her ship, and only forty percent of her launchers were operational, but she had full maneuvering capability again—as long as the radiators were deployed. "Things could be worse," she said to Dinata, who joined her in the combat center.

"You should ready the special ordnance," Dinata said, in her most imperious tone. "We cannot allow this infestation to spread."

Dinata had never struck Andini as a practical person, and this certainly remained true now. "To what end, Minister? Our conversion bombs aren't ship-to-ship weapons."

"The Ileris are clearly dealing in proscribed technologies. You saw the evidence."

"I've seen evidence that a rogue commercial entity has done so," Andini said carefully. "No evidence has surfaced of widespread contamination, or of collusion on the part of the Ileri government."

Dinata snorted. "This rebellion is evidence enough. You've also seen Mizwar's report."

"Are you ordering me to conduct a general planetary bombardment?" Andini said, wondering if this was the moment she'd been dreading. "I'll happily engage any clearly identified targets, but I'm hardly going to sterilize the planet based on the information to date." She was grateful her orders permitted her that much discretion.

Dinata huffed but didn't push further. Andini returned her attention to monitoring the imminent battle.

She didn't have long to wait. Her tactical officer's projections told the story clearly enough. "Ears, call the Ileris." The link came up almost immediately. "Commander, it seems apparent the rebels plan to converge on our formation."

Langiri, on video this time, looked grim. "That's our analysis as well, Captain." A side window popped open to display navigational data. "My orders are that we maneuver on this course in order to link up with reinforcements."

Andini flicked a copy of his instructions onto the main tactical display. Her tactical officer frowned. "That relief force is smaller than I'd expect," she said. Andini relayed that concern to the Ileri.

"Higher command hasn't shared all their plans with me," he said. Andini thought she detected a note of frustration in his voice, but the expert system reading both his verbal and nonverbal cues gave anxiety a higher score. "However, I've been given discretion in the matter of allowing you to launch more busses."

A-ha. Vega's plan—and Andini, having studied the new Prime Minister's career carefully, felt sure it was Vega's plan—became clear. A mix of anger and admiration for the Ileri leader's boldness warred within her. "I see," she said. "Do I have that clearance?"

"My tactical officer suggests waiting until this waypoint," Langiri said, and the point in question flashed once in the projection. "In case we need to maneuver again. That should preserve their operational time."

"Very good. Andini out." She cut the connection and turned to her tactical officer. "We're bait."

The tactical officer nodded grimly. Dinata looked confused. "What do you mean?"

Andini highlighted the bulk of the Ileri formations, which weren't moving to join *Iwan Goleslaw* and her escorts. "The rebels are coming for us. Vega's letting them, sending just enough of her own strength to make it a fair fight, and defend against any accusations that she left us out to hang. She's going to let us bleed her enemies for her."

"You sound like you approve."

Andini sighed. "It's a smart plan. I'd probably do the same in her case." She ordered the ship control officer to maneuver in concert with their escort and put the launcher crews on standby. "Pull in the radiators and set Condition One. Execute."

The second Battle of Ileri played out much the way Andini expected, at least at first. *Iwan Goleslaw* and the Ileri ships with her launched their ordnance at the appointed time, Andini putting everything except for the special weapons and her anti-missile munitions into service. The rebel formations, converging from several different orbits, launched their own array of missiles and weapons busses. Andini and the Ileris knocked most of these down, but some got through. To their credit, Langiri and the other Ileri commanders did their utmost to screen *Iwan Goleslaw's* blind side, at some expense to their own point defense. The rebels, for their part, focused the bulk of their fire on the Ileri vessels, and before long both frigates became expanding balls of plasma and debris.

Andini logged a note commending their bravery and turned her attention to killing as many of the rebels as she could, using her impaired ability to maneuver to keep her damaged side away from the enemy.

Strangely, the oncoming flotillas didn't focus fire on the *Iwan Goleslaw* itself. Instead they poured most of their attacks into the cloud of weapons platforms surrounding the Saljuan ship. They directed the remainder of their fire at the approaching loyalist vessels. Her tactical officer figured it out first. "They're going for CQB," she said. Close quarters battle, where mass drivers and particle beam weapons reigned supreme. Weapons that Andini couldn't use without cooking her ship.

"Swing the surviving busses to the far side of the ship," Andini ordered. "If the rebels aren't shooting at us, we can shield the busses and use our point defense to interdict the incoming fire. Drop the remaining decoys and try to make it look like the busses are still holding station."

Fist moved to comply. Dinata looked confused. "What are you doing?"

Andini's mouth set in a grim line. "I'm holding a knife behind my back so I can stab the fuckers when they get close enough."

Whether the rebels fell for the ruse, or simply didn't care, she didn't know. The first wave of enemy vessels bored in, though her escorts managed to kill two before the range closed. She felt like she could practically reach out and touch the enemy ships. Finally, with less than a minute to go before they reached mass driver range, she gave the order. "*Now.* Dump everything we've got at them."

It was knife-fighting range indeed, at least in space combat terms. The rebels' point-defense systems had scarce seconds to swat down the incoming barrage, and perhaps half of the Saljuan ordnance found its targets. Flowers of fire blossomed above the planet's night side, lighting the heavens. Ships and crews died, some before they realized they were in danger.

But some got through, and then the real surprise came.

"Sweet Mother of the Leap, they're launching shuttles," the tactical officer said. "They're going to board us."

An iron fist gripped Andini's heart as the rebel's plan became plain. "How many?" she asked, wondering if her voice sounded as hollow as she felt.

"Depends on how full they are, but I estimate two hundred to two hundred fifty boarders."

"Target the shuttles," she said, her lips suddenly dry. "Use the mass drivers, too. We're lost anyway if we don't take them out."

But the short range worked in the attacker's favor as well, minimizing the time the incoming assault craft were exposed. And now, at last, the rebels engaged *Iwan Goleslaw* directly, aiming to disable her point defenses with pinpoint fire.

Andini imagined she could feel the moment the first boarding craft clamped on in her very bones, even though it was two hundred meters down the hull. "How long until the reinforcing task force is in range?"

"Twenty minutes."

Too long. Her despair gave way to grim determination. "Right. Major Nkruma's people to repel boarders. All other crew, abandon ship." She locked eyes with her tactical officer as the alarm triggered by her order sounded on the comm of every Saljuan aboard. "Fist. Once the crew is off, we'll scuttle." The tactical officer, face pale, acknowledged. Andini turned to Dinata. "Minister, my yeoman will see you to your shuttle."

Dinata, thoroughly lost, looked back and forth between Andini and the display. "But our mission—"

"Is a failure. So be it." Andini called up the ship control officer as her yeoman dragged the still-protesting minister away. Most of the combat-center crew followed, but a few, mainly those directing point defense against a new wave of boarding craft, stayed at their posts. Pride in her crew pushed back against a new wave of despair. "I need a course that keeps us between the shuttles and the rebel ships. Highest burn you can manage."

The massive ship rotated and thrust returned. It was a paltry one-third gravity, but it would have to do. Andini and the tactical officer unlocked the red panels she'd never once imagined she'd need to open. Long minutes ticked by. Finally, the shuttle pilots reported they had launched.

"How long until they're at minimum safe distance?" she asked. She could hear the fire between the boarders and Nugroho's troops now.

"Three minutes. They've got to kill their initial velocity first."

Shit. She should have held off on maneuvering until the shuttles launched. Too late now, though. She hoped it would be enough.

Barely a minute remained when the tactical officer cried out in surprise. "Captain! Several of the boarding craft are detaching. They're burning hard to rejoin their ships."

"What?" She checked the display, confirmed it with her own eyes. The shooting outside the combat center didn't let up, though. "Why are they doing that?" She flipped the display to show the internal condition of the ship, grimacing at the red blotches denoting the boarders' incursions. They were perilously close to the bridge, the combat center, *and* engineering. But one incongruous tentacle caught her eye, probing deeply but far from the critical stations that would grant the attackers control of her ship.

They had breached the special ordnance store. *The antimatter bombs must be aboard the escaping shuttles.*

She had one card left to play. She prayed the rebels were still close enough for it to work.

"Now," she told the tactical officer, and turned the key.

The nuclear scuttling charges buried deep within *Iwan Goleslaw* detonated, and once again, a new star burned brightly in the Ileri sky. But only for a little while.

CHAPTER THIRTY-SEVEN

TOIWA

GOVERNMENT HOUSE, ILERI STATION, TRAILING RING

POCKETS OF REBELS still held out in the hub and the north ring, but Government House was secure again, with assistance from Captain Gupta's marines. Toiwa and Major Biya delivered their reports to Prime Minister Vega and her cabinet from the huge briefing suite in which they'd first talked with the Saljuans, just a few days before. The conversation was all facts and figures and was totally lacking in narrative, as if the speakers were reporting quarterly-arrest and case-clearance rates. The words felt sterile, banal, and it bothered Toiwa that they seemed to strip meaning from the sacrifices of Zheng and the other dead, from Okereke and Imoke and the other maimed and wounded, from the innumerable stories she'd heard of ordinary citizens who'd found ways to help each other, and to stand up against the rebels. What had these people paid for?

The future? Or just a simple continuation of the present?

"When did I become so dissatisfied with the status quo? Me, the policewoman?" she asked Eduardo, when they finally managed to snatch a few hours of privacy, after *Iwan Goleslaw* burned brightly one last time, as Vega's full plan became clear and her reserve warships hammered the rebel strong points on the ground.

He smiled gently and stroked her forehead. "Love, you've been that way since the moment we met. You've always fought against injustice, and against those who wield power unjustly. You are my bright cavaleira, straight as a sword, bringing judgment to the wicked."

She flushed with embarrassment and not a little shame, thinking about what she'd done these past few days. "I'm not so bright anymore. Rusty and tarnished, more like."

"Only in your own eyes," he told her.

She felt tarnished indeed, as she found herself reciting antiseptic numbers that could never truly represent her dead, her living, her compromised souls caught by some combination of coercive nanoware, loss of opportunity, and demagoguery. Less than ten percent of the rebels tested positive for this strange slow-burning variant of the Unity Plague that Councilor Walla, Ogawa's assailants and a few others carried. How could these bloodless figures ever reflect why so many became caught up in Miguna's movement?

At least, with the nanoware destroyed, she didn't have to worry about a full-blown outbreak of the Unity Plague. At least not yet.

Vega asked to speak with her privately as the conference wrapped up. She withdrew to her new office. Ruhindi's was still ruined and bore the scars of her assassination; Toiwa didn't think she'd ever use it. Instead, she'd installed herself in the former deputy governor's suite. Leaving Sergeant Chijindu at the door, she flipped on the projector, and she and Vega regarded each other's telepresent forms.

"You're doing well," Vega began, her normally gruff voice like dripping honey. "The kind of transition you've made can be difficult under normal circumstances, much less this kind of chaos. You're a credit to the office."

"Thank you, Prime Minister," Toiwa said, feeling uneasy in the face of Vega's praise. It wasn't that she didn't think she was doing well, it was just something about Vega's manner that masked what Toiwa now knew lay inside the other woman. *I know now what you'll do, what—and who—you'll sacrifice to get your way.* She fixed on her politician's face. "Many outstanding people have stepped up into larger responsibilities. I'm pleased you think I'm setting a good example for them."

Vega folded her hands together on the table, leaning forward. "There are some crucial decisions to make, very soon," she said. "We have a chance to put Ileri back together in a way our descendants can cherish, not curse. And our chance to keep the rest of the Cluster from invoking Interdiction, or worse. All that hinges on what we do in the very short term. You see that, I hope?"

She felt the anger, cold and deep, that had lurked beneath her surface ever since Ogawa had told her of the hidden lab and its work. It wasn't clear to her yet just what Vega's involvement was in the government's own dabbling with the Unity Plague, but there was no way she hadn't known about it. Even if those efforts didn't rise to the level of whatever Miguna and his ilk had been up to, they were definitely playing with technology proscribed under the Accords. *An Interdiction or worse, you and yours have almost brought down on us as much as Miguna.*

She kept that latent fury buried, and instead nodded slowly. It wasn't that the bit about putting their world back together wasn't critical. It would be so easy to give in to the desire for revenge, to demand retribution for their losses. History, from that of Lost Earth on through the days of Exile, told her that path never led to a good end.

"I believe so," she said. "We have to chart a response that walks the line between justice and reconciliation. Find ways to reform society and reintegrate those who followed the guidance of the infected, and to expunge the agent from those who did succumb." *The agent* was the euphemism Kala Valverdes had coined to avoid invoking the legendary horror of the Unity Plague. It made Toiwa uncomfortable to dance around the truth, but she'd let herself be persuaded that they needed this fig leaf of deception. "And we have to shore up the weak points in our society that Miguna and his pack were able to exploit."

Miguna, for his part, was *not* among the infected. He'd been abandoned by much of his inner circle, who almost certainly *had* been, judging from the forensic evidence after the fact, and examinations of the few who'd been captured or killed during the first part of the rebellion. The rest had fled aboard the shuttles that launched just before the assault on *Iwan Goleslaw* that rendezvoused with the surviving rebel warships before those jumped out of the system. After the space battle's conclusion,

Vega's forces had cornered Miguna in his command center, alone but for a handful of long-time sycophants, ranting about how incompetence and betrayal had brought him to these straits. He now languished in secure detention somewhere in the bowels of Fort Ali. Was he the puppet master? Or the figurehead diverting attention from whomever truly gave orders to the infected?

Toiwa doubted Vega or her people shared Toiwa's qualms about medically assisted interrogation.

Here and now, Vega favored Toiwa with a smile, the kind one gave a student who'd just given their teacher the proper answer to a pop quiz. "Just so. It's going to be tricky, but I've got some smart people working on it. I'd like you to be part of this effort, but you'll need to decide just what role you want to play."

Toiwa wasn't sure where this was going. "What role, ma'am?" She spread her hands as if to encompass all her new charges. "I thought my role as governor was quite clear."

"That's one option of course," Vega said. "Under the law, you remain governor of the station until we can arrange for elections, which will likely be several months. I suspect you'd probably win the election if you chose to run. But there's another option I feel compelled to offer you."

Toiwa shifted in her seat, uneasy. "I'm not sure what you mean," she said. "Though I admit I haven't given much thought to things beyond crisis control just yet."

"Quite properly so," Vega said, soothingly. "If you were the kind of person who was already planning their next move instead of working their ass off to put out wildfires, we wouldn't be having this conversation."

"Thank you," Toiwa said, confused about just where Vega was going with this. "You mentioned another option?"

"Indeed," Vega said. "The position of High Commissioner of the Ileri Constabulary is open, you might recall." Vega's image leaned back in her chair, watching Toiwa with care.

Oh. Oh, shit.

"I... I hadn't really thought that through, ma'am," she said after a moment. "That... isn't an option I'd considered pursuing." She paused. It wasn't that High Commissioner wasn't, or at least hadn't, been her ultimate ambition, and she wagered Vega knew that. "It's certainly something I aspired to in my career," she admitted. "Just... not now."

"I thought so," Vega said. "It certainly wouldn't be a cakewalk. My social-science advisers are already pushing for a number of reforms. Some of those involve the Constabulary, along with other necessary social rebuilding."

"What do you mean, ma'am?" Toiwa asked.

Vega sighed. "Nearly a third of our citizens are under the age of thirty, the largest single demographic group on the planet. Until recently, we'd managed to mostly avoid the economic bottlenecks that led to the Great Looting back on Lost Earth. But opportunity for our young people has been stagnating, and our leaders have lacked a vision for what our future as a world, as a people, should be. That vacuum is a large part of what Miguna and the One Worlders exploited. They provided a vision, however flawed and toxic it was. That was my predecessor's biggest mistake. She failed to share the message about how joining the Commonwealth would help that."

Toiwa found herself nodding. She understood Vega's arguments intellectually, if not in her own life. Her own drive for truth, for justice, gave her life purpose. But she'd seen that grasping search for meaning in some of her friends. "A better way to help people discover and follow their vocations, for one," she said, and Vega smiled and nodded in approval.

"Indeed," Vega said. "Something the Commonwealth does well. I thought you'd grasp the nature of the work before us. I think that makes you a perfect candidate to help rebuild the Constabulary for the future."

It *was* a dazzling vision, the offer of the very thing she'd worked for nearly twenty years for, though she had expected to work nearly another twenty before getting her shot at it. She knew already some of the changes she'd make, how she'd go about making them, the personnel changes she'd push through... well, that last would depend on who'd survived the rebellion, and their roles in it.

But was Vega telling her what she wanted to hear? Toiwa, as a constable, had learned to look at people's actions to discern their true motives; and the PM had proved utterly ruthless. Biya had privately explained the gambit of using the Saljuans and their paltry escort as bait, and the way Vega seemed to simply tick those lost lives off as acceptable losses chilled her.

That was before one considered the hidden asteroid lab and the government's own work with proscribed technology, and whatever role Vega had played in all that.

So that left her with a question: where would the Governorship lead, if she took that road? If she jumped the tracks to the purely political side? Not that she wasn't something of a political animal already: no one achieved her rank in the Constabulary without being one. But this was a bigger game, and she knew enough to understand the size of her knowledge gaps, to have a clue about just how ill-prepared for this role she truly was.

And yet part of her welcomed the challenge. And if the canvas she'd have as High Commissioner was broad, how much bigger was the one open to her as governor, sitting atop the cable of her world's gateway? Or perhaps, and the thought made her dizzy, as a Member of Parliament, the cabinet, or even the seat Vega now occupied?

She took a deep breath and blew it out slowly. *I can't decide this now.* "Please forgive me, Prime Minister, but I need a little time to consider this," she said. "And to talk with my family. This is something that will affect all of us."

Vega chuckled. "That's putting it mildly," she said. "And that's fine. You don't need to decide right away. I'm pleased, in fact, that you want to think it over." But, Toiwa thought, her eyes told a different story. *She thought I'd jump at the chance to be High Commissioner. I'm not playing the game the way she expected.*

The PM changed subjects. "There's a less pleasant matter we still need to discuss. The Saljuan spies you're holding."

She knew it only *felt* like the room's temperature dropped by five degrees. Dinata and the surviving crew of *Iwan Goleslaw*, their shuttles damaged by the explosion of their ship, had been rescued by the Navy and

416

currently enjoyed Vega's hospitality on one of the orbital bases. The minister's disposition hadn't been improved by her near brush with death and the destruction of her vessel. "Are they upset about how we interrogated their agents?"

Vega chuckled. "Surprisingly, no. Minister Dinata wasn't concerned at all that we used facilitated questioning; it's apparently routine procedure on Salju. No, she claims that we'd never have discovered the truth without their spying. And she maintains that we should be grateful Mizwar and his crew started the housecleaning, discovered the aerosolized plague vector and destroyed most of it."

Toiwa nodded slowly. "She's... not entirely wrong," she said. "We'd have found them soon, after discovering their private network. But maybe not before the coup. Of course, it looks like the coup was triggered prematurely by her arrival and threats, so who's to say?" She realized the fingers of her left hand were softly drumming on the table and put her hand into her lap to still it. "What do we need to decide?"

"Dinata wants us to return Mizwar and all the other agents to their custody and give them safe passage out of the system."

"They're hardly candidates for diplomatic immunity," Toiwa protested, and let a little of her anger show in her voice. "We're to let them go, without justice for their victims?"

"That," Vega said, "is what I want to discuss with you."

Oh. Another test. She wondered if she'd get used to this; if she was going to keep working with Vega, either as governor or High Commissioner, she'd *have* to get used to it. "What are they offering in return for the prisoners?" she said.

"For one, a recommendation against invoking full Interdiction, opting for a temporary quarantine instead," Vega said. "Assuming the government can fully re-establish our authority across the planet and system."

"I see," Toiwa said. From Dinata, at least, that was a major concession. "There's no question about our ability to re-secure the peace, I trust."

Vega shook her head. "Miguna's rebellion died the moment they went after the *Iwan Goleslaw,* and the surviving rebel ships jumped out of the system. We'll have the remaining organized resistance cleaned up within a few days, though unrest will likely continue for some time. Hence the need for the reforms we discussed a moment ago."

She thought things over for a moment. "I'd prefer we not drop the charges against Mizwar and his accomplices," she said. "But we could suspend them. Banish him and his accomplices from Ileri space forever, and if they ever *do* show back up, we throw them into detention immediately, no chance of release." She held up a finger. "Reparations to the victims of his illegal actions, or to their families, must be part of any deal." She thought some more. *What about the big picture? Think like a governor, not a constable.* "And no Saljuan military presence in Ileri space without our express advance permission. If they insist on observers to ensure we're cleaning up, have them come from the Triumvirate, or one of the non-aligned worlds."

Vega nodded. "I think we're on the same page here,"

she said. "I hadn't considered reparations for the victims. I suppose that's something you're more used to. It's a worthy addition. But you're not opposed to a deal?"

"I don't *like* it at all," Toiwa admitted, "but I don't think we have a choice."

"Nor do I." Vega glanced aside at some private window. "That's all the time I can spare at the moment, I'm afraid. My staff will send a draft of the agreement for your review. I expect your full and frank appraisal."

"Thank you, Prime Minister." Vega's image winked out, and Toiwa summoned Valverdes. "What's next?"

MEIKO

COMMONWEALTH CONSULATE, ILERI STATION, SOUTH RING

"THIS CERTAINLY ISN'T the course of events I expected," Kumar said to Meiko as they settled into a pair of deep, comfortable chairs. This meeting room was furnished more like a parlor than the more starkly functional one in which they'd first spoken just a few days and a lifetime ago. This chair would be perfect for curling up and reading in, or taking a nap, or cuddling a puppy, Meiko thought. Neosilk hangings in shades of brown and ochre and burnt orange covered the walls. A bot wheeled in bearing frosted tumblers of chilled pineapple juice and placed them on the low table between the chairs, which were set at the angle one saw in photo-op images.

A much more cordial reception than my first.

Kumar pulled a flask from her jacket, unscrewed the

cap, and poured a generous dollop of something clear into her own glass. Kumar waved the flask over Meiko's glass. "Want a hit? And no, this is not a test."

"What's in it?" Meiko asked, trying to sniff discreetly.

"Vodka. Something the locals do decently."

Meiko considered the offer for a second, then shook her head. "Not right now. I've got a meeting with Dr. Ngila after this, and I have a hard enough time keeping up with her even when I'm not impaired."

Kumar nodded, capped her flask and returned it to her jacket. "I promised myself a drink when this was over," she said, raising her glass. "Not that it's truly over, but nailing that Saljuan bastard and preventing a station-wide nanoware infection seem like milestones worth marking."

"I'll drink to that," Meiko said with a slight smile, and lifted her own glass. They clinked and sipped. The juice was just this side of ice-cold, almost enough to hurt her teeth, sweet but not overly so.

Kumar settled back into her chair and looked at Meiko with the slightly out-of-focus gaze that indicated a private AR window hovered between them. "Do you realize how incredibly lucky you've been? How many rules and protocols you've breached? That if you hadn't delivered the results you have, that your ass would be bounced out of the service so fast you'd beat a driveframe back home?"

Not entirely out of the woods, then. Meiko sipped as she considered her answer and settled on the simplest version of the truth. "I didn't have anything to lose. Even without my career on the line, failure became less and less an option as things unfolded." She shrugged, surprised at how relaxed she felt. "My covert days are done, I see that. So, saving that part of my career? It didn't matter." She set down her glass and slouched deeper into the chair. "Accomplishing the mission became the only thing that mattered, and the rest could go hang. And then, when the situation escalated, things just needed doing. So I did them."

Kumar chuckled. "Assassin caught, Saljuan covert-action cell exposed and destroyed, and this pocket of Unity's Children exposed? Mission accomplished indeed. Helping stop a planetary rebellion and stopping a plague were just bonus actions, then?"

What the... Meiko jerked upright. "What do you mean, 'This pocket of Unity's Children exposed'? What the hell are Unity's Children?"

Kumar's expression turned wry. "Something you're cleared for now," she said, and threw Meiko a data packet.

Meiko's djinn caught it and she popped it open—or started to. A familiar bright and boldly lettered form, a Commonwealth security classification file wrapper, filled the window. She pressed her right thumbprint to her djinn's reader and murmured "I acknowledge," and the wrapper gave way, revealing a smaller-than-expected cache of documents.

She looked over at Kumar, who offered a resigned smile. "Read the abstract. I'll wait," she said, so Meiko did. It took, according to her djinn, seven minutes and twenty-four seconds. And as each second ticked by, she felt more and more disoriented.

She reached the end and held her glass out to Kumar. "If the offer is still open, I'd like to take you up on it."

Wordlessly, Kumar pulled out her flask and poured a generous portion into Meiko's half-empty tumbler. Meiko thanked her and slugged back half of it. The vodka burned pleasantly on its way down her throat. The sensation helped focus her mind, brought her back to here and now. "The infection left Earth with us after all."

"So the evidence tells us," Kumar said with a nod. "There were rumors and suspicions even back in the earliest days of Exile, of course. Some think that there was an outbreak on Sumatra back in PE 61 and that's why they nuked themselves, to keep it from spreading. That's never been proved definitively, though."

So much for being beyond surprise. "People knew that far back?" she said. Her head swam. *For someone who has lived with lies for so long, why does this one hit so hard?*

Kumar shook her head. "Some suspected it for decades, but the first confirmed case of infection was only uncovered fifty years ago. Unity's Children, by the way, is what that first group called themselves. We just adopted the term." She paused to take a drink. "It's possible the Saljuans encountered some earlier. It would explain a lot about the resurgence of their zero-tolerance policies towards innovative nanotech around a hundred years ago, and their aggressive expansion effort ever since."

"I'd thought getting stuck on a world they named *Snow* was enough to fuel their 'never again' stance, personally," Meiko said. She considered downing the rest of her drink but held off. "Why read me in now?" she asked.

Kumar waved her glass at Meiko. "Because you're involved," she said. "The prisoner you took on your last mission is almost certainly from a UC cell here on Ileri. He was after the conversion bombs *Fenghuang* carried, though we still don't know why. That was the biggest UC operation we knew of, until they launched this rebellion." She waved her glass in a circle. "Which you are also involved with. They're getting bolder, coming out of the shadows. Which means we need more operatives on this beat." She pointed at Meiko again. "You broke the rules but doing so was the right call with the stakes what they were, even if you didn't know just how high. Now you do."

Meiko sat back, stunned, trying to take it all in. She was still tired in her bones; she'd pushed herself to the very edge of her envelope. *Not as good as I once was, or able to go on like I used to.* She was sixty-two years old and had been away from home for nearly three standard years and two major missions and now *this*.

Finally, she asked the question which had hung between them since they first sat down. "What happens now?"

"First, we help the Ileris get their house in order, so we can bring them into the Commonwealth," Kumar said. "So that when the next Saljuan warship shows up packing conversion bombs, which I don't doubt is going to happen, those asses won't be quite as ready to threaten to turn a planet of seventy million people, one of the most habitable worlds in the Cluster, into a ball of glowing glass. That means we need to help the Ileris root out the UC here."

"Most of the rebels aren't infected, though," Meiko said. "Less than one in ten. And less than one in three

Ileris backed Miguna and the One Worlders. They were just disproportionately strong in the military and police, where the rate of infection was much higher, from what Dr. Ngila and the Ileri scientists are finding." Somewhere around one in three, in fact, which Meiko found seriously troubling. "Dinata could still call for Interdiction, though."

"Vega's cut a deal with Dinata. Quarantine, but not full Interdiction. At least for now."

The realization hit Meiko then. *I'm not going home. Not yet, anyway.* "We're stuck here, aren't we," she said, unable to keep the note of bitterness out of her voice.

Kumar knocked back the rest of her drink and locked eyes with Meiko. "Some of us are. But you don't have to be."

"What do you mean?"

Kumar waved her hand and called up an image of *Amazonas* as the bot returned with a fresh serving for Kumar. "Captain Gupta will be heading back very soon to report what's happened here," she said. "You could be on *Amazonas* when it leaves. I need someone cleared on all this to carry a report back. You're certainly well qualified to do so."

A spark of hope returned. "I could go home?"

"You've earned it," Kumar said. "But I'd like you to consider staying on."

"What would I be doing?" Meiko asked warily.

"Short term? You're ideally positioned to keep an eye on Dr. Ngila's people and the Ileris, liaise between the boffins and the intelligence services. You've got contacts with the criminal underground here. And Toiwa doesn't hate you."

"She kicked me off the station," Meiko interjected.

Kumar waved that away. "That was before you brought back the assassins, and before you heroically helped save her station. She's a woman who favors results, and she's demonstrating more flexibility than I anticipated given her past record. Plus, she seems to trust Shariff, whose partner and granddaughter seem to trust *you*. I think she'll be fine with you sticking around."

"I doubt the Saljuans are going to be so forgiving," Meiko said.

"You might be surprised. I think they have a lot of respect for you. They're pragmatic, even if they've got iron bars up their asses." Kumar shrugged. "But some of those rebels got away after Andini blew her ship to MC^2. We need to be sure they don't have any footholds left to work with if they come back."

But I could go home. The ache in her heart, unassuaged for the last year, for longer than that, truly, was physical. She had served her time in the darkness, holding the line for the light, had earned her scars and those first gray hairs.

Surely *someone* else could help put things back together here, could take her place on the line.

But could they do the job as well as she could? What if Ileri succumbed to Unity's Children, and she wasn't here to do her part in stopping it? What kind of future had she been serving to build, these last forty years?

"I don't suppose they're going give us hardship pay for this?" she said.

"Now you know why I'm day drinking," Kumar said. She raised her glass, and Meiko raised her own, and together they drank to the onset of their own exile.

Noo

Thanh Victor Medical Center, Ileri Station, Forward Ring

Noo WOKE FEELING positively *fluffy*, which was surprising, since she hadn't expected to wake up at all.

"You're back with us," said a gravelly voice that made her heart skip. Literally, apparently, since one of the monitors squawked alarmingly, prompting a nurse to rush in and paw his way through the monitor fields anxiously.

"I am," she croaked.

The nurse interrupted his examination to raise a squirt bottle of water to her lips and helped her drink. "Don't talk too much yet," he admonished, but he left the water bottle in her hand and skipped out as briskly as he'd come in.

"You gave me a fright, woman," Daniel said. He sat in a power chair, with a brace cradling his head. But his hands were steady and warm as they wrapped around her free hand.

"So did you, old man," she said, her voice sounding less like something to frighten children with. She glanced down, noted the unnatural shortness of her legs beneath the blankets. "I didn't imagine that part, then."

"We're a pair, aren't we?" He patted the arm of his chair. "You're going to get one of these soon, they tell me. And that they can probably regrow your legs."

"Well, we can go dancing afterwards," she said, and he looked away. "Wait, what did I say?"

His eyes found hers. "Dancing seems to be off the table for me," he said gravely.

"Shit." The word was out before her brain caught up to her mouth. "I'm sorry, love. What happened?" She listened carefully as he explained, telling her the story of the doomed assault, and the damage done. "The doctors say I likely won't ever walk again. The rest, they can fix, though it will be a while."

She gave him a smile and squeezed his hand. "I seem to have time."

ONE OF THE cutters tasked with orbital debris clean-up located Zheng's body a few days later, spinning in a long orbit around the planet. Toiwa ordered the cutter to Ileri Station the moment she learned the news and came in person to invite Noo and Daniel to the funeral.

The ceremony was strangely simple in light of the number of VIPs in attendance. In addition to Toiwa and the top brass of the station government and the Constabulary, Major Biya turned up with a military honor guard; the soldiers and police split the pallbearers' duties. Fathya and Fari stood amidst the massed ranks of the Shariff family and associates, to which Daniel, Noo, and Yinwa attached themselves. The young woman turned out to have had a sizable number of friends, and her family— shuttled up at government expense—numbered nearly two dozen. The Commonwealth Consul attended with a respectable contingent, Meiko in his wake. Even Pericles Loh came, though only Myra accompanied him.

No one seemed to mind that Noo dozed off through the brief rounds of chanting and verse-reading, or the series of remembrances offered by Zheng's family and friends. She was awake enough to see Meiko start forward as if to share before a short woman next to her, the science attaché according to her social profile, dissuaded her. Fari did come forward, though, to speak on behalf of their short-lived team.

"There was no finer person to have at your side when the night is dark, danger surrounds you, and desperate action is the only path forward." Fari's voice was thick with emotion. "I would not be standing here today without Maria's skill and steadfast courage." She looked out at the crowd, her eyes glistening, and Noo wept silently herself. "Many of us here today would not. And though I didn't know her long, I miss her terribly."

Afterwards, Noo and Daniel lingered in the temple space rather than try to force their power chairs through the crush of people. Loh found them tucked away in the corner furthest from the incense burner. "Might I speak to your mother privately?" he asked Yinwa, who rolled her eyes before slipping out to wait with Fari and Ifedapo. Daniel made as if to leave, but Loh indicated he should stay.

Loh crouched down before them, bringing his eyes to their level, and snapped a privacy field into place. "I wanted to thank you both for what you did for us all," he said.

Noo shrugged while Daniel, who while not a diplomat, was at least more of one than Noo, made appropriately grateful noises.

"It appears the system is going to be quarantined."

"I watch the news," she said. She flicked her eyes at Daniel, who watched the Fingers boss with a bemused expression. "What are you getting at, Pericles?"

"I can arrange to get people out of the system, for

a little while at least. The Navy has their hands full between helping mop up the last rebels and preventing Kessler syndrome in close orbit. It will be two weeks, three at most, before they can lock down traffic from the outer-system station."

"Why would I want to leave?" she asked, puzzled.

He reached over and bumped his djinn to hers. "I can think of one reason," he said, as she opened the file and found a remarkably detailed dossier on Mizwar, including bits of information about his activities beyond Ileri.

She reached over and touched her djinn to Daniel's. He opened the file and she studied his expression as he perused it. They locked eyes and opened their private channel.

<They'll probably take him straight back to Salju, now that he's burned to both us and the Commonwealth,> Daniel sent.

<That seems likely.> Her hands twisted in her lap.

His eyes flicked downward to his legs, and the space where hers ended. *<We wouldn't exactly be inconspicuous. And neither one of us is exactly in fighting trim.>*

She glanced out the doorway. *<We can bring some highly motivated muscle.>*

His mouth drew tight, and his eyes looked up and out into the middle distance as he thought it through. *<It will delay getting you new legs.>*

<I'm too old to go running after the shits anyway.>

He gave her a faint smile, and she knew his answer.

"I might be open to a bit of travel," she said.

Daniel reached over and took her hand. "*We* would be open to it."

"And possibly a companion or two," Noo amended.

Loh nodded slowly. "I thought you might," he said as he stood up. He shook Noo's hand, then Daniel's. "I'll start making the arrangements. I'll need to know for how many the day after tomorrow."

"That just gives us enough time for the wedding," Daniel said, and Loh broke out into a huge grin.

"Congratulations, and best wishes for a fruitful honeymoon trip."

The Huntress came into her dreams that night, and she knew her path to be righteous.

AFTERWORD

THE STORY THAT became the book you're holding, or perhaps listening to, was first conceived in the summer of 2016 and written over the course of 2018. A lot has happened in that time, and a lot has changed.

Science fiction authors don't really predict the future, but we sometimes wind up a lot closer to target than we expect. (I swear John Brunner's THE SHOCKWAVE RIDER looks more prescient by the day, though.) Little did I know while writing this book that the world would experience a global pandemic, or that the US would see not only an honest-to-goodness attempted coup, but also massive protests triggered in part by the simple notion that the lives of black Americans should no longer be snuffed out by police. Both of the latter went hand-in-hand with widespread misconduct and outright brutality on the part of police; and in parts of the US, the police have played a role in exacerbating the COVID pandemic, not least by refusing in many cases to wear masks.

The summer of 2020 made the notion of having a

sympathetic and mostly justice-oriented police official seem like another speculative element in my novel.

Perhaps the reality is that it's impossible for any police force, no matter how instituted, to uphold the Peelian principles of "Policing by consent" over time. Maybe it's possible that no human driven by an inner sense of justice can keep that fire lit after serving.

The Ileri Constabulary certainly isn't depicted as a wholly virtuous institution. Toiwa, after all, has made her reputation as someone who comes to clean out the corrupt. Daniel Imoke is denied his due because there are lines he won't cross. Can these people not only exist, but eventually rise, within such an institution?

I consider the MD State Police troopers I met at the first protest I attended at BWI in January 2017 who treated the crowd with respect, Capitol Police officer Eugene Goodman who without a doubt helped prevent a massacre during the insurrection on January 6th, 2021, and I think "Maybe?" Perhaps with a lot hard work and a bit of luck, we may be able to restore the "serve" component of "To protect and serve."

I look forward to telling the story of Toiwa and her crew wrestling with these problems.

ACKNOWLEDGEMENTS

THIS BOOK WOULDN'T be what it is, and in fact wouldn't even exist, without the contributions of many fantastic people. First and foremost of course are my wife Michelle, my daughter Alexa, and my son Ben, who are the center of my universe. Their love and support make all things possible.

Thank you to my parents for teaching me to read at an early age, and for advocating for me to be allowed to read things well above my age level ("Yes, I know he's 9, but he can handle THE WINDS OF WAR.") Thanks also for being supportive of me even when you didn't understand or agree with what I was about.

The mighty Maryland Space Opera Collective, or MD SPOC, is my local writing and critique group. They see pretty much everything I write and every bit of it is better thanks to them, so thank you to Kelly Rossmore, Phil Margolies, Martin Sherman-Marks, Beth Tanner, L. Blankenship, and most especially my siblings in ink, Karen Osborne & Jo Miles. (Thanks also to our other members, Jules Whitney, Amy Lynwander, and Vickie

Chen, who didn't see this book, but have made an impact on my writing since.) This crew saw the earliest versions and helped me find the shape of the story that lay within the draft I handed them.

Other readers who provided invaluable feedback include Mary Alexandra Agner, Aimee Kuzenski, Tyler Hayes, Sydney Rossman-Reich, and Tim Shea. Each one of them poked and prodded and asked questions and helped this world and its people come to life.

Having a community of other writers as a support network is invaluable, and the Isle of Write is the community I'm privileged to be a part of. Ever so proud and thankful of my posse.

Elsa Sjunneson provided consultation and sensitivity editing regarding blindness and was instrumental in crafting my portrayal of Josephine Okafor. She also helped create the tactile hacking system Okafor uses. Whatever is true and real in that portrayal is due to Elsa's guidance; the responsibility for any errors, omissions, or mistakes that remain lies with me.

Thank you to Tempest Bradford, Nisi Shawl, and all their guest instructors in the Writing the Other workshop. Anything correct in this book about the portrayal of people who aren't like myself is due to their tutelage; all mistakes are solely my own.

My agent Hannah Bowman saw my pitch of "BATTLESTAR GALACTICA meets THE GOLDEN GIRLS" and very quickly understood what I was trying to do in this story, and what kinds of stories I want to tell. Her feedback provided the final polish. She's a terrific partner and teacher.

Thanks to my editors Kate Coe & Jim Killen, and all the team at Rebellion/Solaris for being fans of the "exploding spaceships" aesthetic, and for publishing adventurous science fiction that's not wrapped up in jingoism and stilted attitudes.

Many established SFF writers welcomed me into the community, and provided all sorts of support and encouragement, most especially Curtis Chen, Tobias Buckell, Derek Kunsken, Mary Robinette Kowal, Fran Wilde, Scott Lynch, and Elizabeth Bear. Closer to home is what Mike Underwood calls "The Greater Baltimore/DC Speculative Fiction Co-Prosperity Sphere," including Mike himself, Sarah Pinsker, Kellan Szpara, Scott Edelman, Dan Lyman-Kennedy, the MD SPOC crew, emeritus members Arkady Martine & Vivian Shaw (may New Mexico continue to be good to you!), and all the rest of the local SFF community.

My thanks to the Viable Paradise community, including all the alumni, instructors, Mac Stone and the amazing staff, and most especially to my fellow Cheese Weasels of VP20.

Speaking of VP: I wouldn't have been able to attend had my mother-in-law, Mary Gingrich Martin, along my son Ben, not taken care of Michelle when she broke her foot the day before I left badly enough to require surgery while I was at the workshop. As Ben put it, they spent a week at the bottom level of Maslow's Hierarchy while I was off living at the top. That formative experience wouldn't have been possible for me without their sacrifice and labor.

And lastly, my thanks to Karen, Trish, Ali, Mackenzie, Alejandro, Becky, and all the rest of the Shadow Council crew, who were there when the Dead Guy With A Sword started telling stories so long ago, and encouraged him to keep going.

ABOUT THE AUTHOR

JOHN APPEL VOLUNTEERED to jump out of planes before he'd ever been in a plane; his friends and family say this sums up his approach to life pretty well. He writes science fiction and fantasy and the occasional tabletop RPG adventure. A lifelong Marylander, he lives in the Baltimore suburbs with his wife and children. He masquerades as a technology risk manager to pay the bills after two decades as an information security pro. When not writing, rolling dice, or keeping the bad guys at bay, he enjoys rum and swords, but not both at the same time. John is a graduate of the Viable Paradise writing workshop.

FIND US ONLINE!

www.rebellionpublishing.com

/rebellionpub /rebellionpublishing /rebellionpublishing

SIGN UP TO OUR NEWSLETTER!

rebellionpublishing.com/newsletter

YOUR REVIEWS MATTER!

Enjoy this book? Got something to say?

Leave a review on Amazon, GoodReads or with your favourite bookseller and let the world know!

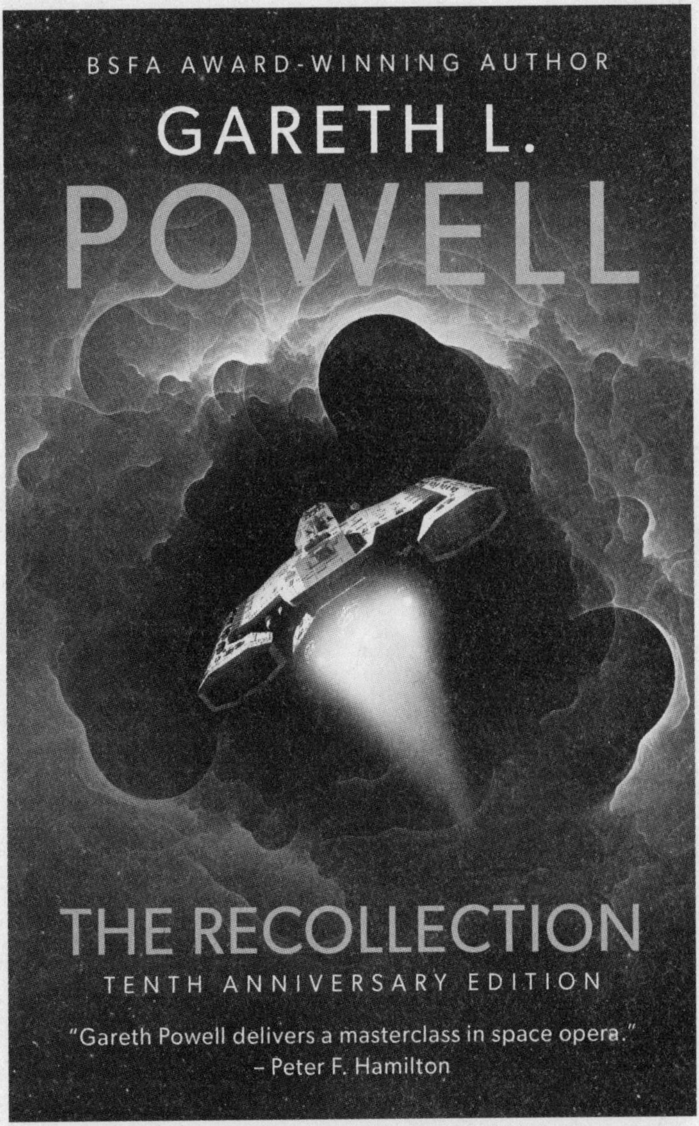
BSFA AWARD-WINNING AUTHOR
GARETH L.
POWELL
THE RECOLLECTION
TENTH ANNIVERSARY EDITION
"Gareth Powell delivers a masterclass in space opera."
– Peter F. Hamilton

MACHINERIES OF EMPIRE BOOK ONE

NINEFOX
GAMBIT

HUGO &
NEBULA
AWARD
NOMINATED

YOON HA LEE

'Yoon Ha Lee has arrived in spectacular fashion.'
Alastair Reynolds

⊙ SOLARISBOOKS.COM